W9-CFV-398

WILLOWGROVE

WILLOW

KATHLEEN PEACOCK

GROVE

Katherine Tegen Books is an imprint of HarperCollins Publishers.

Willowgrove
www.epicreads.com

Library of Congress Cataloging-in-Publication Data
Peacock, Kathleen.
    Willowgrove / Kathleen Peacock. — First edition.
        pages   cm
    Sequel to: Thornhill.
    Summary: Mac and her boyfriend, Kyle, fight to unravel the con-
spiracy surrounding illegal experiments performed on werewolves at
the secret asylum Willowgrove.
    ISBN 978-0-06-204871-4 (hardback)
    [1. Werewolves—Fiction.   2. Conspiracies—Fiction.   3. Mystery
and detective stories.]   I. Title.
PZ7.P31172Wi 2015   55 46 0298   2014022030
[Fic]—dc23   2/15   CIP
                                                             AC

Typography by Torborg Davern
14 15 16 17 18   PC/RRDH   10 9 8 7 6 5 4 3 2 1
❖
First Edition

FOR THE READERS—
  THANK YOU FOR TAKING THE JOURNEY

January

SHE SWEARS SHE CAN HEAR THE ECHO OF STRANGLED sobs and slurred shouts—every sound made under the roof while he was gone—as she stands in the empty hallway.

She doesn't knock. Knocking is asking permission, and that's one thing she almost never does. He doesn't speak as she steps inside and closes the door; he just sits there, on the edge of the bed, staring down at a small black box as he turns it over and over in his hands.

Silence stretches between them and she's the first to break. "You went back there, didn't you?"

"Don't worry about it. Go back to bed."

She leans against the doorframe. She knows the ground isn't really crumbling beneath her, but that's how it suddenly feels. He's going to destroy everything. All of them. "You can't trust her. Whatever she asked you to find or do, you can't—"

"It doesn't affect you." His blue eyes glint like chips of ice as he looks up. Even in the soft glow from the bedside lamp, she can see how tired he is. How lost. Lies and subterfuge are her talents, not his. They wear him out and stretch him thin until you can see every thought and feeling swirl beneath the surface.

"It affects me. It affects all of us." She takes a step toward him. "It's just a handful of empty promises. Everything she told you is a lie." He'd see that, too, if he wasn't so desperate. If he didn't want so badly to be like everyone else.

"Not everything," he says. He sighs and pushes himself to his feet. "Besides, I haven't made a decision."

"Yet." She already knows what he'll do; she just doesn't know how to stop him. She can't get him to see that he's making a mistake. He's two years older and has always been the smart one—the one who cleaned up her messes and looked out for her—but fate has flipped their roles. Now she's the one who needs to stop him from doing something stupid, and she doesn't know where to start.

All she can do is stand there as he crosses the room and comes to a stop in front of her.

He presses a kiss to her forehead.

He's never done that before. The kiss, more than anything, convinces her just how much trouble he's in.

"Go back to bed, Amy," he tells her again, and this time she nods and slips across the hall to her own room.

She doesn't crawl into bed: the idea of sleep is laughable. Instead, she grabs a pair of jeans and a T-shirt from the mess on the floor and dresses as quickly and quietly as she can.

A few minutes later, she hears the shower and sneaks back to his room.

It doesn't take her long to find the black box. It's wedged

beneath his mattress, and she suddenly misses the days when the only things he had to hide there were dirty magazines and the occasional pack of cigarettes.

As she creeps down the stairs and out the front door, she tells herself that what she's doing isn't wrong. She's not just doing it for herself, and that has to make a difference. There isn't a cure—there won't ever be a cure—and whatever he took—*whatever he stole*—might be enough to destroy them all.

It's not selfish, what she's doing.

That's what she tells herself over and over in the twenty minutes it takes her to get where she's going.

Still, she can't help looking over her shoulder. Twice, she turns, convinced she's being followed, but no one is ever there.

Just nerves, she tells herself. *I'm doing the right thing.*

By the time she reaches her destination and finds a grubby pay phone, she almost believes it.

1

WATCHING A HUMAN BODY BE RIPPED TO SHREDS—EVERY bone shattered, every ligament torn—was never pleasant; watching it happen to the person you loved was a special brand of torture.

It definitely wasn't the kind of experience you signed up for—unless you happened to be dating a werewolf.

I shivered and tugged my borrowed sleeping bag a little tighter around myself. November was almost half over; here, in the woods surrounding Hemlock, the night was colder and darker than it had been back in town.

The tremble didn't slip past Kyle. He tossed another log on the fire, sending a spiral of sparks up into the night. He tracked their progress until the last one burned out, and then he turned and pulled his T-shirt over his head.

My heart skipped at the sight of his broad back and all that skin. Almost immediately, though, my eyes were drawn to the five scars that ran from his shoulders to his waist. They didn't mar his beauty—in a strange way they almost added to it—but they would forever mark him as infected. As a werewolf.

I slipped a hand under my jacket and touched the quarter-sized circle of scar tissue—a souvenir from a bullet—on my own shoulder. It wasn't my only scar, but it was the most recent. Neither of us had made it through the past few months unscathed. Our wounds were like stories: they spelled out victories and losses across our skin.

Kyle tossed his shirt toward the tent as he turned back to me. The light from the fire highlighted the strong planes and angles of his face while leaving his eyes full of shadows. "Maybe this isn't such a great idea, Mac." His voice was neutral, but there was an undercurrent of uncertainty beneath the words.

"It is," I said softly.

Kyle had come closer to embracing his wolf side since Colorado, but deep down, part of him still worried he was a monster. I loved and accepted him, but until he accepted himself, his infection would always be between us.

The woods had been my idea.

We both needed a break and Kyle had mentioned, once, that the forest seemed to bring the wolf closer to the surface. He had transformed in front of me before, but always in life-or-death situations when he'd had no choice. For once, I wanted to see him transform when someone wasn't trying to kill us.

I wanted to prove that I really wasn't afraid of him.

He didn't look convinced. "We don't have to do this

tonight. We can go back to town. Do something normal . . ."

I made a small, skeptical noise. Like anything in Hemlock was normal right now. The town had become Tracker central over the past week. Members of the right-wing anti-werewolf group were around every corner; you couldn't throw a rock without hitting someone with a black dagger tattooed on their neck.

"Are you sure all this stalling isn't just fear of me seeing you naked?"

A low laugh slipped from Kyle's throat. "Mackenzie Dobson, if you thought you had to go to this much trouble to get me out of my clothes, then we've got bigger problems than me being a werewolf. Next time, just ask." A dark, mischievous light flared deep in his eyes. "This time, however, the shorts stay on."

My stomach did a slow flip—that thing other people called "butterflies"—as warmth flooded my cheeks. We had agreed to take things slowly and I knew he was just teasing, but . . .

A line of sparks raced down my spine.

Kyle's lips curved up in a small grin at the blush, but like all of his smiles over the past few months, the grin faded quickly. "Whatever happens, stay on that side of the fire."

I nodded. Werewolves didn't always have the greatest control over their movements when they shifted. It was hard to be conscious of every gesture when your body was being pulled apart, and one accidental scratch could infect me with lupine syndrome.

"I usually get a burst of adrenaline after I change. If I

run, don't try to follow, all right? I won't go far. I just might need to burn some of it off before I can shift back."

"Kyle, we've been through this." At least twenty times in the past three hours. "If you really don't want to . . ."

"No. I do." The words were resolute, but he still looked doubtful—like he thought this whole thing was a mistake and that I'd freak and bolt.

Shrugging off the sleeping bag, I stood. I walked around the fire and came to a stop in front of him. Gently, I pressed my hand to his chest. A werewolf's heart beats faster than a reg's, and I could feel the thud under my palm. His skin was hot—as though he had a fever. I stood on tiptoe and brushed my lips against his as I ran my hands over his chest, along his shoulders, and down his arms.

Pulling me close, Kyle deepened the kiss until it felt like his arms were the only things keeping me upright.

I finally eased away—not because I wanted to, but because we would both forget why we were here if he kept kissing me like that.

He brushed a strand of hair back from my cheek. "Have I told you how great you look with short hair?"

I ran a hand through my dishwater-blond locks—too long to be a pixie, too short to be a bob—and shook my head. "Only about thirty times."

"Here's to thirty-one." He was quiet for a minute. "I've been thinking," he said finally. "About Colorado."

"Oh?" I tried to keep my voice casual but it cracked over the single syllable. A little over a month ago, Kyle had left Hemlock to start a new life in Denver. Part of that new life had included joining a wolf pack—the Eumon. There were just a few things he hadn't counted on—like the fact that Jason and I would follow him halfway across the country or that the leader of the pack he had chosen was my estranged father. Now Kyle was stuck between worlds with a decision to make. He could stay here, with me, taking the very real chance that he'd be labeled an oath breaker and blacklisted by the werewolf community, or he could return to Colorado and take his sworn place among my father's wolves.

That pending decision was the big reason we were taking things slowly: Kyle didn't want to hurt me any more than he had to, and I didn't want to make his choice any harder than it had to be.

There wasn't a single part of me that didn't want him to stay, but I loved him enough to want what was best for him. Even if I wasn't it.

There was a time—not very long ago—when I wouldn't have been capable of thinking that way, when I would have fought to keep him by my side because I was too scared and selfish to even consider letting him go, but the past few weeks had changed me.

The thought of a life without Kyle made it feel like parts of me were cold and dying, but I now knew that I could be strong enough to let him go—if that was what he really wanted. I would do anything for him—no matter what the cost.

A shadow passed over Kyle's face, and I wondered how much of my thoughts had shown in my eyes.

He slid his hands over my arms. Even through two layers

of clothing, the touch made me ache.

"I think part of the problem is that we both keep looking at it like an either-or situation—either I go back to the pack or we stay together."

"You're saying you want me to go to Colorado with you?" I raised an eyebrow.

"No," he said. "I'm not sure a wolf pack is the safest place in the world. Plus, you have Tess and school. Serena and Jason." There was a strain around the way he said his best friend's name, one I didn't want to examine too closely. "Lots of people have long-distance relationships. Even if I had never gotten infected, if we had just started dating like a normal couple, there's no guarantee we'd have picked the same college. We might still have ended up doing the long-distance thing."

I wasn't convinced that joining a wolf pack could be compared to a semester away at school with Thanksgiving break and keggers, but I still felt a small flare of hope. Speaking slowly and carefully, needing to know I wasn't misunderstanding, I said, "So even if you go back to Colorado, you're saying you want to stay together?"

He nodded. "I'm still not convinced it's what's best for you, but I tried to make the decision for the both of us and it failed spectacularly." He reached out and traced the curve of my cheek with his fingertips, making me shiver, before gently pressing his palm to my shoulder, right over the spot where I had been shot. Something dark and haunted slipped behind his eyes, and I knew he was thinking of how close I had come to dying just a few weeks ago. "Besides, if I'm being honest, I'm not sure I'm selfless enough to walk away from you a second time."

I pulled him to me, clutching him so hard and kissing him so fiercely that every inch of my body trembled.

"You know," breathed Kyle, easing back just far enough that speech was possible. "We could just forget about this whole shape-shifting thing."

"Mmmm. Tempting, but no." Truth be told, I wasn't entirely sure I trusted myself to stick to the slow path. I placed both hands on his chest and pushed myself back.

My fingers itched to touch him again, but I forced myself to return to my place across the fire.

Kyle stared at me for a long moment over the flames. With a shake of his head and a small sigh, he kicked off his Vans and slipped out of his jeans until he stood in just a pair of dark-blue shorts. "That side of the fire. Remember."

I nodded.

Nothing happened.

I bit my lip.

Nothing continued to happen.

"Would it be easier if—" Before I could complete the sentence, his face contorted in pain. With the sharp, dry sound of a board snapping under too much weight, his spine bowed, driving him to his knees.

Kyle dug his hands—hands that were too long and the wrong shape—into the carpet of leaves on the forest floor as muscles writhed like snakes beneath his skin.

My pulse thundered and a bitter taste flooded the back of my mouth.

Every other time I had seen Kyle shift, we had been under some sort of attack. This time, there was nothing to divert my attention. There was just me and Kyle and the things that were happening to his body as I stood helplessly by.

His mouth stretched in a scream, but no sound came out.

I took a small step forward; I couldn't help myself.

"Stay back!" The words were a growl pulled from deep inside Kyle's chest a heartbeat before his entire body twisted and shattered.

When it was over, I was left staring at a wolf with fur the color of freshly turned earth.

The wolf's eyes—Kyle's eyes, I reminded myself—caught and reflected the light from the campfire as I searched them for some sign of the boy I knew.

The wolf cocked its head to the side and let out a small, questioning bark—almost like he was asking if I was all right.

I let out a deep breath. "I'm okay."

Something painfully human passed behind Kyle's wolf eyes before he turned and ran: relief.

Smoke clawed at my throat and stung my eyes as, thirty stories below, a city burned. Chicago, Phoenix, Seattle— I didn't know where I was and it didn't matter: every few nights, another city tore itself apart.

Twenty-five days ago, I had helped three hundred teens break out of Thornhill Werewolf Rehabilitation Camp. Our only goal had been self-preservation, but our actions had been a spark that lit a fire under the entire country. Within days, there had been uprisings at two other camps and clashes between humans and wolf packs in half a dozen cities.

The reg population was terrified. The camps and the LSRB—the system they trusted to keep the infected safely at bay—had failed. There had always been as many wolves outside the camps as in, but people hadn't wanted to believe it. Thornhill had forced them to believe; and groups like the Trackers, groups that fed on fear, were doing everything they could to keep the public as frightened as possible.

Within weeks, the country had plunged into the kind of violence and fear it hadn't seen since the early days of the LS epidemic. Paranoia was at an all-time high and mob mentality had started taking hold. Anyone with a scar was suspect. The Lupine Syndrome Registration Bureau couldn't keep up with the number of calls flooding its tip lines, and people were taking matters into their own hands. There were states where killing a werewolf wasn't illegal, leaving crowds free to act without fear of repercussion—as long as the target of their violence really was infected. Dozens—maybe even hundreds—of wolves had been murdered since the breakout.

My father, Hank, had warned me this would happen. I should have known he'd be right.

Most of the violence hadn't hit Hemlock. Yet. It was concentrated in cities with wolf packs and large pockets of infected people. But it was only a matter of time—especially with the Trackers in town.

I pressed my palms to the concrete ledge that encircled the rooftop as I counted burning buildings and listened to the distant echoes of shouts and screams. The anonymous city below fell into chaos and all I could do was watch.

I had done this. It had been my idea to take down Thornhill. All of this death and destruction was the result of my actions.

"Martyr, much?"

I turned as Amy stepped out of the shadows. Even though it was November, she was wearing cutoffs and a sleeveless gray shirt. Her pale skin seemed to glow in the moonlight, and her knees were scraped raw and bloodstained.

I should have known she would turn up in a place like this. In death, she lived for places like this.

The air around her shimmered and changed as she crossed the rooftop. Empty space became white tile walls. Darkness became blinding fluorescent lights. The smell of smoke was drowned out by the scent of bleach.

The detention block at Thornhill. The place where dozens of wolves—including my friend Serena—had been tortured in Warden Winifred Sinclair's crazed search for a cure to lupine syndrome. The place I had seen in dreams every night since the breakout.

I shook my head and stepped back. "I don't want to be here."

Amy raised an eyebrow. "And I do?" She tucked a strand of black hair behind her ear and the light caught a flash of silver at her wrist—a bangle her brother had brought her back from Mexico one spring break.

She stared at me expectantly, but then, instead of waiting for a reply, grabbed my hand and began dragging me toward the control room. My heart rate spiked as I tried to pull away. I didn't want to go in there. I didn't want to see videos of Serena being tortured. Not again.

But Amy was always stronger than I was in dreams. No matter how I resisted, I couldn't stop her from pulling me through the door and toward the only source of light in the room: a bank of nine computer monitors. "You need to see," she said.

"I've already seen." I tried to twist away. It wasn't any use.

"Not the videos."

She let go so suddenly that I stumbled forward.

"What do you mean?"

Eight of the monitors displayed a screen saver of the camp logo. The ninth showed an image of Serena behind a metal table, her shirt torn and her eyes wide. The video had been taken the night we arrived in the camp, after we had been separated. I glanced over my shoulder. "Besides the videos, what else is there?"

"Just look, Mac. Please. I need you to look." Amy's voice was uncharacteristically tired and small, so un-Amylike that I couldn't refuse it.

Chest tight, I focused my attention back on the screen. Serena's image filled the monitor—well, almost filled it. Six or seven icons cluttered the taskbar and a spreadsheet was open behind the video player.

"There isn't anything else here." But as I spoke, my gaze

was drawn to the upper left-hand corner of the spreadsheet, where a small splash of black—what looked like part of a logo—was just visible beneath the other open windows.

Amy closed the distance between us. Leaning in so close that her breath left a layer of frost on my cheek, she said, "Everyone always sees more than they remember. And sometimes people see things they're not ready to accept."

I woke with a start, disorientated and confused. I wasn't in my bedroom and I wasn't back in the dormitory at Thornhill. There was a weight across my chest. I started to panic but then the roof of the tent came into focus and I became aware of Kyle—the scent of his skin and the steady sound of his breathing—beside me.

He had thrown an arm over me in his sleep. For a moment, I just closed my eyes and enjoyed being near him, grateful to no longer be trapped in the dream. Being in the detention block once—seeing the videos of what had been done to Serena—had been horrible enough. Having to revisit that place—those images—night after night in my dreams was exhausting.

Everyone always sees more than they remember. A chill swept down my spine as I thought about Amy's words.

As quietly as I could, I unzipped my sleeping bag and carefully wormed out from Kyle's embrace. He rolled onto his back, but didn't wake.

I rummaged in the bottom of my knapsack until my fingers closed around a pen. Digging through my jacket pockets turned up a receipt for the soda and chips I had bought when we stopped for gas, and using my phone as a flashlight, I sketched out what little I had seen of the symbol from my dream.

The result was a thick squiggle that looked like a half-melted version of the Nike swoosh.

I frowned down at the piece of paper, turning it this way and that. Something about the curve of the lines seemed familiar, but I couldn't place it. It definitely wasn't the twisted vines of the Thornhill crest, but it did look like it could almost be part of a logo.

Maybe it was nothing, but there really had been a spreadsheet on the monitor the night we had broken into the detention block. At the time, I had been too distracted to do anything more than note its existence. I had been too focused on the realization that Serena had been tortured and the possibility that we'd all be caught at any moment.

What if I had missed something? Something important. What if that was why I kept seeing the detention block in my dreams night after night?

I snapped a photo of the sketch.

The flash was blinding in the tent. I held my breath until I was certain I hadn't woken Kyle, and then I typed what I could remember of the dream into my memo app. It was one more fragment to add to my growing collection of memories and questions—what Jason and Kyle had dubbed my "Thornhill Files."

They thought I was obsessed.

Maybe I was.

Aside from Sinclair and a handful of her former staff, we

16

were the only ones who knew what had really happened at Thornhill. The employees in the detention block had been so determined to keep their secrets that they had set fire to the camp's main building once they realized the breakout couldn't be stopped.

Every scrap of proof had burned in the blaze.

Everyone else wanted to let go of the camp. They wanted to believe it was over and that we were safe—or as safe as we could be. Thornhill was gone and Sinclair couldn't hurt anyone else. We'd never be able to prove what had happened inside the fences; the only thing we could do was try to put it behind us, try to put ourselves back together. All we could do was try to move on.

And I wanted to move on.

It was just . . .

Warden Sinclair had kept her search for an end to lupine syndrome secret from the LSRB. She had falsified admission records, kept most of her staff in the dark, and paid Trackers to bring in wolves under the table—all to keep the bureau from finding out that she was torturing and killing inmates in pursuit of a cure.

A cure she couldn't possibly have been working toward on her own.

The drugs, the detention block, the research—all of it would have taken money and resources. Way more money and resources than a civil servant could pull together. Someone had to have been helping her—if not the LSRB then someone else—and whoever that someone was, they were still out there, free to start again. Free to hurt people like

Sinclair had hurt Serena. They wouldn't even need another camp. Not really. They could just grab infected people off the street.

Knowing what we did . . . it felt like some sort of responsibility—like we had to figure out how Sinclair had gotten away with so much and who had helped her. How could any of us really put Thornhill in the past when there were still so many questions?

I stared down at the small sketch for a moment, and then sent a text to the person who had been standing at my side in front of the monitor that night. **Need 2 ask u something.**

My phone vibrated a second later. **s'up?**

I rubbed my eyes. Jason's response had come too quickly for my message to have woken him. I tried not to think about what sort of trouble he might be getting into at 3:00 a.m. on a Friday night in a town overrun by Trackers.

Both Kyle's parents and Tess, my cousin and legal guardian, were still having trouble coping with the news that Kyle was a werewolf and that we were both, technically, fugitives. They watched us like they were waiting for the sky to fall. Jason's parents, on the other hand, were happy just to have him back without a scandal. Once he had assured them that he hadn't dragged the Sheffield name through the mud or gotten anyone knocked up, it had been business as usual.

I sent him the picture of the sketch. **Does this look familiar?**

No. Y?

Before I could reply, he sent another text. **Gotta go.**

That was it. No explanation. No good-bye.

Wherever he was and whatever he was doing, I was certain it couldn't be good.

Leaving a group like the Trackers wasn't easy—especially when you had the kind of status and money Jason did. They had gotten their claws into him and they intended to keep things that way. And Jason . . . Jason believed that staying close to them would help keep the rest of us safe—as though he could be a kind of early warning system if someone found out Kyle and Serena were infected or that I was the daughter of a pack leader.

It was the same at school. He continued to play the part of Tracker and alcoholic screwup to draw attention away from the rest of us. He played it so well that there were times when I had to remind myself that he really had changed. He played it so well that sometimes I suspected even he forgot who and what he was.

I stowed my phone and then slid back into my sleeping bag. I rolled over and studied Kyle's shadowed profile. In the morning, we'd drive back to Hemlock and have to face the real world. Trackers. Jason. The fact that Serena still hadn't recovered from Sinclair's "cure" and the knowledge that Kyle would soon have to decide whether or not to return to Colorado.

But morning was still a few hours off.

I reached for Kyle's hand, gently lacing my fingers through his.

For a few hours, if I tried hard enough, I could pretend that everything was fine.

Amy was still alive, Jason had never joined the Trackers,

and Kyle had never become infected. None of us had so much as heard of Thornhill, and Hemlock wasn't at the epicenter of what could turn into a full-fledged war between wolves and regs.

Everything—*everything*—was all right.

I edged closer to Kyle and rested my head on his shoulder.

Sometimes, it was better to fall asleep to a comforting lie than to the truth.

2

I ROLLED MY SHOULDERS AS I LINGERED UNDER THE HOT water. I was about as far from pampered as you could get, but I was a city girl, and my back was complaining about a night spent sleeping in the woods.

Still, every kink and knotted muscle had been worth it.

I closed my eyes and remembered the sensation of Kyle's arms around me and the way his lips had tasted a little like cinnamon. My heart beat a little faster as I turned off the shower and raised my fingertips to the slow smile that stretched across my face. He wanted to stay together. Even if he went back to Colorado, he didn't want it to be the end of him and me. The end of us.

"Mac?" My cousin Tess's voice drifted through the closed bathroom door, jolting me from my thoughts.

"Yeah?"

"Your phone's been blowing up for the past ten minutes."

Shit. Straining, I could just make out the last notes of my ringtone before whoever was on the other end of the line gave up.

I quickly hauled on clothes, wincing as my shoulder twinged. The bullet I had taken during the Thornhill breakout had been Warden Sinclair's last attempt at revenge. I had been warned that my shoulder might never be quite the same, but I wasn't about to complain about the occasional flashes of pain: a few inches either way and the bullet would have left me crippled. Or dead.

For an entire week, Jason had gone around calling me *Miracle Girl*.

I caught sight of my reflection as I pulled open the bathroom door and quickly looked away. Ever since Thornhill, the girl who stared back at me from the mirror seemed somehow . . . less. It was as though I had left some part of myself back at the rehabilitation camp, locked behind its electric fences.

Miracle Girl. Yeah, right.

I beelined for my room and grabbed the phone from my nightstand. These days, I usually took it everywhere— even into the bathroom—but I had been so tired after Kyle dropped me off that I had stumbled to the shower on autopilot.

I unlocked the screen. Three missed calls—two from my father and one from a number I didn't recognize—and a text from Kyle telling me I had forgotten Tess's sleeping bag in his car. I bit my lip and dialed Hank. Not entirely surprising, it went straight to voice mail.

After Trackers had burned down Hank's club and run his pack out of Denver, most of the Eumon had relocated to an old mining town in the middle of nowhere. They were so far out that Hank only had cell reception when they made the trek to other towns for supplies or news. I left a message and then checked my own voice mail.

Two hang-ups. Typical. Messages were footprints and Hank didn't like leaving tracks. Even his cell phone was a cheap disposable: every two weeks, both the phone and the number changed. It was amazing how many of the habits he'd developed during his long career as a jack-of-all-trades criminal could be applied to life as a werewolf. Don't draw attention. Stay on the move. Be ready to leave everything behind and run.

For werewolves who managed to evade the LSRB and the rehabilitation camps, life meant constantly looking over your shoulder and always sleeping with one eye open.

As the reg girlfriend of a werewolf, that was the same life I was signing on for.

My gaze was drawn to the wall above my desk, where I had tacked up dozens of articles about Thornhill and the breakout—more fodder for what everyone else worried was my growing fixation. Life on the run was no picnic, but it was far, far better than ending up in one of the camps.

I gave my head a sharp shake, clearing my thoughts.

I didn't need a crystal ball to guess why Hank had called. He wanted me out of Hemlock until the Tracker invasion was over. We had argued about it twice already this week. My father had changed—I had seen proof of that since Denver—but a sudden paternal interest didn't mean he automatically got to have input into my life. I had been making decisions for myself since he had abandoned me all those years ago, and that wasn't about to change.

I was staying in Hemlock. I wasn't going to let a sudden influx of Trackers run me out.

A voice mail began to play.

"Mac . . . Hey. It's Stephen. I'm back in town—at least for a while. Taking a break from school and working for Dad . . ."

The familiar deep voice threw me for a loop. Of all the people who could have left me a message, Amy's brother was practically the last person I would have expected.

He cleared his throat. "Anyway, I've been going through Amy's room. I thought there might be some things you would want. Photos, books—that sort of stuff. Maybe we can grab a coffee or you can stop by the house. The place is a zoo with the fund-raiser tomorrow night, but call me when you get a chance."

An automated voice told me I had reached the end of my messages.

My hand shook a little as I lowered the phone. I tried to remember the last time I had spoken to Stephen. Last Christmas, maybe. He went to school out East—at least he had until recently. He had flown back for a few days after Amy's death, but he hadn't been at the funeral. Jason said he hadn't been able to make it past the cemetery gate.

And now he was back in Hemlock.

I bit my lip. I couldn't imagine Stephen taking time off from school—not even for a semester. He had always been the golden boy to Amy's black sheep. Straight-A student. Responsible and dependable. The perfect older brother. The kind of older brother I had always wanted.

"Mac, there's coffee." Tess's voice drifted down the hall.

"Okay!"

Hearing Stephen's voice shouldn't have felt strange—even after he had gone to college, I had still seen him when he came home on breaks—but it was impossible to think of him and not think of Amy. Every memory I had of him was tied to her.

I slipped my phone into my pocket as I walked to the bookcase on the other side of the room. I already had the only thing I really wanted of Amy's: a bracelet made from a handful of foreign coins, a flea market find she always claimed was lucky. I reached into the glass bowl I kept important odds and ends in, and lifted it out.

A flash drive on a length of black cord came up with it.

Frowning, I unwound the cord from the bracelet and set the drive aside. Amy had given it to me days before she had been killed. It was a bunch of photos and videos and music—things she thought I might like copies of. After the funeral, I had spent whole evenings just looking at every image and listening to every song, trying to get her back.

I should go through the files again. Some of the pictures were of Stephen and Amy, and a few of the videos were from concerts he had taken us to; there might be a few he didn't have and would want.

But the thought of seeing Amy's brother again, of talking about her in the past tense, wasn't something I felt ready to face.

Like a coward, I tied the bracelet around my wrist and

headed for the kitchen without calling Stephen back.

Tess looked up from a glossy magazine—one of a whole stack—as I entered the room. "Coffee's fresh. I just made a new pot." Her multicolored hair was pulled back in a high ponytail and she had traded her work clothes for a pair of sweats. Tess waited tables at the Shady Cat, a trendy microbrewery/restaurant near the college campus. On a normal Saturday, she headed to bed around 5:00 a.m. and wasn't seen again until midafternoon, but she had stayed up to make sure I got home okay.

She never used to worry when I was out with Kyle, but a lot had changed.

Tess knew almost everything now—everything except that her ex-boyfriend Ben had been the white werewolf who had killed Amy and terrorized the town. Faced with all of the things I had hidden from her, she wasn't sure how to trust me again. And she blamed Kyle for the fact that I had run off to Colorado and almost gotten killed. I think that bothered her more than the fact that Kyle was a werewolf. She had always trusted Kyle to keep me safe, and now she felt like he had betrayed that trust.

"How are you still awake?" I asked, passing up coffee and grabbing a granola bar. The TV was on in the living room, but the sound was muted.

"I had about a gallon of caffeinated goodness before you got home," she admitted with a small shrug. "Plus, I have this whole theory that if I fill out six months' worth of *Cosmo* quizzes in a single sitting, everything in my life will magically fall into place."

"Good luck with that." I unwrapped the granola bar and broke off a piece. "You didn't have to wait up," I said before popping the bite-sized chunk into my mouth.

The look Tess shot me spoke volumes, but instead of pushing, she said, "What are you doing today?"

I swallowed. "I was going to head over to Serena's." Jason hadn't recognized the symbol from my dream and Serena was the only other person I could ask. The last thing I wanted was to remind her of the detention block, but I couldn't shake the feeling that it was important. I had been dreaming of that hallway—of that room—for a month. I wasn't a psychologist, but there had to be a reason my subconscious kept throwing me back there.

"Oh." Disappointment flashed across Tess's face. "I have the night off. I was going to ask if you wanted to go on a mini road trip."

"A road trip?"

"Just a small one. We could leave around three, stay overnight someplace—maybe not the Ritz, but at least someplace with a pool—and come back tomorrow. You've been so preoccupied . . . I think getting away for a day would be good for you."

"Tess, we can't afford that." Saying the words was awkward. Money was almost always tight, but we never talked about it.

The corners of her mouth quirked up. "Actually, tips have been really good the last week. Practically insanely good. Most Trackers may be complete assholes, but a lot of them are pretty generous once they down a few beers."

"More like they're generous once they catch sight of you coming toward their table," I teased.

"That, too." Her hazel eyes sparkled. "So what do you say?"

"It's just . . ." My voice trailed off. Tess, more than anyone, wanted me to forget about the camp. Just the mention of Colorado was enough to make her flinch. "I really wanted to see Serena," I said lamely. "And with everything going on in town, I feel weird leaving." It felt like abandoning my friends.

Tess hesitated just a second too long before speaking. "Okay. No sweat." She flashed me a smile that was so forced it cracked around the edges. "I'm exhausted anyway." She stood and walked past me to the sink.

"Maybe we could do it another time?" I asked hesitantly. Hopefully. "Maybe next weekend?"

Tess rinsed out her coffee mug and set it on the counter. "Sure." She shot me another fake smile. "Besides, I could use a quiet night in by myself. Just me and a tub full of bubbles followed by a bag of Doritos and a *Sex and the City* marathon. Go. See Serena. Maybe call Jason. You don't spend enough time with him anymore."

She headed down the hall before I could say anything else. A second later, her bedroom door clicked softly shut.

I tossed the rest of my granola bar in the garbage: suddenly, I didn't have much of an appetite. Things had been strained since I had gotten back, but that wasn't Tess's fault. She was doing her best to trust me again. She was trying.

Even though she was exhausted, she had wanted to spend time with me.

Maybe I couldn't just up and leave town, but I could have suggested an alternate plan. I liked Doritos and I could make it through at least a few episodes of *Sex and the City* without completely losing my mind.

Suddenly, more than anything, all I wanted was to spend the day with Tess, to show her that I was willing to try, too.

I started toward the hall just as a flicker of movement on the television caught my eye.

Tess had left the TV tuned to CNN. Amy's grandfather, Senator John Walsh, was on-screen, standing on the stone steps of some building in Washington, surrounded by reporters. I didn't bother turning the sound on: I already knew the sorts of things he would be saying. He had become vehemently anti-werewolf after Amy's death, and over the past few weeks, he had been pushing for two things: a public inquiry into security at Thornhill and the authorization of extreme—even lethal—force in recapturing escaped wolves.

I wondered what he'd do if he knew Amy's death hadn't been—as everyone believed—the random act of a crazed werewolf. Branson Derby, then head of the Trackers and Ben's father, had sent his own infected son on a killing spree as part of a carefully orchestrated plan to increase public fear and destroy the pro-werewolf lobby in Washington. To get Amy's grandfather—one of the few politicians who had openly supported increased wolf rights—to become as anti-werewolf as possible.

If the senator knew why his granddaughter had really died, would he change his stance back? If he had seen the torture the wolves had been running from at Thornhill, would he still want them hunted down like they were something less than human?

Heart heavy, I grabbed the remote from the kitchen counter and turned off the television. As much as I wanted a quiet day with Tess, I owed it to Serena and Kyle and everyone else who had been at the camp to figure out if there was anything behind the symbol from my dream. The symbol I had seen in the detention block. It could be nothing, but it might be part of the puzzle that was Thornhill. And maybe, if I figured it out, some of the dreams would stop.

I scribbled an apology to Tess on the notepad by the phone and then grabbed my jacket and headed for Serena's.

"Protect yourself and your fellow regs!" A woman tried to block my path as she forced an object into my palm. I jerked my hand away and stepped around her.

Once I was safely around the corner, I uncurled my fingers. A *Hunt or be Hunted* button. It was a phrase used by the Trackers—one they emblazoned on everything from T-shirts to posters. I tossed the button into the next garbage can I passed and then paused to wipe my palm on my jeans.

I glanced up. I had stopped in front of the music store—closed a week ago after people found out its owner was infected—and the street behind me was reflected in its dark windows. Though the sidewalks were crowded with people rushing to and from Riverside Square, a hauntingly familiar figure stood perfectly still on the other side of the street. Watching me.

Ben.

His blond hair fell over his forehead, obscuring his gray eyes. His jeans were torn at the knee and his hands were shoved deep into the pockets of a battered leather jacket. As he watched me in the window, his mouth curved up in a small smile.

A shudder rocketed down my spine as my heart rate shot sky-high.

I whirled, struggling for breath as I desperately scanned the street.

No one was watching me. Ben wasn't there.

It was just my mind playing tricks on me. Just a ghost.

I willed my heart to stop racing.

It wasn't the first time I had imagined seeing Ben. It had happened in Denver and a few times since we'd been back in Hemlock. "Post-traumatic stress"—that's what Kyle called it. I guess it didn't get much more traumatic than being hog-tied in the woods by the man who had killed your best friend.

Still, each time it happened, I felt like I was going a little bit crazy.

Shivering, I tried to put it out of my mind as I resumed my trek to the park. A few flakes drifted through the air: it looked like winter was coming early this year.

The first winter without Amy, I thought. It didn't seem possible that it had been more than half a year since her death.

The closer I got to Riverside Square, the more people I

saw with black-dagger tattoos on their necks.

On Monday, the twelfth anniversary of the day lupine syndrome had officially been announced to the world, the Trackers would hold simultaneous "unity rallies" in major cities across the country—and Hemlock would be at the center of it all.

Thanks to the Thornhill breakout—and the resulting violence and paranoia sweeping the country—the Trackers were riding a massive surge in popularity, a surge they were milking for all the publicity, donations, and political clout they could get. There were other places the group could have chosen for the main rally—larger cities with bigger venues and the ability to better accommodate a huge influx of visitors—but the name "Hemlock" would forever conjure images of the worst werewolf murder spree in history. It was the location guaranteed to get them the most attention, and they were exploiting that by billing the Hemlock event as both a call to action against wolves and as a memorial to the victims of the attacks in the spring—victims the press had dubbed *The Hemlock Four*.

The mayor and most of the city council had pledged to deny permits for the rally—they were afraid it would turn into a riot—but they had caved when Senator Walsh loudly and publicly voiced his support for the event. The Walsh family were the biggest philanthropists in town; no one wanted to risk alienating them. Amy's parents were even holding a private fund-raising gala the night before the rally to raise money for a memorial sculpture in Riverside Square—one that would be inscribed with the names of each of the Hemlock victims.

I passed a lamppost bearing a flyer with a picture of Amy above the word *Remember* and resisted the urge to tear it down. If it hadn't been for the former head of the Trackers, she would still be here.

Not a single day went by that I didn't wish I could tell people the truth about who had killed Amy and why, but no one would believe me—not without proof—and I couldn't risk anyone finding out I had been in the woods the night Branson Derby had died. Derby had been killed by a were-wolf. By Kyle. If anyone learned I had been there that night, they might start looking at the people closest to me. At Kyle or Serena or Trey.

I couldn't risk that. I wouldn't risk them. Not even for Amy.

All I could do was watch as the rally's organizers used Amy's death like a prop.

It was just one of the reasons I had been avoiding downtown—and the square where the rally would be held—all week.

Unfortunately, there was only one bus that went out to Serena's neighborhood on Saturdays, and the stop that ran along the far side of the park was the easiest place to catch it.

I stepped through the wrought iron arch—one of three—on the square's eastern edge, and tried to suppress the feeling that I had been dropped into enemy territory.

Normally, the only people in the park before noon on weekends were skateboarders, guys sleeping on benches, and the handful of die-hard chess players who met until snow covered their strip of checkered tables. But today, hundreds of people wandered the tree-lined paths and congregated on the grass. Some of them handed out flyers while others paused to watch as mammoth video screens—the kind you saw at outdoor concerts—were erected on three sides of the square.

I gave up trying to count the number of tattoos I saw as I made my way across the park.

Every once in a while, I spotted someone in an RfW— Regs for Werewolves—shirt, but they were few and far between. Advertising the fact that you supported equal rights for the infected in a town on the verge of an anti-werewolf rally was noble to the point of suicidal.

"There is no virus!"

The voice came from a patch of grass to my left, where a man on an upturned crate held a small group in thrall.

"God has sent the werewolves as divine punishment! America has backslid into sin. He strikes the wicked—the sinners and the morally decayed—and unleashes them among us!" The man's wide eyes and his tangled black hair made him look like someone who spent his time wrestling imaginary demons. He was young—maybe only a few years older than I was—but his ragged voice and disheveled appearance made him seem ancient. His baggy trench coat flapped around him like wings, and when he swept his arms back, his collar gaped wide, revealing a pale expanse of unmarked skin.

He wasn't a Tracker, just crazy.

I crossed my arms over my chest and tried to tune out his words as I passed.

Kyle wasn't a punishment.

He wasn't a sinner or morally decayed.

He was the strongest person I knew. The best person I knew.

Besides, God wasn't singling out America. Other countries had lupine syndrome. Maybe they didn't have as many cases, but the virus wasn't an exclusively American problem.

"And God gave the demons human faces so that they might pass among you, but at night the beasts crawl on all fours! That is how you shall know them! Know them and root them out!"

Hello, Salem 1692.

I should have walked around the square. It would have taken longer, but it would have been better than listening to this. I glanced back and tripped to a stop as I spotted a familiar face in the preacher's audience: Amy's father.

Ryan Walsh stood a little apart from the crowd, a faraway gaze in his eyes. He was dressed casually—jeans and a wool coat instead of the suits he so often wore—but there was a briefcase in his right hand. There were more lines on his face than I remembered. He was still handsome for someone his age, but it was a worn kind of handsome. Though Amy had inherited his pale skin, she had missed out on his blond hair and ice-blue eyes. Those had gone to Stephen. Nordic: That was how Amy's mother had always described them. Her Nordic boys. They were so alike that looking at Mr. Walsh was like getting a glimpse of what Stephen would look like in a few decades.

Mr. Walsh's brows pulled together in a frown as he listened to the manic preacher. For a second, something dark crossed his face, but the look was there and gone so fast that I wondered if I had imagined it.

It was odd to see him so soon after Stephen's voice mail, but I guess it was kind of inevitable that he'd be drawn to the square with the rally just around the corner. I debated going back and speaking to him, but what could I say?

When Amy had died, she had taken my tie to her family with her. Anything I said now would come off as awkward and empty.

I turned and headed for the arch at the western edge of the park and the line of waiting buses.

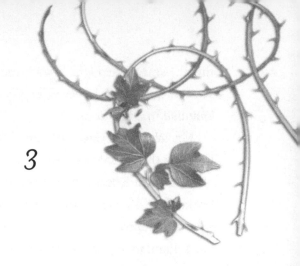

3

THE MEADOWS WAS A FOUR-BLOCK BY TWO-BLOCK
stretch on the southernmost edge of town. The area had
gotten its nickname from the fact that it had almost as many
vacant lots as ramshackle buildings. It was the kind of neighborhood people found themselves in after the last of their
luck had run out, where crack dens sprouted like weeds and
herds of abandoned shopping carts dotted the landscape.

Serena's family had been driven here after a handful of
Trackers burned them out of their home.

As I stepped off the bus, I tried not to think of the part
Jason had played in that event. So much had changed since
then—*he* had changed. Though nothing would ever make up
for what had happened that night, Jason had risked his life
to get Serena out of Thornhill. Hundreds of werewolves had
been saved from Sinclair because of a breakout Jason had
helped plan and execute.

A dark car with tinted windows turned onto the street
as I made my way along the cracked sidewalk. It slowed and
I felt my heart skip a beat. *Probably just a drug deal*, I told

myself, staring straight ahead and trying not to look nervous or suspicious. *Nothing to do with me. Nothing to do with Thornhill.*

I reached the Carsons' rental house—a gray two-story building that seemed to lean precariously to one side—and glanced back. The car had stopped two doors down. It idled at the curb as a man in a bathrobe crossed an overgrown lawn and approached the passenger-side window.

A knot in my stomach unclenched as money changed hands.

You knew you were getting paranoid when you were relieved to see the local crackheads conducting business.

Ever since the escape, I had been jumping at shadows. None of us were from Colorado, and we had all used fake names when we entered the camp, but I still kept expecting the LSRB to somehow find us, to swoop in and grab us the second we let down our guard.

With a small sigh, I headed up the walkway to Serena's house. The blinds on the first floor were all drawn, giving the place a deserted air, but her car was parked in the weed-choked driveway. Even without the car, I knew she would be home. Serena had always been outgoing—a people person—but now crowds and strangers made her flinch. When we'd first gotten back, she had barricaded herself in the house, pacing the rooms and hallways, too afraid to set foot outside or even look out the windows.

She had started going to school again last week—at least some days—but she wouldn't go anywhere else.

Kyle said to give her time, that she was doing remarkably

well given everything she had been through, but there we[r]
days when I wondered if she would ever fully recover from
Thornhill. There were days when I wondered if recovery was
even possible.

Behind Serena's car sat a motorcycle that looked fresh
from the assembly line. One of Tess's old boyfriends had
been a biker. He had tried teaching me how to ride—until
Tess found out and freaked. She thought I would end up
being one of those cautionary tales told by driver's ed
instructors.

I wondered where Trey had gotten the money for a new
bike. Serena's older brother had a reputation as a badass—
a reputation that wasn't entirely undeserved—but I didn't
think he'd steal a ride. For one thing, we were all trying to
keep a low profile. For another, his father would kill him.

I climbed the steps to the sagging front porch and
pressed my thumb to the doorbell.

After a small eternity, Trey opened the door.

His mouth twisted down at the corners as his gaze raked
over me; I tried to ignore the answering pang in my chest.
Trey and I hadn't exactly been friends, but I had always liked
him. As far as I knew, that feeling had been mutual—until
Colorado.

Trey crossed his arms, showing off a set of well-defined
muscles under a slightly too-small T-shirt as he leaned
against the doorframe. "What do you want, Dobs?"

"I came over to see Serena."

"And I should let you in because . . . ?"

I didn't have an answer.

d me for what had happened to his sister, and knew I deserved. I was the one who had asked . I had asked her to come to Denver, kicking events that had led to Thornhill's detention e project Warden Sinclair had dubbed "Willowgrove."

I was the reason Serena had come back vacant and wild and broken.

Silence stretched out between us. "When did you get the bike?" I asked, after a long moment, hoping talk of his new toy would soften him.

It didn't. If possible, his expression hardened into something even more severe. "It's not mine."

I almost asked him who the bike belonged to, but the look in his eyes stopped me.

Just when I was thinking I would have to text Serena to come let me in, Trey muttered something under his breath and stepped aside.

I hesitated, half convinced he would bite my head off— literally—if I crossed the threshold, but after a moment, I stepped into the house and pulled the door shut behind me.

As I followed Trey down the dingy front hallway, I had to step around and over boxes. I glanced in the living room: all of the Carsons' secondhand furniture had been pushed to one side.

"Your dad found a new place?"

"Not exactly." Trey paused at the foot of the stairs and leaned against the banister. He pressed his knuckles to the wood. Soft punches punctuated his words. "Trackers nabbed a werewolf and her boyfriend two blocks over last night. They put the boyfriend in a coma and a bullet in her head. Dad wants to get out of town—at least until after the rally. Our aunt lives in Charlotte. She's taking Noah. Dad left this morning to drive him down."

Noah was Serena and Trey's kid brother. I frowned. "What about you and Serena?"

A muscle ticked along Trey's jaw. "She doesn't trust werewolves around her kids."

I struggled to find something to say—anything to say—but Trey gave a stiff shrug and continued speaking while I was still fumbling for words.

"Dad was able to get a week off work. We're just going to drive until we find some place we feel like stopping. The boxes are in case . . ."

"You decide not to come back." I tried to keep my voice level, but the words wilted at the edges. Serena was one of my closest friends. My only female friend. I didn't want to lose her again.

Trey watched me soberly. "Kyle should think about getting out, too. By the time the rally hits, the whole town will be a tinderbox."

I thought about the number of dagger tattoos I had seen in the park. Trey was right: Hemlock wasn't safe for any werewolf—especially not one who had killed the former head of the Trackers.

Suppressing a shudder at the thought of what the group would do to Kyle if they ever found out, I nodded and slipped past Trey.

"Dobs . . ." Trey's voice stopped me when I was halfway to the top of the stairs.

I turned.

"It's none of my business, but Kyle's a decent guy. If you're the only reason he's sticking around . . ."

I tried to keep the anger and hurt from showing on my face. Did Trey really think I was so selfish that I would put Kyle in danger just to keep him by my side? "You're right," I said softly, "it's none of your business."

I jogged up the rest of the stairs.

The floorboards creaked as I made my way to Serena's room. I raised my hand to knock, but her smooth voice cut me off. "It's open."

Like the rest of the house, Serena's room was in serious need of new paint, but her father and brothers had tried to make the space cheerful. A bright-pink comforter covered the bed while turquoise lace framed the window. A pair of oversized wicker lawn chairs sat in the far corner, each heaped with purple cushions. The only thing in the room that lacked color was Serena herself. Since Thornhill, she'd worn only black or gray, never the bright clothing that had always seemed like an extension of her personality.

It was as though the camp had washed her out. Or like she was trying to fade away.

I walked into the room, and my steps faltered. Serena was curled up in one of the wicker chairs and she had company.

Jason rose from the other chair. His green eyes were bloodshot and there were dark circles underneath them, as though he hadn't slept in days. Had he looked this worn-out yesterday at school? I racked my brain and realized I had barely seen him. We had exchanged a handful of words in the hall between classes, but that was all.

"Mac. Hey." There was a slight, awkward catch to his voice. "I just came over to see how Ree—Serena—was doing."

My gaze darted to Serena. "Ree?" It was a pet name— one Serena's family used. It sounded strange coming from Jason.

Serena lowered her legs to the floor and sat up a little straighter. I tried not to notice how thin she was, how her knees and elbows were like sharp points under her clothes. Her ultrashort hair—another holdover from the camp— gave her face an elfinlike quality, and the slight hollows in her cheeks made me wonder if she had stopped eating again.

But her eyes were sharp and alert. It was a marked change from a month ago. For the first few days after Colorado— the first two weeks, really—Serena had alternated between a horrible sort of vacantness and wild, almost feral outbursts. Being back with her family had helped. There were still moments when she seemed to disappear inside herself, when flashbacks tangled with reality and left her frightened and confused, but the time between those moments seemed to grow steadily longer.

She glanced at Jason. "He was trying to drag me out. He claims going to school doesn't count as leaving the house."

"It doesn't." I stared at Jason, trying to reconcile the

sight of him in Serena's room. "Wait—that's *your* bike in the driveway?"

He ran a hand through his short blond hair. "Not exactly. I sort of borrowed it from the new dealership."

In addition to owning a huge amount of the commercial real estate in Hemlock, Jason's father owned a chain of car and motorcycle dealerships. I cringed. "Your dad will just love that."

"He'll barely notice." Jason shrugged. The gray T-shirt he wore left the black dagger on his neck exposed. The tattoo was incomplete—Jason had never become a full-fledged Tracker—but it was hard to look at the mark and not think of what was happening in the park.

Jason followed the direction of my gaze. He started to lift a hand to his neck and then caught himself. A faint blush crept across his cheeks.

Awkward silence filled the room, and when Jason's phone went off, I felt almost relieved, as though I had been saved by the bell.

He pulled out his cell and glanced at the screen. "I have to get this," he muttered, striding from the room.

A second later, I heard his steps on the stairs.

I turned to Serena and stared.

A slightly embarrassed look flashed across her face. "What?" she said defensively, then added, "He was checking on me. It's not a big deal. He just comes over sometimes."

I crossed the room and sat in the chair Jason had vacated. "Jason Sheffield has been coming over? On his own? To check on you? And it's not a big deal?"

Serena frowned. "You don't have to sound completely shocked."

"I'm not . . . that's not . . ." I bit my lip. "I know Jason can be really sweet. Sometimes. But he usually hides it and you're—"

"A werewolf?" She raised an eyebrow.

"Yeah," I said, feeling guilty even as the admission left my mouth. The fact that Serena was infected didn't matter to me, but as much as Jason's feelings on werewolves were changing, I wasn't sure it was possible for him to do a complete 180 in a few weeks.

"To be fair," Serena said, "I think I'm sort of a last resort. I think Jason's just . . . I dunno . . . lonely." She tugged at a loose thread on the bottom of her oversized gray cardigan. "You and Kyle have been kind of wrapped up in each other." I started to object, but she rushed on. "Which is totally understandable, but it's not like Jason has many people he can talk to about stuff that happened in Colorado or what he's going through now. And I think it's kind of hard for him . . . seeing the two of you together."

I felt my cheeks flush. Before the breakout, Jason had kissed me—and said he loved me—but every time I had tried to bring it up, to make sure we were okay, he dodged the subject.

Maybe I should have tried harder, but not talking about it seemed easier. Safer. Even though the more we didn't talk about it, the harder being around each other became. When the two of us were in the same room with Kyle, the awkwardness was almost suffocating.

"I know I've been spending a lot of time with Kyle," I said. "It's just that we have so much to figure out. . . ."

"Like whether or not he should go back to the pack."

I nodded. "We talked about it more last night. About how we could do the long-distance thing. Kyle said it's not really that different from one of us going away to college."

"Except college is, like, four years, and a pack is a lifetime commitment." Concern darkened her eyes. "And that's something you would want? That you would both want?"

"I want Kyle," I said, "and I want him to be happy." But it wasn't something I really wanted to talk about, not with Trey's words fresh in my mind. "So Trey and your dad are okay with Jason coming over?" I asked, shifting the conversation a degree to the left. "After everything that happened? *You're* okay with him coming over?"

"I wouldn't say Dad and Trey are exactly okay with it. I mean, Jason did try to beat Trey to a pulp, and he stood by while a group of extremists torched our house." Serena pulled in a deep breath and glanced down at her hands as she wrapped the thread from her sweater around her finger. "But he risked his life to help get me out of Thornhill. And given that I apparently tried to kill him, I'd say we're probably even."

"It wasn't your fault." I reached over and took the thread before she could cut off her circulation. "You didn't know what you were doing." Serena had been completely out of it when she attacked Jason—so out of it that she couldn't recall that night at all. She only remembered the detention block in scattered fragments; it was like a puzzle with half the pieces missing.

"Yeah, well . . . it doesn't change the fact that I did it." She raised her gaze to mine. "Trey told you we're leaving?"

I nodded. "Yeah."

Serena glanced out the window. "It's like they keep taking everything. The Trackers . . . the LSRB . . . Thornhill . . . I'm not even a threat anymore. If they wanted to take me back, I wouldn't even be able to defend myself."

I didn't believe that.

Serena had saved my life during the breakout. She had been able to shift just enough of her body to maul the warden and leave her infected with lupine syndrome. According to the news, Sinclair was being held under guard in a transition house—a place where the newly infected were sent to wait out the virus's thirty-day incubation period—while the government tried to piece together how a breakout at Thornhill could have happened. Once they were done with her, she would be shipped off to a camp where she would be just another inmate. As powerless as the wolves who had been in her care. Poetic justice.

"You saved my life back in Thornhill," I said. "You're not helpless."

Serena let out a soft, skeptical snort and held up her hand. The muscles under her skin slowly began to twitch and each twitch was accompanied by the sound of a breaking bone. It wasn't the harsh snap of a rib or femur; it was a small, delicate sound—like the noise a wishbone made.

47

Sweat broke out on her face and the tendons in her arm bulged like steel cables. Bit by bit, her hand transformed into something long and clawed.

But she couldn't hold it.

Serena's breath quickened as she let her arm fall back to her side. When I glanced down, her hand looked completely human.

She closed her eyes. "That's it. No progress since the night of the escape. I can shift my hand and then . . ."

"Nothing."

She nodded.

Sinclair's cure may not have truly worked, but it had changed Serena. For the briefest of seconds, I wondered if the warden would have eventually been able to achieve her goal, but I quickly pushed that thought aside. It didn't matter. No cure was worth the price Sinclair had been willing to pay.

"It's strange," said Serena, "for the first year or two after Trey and I got infected, I spent so much time wishing I could go back to being normal. But this? This feels like something's been carved out of me. It's like I'm hollow inside."

She opened her eyes. "But the hollowness isn't the worst part. The worst part is knowing they took something from me and not being able to remember them doing it. If I could remember, I'd at least know *what* they did. Instead, I keep imagining all of the things that might have happened." Without makeup and her old clothes, Serena looked young—way younger than seventeen—but her gaze held a weight that was ancient and tired.

As much as I hated asking her to think about the deten-tion block, it was hard to imagine there would be a better opening. "I remembered something from Thornhill," I said slowly, "part of a symbol I saw the night we tried to break you out. It was on a spreadsheet one of the program coordi-nators had. I think it could be a logo—maybe something or someone Sinclair was working with."

I pulled out my cell and brought up the picture I had snapped in the tent. "I thought . . . if I showed it to you . . ."

"I could tell you if I had seen it, too?" Serena reached for the phone. "Most of what happened really is a blank," she warned. "I mean, if I don't remember finally trying to stran-gle Jason Sheffield . . ." Her eyes grew wide as she stared down at the picture. She gripped my cell so tightly her hand shook.

She glanced up and her gaze locked on the wall behind me.

I looked over my shoulder. Whatever Serena was seeing, it wasn't in the room with us now.

"Serena?" I turned back to her and reached for her shoul-der. She flinched, but showed no other signs of response. I wasn't even sure she knew I was there.

The pulse in her neck beat like an animal throwing itself against a cage.

"Serena?" I said her name again, louder, as I shook her, gently at first and then harder.

Still, nothing.

"Trey!"

"Dobs?" I heard Trey's voice a second before his heavy footfalls sounded on the stairs.

Her brother's voice seemed to break through to Serena and pull her back. Awareness of where she was slipped through her eyes as her startled gaze darted to mine.

"I'm sorry," she whispered. "There was something, but I couldn't hold it." She pressed the phone into my hand as Trey appeared in the doorway.

Trey took one look at Serena's face and crossed the room in three long strides. "What happened? Are you all right?" He crouched next to her chair and glanced back at me. His gaze narrowed as though he knew, without being told, that I was responsible.

"I'm fine." Serena tried to brush his concern away. "I just tried to shift again."

"We agreed you'd give it a few days."

"No," corrected Serena, "you said you didn't want me trying. That doesn't mean I agreed."

Across the room, someone cleared their throat.

I turned toward the sound. Jason stood in the doorway, a tense, wary look in his eyes. "Did you tell them?" he asked Trey.

"Not yet."

"Tell us what?" I glanced from one boy to the other.

"There was an explosion at a transition house in D.C.," said Trey. "Fire gutted the parts of the building that were still standing—including the cells. They're estimating at least fifty people were killed." He shook his head. "Those places are locked down almost as tightly as the camps. If no one let the inmates out . . ."

"Jesus." The word was a whisper. I thought of all of those people—trapped inside, unable to breathe as the flames closed in—and shuddered. None of them would have been past the LS incubation period. None of them would have had the strength or healing abilities that came with being a full-fledged werewolf.

"That's not all." Jason pulled in a deep breath as his eyes locked on Serena. "So far, it's just rumors, but they're saying it was the transition house where they were holding Sinclair. They're saying the warden's dead."

4

TREY LOOKED UP AS I WALKED INTO THE KITCHEN. "ANY-thing?"

"Kyle's at the garage with his car. He'll be over soon." I sank into the chair next to Serena. "I couldn't reach anyone in Colorado, but that doesn't necessarily mean anything with the reception problems they have."

There was no reason to think Sinclair's death had anything to do with the pack or my father. Early reports were speculating that a gas leak had caused the explosion. Maybe, as unlikely as it seemed, it had just been a tragic accident.

The fact that Hank had called me twice on the same day the warden died was probably a coincidence. According to one of Jason's Tracker sources, Sinclair's death hadn't even been confirmed yet.

So why did the fact that I couldn't reach my father make me nervous?

Trey pushed a cardboard container of pad thai across the table. "Thanks," I mumbled, picking up a fork even though I wasn't hungry. "Jason's not back?"

Trey snorted. "He and his Tracker buddies are probably busy high-fiving one another over taking out a transition house."

I wanted to defend Jason, to tell Trey that he had changed, but the history the two of them shared was stronger than anything I could say.

"It wasn't the Trackers," I said instead, spearing a piece of shrimp on my fork as I glanced out the window. It had snowed in earnest an hour ago—a brief storm that had whited out everything for twenty minutes before suddenly stopping—and small mounds of flakes had gathered on the sill.

"Who else could have done it?" snapped Trey, pulling my gaze back. I guess none of us were buying the gas leak theory. "The Trackers have whole chapters that train guys to clear out packs and dens."

"There's a big difference between a den and a transition house," I pointed out, setting down my fork. "Trackers want wolves to be locked up. They aren't going to hit anyplace where that's happening. And they wouldn't risk pissing off the LSRB."

No. Assuming the destruction of the transition house hadn't been an accident, someone other than the Trackers had to have been behind it.

I sighed and leaned back in my chair as the scar on my shoulder blazed with a flash of phantom pain. I remembered the way Sinclair had looked at me—like I had taken everything from her and would suffer for it—as she raised her gun the night of the breakout.

With her dead, I didn't have to worry about her ever hurting me or the people I cared about again.

I should have been relieved.

It was just . . . of the hundreds of transition houses in the country, what were the odds of something happening to the one house where Sinclair was being held?

Only fools welcome coincidence—that was something Hank had always said.

With both the warden and the detention block gone, it seemed unlikely the truth about Thornhill would ever come out. And that, I couldn't help thinking, might be the reason that particular transition house was no longer standing.

There was a pen on the table. I picked it up and absently began doodling on a paper napkin, turning the edge of a grease stain into the symbol from my dream.

Sinclair hadn't been working alone at the camp. What if whoever she had been working with had wanted to make sure she wouldn't be able to tell anyone about their involvement?

I glanced up as a prickly sensation crept down my spine. Serena was staring at the ink swirls I had made. There was a tightness around her mouth and at the corners of her eyes, an echo of the fear she'd shown upstairs.

She took both the pen and napkin from my hands.

"Serena?"

Without answering, she expanded the sketch I had made, pressing the pen down so hard the paper tore.

"Ree?" Trey stood and walked around the table.

Serena didn't acknowledge his presence—not even when

he stepped between us and put his hand on her shoulder.

He gave her a small shake. "Ree?" he repeated, voice more insistent.

I peered around him. The sketch was now twice as large as the one I had made—it swallowed my original lines whole—but before I could get a decent look, Trey reached for the pen in Serena's hand, blocking my view.

All at once, Serena seemed to snap back to her surroundings. "Sorry," she said, voice small and shaking, as Trey shot me a worried look over his shoulder. "I was just—"

Whatever she was going to say was cut off by a knock at the door.

"I'll get it," I murmured, letting out a deep breath and pushing my chair away from the table. "It's probably Kyle or Jason." I left Trey to watch over Serena. Their voices followed me down the hall. Guilt settled over me as I heard the fear and confusion in Serena's voice as she struggled to explain to her brother what had just happened.

I should never have shown her that picture.

The knocking came again, louder this time.

"Coming," I muttered, knowing that if Kyle were outside, he'd hear me even through the door.

The knocking stopped. Definitely Kyle. Something in my chest unclenched just a little bit.

"I haven't been able to . . ." My voice trailed off as I pulled open the door and stared at the man on the porch—a tall, raven-haired man who was definitely neither Kyle nor Jason.

"Can I help you?" I asked, tightening my grip on the doorknob as my gaze darted to the unmarked skin at the man's neck. Despite the cold and snow, he wasn't wearing a jacket.

He flashed me a smile that probably would have been disarming if I had been a less paranoid person. His teeth were toothpaste-commercial bright, but crooked on the bottom. A swoop of dark hair fell over his pale forehead while stubble softened the harsh angles of his jaw. He was clad head to toe in black and held a manila envelope in his hand.

"I'm sorry—you were expecting someone else." His voice held the faint trace of an accent—Irish or Scottish, maybe—that had been worn down by time. "I was wondering if you could help me."

Before I could reply, he reached into the envelope and slipped out a sheet of paper. "I'm looking for this girl."

I fought to keep my expression blank as he passed me a glossy 8×10 of Serena. The photo had been cropped, but I knew it had been taken at Thornhill. I recognized the metal table with the built-in restraints and the large digital clock on the wall behind Serena's left shoulder. It was the room where they had tortured her.

Every drop of blood in my veins turned to ice water.

How had anyone found her? We had all given fake names, but Serena had been even more of a ghost. In order to hide her work from the LSRB, the warden had kept the wolves from the detention block from being registered in the system—something Jason had discovered while working in the camp. As far as the LSRB was concerned—as far as the official records for Thornhill were concerned—Serena had never existed.

My pulse pounded in the back of my throat until it felt like I was choking on each heartbeat, but somehow when I spoke, my voice sounded normal. "I've never seen her." As inconspicuously as I could, I took a small step to the side and closed the door halfway as I handed the photo back, trying to block as much of the view into the house as possible. "Who is she?"

The man's gaze dropped to my arm. Too late, I realized my sleeves were pushed up. The scar on my forearm—a permanent reminder of the men behind Amy's murder—was fully visible. It was long and jagged and could easily have been caused by any number of things. Including a werewolf.

These days, any scar was suspicious.

A trickle of sweat ran down my spine as a floorboard creaked behind me. I didn't have to look back to know it was Trey. He was careful to stay out of sight, but he brushed past me as he took up a position behind the partially closed door.

The man on the porch pulled his eyes away from my scar and slipped the photo back into the envelope. "She's one of the wolves who escaped from Thornhill."

"Here? In Hemlock?" This time when I spoke, my voice cracked slightly over the words. I prayed it would be written off as a normal reaction to the thought of escaped werewolves hiding nearby.

The man handed me a plain white business card bearing only a phone number. "Wolves are found all over and trouble usually follows." The words were bland, but it was impossible to miss the threat behind them.

I frowned at the card before tucking it in my pocket. The

area code was 713. Houston. Hank and I had lived there for almost an entire year, once—long enough for him to break down and get a landline.

The man on the porch was watching me in a way that made the hairs on the back of my arms stand at attention. "Give us a call if you change your mind about seeing her."

"Sure," I lied, forcing a tight smile as I began closing the door.

"The thing is," he said, stepping forward and wedging his foot against the doorframe to keep me from shutting him out, "the gentleman two doors down swore he's seen her here." Something sharp and predatory slid behind his eyes, a glimpse of the real man underneath the polite veneer.

"The guy two doors down is a crackhead," I said. "Give him twenty bucks and he'll swear on a stack of Bibles that the Easter Bunny lives next door."

I felt Trey's breath on the back of my neck. His arm skimmed mine as he placed his palm flat on the door, ready to shove even if he pulverized the man's foot in the process.

Time seemed to stretch out. Finally, the man on the porch moved back. "In that case, my apologies for the intrusion. And I hope you'll give us a call if you do see her." He turned and headed down the walkway, pausing and glancing back when he was halfway to the street. "Enjoy the rest of your day," he called, lifting his hand in a funny little backward wave.

Trembling, I closed the door and flipped the dead bolt.

"He'll be back," I said, pressing my forehead to the wood. "He knows I was lying about Serena and he saw my scar.

He's not sure whether or not I'm infected."

"We have to leave. Now." Trey headed for the kitchen.

I had to call Kyle and Jason; I had to warn them not to come to the house. I reached into my pocket and came up empty: I had left my phone in Serena's room.

As I headed for the stairs, I heard Trey promise Serena he'd die before letting anyone touch her.

Praying it wouldn't come to that, I took the stairs two at a time. How long until the man returned with reinforcements? Five minutes? Ten? A flash of movement caught my eye through an upstairs window as I reached the second-floor landing. A car with tinted windows—the same car I had seen earlier—had rolled to a stop in front of the house and a second car was pulling up behind it.

"Trey!" I bolted back down the stairs.

The sound of shattering glass came from the rear of the house followed by a ragged, male shout.

I tripped on the last step and collided with Trey and Serena in the hallway.

Blood welled from a gash in Trey's arm and Serena's eyes were so wide that she looked like one of the girls in the manga Tess sometimes read.

There was a thud at the other end of the hall. I turned toward the noise just as something slammed into the front door with enough force to splinter the wood around the dead bolt.

More shouts echoed in the kitchen. They were in the house.

"Go!" Trey shoved Serena and me into the small half

bath underneath the stairs and followed us inside.

The space was little bigger than a closet. Serena and I wedged ourselves into the gap between the toilet and the wall as Trey slammed and locked the door.

"Please tell me your plan has a part two," I said. Next to me, Serena's breath came in ragged, pained gasps; it was like she was on the verge of a panic attack.

Trey swore and tilted his head to the side, listening to the growing amount of noise in the house. "There are too many of them."

He moved to the small window above the toilet. It groaned in protest as he forced it open. He waited for a moment, listening, and then stepped back. His gaze locked on Serena. "Up!" The word was a low, desperate growl.

The window didn't look wide enough for my hips, let alone Trey's, but I didn't argue as Serena scrambled up onto the toilet seat.

She tried to hoist herself up, but whatever they had done to her at Thornhill had left her little stronger than a reg. Trey gave her a boost and supported her weight as she struggled to wriggle through the narrow opening.

I held my breath, almost as though I could make Serena's slight frame even smaller by constricting my own lungs. I let all of the air out in a whoosh as she made it through.

"You too, Dobs," muttered Trey, helping me up as something collided with the bathroom door.

I was so scared that I didn't crack a single joke about him trying to cop a feel.

Serena had barely made it through and I was two sizes

bigger. I twisted and squirmed as Trey shoved me from behind. Like a cork from a bottle, I finally popped free and only Serena kept me from falling on my neck.

We were on the small patch of lawn between her house and the next.

Serena stared up at the window and spoke through clenched teeth. "C'mon, Trey."

A horrendous crash came from inside followed by a wolf-like snarl. Someone screamed.

I grabbed Serena's arm, trying to pull her to the front of the house.

"I'm not leaving him!"

"We have to!" I dug my fingers into her arm as hard as I could, forcing her to look at me. "They're after you, not him. If we run, they'll follow. It'll give Trey a chance to get away." I had no idea if that was true, but Trey would never forgive me if I let anything happen to Serena. *I* would never forgive me.

"Serena, please!" I pleaded. "He'll be safer if he doesn't have to protect us!"

She shook off my grip. For a second, I thought she was going to fight me, but then two men rounded the back corner of the house and raised the alarm.

With an anguished glance at the window, Serena grabbed my hand and broke into a run.

We reached the front yard. Serena's car was blocked in the driveway. By unspoken agreement, we veered left, fleeing on foot and heading deeper into the Meadows.

If we could lose them among the ramshackle buildings

and vacant lots, we might stand a chance.

The sky had started to clear and the snow was rapidly melting. I slipped and slid on the slush-covered ground as we sprinted across lawns and darted around houses. More than once, Serena kept me from falling. She had lost her werewolf strength but was still more graceful than a reg.

My lungs burned and my muscles ached, but I pushed myself to go faster as shouts sounded in the distance. I concentrated so hard on putting one foot in front of the other that when I finally looked up, I had lost my bearings.

We were still in the Meadows, but I wasn't sure where— not until we ran across an expanse of broken pavement that was wet with melted snow and ducked into an alley created by two hulking shipping containers. Not until we came face-to-face with a dead end.

5

THE WOODEN FENCE TOWERED ABOVE US AND STRETCHED for blocks in both directions. Something in me sagged in relief as I stumbled to a stop and wiped the sweat from my eyes.

Serena let out a low, frustrated cry and turned to retrace our steps, but I grabbed her arm.

"Wait," I gasped. Forcing my shaking legs back into action, I jogged to the fence and squeezed into the gap behind the storage container on the left. I scanned each board. It was here; it had to be.

"Mac . . ." Serena peered around the edge of the container.

I finally found what I was looking for: a small carving of a skull in one of the planks. I jumped as high as I could and slapped the top of the board. Both it and the plank next to it popped out, revealing piles of scrap metal on the other side.

We had reached the junkyard on the edge of the Meadows—a place Amy and I used to go on dares. The secret entrance had been used by generations of students and was probably as old as the fence itself. Amy's brother had told us about it one lazy summer afternoon, and we had spent all of the following day searching for it.

I glanced back at Serena. Judging by the surprise on her face, the junkyard was one Hemlock experience she had managed to miss.

"Go!" I said, stepping aside so she could slip through.

The shouting came again—closer, this time—as I squeezed through after her and pulled the boards back into place.

I hauled in a deep breath as my heart hammered in my chest. After a moment, voices drifted over the fence, but I couldn't make out what they were saying.

"They're checking the nearby buildings," whispered Serena.

"Good." The word came out a relieved sigh as I glanced around. We were in a lane between a wall of scrap metal and the fence. Melting snow dripped off stacks of cars, filling the air with the sound of a hundred leaky faucets.

"We can't stay here," I said, straightening. Staying near the fence was practically asking to get caught.

Serena hesitated, then nodded. Together, we made our way deeper into the maze of precariously stacked scrap. The place became more of a mess the farther we went. Walls of cars were piled four and five high, and mounds of hubcaps reflected the light as the sun slipped out from behind a cloud.

Serena pulled her sweater tightly around herself and shivered.

A chill began creeping through my own bones—a contrast to the ache that was spreading through my muscles like wildfire—as the adrenaline started to wear off. My jacket was back at Serena's.

When we were far enough from the fence that conversation no longer felt like a risk, Serena stopped. "What now?"

It was a good question. The man who owned the junkyard—a crotchety old guy with a beer belly that looked as hard as his head—kept the gate locked unless someone was dropping off scrap or looking for parts.

Two years ago, he had been up on charges for taking a shot at a group of teens he'd found prowling among the old cars. God only knew what he'd do if he caught us trying to sneak past him.

I reached for my phone before remembering that it, like my jacket, was back at Serena's.

"I don't suppose you have your cell?"

Serena shook her head. "I bailed on my bio class yesterday and forgot to grab it out of my locker."

Okay: think. We couldn't call Kyle or Jason. Even if we had a phone, the chance of them being able to help without putting themselves at risk was slim to none. As it was, I was praying neither of them showed up at Serena's until the last of those men had left.

Trey was the one we really needed to get a hold of. We had to find out if he was okay and we needed to let him know that we were safe—at least for now.

Unfortunately, I had no idea how to do that.

"I think," I said slowly, each word falling like defeat, "we should find someplace to hole up for a few hours. An old car or van, maybe. We can't go back the way we came in, and even if the front gate isn't locked—which it probably is—we can't go back into the Meadows. Not yet, anyway."

Serena stared at me incredulously. "You want to hide?"

I nodded.

"And Trey?" A hint of her pre-Thornhill stubbornness flashed across her face. "Anything could happen to him— could be happening to him right now—while we're hiding in here."

"Going out there won't help him. For all we know, he's lying low and we'd only draw him out."

"And if they grabbed him because he made sure you and I got out of the house when he could have been saving himself?" countered Serena.

She glared at me, waiting for an answer.

I didn't have one. I cared about Trey—I really did—but I cared about Serena more, and she was safer in here than back out in the Meadows.

"If it was Jason or Kyle, you wouldn't just hide in here."

I opened my mouth, but she cut me off. "You want to stay, then stay, but I'm going to look for my brother." She stepped around me and started walking back the way we had come, head high and shoulders stiff.

I stared after her for a long moment and then broke into a jog.

"Serena! Wait! *Please* . . ." I followed her around a corner and almost steamrolled her when she came to a sudden stop.

"Why me?" she demanded, turning. Her eyes shone with tears that didn't fall. "Lots of wolves were at the camp. Why did they have to come looking for me?" I reached for her arm and she jerked back. "I'm nothing. I'm nothing, and for all I know Trey is hurt or caught or worse all because the LSRB came looking for me."

I swallowed. "You were part of Willowgrove." Serena flinched at the name of the sanatorium the camp had been constructed on, the name Sinclair had chosen for her pet project. I rushed on. "What if the explosion at the transition house wasn't an accident? What if someone targeted Sinclair to keep the truth about the camp from getting out?" I hesitated and then, as gently as I could, added, "If someone wanted to keep Willowgrove secret—wanted to keep it secret so badly that they'd destroy an entire transition house—then going after the wolves from the detention block might be next on their list."

"But I don't remember anything!" The tears spilled over as Serena shook her head.

"I know that," I said softly, "but they don't. And I don't think those men were from the LSRB."

Serena stared at me blankly. "Who else would they be?"

"I don't know," I admitted, "but Sinclair was keeping the wolves from the detention block off the LSRB's records." I pulled out the business card the man had given me on the porch and handed it to Serena. "Just a phone number. No logo. Nothing official. I don't think he was LSRB."

I had no idea who those men were or how they had found Serena, but I had to talk to my father. Two of the wolves from the detention block were with his pack. Someone had to warn them.

Serena crumpled the business card and then wiped her eyes with the back of her hand. She pulled in a shaky breath and opened her mouth to speak, but was cut off by a deep, male voice.

"I'm telling you: I heard something. They're definitely in here."

The gravel bass sounded like it was right on the other side of the wall of scrap on our left.

Serena grabbed my arm and pulled me back. Back around the corner. Back down the lane. We hung turns so sharply that my feet slid in the mud.

A black-clad figure rose up before us as we rounded another corner.

I stumbled, trying to stop my momentum as Serena let go of my arm.

The man reached for a holster at his waist, and a low, animalistic sound erupted from Serena's throat.

She launched herself forward. In the space between one breath and the next, she thrust her hand—a hand that was no longer human—toward the man's stomach.

It happened so fast that I didn't realize what she was doing—not until her claws pierced fabric and tore through flesh.

The man tried to scream. No sound came out.

I didn't want to move forward, but I had no choice: like gravity, the scene before me pulled me in. My eyes struggled to make sense of what I was seeing as I raised my hands to my mouth to stifle my own cry.

The muscles in Serena's forearm writhed under her skin, sending ripples through thick, black fur. Everything from the elbow up was human. Everything from the elbow down was . . . not. Her arm disappeared at the wrist. It was like it had been cut off.

No, I thought, gut churning as I fought the almost overwhelming urge to throw up. *Not cut off, buried.* Serena's hand was buried in the man's body.

I turned away, horrified, as she withdrew her hand. The sound the man made as he crumpled to the ground dragged my gaze back.

Serena stood over him, shoulders heaving. "I won't go back."

She glanced at me, her eyes more animal than human as her bones snapped and knit back together. Her entire hand transformed from the inside out, but somehow, a red stain remained on her skin. "I won't go back!" she repeated, her voice breaking over the words.

My hands were still pressed to my mouth. I lowered them as I slowly walked forward. Serena turned away as I crouched next to the man.

I couldn't bring myself to touch his skin and search for a pulse.

Instead, I stared at his chest, waiting for it to rise and fall. It didn't.

Black spots danced at the edge of my vision as I pushed

myself back to my feet. *It's not the first time you've seen a were-wolf use their claws as a weapon,* I told myself. *She didn't have a choice.*

Serena took a step and stumbled.

Shoving my revulsion aside, I ran forward and caught her weight as her knees buckled. This morning, back in her room, the effort to shift had exhausted her; this time it had drained her batteries dry.

Shouts rang out nearby. They echoed off the walls of scrap, making it sound like the voices were coming at us from all sides.

"Can you walk?" I asked. "We have to move."

Serena nodded. Leaning on me, she managed to put one foot in front of the other. By the time we reached the end of the lane, she was able to support her own weight.

We turned the corner and my heart plummeted as the fence rose up before us. It was a dead end—one without a secret entrance.

The shouts were getting unmistakably closer. There was no time to double back.

I swallowed. "Can you fight?"

"I don't know," admitted Serena. She flexed her blood-stained hand. Pain flashed across her face, but nothing else happened.

"Right. Plan B."

A rusting Chevy straddled the end of the lane. I headed for it, Serena on my heels.

"What's plan B?"

"We hide." I ducked behind the car. Small shards of glass

cut through my jeans and dug into my skin as I knelt in the sludge. I bit down on my lip, hard, to keep from crying out as Serena crouched beside me.

"They went this way." I recognized the softly accented voice of the man from the porch.

Footsteps churned the slush.

"You might as well come out," he said. "Otherwise, we'll just go in and get you."

For a long moment, the only sounds were the melting snow, the creak of metal, and the pounding in my chest.

I glanced at Serena. I couldn't let them hurt her. No matter what, I had to at least try to stop them.

Stay here, I mouthed. Then, before she could argue, I climbed to my feet.

The man from the porch stood seven yards away. His eyes were the color of scotch on the rocks—brown, but cold—and he held himself like someone who was used to fighting. It was in the subtle shift in his stance as I stepped around the car, in the way he curled the fingers on his right hand into a half fist.

"Tell the girl to come out."

"We split up." My eyes darted to the wall of muscle at his back: four men whose barrel chests and tree-trunk necks practically blocked the view behind them. "She's probably halfway across town by now."

"You're lying."

I could hear an engine in the distance. Probably a car they could force us into—assuming they didn't just kill us on the spot.

71

A wave of hopelessness and fear crashed over me, but I refused to let it suck me under. I reached for a nearby piece of metal and hefted the chunk of scrap like a baseball bat. They would get to Serena—there was no way I could stop them—but I would inflict as much pain as I could before they eliminated me.

One of the men glanced over his shoulder. "Donovan . . ."

The man from the porch—Donovan—ignored him. He walked toward me and I met him halfway, hoping to keep him from seeing Serena for as long as possible.

He glanced at the piece of metal in my hand and a flash of amusement lit his cold eyes. "Did no one ever tell you that sometimes it's better to give up gracefully?"

"What can I say? I believe in playing hard to get." My voice shook, betraying the fear underneath the sass.

"Leave her alone! I'm here."

I cringed as I heard Serena stand, but I didn't glance back. Instead, the second Donovan's gaze flicked to her, I swung my makeshift bat as hard as I could.

The metal hit his face with a sickening crack, the impact so strong that it reverberated up my arms.

Cursing, Donovan lurched to the side as blood gushed from his nose.

One man went to his aid while the other three advanced on Serena and me. Two of them drew Tasers while the last pulled a gun.

I backed up until my hip collided with the Chevy. Serena rounded the hood of the car and stepped in front of me.

I knew what she was thinking: if the Tasers were

calibrated to take down a wolf—like the ones the guards had carried at Thornhill—the voltage would stop my heart.

The nearest man pointed his Taser at Serena's chest as the sound of the engine drew closer.

There was something off about the noise. It was the wrong pitch and volume—more like a motorcycle than a car.

"Look out!" The shout came from the man at Donovan's side a split second before the wall of cars came crashing down.

6

METAL AND DUST. THE ENTIRE WORLD WAS METAL AND dust. I couldn't breathe and I couldn't see and the ringing in my ears drowned out every other sound.

Serena pulled me to the side and I felt a rush of air followed by a thud that shook the ground.

When the dust cleared, a green station wagon was sitting in the spot where I had been standing.

Eyes burning, I followed Serena over the hood of the car. A half-dozen vehicles had fallen into the lane, blocking it like a clog in a drain and scattering the men who had been closing in on us. As the ringing in my ears receded, low moans bled through. Not all of the men had gotten out of the way in time, but I couldn't tell how many had been trapped or who might be lying in wait. Just as I squeezed through the gap between a battered pickup and an old Camaro, a hand locked around my ankle.

Donovan had been pinned between the truck and the car. I couldn't see his legs, but his face was a mask of blood and dirt.

"Let go!" I yelled, kicking out as hard as I could. My foot connected with his face, but he just tightened his grip. With his other hand, he pulled a gun from the wreckage.

A low growl sounded from my left. I fought to twist free as a brown wolf launched itself over the nearest car.

Kyle.

His jaws fastened on Donovan's arm, snapping down like a bear trap.

The grip around my ankle fell away as the gun went flying.

"Come on!" Serena was suddenly there, pulling me through the rest of the wreckage and to an open spot where two lanes met.

I turned back to look for Kyle as the drone of an engine—the same drone I had heard earlier—filled the air.

A motorcycle swerved into the intersection, sending up a spray of slush as it came to a stop. A black wolf followed close behind.

Jason and Trey.

Trey raced past us and launched himself at the rubble, taking down a man who was struggling to his feet.

The man's screams bounced off the metal.

Jason was already off the bike. In a heartbeat, he was in front of me, blocking the fight from view. "Are you all right?" His eyes raked over my body, checking for cuts and broken bones, before turning to Serena. His mouth twisted. "Your brother was supposed to send a single car over—instead, the whole damn wall came down."

Werewolf superstrength to the rescue.

Jason shoved his helmet into my hands and pulled me to the bike. "Do you remember how to ride?"

"Not well."

"Not well will have to be good enough." He ran a hand through his hair and shot a nervous glance back at the wreckage. "Get out of town. You and Serena both. Get to the interstate and keep driving."

"I'm not leaving you and Kyle," I said just as Serena said, "I'm not leaving my brother."

Jason swore under his breath. He shot a desperate glance at Serena before focusing on me. "*Please*, Mac. Just for once, listen to me."

Trey was suddenly there. Still in wolf form, he head butted Serena, trying to push her toward the bike. Something dark and wet clung to the fur around his muzzle, and I tried not to think about the screams I had heard moments before.

"I'm not leaving," I insisted.

Jason let out a frustrated, strangled sound and hauled out his cell. His fingers moved over the screen, typing something into a GPS app. He handed the phone to Serena and then gripped my shoulders. "Go to that address and wait for us. If we don't meet you by sunset, then get as far away from Hemlock as you can."

"Jason . . ."

His grip on my shoulders tightened. "How many men are there?"

I swallowed. "Five."

"Trey and Kyle can take them."

I tried to glance back, tried to catch a glimpse of Kyle, but Jason caught my face in his hands, forcing me to look at him. "Please, Mac. You have to get Serena out of here. She's the one they're after."

I could hear the faint sounds of sirens in the distance.

My gaze slid to Serena. I couldn't let those men get their hands on her, and she couldn't be here when the police showed up and found the man she had killed. I was the reason she had been at Thornhill. Without me, this wouldn't be happening to her now.

I nodded—even though doing so left me feeling as though I had been torn in two.

Jason stepped back. "Head to the end of this lane, then take a right followed by two lefts. That'll get you out of the junkyard. The GPS will take care of everything after that." He hesitated, like he wanted to say something else, but with one last glance at Serena and me, he ran toward the sound of growls and screams.

Eyes stinging, I threw my leg over the bike. I tried to pass the helmet to Serena, but she shook her head as she climbed on behind me. "You're human. I'm not."

She slipped her arms around my waist as I pulled the helmet on. *You're doing this for Serena,* I told myself. A storm raged inside me as my body operated on autopilot and the engine roared to life. *You're not running away; you're protecting Serena. You have to protect her. You have to keep her safe.*

We shot forward and dipped dangerously to the side as I underestimated the power of the bike.

Somehow, I managed to keep us upright.

Serena's arms tightened around me as the junkyard dissolved into a sickening blur. I repeated Jason's directions under my breath like a prayer. "A right. Two lefts. A right. Two lefts."

The entrance loomed ahead. The gate was open, but a dark car had been parked across it. At the sound of our approach, a man ran out of the small hut that served as the junkyard office.

"Hold on!" I yelled, aiming the bike at the narrow gap between the car's rear bumper and the gate. The man threw himself out of the way, narrowly avoiding being crushed as we flew past.

The bike bounced as we hit the street and I struggled to maintain control as I hung a sharp right. The sirens were closer now, and when I glanced in my mirror, I caught a glimpse of red and blue lights.

Every muscle in my body screamed at me to turn around, to try and help Kyle and Jason and Trey, but I kept driving, urging the bike to recklessly high speeds until we were out of the Meadows and on the four-lane stretch of road that led to the industrial park.

The cold air rushing past chilled my skin, and everything inside of me felt numb.

I turned off the main drag as soon as I could, taking a series of twists and turns and finally pulling behind an empty furniture warehouse.

I lowered my feet to the ground and killed the engine. Even with the motorcycle supporting most of my weight, I could feel the tremble in my legs as my knees went weak. *How could I have left them?*

Serena slid off the bike. I looked at her, and for a second, flashed back to the way we had found her in the detention block.

You're not real. That's what she had said. Huddled in on herself and so lost that she couldn't tell reality from dreams. *You keep coming, but none of you are ever real.* I remembered the blood on her wrists and the horrible, vacant look in her eyes.

She had spent days and hours thinking we would never come for her.

I couldn't let anyone hurt her again. Not the men who had shown up at the house or the LSRB or the police.

I hadn't abandoned the others; I had saved Serena. It was the truth, but it didn't make me feel any better.

Serena folded her arms over her chest, hugging herself tightly. "What do we do now?"

I raised the visor on the helmet. The world seemed too bright as I struggled to find my voice. "You're going to call your dad and tell him it's not safe to come home. Then I'm going to call Tess." I wished I knew what I was going to tell her. After everything I had put her through when I disappeared to Colorado, I was going to have to leave again—at least for a few days. I didn't like it, but I didn't have much choice: there was no way I was going home tonight.

Serena was staring at me expectantly. "And then?"

"Then we head to the address Jason gave us and wait."

Serena pulled out Jason's phone. Her shoulders rose

and fell as she hauled in a deep breath. "What if they don't show up?"

I didn't have an answer. I couldn't even let myself think of that possibility.

"We just left them." A tremble ran underneath Serena's voice as she echoed my own thoughts. "How could we have just left them?"

I squeezed my eyes shut because looking into her face—seeing a mirror of my own guilt—was too hard. "Call your dad."

After a long moment, I heard Serena walk away.

I opened my eyes and ran my hand over Amy's bracelet.

The universe had an extremely hit-or-miss track record when it came to coming through for me, but I would promise anything—do anything—if it meant Jason, Kyle, and Trey were safe.

"Please," I whispered, "just let them be okay."

The GPS app on Jason's phone led us on a twisting route through Hemlock's historic district before winding past Fern Ridge Cemetery and into River Estates—a half-finished housing development that had fallen prey to the town's real-estate crash.

Some of the homes were completed but half were little more than wooden frames or small stakes marking off foundations. As far as I knew, not a single house had sold.

Nothing hit property values like a string of gruesome werewolf murders.

The place felt like a ghost town—a feeling not helped by

its proximity to the cemetery.

"Take the next right," said Serena, relaying the directions from the phone.

I pulled onto a tree-lined gravel lane and drove up to the only building in the subdivision that wasn't new: an old church on an overgrown plot of land. Ivy had staked a claim on its brick walls and its heavy wooden doors had been chained shut. There was a small manse next to the church, but its bricks were fire-scorched and one wall had caved in.

I rolled to a stop next to a For Sale sign covered in graffiti. "Are you sure this is it?"

"One Douglas Lane." Serena shivered as she slid off the bike. "One of Trey's friends told me about this place. He takes girls out here and tells them it's haunted."

It looked like a perfect place for ghosts. Someone had hammered a No Trespassing sign into the trunk of an ancient elm tree, but empty bottles glinted in the grass and cigarette butts dotted the gravel like tiny white bones.

A small chill crept up my spine. "Why's it just sitting here?"

"The congregation moved to a newer, bigger church on the other side of town," said Serena. "I guess there wasn't much point in keeping this one."

Out with the old, in with the new.

I glanced back at the For Sale sign. The words MS Commercial Realty were barely visible under a smear of blue paint. MS Commercial was one of the companies Jason's father owned—which explained how Jason had known about this place.

"It reminds me of the sanatorium." Serena's voice sounded small and lost as she stared at the church.

"It's just the bricks and the ivy," I said, trying to suppress my own memories as I climbed off the bike. "C'mon. Help me get this thing out of sight." The church wasn't visible from the street, but leaving the motorcycle in the open still felt like pressing our luck.

We wheeled the bike around the back of the church and stashed it behind a pile of broken office furniture.

There was an old tarp tangled in a nearby bush. Serena helped me pull it free and then went to examine the back door of the church as I flung the plastic over the motorcycle.

I glanced up at the rattle of chains.

"I hate this," she muttered, tugging on the huge padlock that secured the door and then turning and walking back to me. "A month ago, I could have torn that door off its hinges. Now I'm just—"

"A typical girl who's flunking History?"

"I was going to go with 'useless.'" Her skin was flushed. The air was cool, but she slipped off her sweater and tied it around her waist as she dropped her gaze to the ground at her feet. Softly, so softly that I almost missed the words, she said, "Do you think I killed that man? Back at the junkyard?" She looked up, and her eyes were dark and haunted.

"No," I lied. "Absolutely not. He was still breathing." I didn't think there was any way the man in the junkyard was alive, but Serena didn't need to know that.

Sinclair had seen infection as a bomb waiting to go off, as something she could diffuse, but the fear and memory of the camp—not lupine syndrome—was what had pushed Serena over the edge in the junkyard.

It hadn't been Serena's fault—not really. Besides, it had been self-defense. Better she believe a lie than spend the rest of her life feeling guilty and looking over her shoulder. No one else had seen her kill the man, and since her hand had been clawed, there would be no fingerprints. Whoever those men in the Meadows had been, I had a feeling they weren't the ones who had called the police and I doubted they'd stick around to answer questions.

Serena was staring at me, brows furrowed.

"He was still breathing," I repeated, more firmly, but I could still see the doubt in her eyes. "Come on," I said, turning away in an attempt to put an end to the subject.

I walked the length of the church, looking for a way in. The stained-glass windows were still intact—I guess even vandals had limits—but several basement casements had been smashed.

I went to the nearest one and crouched down. Jagged shards of glass still clung to the frame, making it look as though the window had teeth. I pulled my sleeve over my hand and carefully knocked out the remaining pieces before sticking my head inside.

The room beyond the window was as dark as a tomb.

"I need Jason's phone," I said, reaching back blindly. Serena handed it to me and I shone its light down into the darkness.

The feeble glow didn't pierce more than three feet into the gloom, but it was enough to tell that the room had been some sort of office. There was a desk underneath the window and the floor was littered with file folders and pamphlets.

I stowed the phone in my pocket before scooting back and swinging my legs over the windowsill.

Serena grabbed my wrist. She was still shivering, shivering so hard the trembles radiated up my arm. "You're not seriously breaking into a church?"

"We broke three hundred werewolves out of a government rehabilitation camp, you can't possibly be squeamish about a little B and E. Besides," I added, "the window was already broken."

"Breaking out is different from breaking in," insisted Serena. "And it's different when it's a church. It's sacrilegious or bad luck or something."

I rolled my eyes and pulled my arm free. "It's not like our luck can get much worse." Slowly, trying not to slice myself open on any remaining glass, I lowered myself through the window.

Shards crunched under my sneakers as my feet hit the desk. "Be careful when you come through," I warned as I hopped down to the floor. The mingled scent of mildew, old books, and mothballs ruffled my nose. I fumbled in my pocket for Jason's phone and used its light to find the door as Serena climbed through the window.

I stepped into a hallway. A rectangle of daylight glowed at the far end of the corridor: a door at the top of a single flight of stairs.

Serena was silent as she followed me up out of the

basement and into the main part of the church.

Light filtered through stained-glass scenes of angels and mangers and illuminated rows of wooden pews—most of which had been turned on their sides. Soft coos echoed above our heads, and I glanced up to spot clusters of pigeons nesting in the rafters. It wasn't hard to see how they had gotten in: patches of the roof had rotted through.

I wandered up the center aisle.

There were scattered signs of habitation. An old sweatshirt. A Bible with pages torn out. Three battered paperbacks and a book of matches from some random cheap motel. A travel mug next to a stack of newspapers. I picked up the topmost paper. It was from last week. "Someone was crashing here. Recently."

I strained my ears, but the pigeons and the creak of old wood were the only sounds I could hear. Hopefully, whoever had been squatting here had moved on.

The paper had been left open to the business section and my eyes were drawn to a photo in the upper left-hand corner of the page. It was a picture of Amy's father standing outside of CutterBrown Pharmaceuticals—the company he had helped take from a niche research outfit to one of the leading drug developers in the United States.

Someone had doodled a circle around Ryan Walsh's head, but all of my attention was focused on the building in the background, on the steel-and-glass sign that stood just a few feet from the main entrance.

A roaring sound filled my ears. It felt like something was prying my rib cage open, like the thoughts and emotions rushing down my throat with every breath were too large for my body to contain.

No wonder the image in my dream had seemed familiar. Even seeing just a small slice, I should have known what it was. A kingfisher in flight: the symbol of CutterBrown. Their logo was everywhere—on everything from the new wing at the hospital to scholarship applications in the guidance office at school. But nowhere had I seen it more often or on more random items—on everything from pens to shot glasses—than at Amy's house.

Amy's father had chosen the symbol himself. He had told me so, once, a long time ago—so long ago that the memory was hazy around the edges.

Before Ryan Walsh joined the company, CBP had been one of a handful of medical start-ups in Hemlock—small companies like the one Kyle's parents and Serena's father worked for—but he had lured away some of the best researchers in the world and then channeled the company's R&D budget into two drugs that had proven very, very popular.

These days, CBP was involved in all sorts of things and was one of the largest employers in Hemlock, making Ryan Walsh a sort of local god.

The paper shook in my hand.

A pharmaceutical company would have been the perfect partner for Sinclair. Hell, even the blood test the camp used to confirm incoming inmates were actually infected was something CutterBrown had been developing. Despite that, not once had it occurred to me that the warden might have been working with—or even for—CBP.

Why hadn't it occurred to me? How could I have been so stupid?

Sometimes people see things they're not ready to accept. Amy's words drifted through my head.

There was a soft thump behind me. I had been so consumed by the paper and the horrible ideas filling my mind that, for a moment, I had forgotten where I was.

I turned. "Serena?"

She was leaning heavily on one of the upturned pews, almost doubled over. "I think . . . I don't . . ." She looked up. Her normally dark skin looked ashen and her eyes were wide and unfocused.

Before I could take a single step toward her, she crumpled to the ground.

7

The flickering glow from four pillar candles filled the pastor's office, illuminating a handful of battered furniture and walls that were dotted with framed Bible verses and motivational posters.

I had found the candles—along with two blankets and a case of water—in a storeroom at the end of the hall.

I knelt on the floor next to an old sofa, ignoring the pain in my sliced-up knees as I tried to coax a sip of water between Serena's lips. That was what you were supposed to do when someone had a fever, right? Make them drink fluids. Try to keep them comfortable.

Not that this was any ordinary fever.

Serena's skin was almost blisteringly hot and her clothes were soaked through with sweat. A temperature like this would kill a reg; it would fry their brain and cook their organs within hours.

I didn't know what it would do to a werewolf. Werewolves weren't supposed to get sick—not unless you counted bloodlust—but whatever had been done to Serena at Thornhill had thrown old rules out the window.

Serena coughed and turned her head away from the bottle. "Are they here?" Her whisper was the sound of dry leaves blowing across pavement. It was the first lucid thing she had said in hours.

"Soon." I didn't know if the word was a lie or the truth, but it was all I had. I clung to the belief that Kyle, Jason, and Trey would walk through the door at any moment because that was the only reality I was prepared to accept. *You can't save everyone.* Kyle had said that to me, once. Or something like it. I pushed the words out of my head. They were all right; they had to be.

"How long have we been here? How long was I out?"

"You've been drifting awhile." I checked the time on Jason's phone, trying not to notice how low the battery was getting. "It's a little after eight thirty." I had sat here for hours, trying to make Serena comfortable, trying to calm her when she became agitated and talked about people and places only she could see.

In the lulls when she was still, the noise in my own head became so loud that I wondered if I was going mad.

The paper. The logo. The idea that CutterBrown could have been involved with Sinclair, that the company could have been part of the very thing that was making Serena so sick.

Amy's father didn't just work at CBP: He was chief operating officer. Even though his name wasn't on the letterhead, most people in Hemlock said he *was* CutterBrown. If CBP had been involved with Thornhill, he would have to have known.

. . . wouldn't he?

I tried to tell myself that there were other reasons that logo could have been at the camp. CutterBrown had been developing a test to detect LS—the same sort of test Thornhill had used during the admission process—and they made all sorts of drugs that Sinclair could have been using in the cocktails she had given the wolves in the detention block.

I wanted to believe there was another reason. One that didn't have anything to do with them knowingly helping the warden in the torture of dozens of teens.

"What if they don't come?" Serena's voice came out choked, as though her throat had constricted around the words. "Jason and Trey and Kyle. What if we wait and wait and they never come?"

"They'll be here." I slid the folded newspaper under the sofa. I had gone back to retrieve it after getting Serena settled, but I didn't want her to see it. She had acted so strangely after I had shown her the sketch from my dream. The last thing I wanted was for her to catch a glimpse of the paper and have some sort of relapse.

"Can I get you anything? More water?"

She shook her head.

Jason's phone let out a small, cautionary beep. It was the same sound it had been making off and on for the past hour as the words *connect charger* flashed across the screen.

My stomach twisted. The phone was our only link to the others. I was too scared to try calling Kyle or Jason—if they were lying low, a ringtone might give them away—but the hope that they would call had been one of the only things to get me through the past few hours.

Once the battery died, that hope would die with it.

"I think I'm going to throw up." Serena struggled to raise herself to a sitting position as I made a frantic grab for a nearby wastebasket.

I made it just in time.

Her shoulders heaved as her body expelled every ounce of food in her stomach. She continued to retch long after the point where there was anything left, so long and hard that I worried things inside her body would tear.

Finally she closed her eyes and lay back.

"Better?" I asked, touching her forehead with the back of my hand. Her skin was just as hot as it had been the last time I checked.

"A bit."

I slipped Jason's phone into my pocket and pushed myself to my feet. I lifted the wastebasket, holding it slightly away from myself and trying not to glance inside. "I'm just going to dump this out."

I waited until Serena managed a small nod, then I grabbed one of the pillar candles and slipped out the door.

The bathroom was at the end of a long, narrow hallway. Inside the black-and-white-tiled room, I set the candle on the edge of the lone sink and then dumped the contents of the basket into the toilet in the far stall. I didn't bother trying to flush: like electricity, the church's water supply had been cut off.

I stepped out of the stall and set the basket down. Cleaning up someone else's puke wasn't anything new: I had cleaned up after Jason more times since Amy's death than I could count.

I leaned against the sink and glanced up.

Amy stared back at me from the other side of the mirror. Her black hair fell around her shoulders like curtains and her eyes were dark, bottomless pits.

The phone rang, startling me so badly that I almost knocked over the candle.

"Kyle? Jason? Are you okay?" I fumbled with the phone as the words rushed out. I glanced back at the mirror. My face, not Amy's, filled the glass.

There was a long pause on the other end of the line and then a familiar, rough-edged voice said, "It's me."

"Hank." I gripped the edge of the sink as disappointment threatened to crush me. I had left a voice mail for my father—one with Jason's phone number—shortly after Serena's collapse.

"Are you all right?"

"I'm not hurt." Unless you counted bruises, exhaustion, and so much worry that I was close to losing my mind.

"Serena?"

"She's . . ." I started to tell him about the fever but the battery warning on Jason's phone went off again. The small interruption gave my tired brain a chance to register the

92

strangeness of the question. The message I had left for Hank had been on the far side of extremely vague. While I didn't think it was likely someone was hacking my father's voice mail, I hadn't felt safe leaving anything more than Jason's number and a request to call. "How did you know something happened to Serena?"

He ignored the question. "Is she all right? Is she safe?"

I didn't want to answer his questions until he answered mine, but I was too worn-out and worried to play games—especially with Jason's phone on the verge of death. "She's sick—some kind of fever. Men showed up at her house this afternoon. They had a photo of her. *From Thornhill.* Serena's brother held them off—along with Kyle and Jason. They gave us a chance to get away."

I hesitated. "I don't know where they are," I admitted. "Jason gave us an address. He told us to wait until sunset and then get out of town if they hadn't shown."

"It's past sunset."

"They'll be here."

"You can't afford to be sentimental, kid. You know better."

"They'll. Be. Here." It wasn't a question. It wasn't a debate. My father had always been great at cutting people loose, but I wasn't anything like him.

Hank sighed. When he spoke again, he sounded like he had aged about forty years. "The remaining two Denver packs were hit last night. Someone is going after the wolves from the detention block. They managed to get three—two from Carteron, one from Portheus. It's why I tried to call you this morning. I thought there was a chance they'd go after Serena."

"They almost got her."

"She's lucky," said Hank, a dark edge to his voice. "I don't know who these guys are, but they're not LSRB. According to the other pack leaders, they killed a couple of people who got in their way, but they weren't interested in anyone else. They were fast and efficient, and they knew exactly who they were going after and how to get in. They were good. Mercenary-level good."

Packs didn't take security lightly. If the men had known how to get in and where the wolves from the detention block were, that meant . . .

"They had moles inside the packs." My blood ran cold as the words left my lips. "What about the Eumon?" Two of the wolves from the detention block were with Hank's pack, and there were members of the Eumon who would have known that Serena, Kyle, and I had gone back to Hemlock.

"I know my pack. If there's a leak, it didn't come from us."

"But they knew where Serena was . . . who she was."

"That doesn't mean anything. You saw what they did to your friend in the detention block. You saw how out of it and confused she was. There's no way of knowing who she may have told what."

It was a fair point, but it still didn't make sense. "It's been almost a month since the breakout. If people knew where Serena was this entire time, why wait for today to go after her? Why wait to go after the others?"

"Maybe they wanted to go after everyone in one fell

swoop. Maybe they were waiting until they could get to Sinclair before dropping the ax."

"You heard about the transition house?"

"I'm waiting until there's a body before breaking out the champagne, but yes."

I swallowed. "So it wasn't you?"

"No—though I can't say I haven't been second-guessing my decision not to kill her when I had the chance."

"Do you think someone's trying to cover up what happened in the detention block?"

"Don't you?"

Of course I did. I just wanted to hear someone else say it. For a split second, I considered telling Hank about the CutterBrown logo and then dismissed the idea. There were reasons that logo could have been in the camp—reasons that didn't point to some sort of evil partnership with Sinclair—and accusing CBP of working with the warden would be like accusing Amy's dad. I couldn't do that. Not without any proof. Instead, I said, "I can't let them get their hands on Serena."

"I'm working on finding out who's behind the attacks. In the meantime, you need to get your friend to the pack. We can keep her safe. And you. Eve is on her way to Hemlock to escort you. She should be there by morning."

Eve had been with us in Thornhill. She was Hank's protégé, and a member of his pack. She was also one of the toughest wolves I had met.

"You sent her without even talking to me?" My immediate flash of annoyance was quickly overshadowed by suspicion. Hank didn't do favors—not unless he was getting something in return. "Serena isn't anything to you. She's not part of your pack. Why would you help her?"

"I'd say common decency, but I think we both know that's not it." There was a rustle and I heard muffled voices in the background. A second later, Hank was back. "Someone is going to a lot of trouble to find these kids. Until I know who, I'd prefer to keep them from getting the whole set. Be ready to leave as soon as Eve gets there."

Jason's phone beeped again. I ignored it. I didn't like the fact that Hank was making decisions for us and giving orders, but this afternoon had been close. Way too close. Like it or not, we needed all the help we could get. Heading to Hank's pack couldn't guarantee Serena's safety—especially not when two other packs had been hit—but it was better than getting picked off on our own. "I can't leave until I know the others are all right. I'll try to convince them we should go to Colorado, but I can't promise everyone will be on board."

"I don't care about everyone. I care about you and that girl." Hank's voice began to break up. ". . . want . . . you out . . . Hemlock . . . don't want you . . . rally."

Silence.

Jason's phone had finally died.

Slowly, steps heavy, I walked back to the pastor's office.

Serena didn't open her eyes as I stepped into the room. Her face glistened with sweat and her breathing was labored. Her cracked lips formed words that were too soft for me to catch.

I crossed the room and leaned over her.

"I promise I'll be good. Clean my plate and wash away the dirt. You don't have to leave me here. Please don't leave me here." Tears leaked out from under her closed lids. "I can be good."

"Serena?" Tentatively, I touched her shoulder. "It's okay. You're not there anymore. You're safe."

She flinched at my touch but then grew calm. Her breathing evened out and she seemed to slip deeper into sleep. I watched her for a few moments and then lowered myself to the floor next to the couch.

I tugged the extra blanket around my shoulders as my eyes roamed over the prints and posters on the walls. Like the furniture, they apparently hadn't been worth taking when the building was cleared out.

My gaze lingered over a framed Bible verse. "'What shall it profit a man, if he shall gain the whole world, and lose his own soul?'" I read the line in a whisper. Mark 8:36.

The words were set in white on a black background and reminded me of the banners at Thornhill—the ones extolling the virtue of control.

"Amy . . ." I whispered her name as I pulled my legs to my chest and rested my forehead against my knees.

After we had found out who killed Amy and why, I had expected the dreams to stop. When they hadn't—when the dreams followed me to Thornhill—I had assumed they were the by-product of guilt at letting her killer escape and fear of losing Kyle and Serena in the camp.

All along, I had assumed the dreams were a trick of my

subconscious. A fun-house mirror version of Amy dredged up by my mind to hurt me.

What if I had been wrong?

What if some part of Amy was still here? What if something she had known was keeping her here? What if something connected to CutterBrown was keeping her here?

Her voice drifted back to me from my dream. *Just look, Mac. Please.*

"Amy . . ." I squeezed my eyes shut and waited, but she stayed just out of reach.

8

"MAC . . ."

The weight of a hand on my shoulder. A familiar voice calling my name. I curled into the touch, still half locked in sleep.

"Trey!" The voice rose to a shout. "They're in here!"

Serena. The church.

I jolted back to reality with a gasp.

I had a second to register Kyle's deep-brown eyes and the relief that flooded them before he pressed his lips to mine in a kiss that tasted faintly of smoke and salt.

My vision blurred, tears fragmenting his face as he pulled back. He was here. He was all right.

I wiped my eyes roughly with the heel of my palm.

Kyle looked dirty and exhausted, but otherwise okay.

His gaze swept over me, cataloguing each scrape and bruise. "Are you all right?"

I nodded as Trey burst through the door.

Trey's gaze locked on his sister. "What the hell

happened?" he asked, going straight to her side.

Kyle stood and helped me to my feet. He wrapped an arm around my shoulders, holding me close.

"I don't know," I admitted. "She tried to shift in the junkyard. She was only able to change her hand—just like every other time—but afterward, it was like she didn't have any strength. She couldn't even walk on her own. After a few minutes, she seemed okay, but once we got here, she just collapsed."

I leaned into Kyle and shivered. "She keeps drifting in and out. She was burning up. I didn't know what to do."

"Ree?" Trey called his sister's name softly as he crouched next to her. Gently, he took her hand and checked her pulse. "Her heart is beating too slowly. Like a reg's."

Pain and worry filled his face. His expression was so unguarded and raw that watching it felt like intruding on something private.

I looked away; as I did, the realization that there were four of us in the room, not five, hit me like a slap. "Where's Jason?" I eased away from Kyle as a wave of dread swelled in my chest.

"He's okay," said Kyle, putting his hand on my shoulder. "We ran into a group of Trackers and they dragged him out on a hunt."

I stared at him, wondering how his definition of okay could be so radically different from mine.

"There was a riot downtown," Kyle continued; "that's part of why it took us so long to get to you. By the time we dodged the cops and were sure we hadn't been followed from the junkyard, we got caught up by the mobs. There was fighting all the way up to Elm Street."

My heart lurched. "Tess?"

"She's all right." He slid his hand down my arm and then threaded his fingers through mine. "We went by the apartment building."

"Thank you." I let out a deep breath and squeezed his hand. "What about your parents?"

"They're okay. The violence hasn't spread across the bridge." His gaze hardened and the light from the candles wreathed his eyes in flame. "Trackers grabbed a suspected wolf at a bar. They practically beat him to death. A few locals tried to step in and it turned into a free-for-all. The bars downtown closed early to try and avoid more trouble, but all that did was drive a bunch of half-drunk, overexcited people into the streets."

A large inebriated group with nothing to do and plenty of pent-up anger and fear? No wonder things had gotten out of control.

"We need to get out of Hemlock," said Trey. Serena stirred in her sleep and he adjusted the blanket over her before pushing himself to his feet. The look on his face as he turned to Kyle and me was filled with threats and barely contained anger. "Before things in town get worse. Before whoever sent those men to the house track us down. I won't let them get near her a second time."

I swallowed. "I spoke to my father. Someone went after three other wolves from the detention block last night. He wants us to go to Colorado. To the Eumon. Eve is on her way here. She should reach town by morning."

"What makes him—or you—think my sister will be safe with his pack?" The look Trey shot me was scathing. "In case you've forgotten: she was with his pack when she was caught and shipped off to Thornhill."

"I didn't forget." I struggled to keep my voice even. As if I could ever forget that.

Kyle tried to smooth out the rising tension. "There might be someone in the pack who can help her," he said. "They have people who were doctors and nurses before they became infected. They might at least be able to figure out what's wrong with her or what they did at Thornhill to cause this. Maybe they can figure out what drugs they gave her or if any of them are still in her system."

The corner of the newspaper was just visible under the sofa. I opened my mouth to tell them about the logo, but Trey's voice cut me off and knocked me silent.

"I already know what's wrong with her." He walked to the room's one small, dirty window and stared at the darkness outside. "This isn't the first time this has happened. Back when we were kids . . ." His voice trailed off as he flexed his right hand and rotated his shoulder. So suddenly that I jumped, he punched the window frame, cracking the glass and splintering the wood.

Trey's shoulders slowly slumped as the tension drained out of him. He turned and met my gaze. Everything about him seemed . . . *defeated*.

"We were just kids when we were attacked. Serena . . . hell, she was so small for her age, most people thought she was eight instead of eleven." The Adam's apple bobbed in his throat as he swallowed. "The first time we shifted, I was fine. But Ree could only hold the change for a minute. Afterward it was like her body tried to burn itself up. Dad couldn't take her to a hospital without them finding out what she was. It took three days for the fever to break and Ree ended up in bed for a month. She almost died."

Serena had told me the story once before. No one knew why, but children under fifteen only had a 40 percent chance of surviving their first shift. The fact that both she and Trey had made it through bordered on miraculous.

A small detail, barely noticed at the time, drifted back to me. "I got a look at Serena's admission form while we were in the camp. They circled the age she was when she became infected. Maybe that's why they singled her out."

A crease formed between Kyle's brows. "Because they figured if she could survive being infected so young, maybe she'd be strong enough to survive what they were doing in the detention block."

I thought of the cemetery in the woods behind the camp as I stared at Serena's small, feverish form. What if they had been wrong? What if she wasn't strong enough, after all?

The narrow staircase creaked under my weight as I climbed up to the choir loft. The flame from the pillar candle I carried jumped and flickered, making the shadows in the small space dance.

Kyle looked up as I stepped through the door. He had pushed two benches together and had retrieved Tess's sleeping bag from his car to form a makeshift bed. It wasn't exactly luxurious, but it was good enough.

Jason had managed to get his hands on a phone and had called Kyle to say he wouldn't make it to the church before morning, and Trey had wanted to be alone while he kept watch over Serena—I think because he hated the idea of anyone watching him wait and worry while his sister fought for her life. The only thing for Kyle and me to do was try to catch some sleep.

"Did you reach your dad?"

Warmth flooded my cheeks. I prayed the darkness would hide my blush as I handed Kyle his phone. "No answer," I lied. "I guess we just wait for Eve to show up in the morning."

His fingertips brushed mine as he took the cell. Part of me almost caved right then and there. I wanted to tell him the truth—I knew how dangerous secrets could be—but for some reason, I couldn't bring myself to tell him about the logo or why I had really wanted to borrow his phone.

Not yet.

It was like CutterBrown was a secret—one shared between Amy and me.

I would tell Kyle—I would tell him everything—once I figured out whether or not there was anything worth telling.

He pulled back the sleeping bag and stretched out on one of the benches.

I watched him for a moment, memorizing the way the candlelight played across his face, before blowing out the flame and joining him.

He slipped an arm over my waist and I scooted back until my shoulders were flush to his chest. Between the sleeping bag and the old jacket Kyle had found in his car, I was truly warm for the first time in hours.

Kyle traced light patterns on my stomach, loops and swirls that I could somehow feel even through layers of fabric. We had never been driven to fill silence with words—not when we were with each other—but the quiet that fell over the loft was somehow thick and heavy.

"Are you all right?" I asked.

It was a stupid question. None of us were all right.

His hand stilled, but he didn't speak for a long moment. "I was thinking about the junkyard," he said finally, pulling away from me.

Kyle and Trey hadn't said much about what had happened after Serena and I took off on the bike.

I rolled over so I could study his face.

Kyle was lying on his back. Moonlight drifted down through the holes in the church's roof, providing just enough illumination for me to make out his profile and the hard line of his jaw.

"What happened?" I asked softly, hesitantly. I thought of Serena and the man she had killed. "Did you . . ."

I cut myself off before finishing the sentence, but Kyle guessed what I had been about to ask.

"I don't know. I hope not." His chest rose and fell as he took a deep breath. "Most of the men were trapped when Trey sent that wall of cars crashing down. I hurt a few of them—the guy who grabbed you, another who was trying to call for backup—but I didn't kill anyone. I didn't have to."

I slipped my hand into his as I waited for the *but*.

"More men cornered us in the Meadows. Not the police. Guys like the ones who went after you and Serena. One aimed a gun at Jason. I didn't think . . . I just . . ." Kyle's hand flexed around mine. "I don't think I killed him—everything was crazy but I'm sure he was still alive—but I cut him up pretty badly."

"You were protecting Jason."

"So?"

"What do you mean, 'so'?" I let go of his hand and raised myself up on my elbow. "Kyle, you were protecting Jason. You were protecting all of us."

"That doesn't make what I did any less awful. Any more human."

"And they were acting like humans? They had guns and Tasers. They drove Serena out of her home and hunted her down. That's not very human."

Looking at him, I felt a sharp, aching sadness. Infected or not, Kyle was the most human person I knew. The best person I knew. I wished there was some way I could make him see that.

After a long moment, I lay back down and rested my head on his chest.

Eventually he put his arm around me.

"We're not coming back here, are we?" I asked, changing the subject. "After tonight, we're not coming back to Hemlock."

"Not for a while," Kyle said. I shivered and he held me

a little tighter. "Those men aren't just going to give up, and if they were able to find Serena, it won't take them long to figure out who the rest of us are. Where we live. Who we know. It's not like Serena has a ton of friends for them to sift through."

My heart flipped and my stomach plummeted. With everything else going on, the thought that whoever had sent those men might try to track the rest of us hadn't even occurred to me. "What if they go after Tess? Your parents?"

I went rigid in Kyle's embrace as panic flooded me.

"They should be okay as long as we don't try to contact them. They'll watch our families in the hope they can lead them to us. As long as they can't, they should be safe." His voice was low and steady as he ran his hand over my shoulder and upper arm, trying to coax my muscles into unknotting.

I didn't understand how he could be so calm. "You sound like you're okay with it. Like leaving isn't the end of the world."

"I'm not okay with it," he said. "But the last time I left, I thought I had lost everything. My past. My future. Everyone I cared about. This time, whatever happens, I have you."

"You had me before," I said softly. "You've always had me."

He pressed a kiss to my forehead. "Yeah, but this time it finally sank in."

I was quiet for a moment. "What happens when we get to Colorado?"

Trey hadn't been thrilled at the idea of running to the

Eumon, but we didn't have a lot of options. We could strike out on our own—run away and try to hide—but there was no guarantee we wouldn't be found. At least with the pack, we would have people backing us up—not that being part of a pack had helped those other wolves in Denver.

Kyle brushed a strand of hair back from my face. "What do you mean?"

"Like you said: those men aren't just going to give up. Until we know who's after Serena and why, how will we ever know when it's over? What's to say we'll ever feel safe enough to leave the Eumon?"

"Maybe we won't want to. There are worse things than being part of a pack."

"For you and Serena and Trey, maybe, but what about me?" Thinking about myself at a time like this felt selfish, but I didn't want any misunderstandings between us—not when Kyle still hadn't decided whether or not he wanted to be a member of the Eumon. "The other wolves won't accept me. Not really. I'll always be Hank's reg daughter or your reg girlfriend."

And even if they did accept me, what would I do there? They were in the middle of nowhere. I wouldn't be able to finish school or get a job. I would be the only person in fifty miles who wasn't infected.

I would be with Kyle, but in a way, I would be alone.

Kyle sat up. His face was completely in shadow and his tone, when he spoke, was carefully neutral. "What do you want, Mac? Because right now we don't have a lot of choices."

"I know. But if we're giving up everything, don't you at least want to know why?" I thought of the newspaper downstairs. Again, I wanted to tell him. Again, I found myself holding back.

"Of course," said Kyle, "but knowing won't change the fact that we can't stay here."

We both lapsed into silence. "I'm not saying we shouldn't go to the pack," I said finally. "I'm just saying I don't want the pack to be a permanent solution. Staying because we want to is one thing. Staying because we're scared to leave just makes the pack a prison."

"Werewolves carry prisons with us no matter where we go," said Kyle. "We have to put up walls because if we don't . . ." He sighed and lay back down without finishing the sentence. He didn't sound angry—not exactly. Just tired and frustrated. He didn't touch me and the few inches of space between us felt like a chasm. "We can talk about it tomorrow," he said. "For now, let's just try to get some sleep."

I hesitated, but eventually nodded. "Okay."

Still, no matter how many minutes ticked by, sleep evaded me.

"Kyle . . . ?"

"Yeah?" His voice came back heavy with sleep. After all, he had even more reason to be exhausted than I did.

"You really do have me. Always."

I waited for his response, but he was already gone.

9

SNOWFLAKES STUNG MY CHEEKS AND CLUNG TO MY lashes. They covered frozen puddles and the remainders of makeshift memorials, turning the alley white.

The snow somehow made things more bearable. I still couldn't bring myself to enter the gap between the buildings, but I could stand at the opening and look inside.

It was the closest I had managed to get.

"Someday, you won't even think about it." Amy stepped around me and into the alley. "You'll be walking down the street, lost in thought, and you'll pass the spot where I died without a second glance. Nothing lasts forever—not even guilt and grief."

I was freezing, but she wore a yellow sundress and her feet were bare. Her only concession to the cold was one of her brother's dress shirts, unbuttoned and tied over her midriff.

"Amy . . ." A lump rose in my throat and I struggled to speak around it. "Is CutterBrown tied to Thornhill? Is that why you showed me the detention block and the logo?

Because of CBP and your dad?"

Instead of answering, she crouched down and plucked a teddy bear from under the snow. She shot me a small, sad smile as she stood. "I never wanted any of this, you know. My death . . . these nighttime visits . . . any of it. I didn't know this was what would happen."

"You're not real." My voice rose at the end like a question. I had been considering the possibility that she was real just a few hours ago, but faced with her now, I didn't want to believe it could be true. I wasn't sure if I believed in Heaven or Hell, but I wanted to think Amy was someplace better than here. "You're just some twisted product of my subconscious," I insisted, trying to squash my doubts.

She raised an eyebrow. A splash of blood appeared on her cheek, but she waved it away with one hand. "Why do I have to be one or the other? Why does everything have to be black or white?"

"It just does."

She tossed the bear back to the ground. As it hit the concrete, the alley changed. The white snow and dark shadows swirled together and pulled apart until there was another alley, one where sprays of blood covered brick walls and puddles were tinged pink. One where Amy lay sprawled on the ground, her arms and legs at angles that were all wrong, a gaping hole where her torso should be.

I stumbled back, tripping and landing flat on my back in my desperation to get away.

I squeezed my eyes shut. I wanted answers, but I didn't want to be here. I wanted to wake up. "Please . . ."

"Shhh. Mac . . . Shhh . . ."

My eyes flew open as cold hands touched my face. Amy was leaning over me, her hands cupping my cheeks. "It's all right," she whispered. Her breath smelled like cherry licorice and rotting leaves. The alley was gone and I could see the choir loft over her shoulder.

I turned my head; next to me, Kyle slept soundly and deeply.

Amy stepped back and then smoothed the skirt of her dress over her legs as she knelt on the floor beside him. She reached out and brushed a lock of hair back from his forehead. He shivered and frowned, but didn't wake.

"He sees me sometimes, you know. Ever since he became infected. Out of the corner of his eye or as a shadow behind his reflection in the mirror. Once, I think he heard me. He was leaving flowers on my grave—pink carnations from the grocery store, but I told myself it was the thought that counts—and I yelled at him as loudly as I could. He looked up and turned, but shrugged it off as the sound of the wind through the trees. Maybe that's all I am: gusts of wind and patches of shadow."

She blurred around the edges as I drifted closer to waking.

"Amy . . ."

"Come and see me," she said softly, pushing herself to her feet.

"You're not real," I said again.

Her hair fell forward as she shook her head. "If you really

believed that, you would have worked harder at keeping me out."

Before I could reply, she faded away.

I woke slowly and reluctantly, clinging to Amy's words as I opened my eyes.

Dawn filtered through the stained-glass windows below. It filled the loft with patches of soft, color-tinged light and fell on Kyle's sleeping form. I had edged away from him sometime during the night. I felt an almost overpowering desire to wake him, to have him wrap his arms around me and hold me close.

My dreams of Amy were usually so bad that I couldn't wait to escape back into reality. This had started out that way, but the ending had been different. It had left a hollow in my chest, like the loss of her was as fresh and raw as it had been in those first few days after her death.

I remembered the weight of Kyle's arm around my shoulders at Amy's funeral, how his touch had been the only thing that kept me from running. It had always been like that, like his presence anchored me.

I started to reach for him but pulled back. As much as I wanted comfort, there were other things that were more important.

I slipped out from under the sleeping bag and swung my legs to the floor.

Kyle shifted in his sleep, but didn't wake.

He had left his cell on the floor. I picked it up and scrolled through the options until I found a memo app.

Something I have to do. Be back soon. M

Guilt brought a lump to my throat. I swallowed it down.

I knew Kyle would freak if he woke to find me gone with only a vaguer-than-vague note, but there was something I had to do. Alone.

Setting the phone on the bench, I pushed myself to my feet.

Hopefully, I'd be back before he woke. Back and with answers.

The chill in the air stole my breath and I burrowed deeper into Kyle's jacket as I carefully made my way to the stairs and down to the first floor.

I paused outside the pastor's office. The candles had all been extinguished, but enough light slipped through the room's one window to let me see the rise and fall of Serena's chest. She looked like she was sleeping peacefully.

Trey was sitting on the floor next to her. His eyes were closed and his head lolled back against the arm of the sofa.

"Where are you going?" he asked as I stepped away.

Startled, I turned back. Trey's eyes were still closed. "Outside to use the bathroom," I lied. "I won't be long."

He nodded and mumbled, "Be careful."

"I will," I promised, hoping he would fall back asleep without realizing I hadn't returned.

Without another word, I made my way to the heavy wooden door at the end of the hall. Kyle and Trey had broken the chains last night. It sure beat climbing in and out through the basement windows.

Outside, my breath fogged the air. I tugged the cuffs of Kyle's jacket over my hands as I walked around the church and headed down the lane. The morning was cold, but the sky was a crisp, cloudless blue. It felt surreally peaceful, given everything that had happened yesterday.

I reached the road and turned left, heading for the entrance to the subdivision.

There was something sad about all of the empty and half-finished houses. It was like they were sleeping, waiting for people to come and wake them up. I wondered what would happen if the market never recovered. Would the houses be left standing or be razed to the ground?

Trees backed the lots on my left, and through their branches, I caught glimpses of a tall brick wall—the wall that encircled Fern Ridge. I wasn't superstitious, but I couldn't understand why anyone would think building a subdivision practically on top of a graveyard was a good idea. Didn't anyone watch horror movies?

My steps slowed as I reached the edge of the development: I could hear engines in the distance. Paranoid after yesterday, I quickly stepped into the shadows behind a billboard as the noise drew closer.

Both the subdivision and the cemetery were located just off a winding road that led up to the interstate. Most of the cars you saw out here were either heading into or out of town.

Into, I determined, as a battered pickup with Illinois plates rumbled past.

Behind it were six motorcycles and two RVs. One of the

RVs had speakers—blessedly silent—mounted on its roof and had been painted with a huge version of the Tracker dagger. I squinted at the license plate: Ontario. People really were coming from all over for the rally.

Two news trucks from major networks followed the caravan.

They proceeded down the hill and around a bend, heading for downtown.

As soon as the last bumper disappeared from sight, I stepped out of the shadows and walked the short distance to Fern Ridge. It was early, just past eight o'clock, but the cemetery gates were open and there was already a black Acura in the small row of parking spaces used by people who preferred to walk the tree-lined paths.

I bit my lip as I passed the car.

I was late.

The graveyard seemed oddly silent—not even the sound of birds or the noise of the breeze through the branches overhead—as I made my way to the far corner of the grounds, and I couldn't quite shake the feeling that I was being watched.

I used to come here a few times a year with Tess—Fern Ridge was filled with family Hank had never told me about—but I hadn't set foot through the gates since Amy's funeral; I hadn't wanted my memories of her tied to a stone slab.

I still didn't, but I couldn't risk going back into town, and the graveyard was one place I felt reasonably sure would be private at this time of morning.

Come and see me—that's what Amy had said in my dream.

Maybe it was right that I had chosen this place.

Like every other Walsh, Amy had been buried in the area reserved for Hemlock's wealthiest and most powerful residents. The closer I got, the larger the tombstones became. The more important the person—the more money their family had—the bigger the marker.

It was a far cry from the small cemetery back at Thornhill. There, only numbered plaques marked final resting spots.

I stepped around a mausoleum that was half the size of my apartment and slowed as Amy's grave came into sight.

A familiar figure stood in front of the tombstone. His hands were shoved deep in the pockets of a black wool coat and his head was bowed.

Stephen.

Last night, when Kyle had thought I was trying to call my father, I had texted Amy's brother and asked him to meet me here.

"Stephen?" My voice came out louder than I had intended, startling us both.

Amy's brother turned, his blue eyes wide. "Mac."

I hadn't seen Stephen in almost a year. He looked a little older—more tired and with more shadows around his eyes—but otherwise just as I remembered. A younger version of his father with tussled blond hair, eyes the color of a winter sky, and a lean frame that I knew—from the countless times he had picked me up and tossed me into the Walsh family pool—was stronger than it looked.

His jacket gaped open, revealing a blue scarf and a gray

T-shirt with an illustration from *Where the Wild Things Are* on the front. The shirt had been a birthday gift from Amy; I had been with her when she bought it. *Stephen needs to be a little more wild,* she had said.

Maybe this had been a bad idea.

The last thing I wanted was to grill Stephen over his sister's grave, but he was the best link I had to CBP. Other kids got summer jobs at the pool or the mall, but Stephen's family had always expected bigger things from him. From the time he was fourteen, he had spent every summer working for CutterBrown. According to the voice mail he had left me yesterday—and how was it possible that so much had happened in twenty-four hours?—he was working for them now.

I swallowed and searched for words. "Thanks for coming. I know it's early."

He shrugged, the gesture oddly graceful. "You said it was important. Besides," he added. "I needed to come here." He glanced back at Amy's grave. "I can't run from it forever."

I closed the distance between us and stared down at the epitaph on the stone. AMY ADLER WALSH. BELOVED DAUGHTER. "You weren't at the funeral," I said, letting the words hang in the air like a question mark. I knew he hadn't gone—I knew he had only made it as far as the gate—but it had been six months; it hadn't occurred to me that he might not have come here in all that time.

"No," he said, answering the part of my question that had been unspoken.

"But you came when I texted?" I couldn't quite keep the

surprise from my voice. "Why?"

Again, he shrugged. "Because you were Amy's best friend. Because you asked. Because it was time."

Three explanations. I was sure all of them were true, but I had a feeling there was more to it than that. "Because you were curious?"

A slight, tight grin flashed across his face. It wasn't a real smile—I doubted Stephen would smile again until he left the cemetery—but it was still nice to see. "That, too."

We fell into an awkward silence as he waited for me to explain why we were here. "I got your voice mail," I said finally, not sure how else to begin. "You're working for your dad?"

"For a little while. I needed a break from school, and I figured I could learn just as much about business working for my father as I could in a classroom."

I couldn't imagine Stephen ever needing a break from anything. He had always had this quiet strength that made it seem like he could tackle any challenge—at least until Amy's death.

Her murder had been an earthquake. All these months later, we were all still trying to survive the aftershocks.

"It must be interesting," I said, "working for a company that does so much cutting-edge stuff—like that LS detection test they were working on." Inside, I cringed. The words felt about as subtle as a wrecking ball.

"It is interesting," he conceded. "But I'm sure you didn't ask me to meet you in a cemetery at eight in the morning to talk about my career plans." His tone was mild, but something in his expression became a little more guarded.

I chewed the inside of my cheek.

How exactly did you work your way up to asking the brother of your dead best friend whether or not their father's company had partnered with a deluded prison warden in the torture and murder of dozens of teens?

As I struggled to figure out what to say, a light breeze kicked up, stirring a scrap of color in the grass near my feet. My heart caught in my throat.

He was leaving flowers on my grave—pink carnations from the grocery store.

I crouched down and plucked the remains of a crushed flower from a tangle of weeds. The petals had withered and turned brown, but you could still tell they had once been pink.

A pink carnation.

A wave of goose bumps swept down my spine.

"What is it?" asked Stephen.

"Nothing," I said. The word caught in my throat as, shivering and standing, I let the mangled petals fall back to the ground. "Just a carnation."

"Where did you—" Stephen cleared his throat. "Where did you get that?"

He was staring at my wrist. My bracelet—Amy's bracelet—had slipped out from underneath the cuff of my borrowed jacket.

I opened my mouth to tell him the truth, but a lie came out instead. "Your mom gave it to me."

A shadow passed behind Stephen's blue eyes as he raised

his gaze to mine. "I asked her about the bracelet yesterday. She said she hadn't seen it."

Blood rushed to my cheeks as every thought of Cutter-Brown was driven from my head. "I didn't think anyone would miss it." The bracelet felt suddenly heavy around my wrist and I fought the urge to cover it with my other hand.

Stephen just stared at me, waiting for an explanation.

"I was at your house a few weeks ago." The words tripped over one another and fell flat. "I went upstairs—I just wanted to see her room again—and I saw the bracelet. I didn't want it to get thrown out."

"So you just took it?" The tone of his voice made me feel small and guilty. "Did it ever occur to you to just ask for it?"

I had come here to question Stephen; now I was the one on the defensive.

"I'm sorry," I said weakly. "I didn't think anyone would notice or care. I didn't think it would be worth anything to anyone but me."

He raked a hand through his hair. "The bracelet wasn't the only thing that was missing."

The accusation behind the words hit me like a blow.

Pressure built inside my chest. No matter how many years I had been friends with Amy, no matter how many afternoons I had spent at the Walsh house, I was still just a girl from the wrong side of the tracks. The kind of girl people thought would steal from her dead best friend.

It didn't matter why I had taken the bracelet or that it didn't have value to anyone other than me. The only thing that mattered to Stephen was that I had taken it.

Eyes burning, I fumbled with the leather tie that held the bracelet in place. I tried not to think about how much I had risked to keep the bracelet in Thornhill or about how I had almost lost it during the hunt for Amy's killer.

And I tried not to notice how naked my wrist felt without it as I reached out and laid the coins on the cool granite of Amy's headstone.

"That's the only thing of hers I had." My vision blurred but my voice was as hard and final as the stones around us. "I didn't take anything else."

Before Stephen could reply, I turned and walked away.

10

I MADE IT HALFWAY TO THE GATE BEFORE I HEARD STEPS behind me.

"Mackenzie! Wait . . ."

I spun and crossed my arms. My breath fogged the air as I exhaled in a rush. "I gave you the bracelet. I don't have anything else. Do you want to frisk me?"

"Frisk you?" A flash of amusement crossed Stephen's face. "We both know you'd slug me the second I put a hand on you."

He waited for me to soften. When I didn't, his expression slid into something that was almost contrite. "What I said back there . . . it came out wrong." He held out the bracelet. "Here. Take it."

When I didn't move, he took my hand and pressed the bracelet to my palm. "I was planning on giving it to you, anyway. That's why I asked my mother if she had seen it."

I felt my cheeks flush as my fingers curled around the small bundle of coins. "I guess . . ." I stumbled over the words and started again. "I guess I kind of overreacted.

The last couple of days have just been kind of . . . crazy."

It wasn't an apology—not quite—but Stephen shot me a small, wry smile. "Tell me about it. With all the civil unrest last night, I thought my parents would cancel the fund-raiser, but the first catering truck pulled up at five this morning."

He thought I was talking about everything going on in town. If only. Nevertheless, I felt myself relax a fraction of an inch as I carefully tied the bracelet back onto my wrist.

I pulled in a deep breath. I needed to ask him about CBP, but something he had said back at Amy's grave was still bothering me. "What else did you think I had stolen?"

"Stolen is the wrong word," Stephen said quickly. "Someone should have asked you, months ago, if there was anything you wanted. I just don't think anyone was up to going through Amy's things." His gaze sharpened, the blue somehow becoming darker. "Most of her stuff was all there, but her diary and her old iPod are missing. And an external hard drive."

An external hard drive? I guess one of Kyle's lectures about backing up her computer had finally sunk in. In the years I'd known her, Amy had managed to lose four laptops—if you counted leaving a laptop on the front seat of your unlocked car as "losing."

Stephen slipped a hand under his jacket collar and rubbed his shoulder, kneading it lightly as though it ached. "Rugby injury," he explained when he realized I was watching. "The cold makes it ache."

"Rugby?" I raised an eyebrow. Stephen had always been

athletic, but he hated team sports.

He shrugged. "Ivy League school. They're big on things like rugby and rowing and secret societies that meet in caves under frat houses."

I shook my head. I would have to take his word for it. The Ivy League wasn't exactly in my future. Hell, as things stood now, I wasn't even sure graduating high school was a certainty.

"The hard drive just had a bunch of pictures and movies on it," said Stephen, steering the conversation back on track. "Stuff that's not on her laptop. It's not important." But the expression on his face contradicted the words.

I knew what it was like to desperately want to hold on to pieces of someone. Of Amy. "She never said anything to me about a hard drive, but I have a bunch of photos she gave me on a USB key last spring. I could email some of them to you."

I cursed myself the second the words left my mouth. The USB key was back at the apartment. I didn't know how, if, or when I would ever be able to go back for it.

Stephen didn't notice my insta-regret. An oddly relieved look crossed his face as he said, "That would be great. I can come over and get it."

I hesitated. I couldn't go back to the apartment but I couldn't exactly tell Stephen the reason why. "I think it's in my locker, actually," I lied. "I won't be able to get it until Monday."

He hid it quickly, but the flash of disappointment on Stephen's face was impossible to miss. "Well, at least let me walk you to the gate."

I nodded and fell into step beside him.

We walked in silence. After a few minutes, the cemetery gates came into sight in the distance. I felt a small rush of panic. I still hadn't asked Stephen about CutterBrown. Once Eve arrived at the church, we'd be leaving Hemlock. There was no telling if or when I would see him again.

"I wanted to talk to you about CBP," I blurted awkwardly, deciding that some version of the truth—an extremely watered down, hole-riddled version—was the best approach.

I glanced at Stephen out of the corner of my eye. He inclined his head slightly, curiously. "And you thought you had to get me out here to do that?"

"I was scared someone might overhear if I met you anywhere else," I admitted. "I'm taking a big risk just by being here."

Stephen stopped and turned to face me. A stone angel was just visible over his left shoulder. Wind and rain and time had worn away most of her features, but her sightless eyes still seemed focused on us.

"What do you mean, you're taking a risk?" The look on Stephen's face was so earnest, so full of concern, that I almost wished I could be honest with him. Not for the first time, I wondered how my life would have been different if I'd had a brother like Stephen growing up.

He was staring at me, waiting for an answer. "Mac, are you in some sort of trouble?"

I shook my head. "I'm not—but someone I know is. They have LS."

His brows knotted. "Your cousin?"

"No." My voice was a startled squeak; I could practically see Stephen running down a mental list of the people in my life, and the list wasn't terribly long. "Someone from school. Not anyone you know, but someone who's been a good friend to me since Amy. Someone I care about."

"I'm sorry." Stephen hesitated for a moment, then added, "I'm not sure what this has to do with CutterBrown, though. Or me."

I started walking again, more slowly this time. Movement was better: it gave me an excuse not to look into his eyes and made it easier to sling half-truths. Some people were harder to lie to than others; Amy's brother was one of them.

"I remembered that CBP was working on a test to detect lupine syndrome. I thought, maybe, if they were working on a test, they'd also be working on a cure."

"They're not." Stephen's voice was gentle, but firm. "Every pharmaceutical company in the world has tried to find a cure and they've all hit brick walls."

His black Acura came into view as we reached the strip of parking spaces.

"The best thing your friend can do is keep her head down and try to go unnoticed. Tell her to forget about a cure. The sooner she accepts that her condition is permanent, the easier things will be."

Stephen's words took me by surprise. Especially after what had happened to Amy. Especially when his grandfather was pushing for harsher laws against werewolves. "Most people would say she should turn herself in to the

LSRB," I said slowly, "that I was wrong to want to help her."

"Guess I'm not most people." Stephen frowned as we reached his car. He glanced around the empty parking lot and his mouth hardened into a thin, straight line. "Please tell me you didn't walk here?"

When I didn't answer, a familiar, exasperated look crossed his face. I had seen him turn that look on Amy dozens—maybe hundreds—of times. "It's the morning after a riot and there are God only knows how many still-drunk extremists running around Hemlock like it's the Wild West. I can't believe you walked out here alone."

He looked like he wanted to say something else, then seemed to think better of it and just sighed. "Get in," he said, pulling out his keys and heading for the driver's side of the car. "I'll take you home."

I followed him to the Acura. I opened my mouth to tell him that I didn't need a ride, that I had somewhere else I had to be, but my gaze fell on a messenger bag on the passenger seat. An ID badge with Stephen's photo on the front was clipped to the strap.

"Shit." Stephen reached into his pocket and pulled out a vibrating cell phone, then frowned as he glanced at the display. "I have to take this." He gestured at the car before turning away. "Get in. There's no way I'm letting you walk home."

This time, I didn't think of arguing. I trusted Stephen and didn't believe he would intentionally lie to me about what CBP was working on, but when you got right down to it, he was just an intern. An intern whose father ran the company, sure, but he might not know everything that was going on.

The faint scent of lavender ruffled my nose as I lifted the messenger bag and slid into the car. Ever since Thornhill, I had hated that smell. Tess had a bottle of lavender shampoo and I had begged her to throw it out because it reminded me of Warden Sinclair.

I glanced out the window. Stephen had wandered to the edge of the parking lot. I didn't know who was on the other end of the line, but the conversation was obviously private.

I checked his ID badge and frowned. It had his picture and name along with a four-digit employee number, but no magnetic strip. It wasn't anything that could help us get inside CutterBrown.

Get inside CutterBrown? scoffed a small voice in the back of my head. *Aren't you supposed to be leaving town this morning?*

I told the voice to shut up. At the other end of the parking lot, Stephen had begun to pace. He looked angry and frustrated.

Anger was good. Anger meant he wasn't paying attention to me.

Feeling slightly guilty, I unzipped the bag. I didn't know what I was hoping to find. A laptop, maybe, or a stack of files and memos. Instead, all I found were a couple of books. I pulled one out.

Managing an Epidemic. Our school library had the same book—I had borrowed it after finding out Kyle was infected. I frowned. It wasn't exactly light reading. I started to slip it back, but a piece of paper sticking out of the middle of the book caught my eye. A slice of a photo was visible on the top of the page. A black-and-white picture of an imposing old building. A building with a peaked roof and ivy-covered walls. I remembered looking at the harsh angles of that building in the early morning light and thinking it was a photographer's dream.

Willowgrove.

Only half of the picture was visible, but I didn't need to see the whole image to recognize the old, repurposed sanatorium.

I couldn't breathe. My lungs, my heart, everything in my chest was turning to ice and the ice was threatening to crack.

I forced myself to look up, to make sure Stephen was still engrossed in his conversation, and then I slipped the piece of paper from the book.

It was a pamphlet for an art exhibit. Some sort of retrospective by a group of Colorado photographers. The Willowgrove in the picture wasn't exactly the one I had known. The ivy was so overgrown that it threatened to pull the walls down, and the doors and windows were all boarded up. It was the sanatorium—there was no doubt of that—but the photo had been taken sometime during the decades the old hospital had stood empty.

Before Sinclair.

Before Thornhill.

My eyes drifted down to the location of the exhibit.

Flagler Public Library.

The name of the town was a knife in my stomach. Flagler was a forty-minute drive from Thornhill and was so small it barely registered on the map. Most of the camp's personnel who chose not to stay in the staff dormitories had lived in Flagler and commuted—at least that's what Jason had once said. Without the nearby camp and the jobs it provided, Flagler would have been a ghost town.

I turned the pamphlet over. A phone number and what looked like a room number had been jotted on the back in Stephen's looping, off-kilter handwriting. *Chicken scratches—* that's what Amy had said any time she had been forced to decipher a note he'd left.

I glanced up. Stephen was walking back to the car, his face set in hard, grim lines.

Hastily, I shoved the book back into the messenger bag and tucked the paper into my jacket pocket.

I pushed open the passenger door and climbed out of the car just as Stephen rounded the hood.

He shot me a piercing look. "What's wrong?"

I stared at Amy's brother. Everything about him suddenly seemed different. Suspect.

My hand shook as I shut the car door. A thousand questions flew to my lips, but I choked them back. I wouldn't be able to trust anything he said. Stephen had been at Flagler. He must have been at Thornhill: the camp was the only reason anyone would go there.

Someone had sent those men after Serena. If Cutter-Brown had been working with Sinclair, then they had the most to lose if the truth ever came out. It would be a public relations nightmare. Admitting I knew anything about Thornhill could be suicide.

Would be suicide, I amended, thinking about the explosion at the transition house.

"I have to go." Four words that shook as they left my lips. "I don't need a ride."

Before Stephen could respond, I turned and headed for the gates. My legs trembled, but I crossed the distance in record time, walking so fast that I was practically running.

"Mac! Wait!"

Stephen caught up with me as I reached the street. He grabbed my arm and pulled me to a stop.

I stared into his blue eyes—the icy-blue eyes he had inherited from his father.

"Why are you staring at me like that?" His voice was filled with something. Worry or suspicion: I couldn't tell the difference.

I tugged my arm free and tried to throw up walls to keep my thoughts and emotions from showing on my face. "Like what?"

"Like you're scared of me. Mackenzie, what the hell just happened?"

"Nothing." The urge to slip a hand inside my pocket, to make sure the pamphlet was still there, was almost overpowering. "I'd rather just walk home. Walking is good. I'm totally fine."

"You're obviously not fine." Stephen's voice was slow and careful; it was the kind of tone you'd use with an idiot or someone who was up on a ledge. He started to slip the scarf from his neck and froze when I tensed. His nostrils flared as he inhaled deeply. "You look like you're going to throw up or pass out. Just let me drive you home—or at least wait while I call your cousin to . . ." His voice trailed off as engines approached on the street behind me.

Great, I thought, turning and glancing in the direction of the interstate, *another Tracker caravan*.

But instead of an RV, a green transport—the kind soldiers rode in—rumbled past. A dozen more followed in its wake. Like the Trackers and news vans I had seen earlier, they were headed toward the center of town.

A National Guardsman leaned out the back of the last truck.

"Jesus," muttered Stephen. He walked past me and stepped out onto the street, staring after the trucks as they disappeared around the bend. For a second, he forgot all about me.

I backed away from the street and whirled. Stephen yelled my name as I ran back into the cemetery, but he didn't follow.

Fern Ridge was surrounded by a brick wall, but there was another gate on the far side, one that was used by the groundskeepers and gravediggers.

Muscles aching and lungs burning, I reached the wall and slumped against the bricks.

I pulled the crumpled paper from my pocket. My hand shook as I tried to smooth out the creases. The date of the exhibit had been July 29—just weeks before Thornhill had opened its doors. I had suspected CutterBrown was involved with the camp, but part of me had desperately been hoping I was wrong.

And never, in a million years, could I have imagined that Stephen would somehow be involved.

"I'm not leaving Hemlock." My words were a whisper. Serena and the others had to get away—now, with the National Guard in town, more than ever—but I wouldn't be going with them.

Amy's family had been involved with Thornhill. I had to find out how deeply.

I squeezed my eyes shut. "What did you know, Amy? Is this the reason you're still here?"

The wind through the trees was my only answer.

11

I RETURNED TO THE CHURCH TO FIND FOUR ANGRY WERE-wolves and one seriously pissed-off Tracker.

Kyle, especially, was furious. He couldn't believe I hadn't told him about the logo last night or that I had gone to the cemetery to meet Stephen by myself.

My excuse—that I had thought Amy's brother would be more likely to talk to her best friend than a group—fell on deaf ears. I understood why they were upset—I would be furious if the situation had been reversed—but I didn't regret going.

After what felt like an eternity of apologies and lectures, we reconvened in the front of the church—all of us but Serena, who was sleeping fitfully in the pastor's office. Eve and Trey sat on the pews, Jason and Kyle on the steps leading to the pulpit. Me? I paced between them because I was too full of too many emotions to stand still.

"So this friend of yours—Amy—you think her father was working with Sinclair?" Eve pushed a red curl away from her forehead and climbed up onto the backrest of her pew. She was so short that her cherry-red Doc Martens hung a few inches above the bench, but I knew better than to judge her on her size; Eve was one of the toughest people I knew—both physically and mentally.

She looked remarkably well rested for someone who had been on the road all night—not that I was about to tell her that. Though my attitude toward her had changed inside Thornhill, she was still Hank's protégée, the adopted daughter my father had taken in after abandoning me. That made my feelings toward her . . . complicated.

"I saw the CutterBrown logo in the camp, and Stephen—his son—was in Flagler." I twisted Amy's bracelet around my wrist. "CutterBrown was already working on a test to detect LS. If they could develop a cure—even just a treatment—it would be worth millions."

"Billions," corrected Jason. "But that doesn't mean they were testing one at the camp." His eyes glinted like pieces of broken glass. "All the logo proves is that Sinclair might have been using one of the drugs CBP already makes—a sedative, a chemo drug, anything. And all the pamphlet proves is that Stephen was in Flagler."

After I had gotten back to the church, I had called the number on the back of the pamphlet. It had been a motel: the Flagler Motor Lodge. The girl working the desk even remembered Stephen—once I had given her a description. I'd gotten the impression that there was a shortage of young, handsome men checking in and out.

I shook my head. "Flagler isn't exactly a tourist destination. Why would Stephen have been there unless there was a connection between CBP and the camp?"

I expected Jason to answer, but it was Kyle who spoke. "It could have been for the blood tests," he said, leaning forward, resting his elbows on his knees. "Every wolf who passed through that gate was tested for LS. The whole admission process could have been a clinical trial." He met my gaze. "It's possible Stephen was sent to check on that and CBP didn't know anything about the detention block."

He was grasping at straws, just like I had been.

"A major pharmaceutical company involved with the camp and they didn't know Sinclair was looking for a cure?" Eve shook her head and ran a hand over her wrist, encircling it with her thumb and forefinger as though remembering the cuffs we had worn in Thornhill. "Sorry, but that requires a little too much suspension of disbelief. Sinclair was smart but it's not like she magically whipped up a cure in the basement with a chemistry set. Someone had to have helped her."

After a moment, Kyle nodded, the gesture gruff and a little reluctant.

Jason pushed himself to his feet. His gaze darted between Kyle and me. "You can't really think Amy's father would be part of something like the detention block or that he would involve Stephen in it."

I stopped pacing and let out a deep breath. "I didn't think Ben was a mass murderer," I pointed out. "Once you accept something that horrible, it gets a little easier to wonder how well you really know anyone."

"That's different. You knew Ben a few months." Jason

glanced to his best friend. "Kyle?"

It usually felt as though I had known the two of them forever—as though the years before I had met them had been someone else's bad dream—but there were times when the history they shared was a gulf I couldn't cross.

It was there now, in the way Jason expected Kyle to back him up because they were best friends. Because they had known Amy and her family practically their whole lives.

Kyle didn't say anything, but the expression on his face made it clear that he agreed with Eve, that he thought it was too big a coincidence.

Jason turned away from him. To the rest of us, he said, "I've known Amy's dad my whole life. He wouldn't have signed on for something like this. I don't care how much money was involved."

Up in the rafters, a few of the pigeons took flight. For a moment, the only sound was the flap of wings.

And then Trey spoke.

"Because Ryan Walsh was such an outstanding guy, right?" He had been so silent that I had almost forgotten he was in the room.

Jason glared. "You think being Amy's toy makes you an expert on her family?"

Trey pushed himself to his feet, and Kyle quickly stood and stepped in front of Jason.

"Let me guess," said Eve. "Amy was the star of her very own love triangle."

"Not helping," I muttered. Amy had begun sneaking around with Trey after finding out Jason had feelings for me. Revenge probably tasted sweeter when it came with washboard abs.

"Amy was miserable in that house." Trey's voice held the undercurrent of a growl. The light shining through the stained-glass windows edged his skin in gold. "She wouldn't talk about it and she tried to hide it, but every time I saw her, she smelled more desperate and more lost."

"Werewolf powers at their most charming," muttered Jason. "Who cares about the scent of perfume when you can sniff out desperation?"

"You think I'm kidding?" Trey tried to push past Kyle and almost succeeded.

"Time out!" I moved forward and grabbed Trey's arm. His muscles tensed under my hand, a reminder that he could toss me around like a rag doll. *"Please, Trey. Fighting isn't going to help anything."

"Maybe not, but it would be satisfying." Despite his words, he pulled in a deep breath and let me guide him back to one of the pews.

"Even if Amy was unhappy, what makes you think it was because of her father?" I asked, sitting next to him and resisting the urge to glance at Jason. We had made her unhappy, too—Jason because he hadn't loved her enough and me because I had missed the signs that he cared about me too much.

"I don't—not for sure," said Trey, "but something in that house scared her. There were times when I would drop her off and it was like she had to force herself to get out of the car. Once, she called me in the middle of the night from a strip mall. She had left the house without her jacket or purse. In January. She called me from a pay phone, begging me to come pick her up. A few weeks later, she started talking about running away, saying we should just take off together, but wouldn't tell me why."

This time, my gaze did dart to Jason. No matter his feelings for me, Amy had been his girlfriend. Hearing that she had asked Trey to run away with her had to hurt, but his face gave nothing away. Instead, it slid into something cold and hard, as if he'd been carved from stone.

"It doesn't make sense." Kyle ran a hand through his hair. "If something was wrong, why didn't she say anything? Even if she didn't want to tell Mac or Jason, she could have talked to me."

Could she have? I tried to put myself in Amy's shoes. "What if whatever was going on was too awful to tell anyone? What if she was scared of getting her family—her dad—in trouble?" The weight I had been carrying since last night grew sharply. "I need to find out what she was scared of. I need to know if it had anything to do with Thornhill."

"And if you're right and there's a connection between CBP and the camp? If it turns out that's why Amy was scared? What then?" Jason's voice was the lash of a whip. I flinched, but he continued. "You think Amy would want this? If CutterBrown really was behind what happened at the sanatorium and Amy's father was involved . . ." He shook his head. "Amy was your best friend and her family was never anything but good to you. Finding proof would destroy them."

"And might stop what happened to Serena from happening to anyone else," I countered. "And maybe give us some leverage in case those men come after her again." I stared at him, willing him to understand. "What happened at Thornhill is bigger than me or you or even Amy. If there's even a chance we can find out what really happened . . . if there's a chance we can find proof . . ."

"You saw what they did to Serena in the detention block. How can you think Amy's dad could be a part of that?" Jason waited for me to say something. When I didn't, he cursed under his breath and strode from the room.

I rose and started after him, but Kyle stopped me as I reached the door. "I'll go."

"But—"

He cut me off. "Even before he and Amy started dating, Jason practically grew up at the Walshes'. Ryan Walsh was more of a father to him than his own ever was."

"I care about Amy's family, too." I didn't want this; I hadn't asked for this.

"I know." Kyle pressed a quick kiss to my temple and then he, too, was gone.

"How much did you hear?" asked Trey, handing Serena a half-empty bottle of water.

"Pretty much all of it," she admitted.

She had been awake when Trey, Eve, and I had gotten back to the pastor's office. I had no idea where Kyle and Jason had gone—the grounds or the burned-out manse, maybe. I wanted to go after them, but I was holding myself back. I had a feeling my presence would just upset Jason more than he already was.

Serena touched my hand as I sat next to her on the battered sofa. "It'll be okay," she said. "Jason will get over it." Her eyes were bloodshot and the hand that touched mine shook a little, but she seemed otherwise okay. Last night's fever had finally broken. "So what now?" she asked, her gaze going to her brother. "We're staying, right?"

Trey's eyes darkened. "Ree . . ."

"You guys need to get to the pack," I said. "Hemlock isn't safe. The men who attacked your house are still out there and the rally is tomorrow night." To say nothing of the National Guard trucks I had seen rolling into town.

"While you stay here and investigate CBP?" Serena shook her head. "No way. Besides, Jason and Kyle are staying."

I wasn't actually sure that was true. Jason was furious with me, and I hadn't had a chance to speak with Kyle privately. Even though I knew the effort would be futile, even though I didn't really want to do this alone, I had to at least try convincing him to leave town. It wasn't safe here. For any of the wolves.

Trey glowered at his sister. "Harper and Sheffield aren't the ones who had a squad of mercenaries show up on their doorstep."

Serena opened her mouth to argue, but I cut her off. "Trey's right. The best thing for you to do right now is to go back to the pack with Eve."

"And what makes you think I'm going back?" asked Eve

from her perch on the windowsill. Sunlight filtered through the glass behind her, throwing fiery highlights over her red hair.

I stared at her dumbly. "A: Hank told you to, and B: You didn't know Amy or her family. Why would you want to stay?"

"You're joking, right?" She pushed herself off the sill and landed lightly on the balls of her feet. "This isn't just about your friend. Finding proof of the detention block would be huge. Game-changer huge. It might be enough to make people really start questioning the existence of the camps."

Trey snorted. "What makes you think anyone who isn't infected will give a damn about what happened at Thornhill? People already know the other camps are horrible, and they're still open for business."

"People have heard rumors," corrected Eve, the colors in her gray-green eyes swirling like fog. "And what went on in Thornhill was way beyond overcrowding and food shortages. It was torture." Her gaze slid to Serena. "They were recording the tests. Imagine if those videos got out. Videos of teenagers strapped to tables while guards break their bones? Most people don't have the stomach for that—not even when it comes to werewolves."

"Eve . . ." I shot a nervous glance at Serena. Her hands were clasped on her lap and she was staring down at her fingers. Eve's example hadn't been random; it was one of the things they had done to Serena, one of the things she couldn't remember.

"Eve's right," said Serena softly. "People need to know

143

what happened. We need to find proof."

"Not at the risk of losing you," said Trey. "If Harper and Sheffield hadn't shown up yesterday . . ." His mouth twisted around Jason's name as though the admission left a bitter taste on his tongue.

"All the more reason to stay and find out if those men are connected to CutterBrown. You heard what Mac said about leverage." She hesitated, then added, "Besides, you want to know what Amy was hiding, too. I know you do." She stood and put a hand on her brother's arm. "Eve's right: finding proof could change everything. And I need people to know what they did to me. *I* need to know what they did to me."

Next to her brother, Serena was tiny—a mouse next to a lion—but the determination on her face was more than a match for Trey's physical strength.

She stared at him and waited.

After a long moment, Trey sighed, swore, and then nodded.

"Thank you," Serena breathed, sitting back down.

"Don't thank me," said Trey miserably. "For all I know, this is the biggest mistake I've ever made." He didn't look at any of us. "I think I'll go check the radio in Kyle's car, see if I can find out anything about those trucks Dobs saw."

"You do realize my father is going to kill you, right?" I asked Eve as Trey headed down the hall.

"Serves Curtis right." Eve toyed with a pewter charm on a leather cord around her neck. The small disc had been engraved with a symbol that resembled three interlocking teardrops. It was the symbol of Hank's pack. I had worn a similar one on Amy's bracelet while in Thornhill. Eve was one of the few wolves who knew about my father's past. Everyone else believed he was Curtis Hanson, an alias he had adopted after becoming infected. "He's been keeping so many secrets since the breakout that he can't say three words without two of them contradicting. Besides," she added cryptically, "the National Guard and the Trackers aren't the only ones flooding Hemlock."

"What's that supposed to mean?" My voice was sharp; I was emotionally exhausted and way too tired for riddles.

"Curtis and the other pack leaders are planning something for the rallies. Something big. He won't tell anyone what. Not even me. No matter how much I ask." She kicked at a piece of chipped tile. "He's never not trusted me before."

I wanted to tell Eve not to take it personally, that Hank didn't really trust anyone, but she looked so miserable that I kept the comment to myself.

"Anyway," she said, "he sent Dex to Chicago and a bunch of wolves to Atlanta and New York. More are headed here. He told them they'd find out what was going on when they got where they were going. That was a week ago. And it's not just the Eumon. Other packs are sending people to almost every place a rally is being held. Small groups—usually no more than five or six—but if every pack is sending them . . ."

"It would be a small army," breathed Serena. "Maybe even enough to attack the rallies."

I shook my head. My father had a lot of flaws, but stupidity had never been one of them. He had to know that a hit on the rallies would result in an even bigger backlash against wolves. "Attacking the rallies would just make things worse. Hank knows that." But even as the words left my mouth, I thought about how adamant he had been that I leave Hemlock before Monday night.

Something was coming. Something he didn't want me anywhere near.

"Things can't get much worse, Mac," said Eve. Her expression settled into something hard and sad. "We're being hunted down and exterminated, and the news is only reporting a fraction of what's happening. If Hank and the other pack leaders don't do something . . ." She ran a hand over her wrist, over the scars she had gotten when she became infected. "The way things are going, the wolves we broke out of Thornhill might have been safer where they were; at least Sinclair was only killing a few at a time."

I stared at her in disbelief. "There's no way you believe that."

Her shoulders sagged as she let out a deep breath. "No. I guess not. Not yet. But I'm getting there. Things haven't been as bad in cities where rallies are planned because the Trackers are trying not to rock the boat too much until they have their moment in the spotlight. Everywhere else, though, it's open season on anyone who's infected. Trackers wiped out an entire pack in Miami three days ago. A hundred and fifty wolves dead, and not one news outlet picked it up. I passed through a town on my way here—some two-bit hick place I only pulled into because I needed gas." She swallowed roughly. "It was dark, but I could see bodies hanging from trees by the town limit. A dozen of them. Maybe more. Some of them had signs around their necks, but I didn't stop to read them. I just turned around and drove as fast as I could. I passed two more towns and was running on fumes before I felt safe enough to stop. And that's just two places. Two stories out of hundreds. The country is tearing itself apart and no one wants to talk about it because no one wants to admit who the real monsters are."

My stomach twisted as I pictured dozens of bodies swaying from trees. I knew I should say something, but I couldn't find the words.

Eve sighed and glanced at Serena. Her eyes widened and her mouth formed a perfect, horrified O. "Jesus . . ."

I turned and then scrambled off the couch. "Trey!" I screamed for Serena's brother as tracks of blood ran from her eyes and dripped onto her clothes.

I reached for her shoulder, but Eve grabbed my arm and yanked me back. "Don't touch her, Jesus—whatever you do, don't touch her."

"Her blood can't hurt me." I struggled against Eve's grip as she pulled me across the room. "Blood doesn't transmit LS."

"And werewolves don't normally bleed from their goddamn eyes." Eve wedged me into the corner as Trey burst through the door. "We don't know what Sinclair did to her."

Serena pushed herself to her feet. *Trey?* No sound came out as her lips formed her brother's name. Thin rivers of blood began running from her nose and ears.

Trey caught her as a spasm rocked her body. Her head

whipped back so hard and so fast that something cracked while blood hit the wall like a Rorschach test.

Trey's arms locked around Serena, trying to keep her from hurting herself as spasm after bone-snapping spasm threatened to tear her apart. The convulsions were so strong that he had to struggle to hold her.

"Get Kyle!" he shouted as he tried to ease Serena to the ground.

I couldn't think and I couldn't move. I just stood there, staring at the flecks of blood on the wall.

"Mac!" Eve shook me, snapping me out of it. "Get Kyle. Now!"

She pushed me to the door, trying to keep her body between me and Serena.

I didn't fight her. I let her shove me out of the room, and then I raced down the hall and out the door, raced as though I could outpace the sight of Serena's blood splattered across the wall.

Kyle's car was still parked behind the church, but it was empty. Heart in throat, I ran around the front of the building. Where would he and Jason have gone? Not far—not when the men who were after Serena were still out there— but somewhere they could talk without being overheard by the other wolves.

The housing development.

My sneakers skidded on gravel as I sprinted down the lane.

"Mac?"

Kyle's shout spun me around and pulled me up short as I reached the street. I gasped for air and tried to find my voice as he and Jason jogged toward me. "Serena," I managed. "Seizure."

Kyle didn't wait to get the rest. He sprinted for the church, moving far faster than a reg could. Jason started after him, but slowed when he realized I was having trouble keeping up.

"Something's really wrong." I forced the words out between gasps. "She was okay and then she started bleeding and shaking. . . . Trey . . . he said . . . to get Kyle."

Jason threaded his fingers through mine. In that moment, our argument in the church didn't matter. "Come on."

Together, we ran back up the lane.

Kyle had already disappeared inside. As Jason let go of my hand and reached for the door, we heard the first scream.

Every hair on my body stood at attention.

Jason's fingers curled around the door handle, gripping it so tightly his knuckles were white. He glanced at me, eyes wide, as a second scream followed on the heels of the first.

No throat—wolf or reg—should have been capable of making a sound like that.

Swallowing roughly, Jason pulled open the door.

"Hold her arm! Don't let—" Trey's voice was lost under a large thud and a sharp crash.

Jason reached the office first. He choked out a stream of curses and then turned and tried to block the door with his body.

I ducked under his arm. He should have been able to stop me, but whatever he had seen had left him slow and shaken.

"Mac, wait—"

The acrid scent of vomit and the tang of copper hit me like a slap as my eyes struggled to make sense of what was happening.

The room was a scene from a horror movie. It was blood and breaking bones; 3-D gore with surround sound.

Serena thrashed on the floor. Eve held her legs down, while Trey and Kyle each fought to restrain an arm. For weeks, Serena's strength had been reduced to little more than a reg's; now it took three werewolves to hold her down.

Kyle's hands were slick with blood. He lost his grip and in the three seconds it took him to regain control, Serena reached up and clawed at the skin on her neck, peeling it back the way you'd peel an onion.

A wave of bile rushed up my throat and I stumbled back against Jason.

Kyle's gaze snapped to the door and went wide. "Get out of here!" he yelled as Serena managed to shake off both him and Trey.

Jason's arms locked around my waist. If he was trying to keep me from running forward, it was a wasted effort: it was all I could do not to bolt from the room.

Eve threw all of her weight down as Serena's muscles began to twist and jump under her skin.

The amount of time it took each werewolf to transform varied, but it was never like this. As Serena shifted, I was able to see every muscle tear beneath the skin and I could hear every bone snap—all 206 of them. It was like it was happening in slow motion.

I tried to watch, but in the end, I turned in Jason's arms and buried my face against his chest. He tightened his arms around me, but the embrace offered no comfort. Not when I could still hear the noises Serena's body made—sounds that somehow managed to be both brittle and wet.

And then it was over.

I felt Jason let out a deep, shuddery breath as silence filled the room.

Nerves humming like a power station, I stepped away from Jason and turned.

"Serena." Her name was a raw whisper as relief made my knees weak.

She was alive.

A large, black wolf pushed itself—herself—up onto shaky legs. She turned to Trey and let out a high-pitched, almost apologetic whine.

Trey, Kyle, and Eve all looked decidedly worse for wear. Their clothing was ripped and stained, and both Eve and Trey were sporting gashes. The cuts would only take a few minutes to heal—one of the perks of being infected—but for now they looked painful.

Kyle climbed to his feet and reached for me before remembering his hands were covered in blood.

Jason cleared his throat. He stared at Serena for a long moment and then glanced at the blood splatters on the wall. He looked ill, so ill that he was practically shaking. "Is she . . ." He turned to Trey. "Is she all right?"

Serena let out a sharp bark.

"I guess that's a yes." Relief flashed through Jason's eyes as he ran a hand over his neck.

Eve pushed herself to her feet and headed for the door. She held her hands slightly in front of her as Jason and I stepped aside to let her pass.

"I don't mind getting my hands dirty, but this is just gross," she muttered. She glanced over her shoulder at Kyle and Trey. "I've got a jug of water in the trunk of my car if you want to clean up."

Trey hesitated, watching his sister for signs of further trouble, but Kyle followed Eve out into the hall.

"Wait," said Jason. His shoulders tensed and he dropped his gaze to the floor.

Everyone stared at him expectantly, even Serena in her wolfish form.

"I was wrong." He raised his head. "Before."

Silence greeted his statement. His voice took on an edge that was harsh and a little defensive. "CutterBrown has billions tied up in research. Their security system makes the one at Thornhill look like a joke. Getting past it won't be easy."

I stared at him, unsure if I had heard him correctly. "You changed your mind? About CutterBrown?"

"I'm still hoping you're wrong, but if there's even a chance you're not . . ." Jason didn't look happy; if anything, he looked like someone getting ready to face a firing squad. "One way or another, we have to find out—though how you think we'll get through the front door is beyond me."

A ridiculous, goofy grin split my face and I had to fight the urge to throw my arms around him. I knew it would be safer for everyone to leave town, but selfishly, I was glad I wouldn't have to do this on my own. "I don't want to break into CutterBrown."

Four pairs of confused eyes stared at me while Serena cocked her head to the side like she was waiting for the punch line.

To Jason, I said, "Do you still have that tux?"

12

LIKE EVERY INCH OF THE SHEFFIELDS' SPRAWLING HOUSE, Jason's bedroom had been placed at the mercy of his mother's interior designer. The result was a lot of mahogany, black-and-white pictures of skyscrapers, and leather-bound books that Jason had no intention of ever reading. It was a space that was as metrosexual as a subscription to *GQ*.

I couldn't remember the last time I had been up here. Not since Amy had died. Even before that, I had rarely been in Jason's room.

Paula Sheffield had never bothered hiding her dislike of me. She couldn't understand how someone like Amy could be friends with a girl she considered trailer trash. And when it came to her son, she saw me as a walking pregnancy scare in the making. The handful of times Jason and I had been alone up here—waiting for Amy or Kyle or working on homework—she had found about a hundred reasons to interrupt.

Amy said not to let it get to me, that I reminded Jason's mother of her past. Paula had been waiting tables in the middle of Nowhere Kansas when she snagged Matt Shef-field. If you looked at the wedding photos from the right angle, you could see the baby bump.

I didn't know if that was the real reason she hated me and I didn't care—or at least I tried not to—but I could just imagine how ballistic she would go if she knew I was stand-ing in the middle of her son's room wearing a towel.

Thank God she and Jason's father had left for the party before we arrived.

There was no use in pretending we could get past secu-rity at CutterBrown: They had the best system money could buy. It would take months of planning and an unbelievable amount of luck. Even if we could get in, it wasn't like we had any idea where to look. But if CBP had been involved with the detention block at Thornhill—if Amy's father had been involved—then the corporate headquarters might not be the only place to find proof.

Ryan Walsh was a workaholic, and his private study was the one room in the Walsh house that was completely off-limits. Only Amy's father had the key—in theory. In reality, Amy had managed to sneak it out and make a copy after her father had revoked her shopping privileges and confiscated her credit cards.

I knew where she kept the key. Or at least where she used to keep it.

Tonight, the Walsh residence would be filled with guests. It would be our one chance to move freely around the house without being noticed or explaining our presence. It was the perfect opportunity. Maybe our only opportunity.

Of course, crashing a fund-raising gala filled with politicians, bureaucrats, and rich Trackers meant looking the part.

I stared down at a white dress box that had come tied with a black velvet ribbon. Almost timidly, I trailed one finger along the edge of the velvet before unraveling the neatly tied bow. I lifted the top of the box and set it aside and then parted layers of gold and white tissue paper to reveal yards of midnight-blue fabric.

I had balked at the idea of Jason buying me a dress, but he had been right: castoffs from high school dances wouldn't help me blend in at one of the Walshes' parties.

So I had given in and let him call one of the chic boutiques where his mother had an account. I had listened as he arranged for a dress to be sent over and tried not to be too unnerved when he was able to tell them my dress size without asking. *He's lending Kyle clothes*, I had told myself. *This isn't any different.*

I glanced at the clock on Jason's nightstand. The two of them were probably getting dressed and bonding over their mutual hatred of bow ties at this very moment.

I turned my attention back to the bed.

Another box, long and narrow, sat next to the first.

I peered inside and withdrew a pair of opera gloves that were the same deep blue as the dress and just long enough to cover the scar on my arm. Jason really had thought of everything.

I tossed my towel over the back of a leather armchair and slipped on the dress, careful not to wreck my hair as I slid the fabric over my head. Locks this short didn't come with a lot of options, but I had still attacked my hair with mousse and a curling iron until it looked a little like something from one of those old Audrey Hepburn movies Tess liked so much.

The dress fell around my legs in soft waves, almost reaching the floor. I ran a hand over the fabric, smoothing out the few small wrinkles, and then pulled on the gloves. I frowned down at my hands. Though the gloves covered the scar on my arm perfectly, the fit was too snug to wear Amy's bracelet underneath.

I glanced at Jason's desk where I had left the small jumble of coins while I showered. Maybe it was better not to wear it. Given that we were on our way to look for information that might hurt Amy's father and brother, I wasn't sure I should wear it.

Swallowing back a wave of guilt, I turned my back on the bracelet and walked to an antique mirror in the corner of the room.

I blinked at my reflection. The girl who stared back didn't look like me.

The mousse made my hair seem darker—less dishwater blond and more honey brown—while the deep-blue fabric of the dress made my skin look like porcelain. The cut dipped dangerously low in the front and hugged my hips, giving the illusion of curves. Miles of them. Tiny bits of metal had been sewn onto the stretchy fabric of the skirt; it was like someone had taken a handful of stars and cast them over the night sky.

It wasn't a dress for a girl like me. Hell, the money Jason had spent on this one piece of clothing was probably enough to cover my rent for a month.

There was a soft knock at the door.

"Mac?" Jason eased the door open and stepped inside. "Kyle's on the phone with Eve. Checking in . . ." His voice trailed off as he saw me standing in the corner.

"Wow." The word was soft. Almost reverent.

Our eyes met in the mirror as he crossed the room. Warmth flooded my cheeks. Even though I was completely dressed, I felt the strange urge to cover up.

Jason was clean shaven, and as he drew closer, I could smell the faint trace of expensive aftershave. He had styled his hair so that it was an artfully disheveled contrast to the sharp, crisp lines of his tux. He looked like he had stepped off a movie screen.

The only thing that ruined the picture was the black dagger tattooed on his neck.

"Is everything okay at the church?" I asked.

He nodded.

It had taken Serena a while to change back to her human form, but once she had, it was as though she had fully recovered from what they had done to her at Thornhill—physically, at least. She and Trey had stayed behind at the church. If CutterBrown had sent those men after her, going anywhere near the fund-raiser would be beyond insane.

Eve had balked at the idea of staying with them, but Jason had only been able to get two tickets. As it was, we were one person too many, but I had refused to tell either

Jason or Kyle where Amy had hidden the key to her father's study and neither of them was willing to stay behind while the other went with me.

Besides, I wanted Eve to stay with Serena and Trey. I trusted her to protect them in ways I couldn't.

The corner of Jason's mouth lifted in a crooked grin. "Need someone to zip you up?"

I hesitated, then nodded.

Jason stepped closer. His fingers grazed my lower back, raising goose bumps on my skin as he reached for the zipper and slowly pulled it up. "You look gorgeous," he said.

"It's the dress." I shook my head. "Anyone would look good in this."

The memory of the way Jason's body had covered mine as we kissed swept through me. I pushed it away, but not before he caught a glimpse of the flashback on my face.

He gave his head a small shake as though trying to clear it. "You know, someday you might actually learn to accept a compliment." A faint blush crept across his cheeks. "I was wondering . . ." He reached into his pocket and pulled something out. He kept his fist closed, hiding whatever was tucked inside. "I bought this last year. For Amy. Before everything happened." He opened his hand and a flash of silver tumbled out. A small disc spun at the end of a dainty chain, catching the light as Jason dangled the necklace between his fingers.

I turned and captured the pendant in my palm. It was a small silver compass. North, South, East, and West. A star between them and tiny letters that wound their way along the outer edge. *May you always know the way home.*

"It's stupid and sentimental," said Jason, raking his free hand through his hair, disheveling it even more, "but part of me always felt like she was pulling away—especially this last year. I saw the necklace in a store window and I felt bad about how much we had been fighting and I just, dunno, wanted to try and do something nice for her. I knew it was too little too late, but I still wanted to try."

He pulled in a deep breath. "I never got the chance to give it to her, and after the funeral, I couldn't bring myself to get rid of it. I just . . . I thought it would look nice with your dress."

His hands went to the clasp, a silent question in his eyes. It felt wrong—as wrong as wearing Amy's bracelet—but looking at the earnest, slightly lost look on Jason's face, I found myself nodding.

I turned so he could fasten the chain around my neck. The silver felt warm against my skin. Almost hot.

My chest felt suddenly tight. I was standing in Amy's place. I was wearing the kind of dress she belonged in and a necklace that had been meant for her. I was standing with the boy who should have loved her more than he loved me.

I felt like a thief.

Jason traced the edge of the chain with the barest brush of his fingertips. "I keep thinking about where we're going tonight, and I keep wondering how many ways you can betray a person. Amy's gone, but I still keep finding ways to hurt her."

"You don't have to come with us." It was hard to say

the words—now that I had accepted that he and Kyle were staying, I couldn't imagine doing this without them—but I needed Jason to know he had a choice. To know that he *always* had a choice. "Kyle and I can go. You could head back to the church and wait with the others."

"No," he said, voice low and serious. "I can't."

He held my gaze in the mirror. Like the ocean during a storm, his eyes pulled me under. "Why?" I asked. "What changed?" It was the question I had wanted to ask him for hours.

"Serena." He continued to hold my gaze. "Until this afternoon, I didn't think I would ever see anything as horrible as those videos of them torturing her in the camp. After what happened to her—after what keeps happening to her—she deserves to know who's responsible. You were right: this is bigger than us. I hate where we're going and why—I hate everything about this—but it's necessary."

He started to lower his hand, but I reached up and held it in place. "I don't want to lose you over this. I don't want you to hate me if we go there and find something."

A small, sad smile crossed his face. "You won't lose me. As long as you want me around—however you want me around—I'm here. Don't worry," he added, catching my flicker of unease and the way I bit my lip. "I know it's him. It should be him. He's better than either of us."

"Jason . . ." My heart twisted. I loved him—just not the same way he loved me. Not the way I loved Kyle. I didn't feel guilty for the feelings I had for Kyle—it would be like feeling guilty for breathing—but I wished there was some way I could keep those feelings from hurting Jason.

A floorboard creaked behind us.

I released Jason's hand and turned.

Kyle stood in the doorway, a blank, careful expression on his face that I couldn't decipher.

Jason stepped to the side, putting plenty of space between us. We hadn't done anything wrong, but another blush flared across my cheeks. That one, stupid kiss after Thornhill made everything so awkward and complicated.

Kyle stared at the two of us for a handful of heartbeats before stepping over the threshold.

My pulse sped up as I watched him cross the room. Kyle wasn't as comfortable in a tux as Jason was—he tugged at the collar and the cuffs—but that didn't change the way the jacket emphasized his broad shoulders or how he moved with an impossible amount of grace.

For a second, I forgot the awkwardness of the moment as a single word filled my brain: *Damn*.

My approval must have shown on my face because the corners of Kyle's mouth quirked up in a slightly cocky grin. His gaze took in every inch of my dress and the skin it didn't cover as he walked toward us. He stopped just in front of me. Without glancing at Jason, he placed his hands on my hips and brushed his lips against mine.

The kiss was brief and light, but it still left my knees shaking.

"You look amazing," he murmured, pulling back as heat spread slowly through my body, warming me from the inside out.

His eyes lingered on the necklace for a moment. He glanced at Jason and raised an eyebrow, eliciting a barely perceptible shrug. I wondered if he had been with Jason the day he bought it.

"Aren't you going to tell me how pretty I look?" Jason ran a hand over his lapel. His eyes were dark and the joke was forced, but a small grin still flashed across his face.

"You're a gorgeous specimen of manhood," deadpanned Kyle.

"Not to interrupt the bromancing, but . . ." My gaze darted from one boy to the other. "Are you guys sure you want to do this?"

The look Kyle shot me was pure exasperation. "Do you even need to ask?"

I shrugged. Of course I did.

"Free drinks, hors d'oeuvres, and women in low-cut dresses." Jason let out a small, very male laugh. "Your concern for our well-being is touching, but I think we can handle it."

Half of those women in low-cut dresses would probably be anti-werewolf zealots, and the idea of Jason and free drinks didn't exactly give me warm and fuzzy thoughts, but I tucked a hand into the crook of each boy's arm. "Let's go sparkle."

If Jay Gatsby had lived in Hemlock, he would have crashed parties at the Walsh house.

Amy's family was the closest thing the town had to royalty and their parties were legendary. Even an invitation to something like this—a boring fund-raiser where wealthy socialites and politicians could mingle with prestigious Trackers and high-ranking LSRB officials—was highly coveted.

Despite the fact that the National Guard was patrolling the streets and the entire town was under a ten o'clock curfew, plenty of people had turned up—way more people than had invitations. The party had been under way for over an hour and the line outside the gates kept growing.

"Do you want my jacket?" asked Kyle as I stood between him and Jason and hugged myself for warmth.

I shook my head. I'd be okay—for now—though I was seriously regretting our decision not to don coats before walking the short distance from Jason's house.

We inched our way forward as the security team turned away another group of gate-crashers. I had watched more than one party at Amy's house from the shadows, but I had never seen security precautions like this. Five men worked the gate. They didn't allow any cars to remain within fifty feet of the driveway, and each guest who made it through was scanned with a portable metal detector before being allowed to proceed up to the house on foot.

But that was only the second layer of protection. Before you could even approach the gate, you had to make your way through a gauntlet of Trackers. Like a living wall, dozens of them lined each side of the street, stretching from one edge of the Walshes' property to the other. Something about the way they carried themselves—the set of their shoulders and the way they snapped to attention whenever someone spoke

164

to them—made me wonder if they'd had military training. Some of the more extreme Tracker chapters trained their younger, fitter members for what they saw as an impending war between wolves and regs.

The Walsh family hadn't asked for the added security—not according to the snatches of whispered conversation I caught around us—but with so many important Trackers inside, the group wasn't taking any chances.

With a miniature riot last night and the National Guard crawling over Hemlock, I guess I couldn't blame them for wanting the extra protection—and that was without factoring in the idea that an unknown number of werewolves were planning God only knew what for the night of the rallies.

I remembered Trey's words about the town being a tinderbox and shivered.

Even though contacting our families felt like a risk, I had called Tess and tried to convince her to get out of Hemlock for a few days—without luck. She had insisted she'd be fine as long as she stayed inside. With the National Guard controlling the flood of traffic in and out of town, she felt safer in the apartment than stuck for hours at a checkpoint. Kyle'd had better luck with his parents. Despite the delays on the roads, they were now safely on their way to visit his grandparents out of state. By the time they figured out he was not—as he had promised—already on his way there, it would be too late for them to make it back before the rally.

They'd be safe.

I twisted the chain at my throat as we neared the front of the line.

"Are you all right?" asked Kyle.

I opened my mouth to tell him I was just thinking about Tess, but was cut off by a man with an earthquake of a voice and a face that would have looked at home in the Neanderthal exhibit of any natural history museum. "Names?"

"Jason Sheffield, Mackenzie Dobson, and Kyle Harper," said Jason as he handed over two invitations.

The man's thick fingers danced over a tablet. "You and the girl are on the list. He's not."

"He's supposed to be," bluffed Jason. "Must be an oversight. Call the house."

"Kid, I've turned away thirty 'oversights' in the past hour. If he's not on the list, he doesn't get past the gate."

Kyle stiffened, but Jason just shrugged, the gesture long and languid. "He was a friend of Amy Walsh's."

"I don't care if he's the Pope," replied the man. "He's not on the list."

Jason held his arm out to me. "Come on, Mac. I'm sure Senator Walsh will be thrilled to find out one of his granddaughter's closest friends wasn't allowed through— especially when he asked the three of us to come and say a few words."

A small flicker of doubt crossed the Neanderthal's face.

One of the other guards recognized Jason. "You're the boyfriend, right?"

"I was." Whispers broke out in the line behind us; Jason ignored them. He inclined his head toward Kyle and me. "They were Amy's best friends. The senator thought our presence would help underscore the importance of

166

tougher anti-werewolf legislation."

It was sometimes frightening how good Jason was at lying.

The Neanderthal stared at Jason. Jason stared back. Finally, the second guard—the one who had spoken up— broke the stalemate.

"They're fine. He's a Sheffield and his parents are already inside."

I held my breath.

For a moment, it looked like the guard with the tablet wasn't going to listen, but he eventually stepped aside and let us pass.

"Remove any metal items from your person and stand with your arms out, sir," said another member of the security team as Kyle stepped through the gate.

Kyle did as he was told, staring straight ahead as the man passed a handheld metal detector over him.

Jason and I were each subjected to the same search before we were allowed to proceed to the house.

Ahead, other people were making their way up the long, cobblestone driveway. Glowing paper lanterns had been placed every few feet and the trees had all been strung with small, white lights.

High heels and I didn't get along at the best of times; throw cobblestones and a long skirt into the mix and I tee-tered like a tower of Jenga blocks.

I stumbled and made a desperate grab for Kyle's arm.

He grinned as he steadied me. "I thought walking in ridiculous shoes was a trait all girls were born with."

"Not all girls," I muttered.

"Another illusion of femininity shattered." Jason's tone was distracted as his eyes swept over the lone guard posted at the entrance to the house.

"Shut up. Both of you." I'd be fine once we made it to a flat surface. Despite the fact that my legs were still shaking, I let go of Kyle's arm. In the past month and a half, I had survived a murder attempt and life as an inmate inside a werewolf rehabilitation camp. One evening in formal wear should be easy. Theoretically.

The guard greeted us with a polite nod as he opened the door and stepped aside.

I paused to study the door's four intricately carved panels as I followed Jason over the threshold. Each panel had been handcrafted in Europe and depicted a different nature scene. My eyes swept over mountain vistas and lush forests before coming to rest on a carving of a river. A trout jumping out of the water. Cattails and reeds. A small bird in flight. I reached out and traced the edge of the bird's wing. It was a kingfisher, the same bird used in CutterBrown's logo.

With a deep breath, I stepped into the house.

Waves of conversation crashed over us as we entered the foyer. A huge photograph of Amy stood on an easel next to the staircase, and two tall vases overflowing with calla lilies framed each side of her bright, smiling face. It was a lovely picture—provided you didn't know the smile was fake. Amy's real smile always filled her eyes and this smile hadn't even come close. Genuine-looking smiles were one of the few things she had never been able to fake.

I glanced away from the photo because staring at it was too hard.

Instead, I tried to focus on the ebb and flow of voices and the subtle strands of classical music coming from a string quartet in the living room.

My gaze slid to the stairs. We needed to get to Amy's room, but a velvet rope was strung across the bottom step.

"Jason Sheffield!" A man with a bald head and too much girth for his suit latched on to Jason, pumping his hand enthusiastically. "Your father didn't tell me you would be here. There are people I want you to meet."

The scent of alcohol followed the man like exhaust from an engine, and as he tried to draw Jason into the living room, he tripped over his own feet. Bystanders scrambled to get out of the way as he crashed to the ground. A few didn't move quickly enough.

"Come on." While everyone's attention was diverted, I unlatched the rope at the bottom of the stairs.

I glanced back when Kyle and I were halfway to the second floor.

Jason met my gaze and nodded. He mouthed something that might have been "Be careful," but I was too far away to be sure.

The noise of the party faded as Kyle and I stepped into the shadows on the landing. Small lamps with Tiffany shades glowed on half-moon tables placed at regular intervals in the hall, but the overhead lights were dark.

Thick carpet muffled our footsteps as we made our way to Amy's room. This was only the second time I had been up here since her death, and the place filled me with a mixture of sadness and déjà vu.

Despite all of the people downstairs, the house felt empty. It was almost as though Amy's presence had been the thing that had given it life.

"Wait!" Kyle's voice, low and urgent, stopped me in my tracks as I reached for Amy's door. Before I could ask what was wrong, he held a finger to his lips. With his other hand, he drew me past Amy's room and to a door at the far end of the hall.

The master bedroom.

Kyle stopped when we were a few feet from the door. I stood just behind him, leaning into him as I tried to make out the murmur of voices on the other side.

"—isn't the time and place," said a smooth, masculine voice. A voice that belonged to Amy's father.

"When is the right time, Ryan?" said a woman—a woman who was definitely not Amy's mother. Her voice rose in frustration. "You won't return my calls and you ignore my emails. I flew in to see you and you wouldn't give me five minutes of your time."

"Because there isn't anything left to say. You made your decision."

"You didn't give me any choice!"

"You had a choice." Mr. Walsh's voice was so cold that it sent a shiver down my spine. "You chose to leave."

"After Van Horne, can you blame me? It's like you became an entirely different person. You threw everything we had away."

My heart thundered in my chest.

Van Horne was the name of one of the other camps. One of the worst camps. It was what they threatened us with at Thornhill: step out of line and you'd be sent to Van Horne.

"I can help you, Ryan. I want to help you. Maybe it's stupid, but I still care about you. I came here tonight because people are talking—and not just at CBP. There's even a rumor that your son was behind the breach in January, that he was the leak and that the board is losing faith in you."

Kyle and I were both so intent on the conversation that it took us a moment to realize the woman's voice was drifting closer to the door.

I grabbed Kyle's arm and beelined for Amy's room. We tumbled inside just as the door to the master bedroom opened.

Kyle eased Amy's door almost all the way shut, leaving just enough of a gap for us to see a small slice of hallway. He stood behind me, so close that his chest was flush to my back.

"There was no breach." Ryan Walsh's voice held an unmistakable threat, a threat that contradicted the calm, quiet man I knew. "Stephen wasn't behind any leak."

"Ryan, I really think—"

There was a yelp followed by a thud. "I don't care what you think." The voice still belonged to Amy's father but it was so hard that it was almost unrecognizable. "You gave up the right to an opinion the second you walked out."

I held my breath and eased the door open another inch. Amy's father was standing a few feet away, his back to us.

Behind him, I could just glimpse a brunette in a curve-hugging red dress. Her back was to the wall, her body pinned in place by Ryan Walsh's arms.

My stomach rolled. For a horrible moment, I thought he would hit her, but then she pressed her lips to his.

I thought of Amy's mother and winced. She was downstairs, coordinating a gala in memory of her dead daughter while her husband was kissing another woman just outside their bedroom.

Amy's father pulled away.

"I want to come back," said the woman, voice breathless. "Leaving was a mistake. I want to come back."

"You think it's that easy? You think things can just go back to the way they were?" Ryan Walsh let out a short, bitter bark of a laugh. "I'm giving you five minutes to leave before I call security and have them toss you out." Without waiting for a response, Amy's father turned on his heel and strode away.

Behind me, Kyle tensed as we got our first real glimpse of the woman in the red dress.

A ringing sound filled my ears as she reached up to adjust her glasses.

Though I had only encountered the woman a handful of times, I saw her face behind my closed lids on nights when memories of Thornhill made sleep impossible.

The woman who had signaled out wolves for torture in Thornhill's detention block.

The woman who had tortured Serena.

13

A GASP ESCAPED MY THROAT BEFORE I COULD STOP IT.

The woman's brows pulled together as she turned toward Amy's door. "Is someone there?"

Kyle tried to ease me back, tried to place himself in front of me, but I couldn't move. Every cell in my body had turned to stone.

The woman took a step forward and only the absence of light in the room kept her from seeing us.

"Excuse me, ma'am." A deep male voice stopped her as she reached for the doorknob. "I was told to escort you downstairs."

She frowned and glanced over her shoulder, then looked back at Amy's door, hesitating as she ran a hand over her glossy brown hair.

"Ma'am?"

"Of course," she murmured, turning and heading for the stairs as the owner of the voice followed in her wake.

I was pressed so closely to Kyle that I could feel the tension drain out of him as he reached around me and softly shut the door. He stepped back, but I still couldn't move.

I flashed back to a Saturday, years ago, when Mr. Walsh had helped Amy and me create a diorama of the Globe Theatre for history class. Halfway through the evening, he had ordered a pizza big enough to feed a troupe of actors and rented *The Lion King*. We ate pizza and worked on the miniature theater, and as we watched the movie, Mr. Walsh explained the ties the story had to Shakespeare. The whole time, I kept thinking, *This is what a family is. This is what a father is supposed to be.*

Something inside my chest shattered.

It was one thing to believe in the possibility that Amy's father could have known about Thornhill, but another to have proof—and what else could that woman's presence here be?

Another thought occurred to me as I replayed their conversation in my head. She had said she wanted to come back, that she had made a mistake by leaving.

"Do you think he was cheating on Amy's mom?" I asked Kyle softly.

I already knew the answer; his silence just reinforced it.

I thought of Amy's life and how perfect it had seemed from the outside. How could so much have been wrong beneath the surface?

"Mac? Are you all right?"

I turned to Kyle. The room was so dark that he was just a jumble of shapes.

"I'm fine," I lied. I tried to pull in a deep breath, but my lungs felt tight. "Let's just get this over with."

Kyle caught my hand as I reached for the light switch. "Someone might see the light under the door," he said, voice low.

I was pretty sure we were the only ones left upstairs, but he was right: someone could come back.

The touch on my hand fell away and I heard the rustle of fabric as he crossed the room and pulled open the heavy drapes.

Moonlight and the glow from the gardens below shone through the window, illuminating the empty space.

I blinked.

"We're in the wrong room." But as the words left my lips, my gaze fell on the purple-and-silver fleur-de-lis wallpaper Amy had picked out the last time she redecorated.

"All of her stuff is gone." My voice was a choked whisper. The tightness in my lungs grew, as though someone had laced them up and was pulling on the strings. There were no posters on the walls. No furniture or pictures or mirrors. My shoes sank into the plush carpet as I walked to the closet and pulled open the double doors. It, too, was empty.

Everything that had made the room Amy's had been stripped away. For a moment, it felt like losing her all over again.

I hugged myself tightly as I turned back to Kyle. "Stephen told me he was going through her things, but I didn't think it would be like this. How could they get rid of her stuff? It hasn't even been a year."

I couldn't read the look in Kyle's eyes, but his expression

175

had slid into something hard and closed. "I don't know, but we don't have much time."

He was right. I allowed myself one last look around the empty room and then forced myself to walk to the window seat. Even the cushions were gone. Amy had always stashed things underneath them—her diary, notes from teachers, pictures of Trey—but that hadn't been her only hiding place.

If they find that stuff, no one will ever go looking for anything else. That's what she had told me, once, after I'd pointed out what an obvious hiding spot it was. *It's misdirection, Mac. Let them find the little things so they miss the big stuff.*

I wasn't sure a diary counted as a little thing, but the theory had seemed sound.

Clumsily, I knelt on the carpet. I ran my fingers along the beveled wood that edged the seat until I found a small groove. I tried lifting up and pulling out, but the wood refused to budge. There was a trick to it, and it took me several moments before I found the right combination of angle and force. Finally, a small section popped out, revealing a gap that was no more than five inches wide.

Kyle began to pace as I pulled out a tangle of objects: a ring Amy had stolen from her grandmother's jewelry box and been too ashamed to put back, a prescription for the birth control pills her parents hadn't known she was on, parking tickets, and a wad of cash in a folded envelope marked *California Fund*.

"What did that woman mean when she said people thought Stephen was responsible for a breach in January?" Kyle's voice was low and rough as his steps took him from one side of the room to the other. "What breach? What people? And that stuff about Van Horne . . . was CBP experimenting on werewolves at more than one camp?"

"Stephen's worked in his dad's office as an intern every summer I've known him. Maybe he saw or found something he wasn't supposed to. The Van Horne stuff . . ." I bit my lip as I struggled to remember everything the warden had said to me while I'd been in the camp. "Sinclair told me she had worked at other camps, but she never said which ones."

"So maybe one of them was Van Horne. Maybe they started looking for a cure there and then moved things to Thornhill once Sinclair was installed as warden." Kyle came to a stop and crouched next to me. "We need to find out what—exactly—that woman was talking about. We need to talk to Stephen."

I made a thoughtful, noncommittal noise as I reached back into Amy's hiding spot. After the way I'd freaked out at the cemetery, it would be a minor miracle if Stephen told us anything. Even if he was willing to speak to us, how could we trust him? How could we know he wouldn't just turn us over to CBP? My fingers closed on a small jumble of metal, and I withdrew two keys: the key to Ryan Walsh's study and a second, smaller key that I didn't recognize.

The problem with formal dresses? They never had pockets when you needed them. I hesitated a moment and then tucked the first key into my bra. Just one more secret between me and Victoria.

I glanced up in time to catch Kyle sneaking a glance at my cleavage.

Guilt flashed across his face, and despite the situation, I laughed before I could stop myself. It was so deliciously normal. Everything in our world was going to hell, but my boyfriend was still taking time to check out my chest.

Once I started laughing, I couldn't stop. I tried clamping my hands over my mouth, desperate to silence the sound in case someone wandered upstairs and heard the noise, but the laughter kept bubbling up from deep inside my chest, so hard that breathing became a struggle and tears streamed down my face. *Maybe this is what people mean when they talk about hysterical laughter,* I thought, and that just set me off all over again.

Kyle was staring at me as though I had lost my mind. He shot a nervous glance at the door and that small gesture helped me regain control.

"I'm okay," I managed, lowering my hands from my mouth as the laughter finally subsided. "It's just funny, y'know. Of all the times to sneak a peek . . ."

"Sorry," he said, but the grin that crossed his face looked anything but contrite.

On impulse, I leaned over and kissed him.

I meant it to be a quick, light peck, but Kyle pulled me close and I found my lips parting under his. His right hand slid up the back of my neck to tangle in my too-short hair as my own hands slipped under his jacket.

I kissed Kyle hungrily, greedily, as though I could borrow some of his warmth and use it to chase away the cold sting of everything we had seen and heard over the past few minutes.

"Everything will be okay," he whispered, minutes later, somehow knowing they were words I desperately needed to hear. He pulled back and tucked a stray strand of my hair back into place.

"How?" I asked, trying not to cringe at how small and weak the single word sounded.

Kyle trailed his fingers along my temple. "I don't know," he admitted, "but it will be."

He lowered his hand and then reached past me to begin slipping Amy's things back into their hiding place.

"Wait." I grabbed the second key before he could tuck it away with everything else. It was small— not as small as the key to a suitcase, but smaller than the key to any door. There was something slightly familiar about the size and shape of it. A locker key, maybe? Or the key to a desk drawer.

"What is it?" asked Kyle.

I shook my head. "I don't know. But Amy only kept things in here that were important. It was with the key to the study; maybe it opens something in there." I slipped the key into my bra with the other one, rolling my eyes when he smirked.

I fitted the small section of the window seat back into place as Kyle stood. He reached down and I let him help me to my feet, teetering a little on the dreaded heels.

"Ready?"

I nodded. We crossed the room and Kyle cracked the door, checking the hallway before stepping outside.

I shot one last glance back at Amy's room before following.

She wasn't here, not anymore, and that somehow made it easier to walk away.

I pulled the door closed and headed after Kyle, pausing for a moment to check my makeup—makeup I had borrowed from Jason's mother—in a mirror with a gilded frame. Kyle stopped and waited for me, and I shook my head, amused, as I walked toward him.

I wiped away a small smudge of lipstick at the corner of his mouth. "Jason will never let either of us hear the end of it if you go down there wearing lipstick."

I expected Kyle to laugh or blush, but something dark and uncertain passed behind his eyes. "C'mon," he said, the single word soft and gruff, as he headed for the staircase.

Confused and a little off-balance by the sudden change in his mood, I followed.

The sound of voices stopped us on the landing.

A trio of silver-haired men in suits were locked in conversation at the bottom of the stairs. Amy's grandfather walked by. They called out to him, but the senator waved them off and continued to the hallway on the far side of the stairs, a hallway that wound past the billiard room and the study before eventually leading out to the pool.

The group gave a collective shrug and went back to their conversation.

"It's like I told her: if you lie with wolves, you'll get fleas."

"Or have puppies."

They broke out in alcohol-thickened chortles.

I glanced at Kyle and slipped my hand into his. His expression was studiously blank, and his hand felt hard and unyielding, almost as though metal ran beneath his skin.

"Are you okay?" I whispered.

"Why wouldn't I be?" He slid his hand out from mine and turned. "We'll have to take the back stairs and go through the kitchen."

I watched his retreating form for a moment. I wanted to tell him that I was sorry, but I didn't know how. There would always be men like that; there would always be people who hated and feared Kyle for something that wasn't his fault. Any apology I gave would be useless and inadequate.

In the end, I said nothing and trailed him down the hall.

The back stairs were located behind a door that had been cleverly camouflaged to look like part of the wall. A casual visitor would walk right past it, but Kyle and I were not casual visitors. He pulled it open and held it for me as I stepped through.

The narrow passage was just wide enough for one person. Bare lightbulbs hung from the ceiling at regular intervals, but they didn't do much to dispel the gloom. The space had been a servants' stairway when the house had first been built, and no one had ever tried to make it look anything other than plain and functional.

The din of clanking dishes and the shouts of caterers drifted up from the kitchen below, more than masking the noise my heels made on the wooden steps.

Kyle put a hand on my shoulder when we were halfway to the first floor. "Mac, hold on a sec . . ."

I paused and turned. I was standing two steps below, and even with the advantage of heels, the difference in positions accentuated Kyle's height. I looked up into his eyes and saw that same blend of darkness and uncertainty I had noticed moments before.

He ran a hand through his hair. "Did something happen between you and Jason. Back at Thornhill? Or in Denver?"

My heart skipped a beat and the hand I placed on the railing to steady myself shook slightly. "Why would you ask that?" There was a catch in my voice, one that I hoped sounded more disbelieving than defensive.

"The two of you have been avoiding each other since we got back from the camp. And earlier—up in Jason's room—it felt like I walked in on something."

"You didn't."

Kyle stepped down a stair, closing some of the distance and making it easier to meet his gaze. "I'm used to the way Jason stares at you—I don't like it, but I'm used to it—but there was something in the way you were looking back. It was like there was a charge in the room."

I hesitated. In a way, telling Kyle about the kiss would be easy. I knew he would eventually forgive me and I could stop feeling like I was keeping something from him. I could stop feeling guilty and I could stop worrying that someday, somehow, Kyle would find out about what had happened in the town car.

But while I was certain Kyle would forgive me, I wasn't so sure he would forgive Jason. I wanted to believe their friendship was stronger than the feelings each of them had for me, but I had seen enough talk shows and movies to be scared to put that to the test.

All I knew was that I couldn't be the thing that came between them—not permanently. I would never forgive myself, and in the end, they would both end up resenting me.

Besides, what had happened with Jason would never happen again. It had been a mistake. I had chosen Kyle. I would always choose Kyle.

He was staring at me, waiting for an answer.

I reached up and placed a hand against Kyle's neck. I could feel his pulse jump under my palm, his heart beating so much faster than mine. "I tore down an entire prison to get back to you," I said, throat tight. "There will never be anyone else for me."

I met Kyle's gaze and held it, letting the depth of the feelings I had for him flood my eyes.

After a long moment, he nodded. Leaning down, he folded me into a hug.

14

An army of catering staff filled the Walshes' cavernous kitchen as trays of food and drinks came and went with the precision of a military operation.

Kyle and I tried not to get trampled as we made our way to the open door at the far end of the room. A trickle of perspiration ran down the back of my neck, and I wondered how it was possible for all of the waitstaff to look freshly pressed when the room had to be 110 degrees.

"We need more champagne. There should be at least two more cases."

I shot a startled glance over my shoulder. Amy's mother stood ten feet away, her face slightly flushed as she consulted with one of the caterers. She should have been in her element—Mrs. Walsh had always lived for throwing parties—but there was a tightness around her eyes and mouth. She looked pinched and spread thin.

Blushing, I thought about what Kyle and I had seen and heard upstairs. Amy's parents had always seemed happy—well, as happy as anyone. I knew there were a lot of reasons people cheated, but looking at Mrs. Walsh, I couldn't think of a single excuse that would be good enough.

She half turned in our direction and my heart lurched. *Don't look this way. Don't look this way.* I repeated the words under my breath as Kyle and I quickly crossed the rest of the kitchen.

I didn't think Amy's mother would throw us out, but she would definitely wonder what we were doing here. She would ask questions and maybe tell Amy's father—or Stephen—that she had seen us.

It was as though my thoughts had some sort of strange, summoning power.

"Stephen! Where have you been?" Mrs. Walsh's voice rang across the room. I looked back just in time to catch a glimpse of a blond head as Amy's brother ducked through a door that led to the sprawling backyard.

Mrs. Walsh called after her son a second time, but he was already gone.

"Because that's not at all suspicious," I said.

"He's bleeding. I can smell it over the scent of the food."

I resisted the urge to say *eww*. Werewolf supersenses were handy, but there were times when they walked the line between beneficial and kinda gross.

"Come on," said Kyle, starting after him.

I caught his hand. "Wait—" The longer we stayed at the party, the more we were pressing our luck. "You go after Stephen. I'll find Jason and we'll check the study."

"You can't seriously think splitting up is a good idea." Kyle stared at me in disbelief.

"We're running out of time. People are going to start leaving soon to avoid breaking the curfew. The fewer people in the house, the less chance we have of getting in and out of that room."

Kyle hesitated. He shot a glance at the door Stephen had slipped through, and I could tell from the frown on his face that he knew I was right.

"I'll be fine," I promised. "I'll be with Jason."

"You know that's not as reassuring as you think it is, right?"

I grinned and pressed a quick kiss to his lips. "Be careful."

He nodded, the gesture tight and reluctant. "You too."

I eased into the shadows along the side of the room and watched as Kyle gave Mrs. Walsh a wide berth before disappearing through the back door. Trying to tell myself that the big, strong werewolf would be all right on his own, I made my way out of the kitchen and back to the party.

Conversations engulfed me as I wove past groups of guests. You couldn't have a fund-raiser attended by the LSRB and the Trackers without plenty of werewolf slurs, and while I tried to tune them out, the worst ones slipped through.

"None of this would have happened if they would just treat those creatures like the vermin they are."

"When you have a pest problem, you don't wait to call in an exterminator."

"My husband hunts big game. Can you imagine the thrill he'd get from hunting one of them?"

Heat flooded my cheeks and crept down my neck. Walking by in silence felt like cowardice, but I couldn't afford to draw attention to myself. I forced myself to stay quiet and kept walking.

My eyes roamed over the crowd, searching for Jason as I moved from room to room. I only spotted two dagger tattoos, neither of them his.

He had told me once that most of the influential Trackers—the ones who were high up or wealthy—didn't get the brand. It made it easier for them to mingle with politicians and attend fund-raisers. No matter how popular the Trackers became, some people still found the tattoos unnerving. It reminded them too much of the group's early roots as an offshoot of white supremacy organizations—a past the Trackers had spent a lot of money trying to make people forget.

I tried not to think about the fact that the tattoo had been optional for Jason. As someone who was both wealthy and politically connected, he could have forgone getting marked. Instead, he had voluntarily gotten the tattoo—or at least most of it.

I finally spotted him just past the entrance to the living room, surrounded by a group of laughing girls who all looked as though they had stumbled in from an episode of *The Bachelor*. All Jason needed was a rose to hand out.

Relief flashed across his face as he caught sight of me but quickly changed to confusion when he realized I was alone. He doled out apologies and parting smiles before breaking away from the gaggle of groupies and making his way to me.

"We leave you alone for twenty minutes and you pick up an entourage?"

"Being blond and ridiculously rich is a heavy burden. Where's Kyle?"

"Following Stephen. We saw Amy's father upstairs." I bit my lip, unsure how to tell him what we had found. Of all of us, he had been the closest to Amy's family and the most reluctant to believe in a possible connection between CBP and the camp. "Mr. Walsh was talking to one of the women who tortured Serena at Thornhill. He seemed to know her *really* well. Like, intimately."

"Shit," muttered Jason. He grabbed two drinks from a passing tray as we made our way across the foyer. He downed the first and ditched the glass before starting in on the second.

"Tell me you at least found the key to the study."

No one was looking our way. I nodded and slipped the key out from my bra.

"Safer than Fort Knox." The joke fell flat and he took another drink.

"Is there some twisted part of you that *wants* to see if I'll beat the crap out of you?" I plucked the glass from his hand and took a sip for courage before tipping the rest down a potted plant.

"Jason?"

Mr. and Mrs. Sheffield materialized out of nowhere.

Panicked, I shoved the empty glass back into Jason's hand.

In some ways, Matt Sheffield looked like an older, colder

version of his son. He had the same eyes without the spark of warmth. The same mouth without the capacity for laughter. But as cold as Jason's father was, he had nothing on his wife.

The temperature around us dropped as her gaze settled on me. "Jason, you didn't tell us you would be here. Or that you were bringing Mackenzie."

Somehow, just the way she said my name made me feel like a piece of gum that had been dragged in on the bottom of someone's shoe. I was suddenly achingly aware of the fact that I didn't belong here. I tugged on the sleeve of my dress—the dress Jason had paid for—self-consciously and prayed she wouldn't look down and recognize the shoes.

"Would have," said Jason, wrapping an arm around my shoulders, "but then we would have had to have an actual conversation, and I know how much you detest those mother-son moments."

"I don't know why you always say such things." The ice in Mrs. Sheffield's voice cracked artfully. The words were a show for anyone who might be within earshot. "You know I try."

"Darling," said Jason's father, completely oblivious to— or just ignoring—the tense exchange between his wife and son, "I see some people I need to say hello to." He turned and held out his arm.

Before taking it, Mrs. Sheffield shot a pointed glance at the empty glass in Jason's hand. "Do try to remember where you are and behave yourself."

"Love you, too, Mom," called Jason as she walked away.

"Not a word about the fact that I didn't go home last night or the National Guard or the curfew." He set the glass on the floor. "Someone really needs to send that woman a subscription to one of those parenting magazines."

"I think it's about eighteen years too late." I shook my head. "Come on. I just want to get out of here."

I gripped the key tightly in my hand as we made our way to the study. The tap of my heels echoed in the empty hallway and I couldn't stop glancing over my shoulder.

"Don't look so nervous," said Jason, though he seemed just as off-balance as I felt.

I can't believe we're doing this, I thought. You'd think anything would be easy after taking down a rehabilitation camp, but the closer we got to the study, the more my stomach twisted into knots.

"What the . . . ?" Jason's steps faltered and his shoulders tensed as we neared the door.

There were scuff marks around the lock and gouges in the doorframe. The door was closed, but not all the way. "Someone broke in." It was a clumsy job—the kind Hank would have chastised me for—and the noise probably would have drawn attention if it hadn't been for the background din of the party. I strained my ears, but couldn't hear anything inside.

Jason pushed the door open with his shoulder. It groaned on its hinges, but slowly swung inward to reveal a dimly lit ruin.

Bookcases lined each wall, but their contents had been strewn around the room. Shards of broken antiques and torn pages from heavy leather-bound books covered the floor. Near the far wall, a large desk had been turned onto its side. Its drawers had been reduced to kindling—it almost looked as though someone had destroyed them in a blind rage.

"The room is soundproof," I murmured. Amy had always said her dad needed complete quiet to work. "That's why no one at the party heard the noise."

Jason swore under his breath. I thought he was responding to the destruction, but as he strode toward the desk, I saw what had captured his attention.

Bile rose in the back of my throat as I followed him to a crumpled figure half hidden by the desk. It was a man with dark hair and the same sort of suit the security staff were all wearing. He was lying on his stomach in a pool of blood. It seemed impossible that one body could contain so much blood.

The outer edges of the puddle had already started to dry: he had been here for a while.

I reached for the man's shoulder, and then stopped. Whatever had happened to him, he was obviously beyond help.

Nauseous, I stepped back and turned to stare at the remains of the room. "What do you think happened?"

"Just a guess: we aren't the only ones looking for something." Jason nodded down at the body. His voice was even, but he looked slightly green. "He probably walked in on whoever trashed the study."

A low groan drifted through the room. For a second, I

thought the sound had come from the man at our feet, but then the noise came again, from behind us.

"Oh, God." I ran to the far corner where a familiar, silver-haired figure lay on his side. I pulled off my gloves and let them fall to the floor as I crouched next to Amy's grandfather. He groaned softly as I pressed two fingers to his throat. His pulse was weak and erratic. "I think he had a heart attack." I fumbled for his hand. "Senator Walsh? John?"

The old man's eyes fluttered open. They locked on my face, but seemed to stare right through me. "Amy." His voice was a rasp but his fingers gripped mine so tightly that it was almost painful.

"No, it's—" I started to correct him, but couldn't.

"Stay with me." He closed his eyes but continued to squeeze my hand.

I looked up at Jason. "You have to go get help."

"I'm not leaving you alone in here. You go. I'll stay."

"He thinks I'm Amy." A lump rose in my throat. "I can't leave him."

Jason ran a hand roughly over his face and stared down at Amy's grandfather. When he spoke, the words sounded strangled. "Three minutes. I'll be back in three minutes."

I nodded and turned my attention back to Senator Walsh. "It'll be all right," I said, even though I wasn't sure it would be all right at all. "You'll be okay. Jason's getting help."

The door clicked shut as Jason left the room.

Amy's grandfather struggled for breath. When he spoke, each word was labored. "I don't know how to fix it."

"Shhhhh. It's all right. You don't have to fix anything."

"Amy . . . I didn't know." His voice became a barely audible rasp, forcing me to lean closer. "He didn't mean to hurt anyone. He's a good boy."

A shiver slipped down my spine as I remembered Stephen's hasty exit from the kitchen and the blood Kyle had smelled. "Do you mean Stephen? Was Stephen here?"

From the other side of the study came the rustle of fabric and a thick, wet cough. "He's talking about his son."

Yanking my hand free of the senator's grip, I twisted around just as the figure by the desk rolled over and struggled to a sitting position.

I stared, horrified, at a familiar face and a pair of flat, gray eyes.

"He's talking about Ryan Walsh." Amy's killer smiled at me weakly. "Hello, Mac."

15

My shoulder blades collided with the door. I didn't remember standing or moving.

I stared at Ben from across the room as sweat soaked my skin and my heart thundered in my chest. For a horrible second, I was back in the forest outside Hemlock, my shoulders pressed to a tree as a white werewolf—as Ben—loomed above me.

I dug my nails into my palm, using the pain to keep the past from pulling me under.

Ben was thinner than I remembered, and he had dyed his normally blond hair a rich, deep brown, but it was unmistakably him. The front of his shirt was soaked with blood. It clung to his lower torso and his left shoulder in large patches.

A reg would already be dead from blood loss; given the way Ben stayed on the floor, leaning against the upturned desk for support, the wounds might be too much for even a werewolf to heal.

He didn't look like he was going anywhere, but I wasn't

taking any chances. My gaze swept over the mess on the study floor and settled on a letter opener a few feet away. Locking my eyes on Ben, I walked over to it and crouched down. My fingers skimmed torn books and the remains of a Chinese vase before closing on the ebony handle.

"Don't worry: I couldn't hurt you even if I wanted to." Ben laughed—or tried to—as I straightened. The laugh turned into a cough as a thin trail of blood ran down his chin. "I don't want to hurt you, incidentally. What happened that night was never part of the plan."

I glanced at Senator Walsh. He lay unnervingly still, but I could just see the rise and fall of his chest. "What did you do to him?" I asked, voice steady even as I fought an almost overwhelming urge to run. "Killing his granddaughter wasn't enough?"

Another wet cough bubbled up from Ben's chest. "I didn't do anything to him. The senator found out his son is a monster. Too much knowledge can be fatal at his age."

"What do you mean? What did he find out?" My gaze flickered down to Ben's bloodstained clothing and my stomach rolled as I tried to picture Amy's father killing—or at least trying to kill—someone. "Did Ryan Walsh do that to you?"

"In a manner of speaking."

My grip on the letter opener tightened. "That's not an answer. What happened?"

"Of course it's an answer. You just don't know the right question."

"What are you doing here, Ben?" I asked, a fraction of

my fear giving way to anger. "Why did you come back? Why couldn't you just have disappeared and stayed gone?"

Ben hesitated. For a moment, I thought he wasn't going to answer, but then he said, "I needed to get into this room and this party was my best chance to do it." His gray eyes clouded with pain and then narrowed. "Maybe I should be asking you the same question. What are you doing here, in this room?"

The letter opener shook in my hand as I crossed my arms over my chest. I ignored his question for one of my own. "What in this room could possibly be so important that you'd risk coming back to Hemlock?"

"*Proof.*" Ben studied my face intently. "Why are you here, Mackenzie? How did you get tangled up in this?" He looked oddly concerned for someone who had been ready to kill me less than a month and a half ago. "Is it Kyle? Or is it those friends of yours—the brother and sister?"

"How do you know about Trey and Serena?" Tendrils of fear crept down my spine. "You didn't just come back. You've been here awhile. You've been watching me." I thought of the things I had found in the church—the newspaper with Ryan Walsh's face circled and the battered paperbacks. Ben had never gone anywhere without a book; the spare room in his apartment had been crammed full of them. "Those were your things in the church. That day I saw you on the street— I thought I imagined it, but you were really there."

Ben shook his head weakly. "I spent weeks worried I'd run into you or Tess, then yesterday I go back to the church and hear your voice coming from inside."

I flinched at the sound of my cousin's name. "Don't you dare talk about Tess. You ripped her heart out and never once told her who you really were. If she ever found out about the things you've done . . ."

Ben's gray eyes darkened as he struggled to haul in a deep breath. "You won't tell her. You and I both know it would destroy her."

He sounded so sure. So utterly certain. And he was right. I hadn't told Tess. I was too scared it would kill something inside of her to find out the man she had loved—the man she had wrapped her arms around and trusted and slept beside at night—was a monster.

I squeezed my eyes shut. Just for a second. My memories of Ben were so twisted and tangled that it was hard to look at him. "Why did you come back, *Ian?*" I used his real name, hurling it like an insult. "You said you were looking for proof. Proof of what?"

Ben's eyes took on a faraway, lost look. When he spoke, his voice held that same lost quality. "I wanted to know if it was true. Everything my father said. I let him talk me into killing Amy because he told me it would be payback for the things her father had done to me, that it would stop Ryan Walsh."

A sick feeling wrapped itself around my core. "What did Ryan Walsh do to you?"

It was like he hadn't heard me. "I didn't know there would be others before Amy," he said, "not when I agreed to come to Hemlock. After, I told myself that a few more deaths didn't matter—not if it stopped all the others."

"The others?"

He squeezed his eyes shut as his face twisted with pain. "We weren't supposed to ask about them, you know. At Van Horne. That was the worst part. They would disappear in the middle of the night, and you had to act like they had never existed."

His words were a hook in my chest, reminding me of the disappearances at Thornhill and pulling me closer even as every survival instinct I had told me to stay back. "You were at Van Horne?"

Ben didn't answer.

There was a radio at his waist. It burst to life with a crackle of static. "We've got reports of a medical emergency in the east wing. Heading there now."

"Ben?"

Silence.

His chest rose and fell, but the time between breaths seemed to grow longer. I glanced back at the door. Any second, the security staff would come bursting into the room. Once they did, I'd lose any chance I had of getting information.

I eased closer. "Ben . . . what happened at Van Horne?" I swallowed. "Was CutterBrown experimenting on wolves at the camp? Was Ryan Walsh there?"

He coughed, ragged and violent. Flecks of blood dotted his lips and splattered my dress.

"Ben?" Desperate, I closed the remaining space between us and reached out to shake his shoulder. His shirt was so saturated with blood that the fabric stuck to my hand.

Disgusted and horrified, I pulled back, but Ben grabbed my wrist. The gesture was so fast that I dropped my make-shift weapon and flailed for balance. I struggled to pull free, but even gutted and dying, Ben was a werewolf and I was just a reg.

His eyes flew open. They were wild and unfocused. "They wanted to see if they could give me more scars. Each one had a name, but no one would ever tell me the order of the words."

He coughed again.

"Mac?" Awareness filled his eyes, but he didn't release his grip on my wrist.

Ben reached into his jacket pocket with his other hand. I flinched back, expecting a weapon, but he hauled out a folded sheet of bloodstained paper and pressed it into my hand. "Those are the ones I can remember. It's why I came here. Had to make sure it didn't happen again . . . that they couldn't do it again . . ." He shook his head weakly. "I never wanted to lie to you and Tess. I never meant for you to get hurt."

He had said those last eight words to me once before— right after he had forced me to the ground and slid a needle into my arm. "Maybe not, but you did and I was."

Ben let go of my wrist.

I stumbled back as the muscles under his clothing began to twitch and writhe.

The movement lasted only a second and then stopped as Ben let out a long, ragged sigh. The damage to his body seemed to be preventing the shift, and without shifting, he was too far gone to heal himself.

"You and my father are alike, you know." The words were a low, pain-choked rasp. "The two of you are . . ."

But I didn't get to find out what the two of us were. The light drained out of Ben's eyes as his body went limp.

Something inside my chest twisted. I bit my lip, bit it so hard the tang of copper flooded my mouth. "Ben?" His name came out a whisper. He didn't react. He was gone.

I wanted to feel relieved. Satisfied. He had killed Amy and would have killed me. All those weeks ago, I had trained a gun on his retreating form and hated myself when I couldn't pull the trigger. He deserved to die for what he had done to Amy. For what he had done to Tess.

But . . .

Looking at him, the scene that flashed through my mind wasn't that night in the woods, but a snowy Sunday morning, months and months ago, when Ben had stood at the stove in our kitchen, laughing as he made pancakes for Tess and me.

The study door burst open.

Four men—all wearing the black outfits of the party's security staff—rushed into the room, Jason on their heels. Each of them came to a stop when they saw Ben. One man managed to tear his gaze away and go to the senator's side, but the rest stood frozen, staring at the blood and Ben's lifeless form.

After a handful of heartbeats, one of the men walked forward and knelt next to Ben's body, checking for a pulse. He looked over his shoulder and shook his head.

Someone should have stopped me as I stumbled out of the room, but no one did.

No one looked at me. Not even Jason.

Never in my life had I needed fresh air so badly. The smell of blood clung to the insides of my nostrils and coated my throat and made it hard to breathe in and out.

I made it to the end of the hall on trembling legs, to the French doors that led outside. I fumbled with the lock. My hands were tacky with blood—*Ben's blood*—and left a scarlet smear on the white paint.

Cool air surrounded me as I stepped outside, but no matter how deeply I inhaled, it failed to clear my head.

A wave of vomit rushed up the back of my throat. I stumbled to an oversized flowerpot in the nick of time. My stomach heaved and my throat burned and I struggled to keep my eyes open because every time I closed them— even just to blink—I saw Ben's lifeless body lying in a sea of red.

After a while, when there was absolutely nothing left in my stomach to bring up, I wiped my mouth with the back of my hand.

A scrap of white near my foot caught my eye and I bent to retrieve the paper Ben had given me. When I straightened, a wave of dizziness made my knees weak.

Even though it was November, the pool was uncovered. I crossed the deck and knelt at the edge of the shallow end. I set the paper aside and thrust my hands into the water, trying to scrub them free of Ben's blood.

The effort felt futile, like my hands would never really be clean again.

Shivering, I wiped my palms on my dress, spying bloodstains on the fabric as I did. I hoped Jason hadn't been planning on returning it.

I knew I should go back inside—it wouldn't take Jason long to realize I had slipped out and I had no idea where Kyle was—but I couldn't seem to make my legs work. Dimly, I wondered if I was in some sort of shock. It felt like what I imagined shock would be, like I was detached and everything around me was distant.

Ben had been at Van Horne.

I unfolded the paper he had given me. There were two sheets. The first was thin, almost translucent—a page torn from a Bible. I remembered the Bible I had seen at the church, the one with the pages missing.

I squinted at the tiny type in the light from the house.

It was from Isaiah. One verse had been circled in red.

Prepare slaughter for his children for the iniquity of their fathers; that they do not rise, nor possess the land, nor fill the face of the world with cities.

Great. Ben had killed Amy not just because her grandfather was a senator but because of something her father had been involved with. That was really fair; that was really just.

I shredded the piece of paper and threw the scraps into the pool. They floated on top of the water as I rubbed a hand over my eyes and turned my attention to the second sheet of paper.

Half the page was missing and what remained bore

two columns of names. Twenty in all, seven of which had been circled. Each name was followed by a four-digit number—four-digit numbers like we had all been assigned at Thornhill.

Those are the ones I can remember—that's what Ben had said. If experiments had been going on at Van Horne, too, these were probably the names of wolves they had used as guinea pigs. *It's why I came here. Had to make sure it didn't happen again* . . . I glanced at the pool, at the small pieces of torn Bible verses. What if Ben had been experimented on in Van Horne? His father had said something about the camps that night in the woods. Ben hadn't wanted to hurt me, and Derby had said . . .

Remember why you agreed to do this . . .

I struggled to grasp the words as they hovered just beyond reach.

. . . *so no one else* . . . *so no one else has to endure what you did inside the camps.*

At the time, I had assumed he had been talking about the horrible conditions that plagued all of the rehabilitation camps—food shortages, violence, overcrowding—but what if he had been referring to something much worse?

I thought of how we had found Serena in the detention block. She had been so lost and in so much pain that she had been almost feral. If Ben had been in half her condition when he had gotten out, it would have been easy for Derby to twist him to suit his needs.

Derby had turned his son into a monster, but maybe CutterBrown had given him a head start. Maybe they had done something so awful that Ben had willingly signed on for a killing spree to stop them.

I folded the list of names and tucked it into my dress as I pushed myself to my feet. I had to find Kyle and Jason. I had to let them know I was all right and tell them about Ben. I had to find them so we could get out of here.

I could hear sirens in the distance as I headed for the house. An ambulance for Senator Walsh, probably, and the police to investigate Ben's murder and take his body away. The thought brought me to a sudden stop in the shadows.

To hurt a werewolf that badly, to wound him so critically before he could defend himself . . . you'd have to hit more than just an internal organ or two. A knife wouldn't have done it. Even bullets might not have done the trick.

I flashed back to the junkyard, to the memory of Serena's claws gutting that man as easily as a knife sliding through butter.

A spike of fear slid through me. What if there was another werewolf at the party?

Kyle couldn't be here when the police arrived. It wouldn't matter that he hadn't been anywhere near the study. If a werewolf had been involved and anyone suspected, even for a second, that Kyle was infected—

Rough hands grabbed my shoulders and thrust me up against the house.

The bricks scraped my shoulders and dug into my spine. I struggled to break free but an arm locked across my chest.

I pulled in a deep breath, preparing to scream, just as the person holding me shifted his weight. Light from the house lined the edge of his jaw and threw highlights over his blond hair.

"Stephen—"

I strained against him, but it was like trying to move a boulder. Desperate, I brought my right knee up, aiming for the one spot that reduced all boys to quivering lumps of Jell-O. The long skirt slowed me down, but the blow still connected with enough force that it at least should have made Stephen loosen his hold.

He didn't so much as blink. "The blood on your dress: Where did it come from?" His voice was an unfamiliar growl.

My knees went weak as the truth crashed over me. If Stephen hadn't been holding me against the wall, I would have staggered.

"You did that. In the study." The words came out in a rush. "You're infected."

Surprise flashed across his face. Suspicion immediately followed. He opened his mouth, but before he could utter a single word, a shape rose out of the darkness behind him, ripping him away from me.

Kyle's voice, thick with the promise of violence, sliced through the night. "Let her go."

16

THE GNARLED GROVE OF CEDAR TREES ON THE EDGE OF the golf course had always been one of Amy's favorite places. It bordered one of the water traps and was barely visible from the road. The tree trunks were so twisted that some of them curved down toward the ground and formed natural benches.

It was a strange place to discuss evil corporations and secret medical tests, but it wasn't like we'd had many places to choose from. Though we were a ten-minute walk from Stephen's, we could still see the lights in the distance—both those of the house and the far-off red-and-blue glow of police cars and ambulances. It was as far away as Stephen would go.

I think he would have insisted on staying even closer if the Trackers hadn't started swarming the grounds surrounding the house. They had tried to keep us from leaving—until they realized who Stephen and Jason were.

They knew there had been a werewolf attack at the party, but no one suspected the grandson of Senator

Walsh—especially not when he was with Branson Derby's former protégé.

I shivered. Both Jason and Kyle moved to shrug out of their jackets, but Kyle was faster and closer.

"Are you sure you're all right?" he asked as he draped the jacket over my shoulders.

I nodded and slipped my arms through the sleeves. "Yeah." I wasn't—not even remotely—but I would be. Since seeing Ben, though, I couldn't stop shaking.

I glanced at Stephen. The dark fabric of his clothing hid most of the bloodstains. I pictured him doing that to Ben—*gutting Ben*—and the shivers grew a little worse. According to Stephen, he and his grandfather had walked in on Ben trashing the study. When the senator had tried to call for security, Ben had attacked.

Getting Amy's brother to follow us to the grove had been relatively easy—at least once the Trackers had arrived. Keeping Stephen here and getting answers out of him? That was proving a lot harder.

His attention kept drifting back to the flashing lights. I couldn't blame him. A short walk away, his grandfather was fighting for his life.

"He'll be all right," I said, momentarily putting aside my suspicions and distrust. As freaked out as I had been by what I'd found in Stephen's car this morning—as scared as I had been when he pushed me up against the house—he was still my best friend's brother. "Your grandfather is tough."

Stephen glanced at me, eyes wide and a little surprised, like my words were the last thing he expected. "Thanks."

He straightened his shoulders as his gaze shifted to Kyle. "You asked me about Van Horne a few minutes ago. It's a camp, that's all I know."

"But you did know about Thornhill." Leaning against a tree with his arms folded loosely across his chest, Jason looked casual, but the tension radiating off of him was so strong it seemed to make the shadows around him darker. He had been the most reluctant to consider the possibility of a connection between Amy's family and the camp, but he seemed to be taking the bombshell of Stephen's infection—and the revelation that Amy's brother had been hiding his condition for two years—almost personally. "Mac found a pamphlet from Flagler in your car. You were there just before the camp opened."

"Is that why you ran away this morning?" Stephen's brows rose as he looked at me. "Because I'd been in Flagler?"

"Because you were in Flagler and you work for Cutter-Brown," I corrected.

Genuine confusion—at least what looked like confusion—filled his eyes. "Why would my being there have anything to do with CBP?"

"Let's cut the bullshit." Jason pushed off from the tree. His eyes seemed to glint in the moonlight as he drew closer. "CutterBrown was testing a cure for LS at Thornhill and using the inmates as guinea pigs. You really expect us to believe you were there and it had no connection to your dad's company?"

Stephen's face—already pale—turned ashen at Jason's words. "They were testing a cure? On inmates? And you think CBP was involved?" He shook his head, the gesture sharp. "Not possible."

"They weren't just testing a cure," I said. "They were torturing people." The thought of Sinclair and what she had done filled me with so much anger that it made my voice shake. "They pumped them full of drugs and then hurt them to see how long it took them to shift, how effective their cure was. They strapped them to tables and broke their bones and injected them with poison. And the wolves who weren't strong enough—the ones who died during their tests—were taken out into the woods and dumped like garbage."

An ache formed in the pit of my stomach as I thought about the small cemetery in the woods behind Thornhill.

"There are a lot of rumors about the camps," said Stephen, making no effort to hide his skepticism. "No one knows how many of them are true."

"It's not a rumor. I was there. We all were." I crossed my arms and huddled deeper in Kyle's jacket. "We saw the tests and the wolves they experimented on."

Stephen's gaze darted from me to Jason and back again. "You're regs. How did—"

Jason cut him off. "It doesn't matter how we got in or why. What matters is the tie between CutterBrown and what was happening at Thornhill. That's the only reason you're here and not lying in an unconscious heap for the police to find."

"Jason." Kyle's voice held a sharp note of warning. Kyle was a werewolf, but so was Stephen. Force wouldn't get us far.

209

Stephen's eyes narrowed as he stared at Jason. With their blond hair and tuxedos, the two boys could have passed for brothers. If things had worked out differently—if Amy hadn't died and she and Jason had miraculously stayed together—maybe they would have been. "What makes you think there's a tie between CutterBrown and the camp or that I would even know about it if there was? I'm just an intern."

"An intern whose father runs the company," countered Jason. "Plus, there's the fact that Mac saw the CBP logo inside the camp and you still haven't explained what the hell you were doing in Flagler."

Though he hid it quickly, it was impossible to miss the flash of annoyance that crossed Stephen's face. "You really want to know why I was in Flagler?"

No, I corrected myself, *not annoyance, anger.*

"I was good at control. Great, even. No one but Amy knew I was infected. My parents, my friends, the girls I dated—none of them had a clue. And then Amy died. She was murdered by someone like me. After that, control got harder. A lot harder." His face twisted, almost as though the admission had cost him. For Stephen—someone who had always excelled at everything—it probably had. "I was taking a class on the LS epidemic and how the government was managing it. We learned about this woman who had these new ideas about behavior modification and control. She had just been given a new camp to test her methods."

"Sinclair." The warden's name was little more than a breath on my lips, but Stephen nodded.

"I thought maybe some of the things she was doing could help me. A few months after Amy's death, when things hadn't gotten any better, I went to Flagler to try and meet her. I figured I could say I was interested in her theories and methods, that I was writing a paper on them."

"Sinclair would have eaten that up." The class explained why that copy of *Managing an Epidemic* had been in Stephen's bag.

Stephen shrugged. "Maybe, but I couldn't get a meeting with her. I stayed for a couple of days and then headed back. That's why I was in Flagler. It had nothing to do with CutterBrown or my father." His eyes locked on each of us in turn. Bright and blue and earnest, they seemed to reinforce everything he had just said.

And it seemed plausible. More plausible than the idea that Stephen could have knowingly been embroiled in anything as awful as what had happened at Thornhill.

Jason reached into his jacket pocket and withdrew a silver flask—one I was certain he hadn't had before the party. "Why should we trust anything you say?"

"I've known you your whole life," countered Stephen. "You dated my kid sister for *years*. Why *wouldn't* you trust me?"

"Oh, I don't know." Jason took a deep swig from the flask. "Maybe it has something to do with the mess you left in your father's study. I hope your parents have a good cleaning service. All that blood is going to be a bitch to clean up."

"Jason!" My voice sliced the air as Kyle walked over to

Jason, unceremoniously plucked the flask from his hand, and hurled it into the trees.

Stephen didn't flinch at Jason's words. "That guy lunged at my grandfather and I attacked. What else was I supposed to do?" Maybe it was my imagination, but I thought I saw the muscles in Stephen's arms twitch underneath his jacket.

Kyle returned to my side, standing a little closer, a little more in front of me, than he had a moment before.

Not my imagination, then.

I cleared my throat, trying to draw Stephen's attention away from Jason. "When I asked the man in the study about your grandfather, he said, 'He found out his son is a monster.' What did he mean? What did your grandfather find out about your dad?"

"Nothing." The word came out harsh and bitter. "He was probably talking about me. My grandfather didn't know I was infected. When he saw what I did . . ."

His heart gave out.

It made sense. Sort of. Stephen did look an awful lot like his father. In the rush of an attack, in the dim light in the study, it would be possible to confuse them.

Stephen flexed his right hand and turned it over, studying his palm before glancing back at the house. "I keep expecting it to feel different. You think it would, after what I did."

I wanted to tell Stephen who Ben was and what he had done to Amy—and I would—but now wasn't the time. Knowing would help ease Stephen's guilt, but it wasn't an easy or quick conversation and we couldn't afford to stay here much longer. More police would arrive. Soon. It was only a matter of time before they—and the Trackers—started searching the rest of the neighborhood. There was no time for lengthy explanations.

So instead of telling Stephen about Ben, I said, "We saw your father talking to a woman who had worked at Thornhill. They knew each other." There was no need to tell him just how well. "She mentioned you. She said you had been behind some sort of breach at CBP. Why would she say that?" I tried to keep my voice neutral, but hints of distrust bled through. I wanted to believe Stephen's story about Flagler, but it was hard when I had seen his father with the woman who had singled Serena out for torture, when they had been talking about *him*.

Stephen opened his mouth and then closed it. His shoulders slumped as he ran a hand over his face. It was a long moment before he spoke. "I knew my father was involved with something—something serious—but I didn't know what. I didn't know it had anything to do with Thornhill. I still don't think it could—not if the things you said about that place are true."

He glanced back at the flashing lights outside the Walsh house. "My father's been different over the past year and a half. Drinking a lot. Losing his temper. Board members and people from his office would show up at the house in the middle of the night and there were days when he wouldn't leave his study. He wouldn't tell us what was going on. Not me or Amy or even our mother. It got worse while I was away at school. Amy said he was getting obsessive. He kept asking where she and Mom were all the time and who they were with. By the time I came home for Christmas break last year, she was really scared."

I swallowed. "So you broke into CBP to try and figure out what was behind the attitude change?"

Stephen nodded. "I figured it had to be something with work. Work is practically the only thing he does."

"How did you get in?" asked Jason.

Stephen's eyes flashed. "Whatever you think he did, he's still my father. I'm not going to tell you how to break into his company."

"You found something, didn't you?" Kyle tried to keep things on track. "You took something. That woman we saw your father talking to—she said something about a breach *and* a leak. It wasn't just that you got in. It was that you got in and took something."

"Maybe." There wasn't much open space in the grove, but Stephen began to pace, his steps taking him on a winding path around the trees. "I didn't have much time—even with . . . well, let's just say I was lucky to get in at all. I copied as many high-level access files as possible onto an external hard drive. I barely even looked at what I got. I figured I could decipher it all later."

"So what happened?" Jason's voice was sharp and impatient. He cast a glance toward the road; we had already stayed here too long.

"Amy." Stephen came to a stop and turned back to us. "She knew where I was going that night. She wanted to know what was going on, too, but she was scared I'd find something that would ruin the family. She waited until I got back. As soon as I left the room, she took the hard drive and disappeared. She turned up in the morning but wouldn't tell me where it was. She said I didn't want to know what was on it. No matter what I said or did, that was all she would say. I went back to school a couple of days after New Year's because I didn't know what else to do. A week before she was killed, she called me. She was scared and angry. She said I never should have gone to CBP that night, but she wouldn't tell me why."

His eyes locked on mine. "This whole time, I thought maybe I was the reason she had been killed. I knew it was a werewolf attack, but she was so frightened the night she called . . . I kept wondering if it could have been tied to the files I had taken. That's why I didn't go to the funeral. I couldn't—not when I thought I might be the reason she was dead."

"You weren't." To my surprise, it was Jason who spoke. Some of the hostility had dropped from his voice. More than any of us, Jason had struggled under the weight of guilt after Amy's death. He started to reach for his jacket pocket before casting a slightly mournful look at the spot in the trees where the flask had disappeared. "You don't have any idea where Amy hid the hard drive?" he asked, turning his attention back to Stephen.

"No."

"Would you tell us if you did?"

"I don't know," Stephen admitted. "Would you—if your father was potentially involved in something like this?"

"Completely different situation. I hate my father."

Another thought occurred to me. "That's why you were going through Amy's things. That's why you wanted to know if I had taken anything."

Stephen nodded. "I finally ran out of places to check. You were her best friend. I thought she might have given the files to you. Or told you where they were. When you said she'd given you a USB drive, I thought maybe she had copied some of the data from the original hard drive onto it."

"It was just photos and songs." I was beginning to think Amy hadn't told me anything. Nothing important, anyway. I stared at the red and blue lights pulsing in the distance. It looked like the ambulance was leaving. How could Amy have lived there, in that house, with so many secrets? How was it that Trey was the only one who had noticed something was wrong?

Why was Trey the only one she had turned to? The one she had called when she needed help.

Trey.

An idea hit me so hard that I reached out to steady myself against a nearby tree. I suddenly knew why there had been something familiar about the second key we had found in Amy's room.

I reached into Kyle's inside jacket pocket and fished out his phone. Turning my back on the others without explanation, I walked deeper into the grove of trees, teetering dangerously and trying not to break an ankle in my ridiculous shoes.

Behind me, the voices of the boys faded.

I stopped at the edge of the water trap and dialed.

Trey answered on the third ring.

"The night you picked Amy up at the strip mall—do you remember the date?"

"Dobs? Where the hell are you?" Trey's voice was rough and unsteady, almost breathless.

My stomach twisted as I heard shouts and sirens in the background. "What's going on? Is Serena—"

"She's all right. We couldn't stay at the church. Someone started a rumor that wolves were hiding in the empty houses in River Estates. Trackers flooded the development and set a few places on fire. The whole town is going crazy."

"Where are you now?"

"The ball field at the end of Elm. Taking Eve's car would have drawn too much attention, so we left on foot. We're headed for your place. It's the closest spot we could think of and Ree said your cousin would let us in."

"She will. She knows Serena." The last thing I wanted was to drag Tess into this mess, but it wasn't like we had a lot of alternatives.

"What about you?" Trey asked. "Will you meet us there?"

"Yeah. As soon as we can." I glanced over my shoulder. Kyle and Stephen looked like they were deep in conversation. Jason was watching me, but he was too far away for me to make out his expression. "We're still on the north side.

Right now, I just really need to know what night you picked up Amy at that strip mall and if it was the one on this side of the river."

"What does it matter?"

"Amy might have had proof that CutterBrown was involved in something. I promise to explain everything when we see you, but right now I really need you to answer the question. *Please*, Trey."

"Around New Year's. I don't know the exact date."

Which probably meant it had been the same night Stephen had broken into CBP.

"Which strip mall was it?" I prodded. "Was it the one on this side of the river? The one with the mail supply store?"

"Yeah. Just before the exit for the bridge."

I gripped the phone tightly as something unraveled in my chest. Maybe I hadn't known most of Amy's secrets, but I was suddenly very sure I had the key to at least one.

I heard a commotion in the background. There was a muffled, scraping noise and then Trey told Eve and Serena that they had to get off the street. A second later, Eve's voice came over the line.

"Trey's indisposed."

Fear slid over me. "What happened? What's going on?"

"Nothing we can't handle." There was a harsh, vehement edge to her voice, an edge that reminded me of my father.

"Eve . . ."

"We'll be fine, Mac. Trey and Serena will be fine. I'll make sure of it. I promise I'll take care of them."

I heard Trey make an indignant noise in the background

and couldn't keep a small smile from flashing across my face. Trey was tough, but Eve was my father's protégée. Of all the wolves in his pack, she was the one he trusted to send to Hemlock. To protect us.

And I trusted her to protect them.

"Thanks," I said. The word came out thick and slightly choked.

"Are you close to finding anything?"

"I think so."

"Then do whatever you have to. Don't worry about us, we'll be okay."

"Mac—" Kyle's voice was a terse warning from across the grove. Something was happening.

"Eve, I have to go."

"Be safe," she said.

"You, too," I replied, but she had already ended the call.

I hastily made my way back through the trees. The boys had moved to the very edge of the grove. As I joined them, I spotted a half-dozen shadows walking along the road. They were too far away to make out clearly, but the women were obviously wearing dresses. Refugees from the fund-raiser.

A pair of headlights rounded a bend in the street and came to a stop in front of them. Two men stepped out of the car. One walked slowly with a pronounced limp, and we were just close enough to overhear what he said as they confronted the group of party guests.

"We're looking for Stephen Walsh." The familiar accent slid down my spine like a chip of ice.

Donovan.

I glanced at Amy's brother. Ryan Walsh had been adamant that there had been no breach, that Stephen had nothing to do with any leak. Did he really believe that or had he been lying? Was it possible he had sent Donovan after his own son?

For years, I had seen Amy's father as an example of what a dad should be, but maybe he was more like my own father than I ever would have guessed. Hank could be utterly ruthless and wouldn't let anything get in his way. Not even family.

"Come on," muttered Jason, turning and putting a hand on Stephen's shoulder. The gesture was stiff and awkward, but seeing Donovan seemed to have killed the last of his suspicions about Amy's brother. At least temporarily. "They know you're not at the house. We have to get moving."

Stephen hesitated as, up on the road, one of the party guests was shoved into the back of the car. "I don't understand. Are they Trackers? Is it because of what I did in the study?" There was an odd, false note to his voice, like maybe he already suspected who the men were and what they were after but didn't want to admit it.

"No." I wished there was some easy way to tell Stephen that his father might have sold him out, but the truth was a Band-Aid best ripped off quickly. "It's probably because of the files you took from CutterBrown."

"If I go back . . . if I explain things to my father . . ."

"For all we know, your father's the one who sent them," said Jason, echoing my own suspicions as he let go of Stephen's shoulder. "The only way this will be over is if we find out what was on that hard drive. That will at least give us something to bargain with."

"Unless you're planning on holding a séance," said Stephen bitterly, "I think you can rule out my sister telling any of us where it is."

"We don't need a séance." Three pairs of eyes locked on me as sirens echoed in the distance. "I know where Amy hid the hard drive."

17

EVEN ACROSS THE RIVER, THE GLOW OF FLAMES WAS impossible to miss. Trey had said houses in the empty subdivision had been set alight, but I counted at least three fires in the downtown core.

None of them looked close to Elm Street. That was something, I guess.

"That's one of the warehouses near Bonnie and Clyde," said Kyle, closing the driver's-side door of his car and coming to stand beside me at the edge of the parking lot. He pointed to the largest blaze.

"How can you tell?" The smell of smoke drifted across the river. It clung to my nostrils and the back of my throat, reminding me of the night the old sanatorium—Willowgrove—had burned.

Kyle drew an invisible line with his finger. "See that big cluster of lights?"

I nodded. They shone like the lights in a football stadium and were impossible to miss.

"That's Riverside Square. The Trackers put extra lighting

in the park for the rally tomorrow night. The fire looks like it's about six blocks over."

Behind us, Jason and Stephen got out of the car. Jason came to stand next to Kyle while Stephen walked to the opposite corner of the parking lot, phone in hand as he continued trying to get news on his grandfather's condition.

"I'm still not sure I trust him," said Jason, voice low.

"He wouldn't have lied—not about Amy," I said. "I believe him. Besides, we need him. Even if we find the hard drive, we may need his help deciphering the files."

The three of us fell into silence as we watched patches of Hemlock burn.

"What about the smaller fires?" I asked after a few moments, roughly scrubbing my eyes with the heel of my hand. "What are those?"

Kyle wrapped an arm around my shoulders. "I don't know."

I thought of all the places I loved downtown: the coffee shop, the fair trade store where Tess bought handmade paper and funky scarves, the used-books store where you could get four books for two dollars, and the restaurant where I had worked before taking off to Colorado without giving notice. Any one of them could be burning right now.

Hemlock was the only real home I had known and it was being torn apart.

"Why would anyone do this?" I asked, chest aching.

Kyle didn't answer; he just pressed a kiss to the crown of my head. Next to him, Jason was equally silent. I was starting to think maybe there were never any reasons for the horrible things people did. None that mattered, anyway.

The knowledge that this wasn't even the night of the rally—that things would probably get worse before everything was over—made my stomach flip. I wished I knew what the packs were planning. If the Trackers and the wolves went to war in the middle of Hemlock, the violence would consume the city, catching a lot of innocent people in its wake.

I pulled in a deep breath and forced myself to turn my back on the fires.

I still had Kyle's cell, and as we crossed the parking lot, I tried calling Hank. No answer. I don't know why I bothered. Eve had called this afternoon and gotten nowhere closer to finding out what the wolves had planned for tomorrow night. If he wouldn't tell Eve, there was no way he'd tell me.

With a small sigh, I slipped the phone back into the inside pocket of my borrowed jacket.

"Any news?" Kyle asked as Stephen approached.

Stephen shook his head. "I didn't want to tell the hospital who I was and they're not big on releasing patient information to complete strangers. I left messages and texts with a couple of friends. Maybe one of them can find out something." With a dejected shrug, he turned his attention to the building in front of us.

Hemlock's north side had strict zoning rules to ensure the area stayed free of fast-food joints, big box stores, and just about anything else the town's wealthier families thought would drive down property values. The one exception was the small strip mall near the bridge. It was a miniature oasis for tired nannies, frazzled parents, and kids looking for a quick sugar fix.

Like a lot of the retail property in town, the strip mall was owned by Jason's father, but unlike the drab, boxy strip malls he owned on the other side of the river, Matt Sheffield had built this one to be as attractive and inviting as possible. It was practically the anti–strip-mall strip mall. The U-shaped building was a strange mix of Italian and Oriental architecture—a mix that shouldn't have worked, but somehow did—and the stores all faced a large, shady courtyard—a courtyard complete with a fountain that bubbled away during the summer months.

There was a convenience store, a Chinese restaurant, a dry cleaner's, a yoga studio, and two cafés. There was also a store that sold mailing supplies and rented mailboxes. I headed straight for the latter. Amy had mentioned getting a box last year after her mom had freaked out over a seven-hundred-dollar pair of shoes she had ordered online.

While Amy hadn't told me she had actually gone ahead and rented a box, it was the only reason I could imagine her getting Trey to pick her up here, a twenty-minute walk from her house, in the middle of January.

Our only hope was that the box was still under her name. Hank had rented a lot of mailboxes from a lot of different places when I was a kid—it was amazing the number of illegal things you could move through the mail. Most places let you pay for the boxes up front for a set number of months. Depending on how long Amy had rented the box for, we might still be able to get into it—assuming that was what the second key we'd found in her room actually unlocked.

Fallen leaves crunched under my feet as I crossed the courtyard. Christmas was more than a month off, but small blue lights had been strung in the bare branches of the trees. I glanced at the fountain as I passed. It had been emptied in preparation for the cold, but a layer of leaves had gummed up the drain and several inches of old rainwater and melted snow filled the basin.

We reached the store.

Most of the lights were dark, but one row of flickering fluorescent bulbs lit a wall of mailboxes in an alcove between two sets of glass doors.

Kyle tried the door. It was locked.

"Attention customers," read Jason, leaning toward a small sign taped in the window. "For twenty-four/seven access to mailbox, please speak to management."

"You probably pay a deposit and they give you a key to the door," I said.

"So where's Amy's key?" asked Jason, stepping back.

I shrugged. "We only found the one extra key in the window seat."

"Great. So we have no way in."

"For someone who tries so hard to make everyone think he's a tortured bad boy, you are shockingly inept at being a badass," muttered Kyle. He walked over to a nearby bench. The thing was made of cement and must have weighed a ton. He glanced at Stephen as he bent to lift one end. "Give me a hand."

With an uneasy look, Stephen did as he was told.

"I don't think . . ." Jason started to object, but I put a hand on his arm and pulled him away from the front of the store as Kyle and Stephen prepared to hurl the bench.

The sound of breaking glass was unbelievably loud. I held my breath and waited for an alarm to go off, but things stayed mercifully silent. I guess the store wasn't too worried about people breaking into the alcove.

The bench lay across the door like a beached whale.

"My father is just going to love this," muttered Jason. Given how much he enjoyed pissing off his parents, I had a hard time believing he was actually that upset at the destruction.

Kyle climbed inside, then reached back and helped me over. Broken glass crunched under my feet and I was glad he had found an old pair of my sneakers in the trunk of his car.

"Someone driving by is going to notice this," I said, glancing back across the courtyard. The store was one of three that faced the street: anyone who looked would be able to see the broken window.

"With everything happening on the other side of the river, they may not care," said Kyle, letting go of my hand.

He had a point.

I pulled out Amy's key as I headed for the bank of mailboxes. The key wasn't numbered; there was nothing to indicate which box it belonged to.

The stirrings of a long-overdue headache danced at my temple as I went to the mailbox at the top left corner and got to work.

Sometime after box 30, Kyle and Jason went outside to

keep an eye on the street. Not Stephen. He watched me try lock after lock with an intensity that was almost unnerving.

"You don't have to stay in here with me," I said, pausing to rub my forehead after I had passed the halfway point. With every lock the key failed to open, the pounding in my skull grew a little bit worse. I didn't care how chaotic it was across town: sooner or later, that broken window was going to draw attention. We couldn't afford to stay here long.

Stephen's eyes flashed. "If you're right, one of these boxes holds whatever Amy was scared of. I'm not waiting outside." We were only a few years apart in age, but Stephen's eyes suddenly made him seem so much older. A lot of the wolves had eyes like that. Including Kyle.

"Okay," I said—or started to say—as I slipped the key into the next lock. It turned. Box 175.

"Kyle. Jason." I tried to shout, but my voice came out a whisper. Nevertheless, Kyle was at my side in an instant, Jason right on his heels.

A sudden sense of trepidation flooded me as I stood there and gripped the key. Amy had kept so many secrets, and I wondered if any of us were really ready for what was hidden inside. Steeling myself, I opened the door.

The small pigeonhole was crammed full.

I pulled out old phone bills and credit card statements, delivery notices, junk mail, and a reminder that the one-year rental term on the mailbox ended in December. Nothing looked out of the ordinary—except for a padded envelope near the back.

I let the junk mail and bills fall to the floor as I pulled

the envelope free. There was a note on top of it, held in place by a rubber band. The familiar loop of Amy's writing was a hand reaching out from the past. It wrapped itself around my lungs and squeezed.

If lease on box runs out, please mail to address on front.

I turned the envelope over. The postage had been paid and a name and address had been written on the front in purple marker.

My name.

My address.

Amy?

It was too much. The tightness in my chest grew to almost unbearable levels.

Without bothering to close the box, I made my way out of the store and to a bench in the courtyard.

I sank down and stared at the envelope, raising my eyes only when the others approached.

"She addressed it to me. Why would she do that?" My gaze locked on Stephen. He was her brother; he was the one who had stolen the files in the first place. Why send the envelope to me and not him?

"Maybe she thought it would be safer," said Jason. "Maybe she thought her father or someone from CBP would get their hands on it if she sent it to Stephen."

Hands shaking, I ripped open the envelope and reached inside. "A DVD?" I turned it over in my hand and then reached back inside. I hauled out a second plastic jewel case and a battered iPod. That was it. No hard drive.

The discs were numbered—*1* and *2* written in the same

purple ink as my address—and the iPod was Amy's old one. Stephen had said it was missing from her room. I turned it over and touched the small rabbit sticker on the back. It was an older model, one she had tossed in a drawer as soon as something better came out.

I pressed the power button. Nothing happened.

"It's been in that envelope for months," said Jason. "The battery must have drained." He glanced at Kyle. "You have a charger in your car, right?"

Kyle took the iPod from me. "Yeah."

I slipped the DVDs back into the envelope as I stood and then cradled the small bundle against my chest as I trailed Kyle and Jason to Kyle's Honda, Stephen at my side.

As we reached the parking lot, I noticed him tuck a stack of envelopes into his pocket.

He followed my gaze. "I know it's just junk, but it felt wrong to leave it there."

"I'm sorry," I said, the words stiff and awkward and half a year too late. "About Amy. I never really said that."

"You lost her, too."

I nodded even though I knew it wasn't the same.

Jason pulled the passenger-side door open for me as we neared the car. The engine was idling and Kyle had already plugged the iPod into the charger.

I slid into the Honda and opened my mouth to say we should head to my place, but before I could get a single word out, the iPod's screen flashed to life.

The battery was still down to next to nothing, but there was just enough juice for it to work while plugged in.

I picked it up and entered Amy's password: Jason's birthday. The screen unlocked.

"Now what?" I whispered to myself as Stephen and Jason edged closer to my open car door to get a better look.

Amy had put the iPod in the envelope for a reason; there had to be something on here that she wanted me to see.

I frowned. All of the apps were gone—all but the video app.

I tapped the icon.

There was only one file.

I knew we shouldn't linger here, but there was no way I could wait until we reached the apartment to find out what was in that video.

Swallowing hard, I hit play.

Amy's face filled the small screen.

"Mackenzie Dobson, this is your life, and if you're watching this, something has either gone horribly wrong or I've finally skipped town." Amy stared melodramatically at the camera. A small slice of her bedroom was visible behind her. The light was dim—obviously nighttime. She was sitting on the window seat, her back pressed to the wall. Her long, black hair had been pulled into a ponytail that curled over one shoulder and her face was free of makeup. She was wearing a tank top, and I caught a glimpse of a wicked bruise on her upper arm. A week before she had died, Amy had slipped in the hallway at school and crashed into a wall of lockers. The video had been made no more than a week before her murder.

For months, I had only seen Amy in dreams or in

photographs and videos I had looked at a hundred times. Seeing her now, like this, made it hard to breathe.

"I'm not sure where to begin," she admitted. She chewed on her lower lip. "Things have happened—been happening—things I haven't been able to tell anyone." There was a knock in the background and Amy glanced at the door. "Shit."

The room spun sickeningly for a moment and then the screen went black, as though Amy had set the iPod face-down. There were faint sounds in the background, the slam of a door, a hushed voice that was too muffled to make out.

Stephen crouched next to me.

With a flash of light, the room flipped and Amy was back. Her eyes were red. "I don't know how much time I have or what to do," she said. "I found out something. Something I wasn't supposed to. Something bad. Really, *really* bad. And my dad's wrapped up in it." She tugged on the end of her ponytail, winding it around her fingers. "I wasn't going to tell anyone, but things have been happening. I feel like I'm being watched. Sometimes, I walk into my room and I can tell someone else has been in here. The other night, someone followed me all the way from school to Tre—to the outskirts of town."

At the almost-mention of Trey, I glanced up at Jason, but his face was impossible to read.

"I'm scared, Mac." The slight tremor in Amy's voice pulled me back. "I'm scared something will happen to me and no one will know what was going on. I don't want to drag anyone else into this, but I figure, if something does happen—if things get so bad that I have to split—by the time you get this, maybe everything will have cooled down."

I fumbled with the iPod and hit pause. *It was Ben.* Pain spread through my chest and radiated outward, making my hands shake. Someone had been watching Amy. Someone had been in her room and stalking her—just not for the reasons she had thought.

Somehow, a fraction of the weight I had been carrying since Amy's death lifted. It wouldn't have mattered what any of us had done on the night she died. Ben had been watching Amy long before he had killed her; if we had been with her that night, he would have just picked another.

On some level, I had already known that, but Amy's words finally made it sink in. It hadn't been my fault.

My gaze darted to Stephen. His face was set into hard lines as he stared down at the image of his sister.

Bracing myself as though I were about to dive into very cold water, I hit play.

"So here's the deal," said Amy, "and I know it's not a very good one. If you're watching this, I've gone AWOL. Or worse. In the envelope are two DVDs containing the information I was never meant to find. It's not all of it—not by a long shot—but it's the important stuff. There's a password on the discs, Mac, and you're the only one who has the key and the drive to figure it out." Tears filled her eyes and she rubbed them away with the heel of her hand. "You're the smartest person I know. And the best. Once you know the truth, you can decide what to do with it. Keep it secret or tell everyone. Toss the DVDs or forward them on. I thought keeping it secret was the right thing to do, but now . . . the more I think about the things I saw, the worse keeping it secret feels. Some days, I'm not sure what's right or wrong anymore." More tears filled her eyes, but her voice seemed to grow stronger with each syllable. "Maybe some secrets are just too big to keep. I'm sorry for putting this all on you. There just isn't anyone else I trust."

The video stopped. Three minutes and eleven seconds. That was how long Amy's last words had taken.

No one moved. No one spoke.

Finally, Stephen straightened. "Amy must have hidden the hard drive in her mailbox until I left for school. Once I was gone, she went back and moved it." He swore under his breath. For a second, it looked as though he was on the verge of ripping the iPod from my hands and hurling it.

The anger in his blue eyes took me aback. I wanted the hard drive, too—I wanted to see everything Amy had seen—but it almost seemed as though Stephen was mad at his sister, as though he was taking her actions personally.

I wasn't the only one who noticed. Next to me, I felt Kyle tense.

Shooting Stephen a wary look, Jason said, "So if the original hard drive wasn't in the mailbox and it isn't at the house, where did Amy stash it?"

"Yes," said a smooth female voice from behind him, a voice I heard in nightmares and thought I would never have to hear again. "I think we'd all like to know the answer to that question."

18

KYLE WAS ALREADY OUT OF THE CAR AND MOVING AS Jason and Stephen placed themselves in front of me, trying to block me—and the contents of the mailbox—from view.

Fear stole my breath and made every muscle shake as déjà vu crashed over me. The scar on my shoulder blazed to life, burning so hot the wound felt fresh.

It's not possible.

The voice—that horribly familiar voice—came again. "Get out of the car. Before we start shooting."

I glanced out the windshield. Kyle had stopped near the hood of the Honda, his hands slightly raised. Heart hammering, I shoved everything back into the envelope and wedged it under the driver's seat before sliding out of the car.

I squeezed between Jason and Stephen. Jason tried to stop me, but I slipped past him.

I had to see for myself.

I had to see her.

Winifred Sinclair stood just a few feet away. She stepped

forward and into the glow from a nearby lamppost. Her brown hair had been pulled back in a twist, but strands of white had fallen free. They hung around her face in delicate wisps. The last time I had seen her, she'd had just a single streak of white at her temple; now her entire face was framed in white.

She wore a black trench coat, and when she glanced to her right, I saw deep gouges in her neck: the tail end of scars her collar didn't quite hide.

It had been twenty-seven days since the breakout. In seventy-two hours, Winifred Sinclair would be capable of ripping my throat out with her claws. For now, she was still, essentially, just a reg.

But that didn't mean she wasn't dangerous.

My gaze slid to the man at her side. Donovan. His mouth twisted into a bitter half grin as his eyes met mine. The smile chilled me almost as much as Sinclair's return from the dead. A line of bruises ran down the side of his face, and the way his eyes narrowed made me think I'd be paying for each mark. There was something slightly off about the way he held his arm, and I flashed back to the memory of Kyle attacking him in the junkyard.

Like Sinclair, Donovan would soon be joining team werewolf.

He made a slight gesture with his left hand and six men broke away from the shadows at the edge of the parking lot. Each held a gun at the ready.

We had been so consumed by Amy's video that we hadn't noticed the noose closing around our necks. Even Kyle and

Stephen, with their werewolf supersenses, had been oblivious to the threat.

"Isn't this . . . surprising." Sinclair's gaze passed over the boys before snapping back to me. "I probably should have guessed you'd be tangled up with Serena Carson after the trouble you caused at Thornhill, but I certainly didn't expect to see you here. It's like fate keeps twisting us together."

"You know them?" Donovan shifted a hand to the holster at his hip. "The girl was at the junkyard. Thanks to her friends, three of my men are in the hospital."

"Perhaps if your men had demonstrated more competence, there wouldn't have been an issue."

Given that an entire rehabilitation camp had fallen under Sinclair's watch, I wasn't sure she should be accusing anyone else of incompetence, but I kept my mouth shut.

She turned her focus back on me. It was an effort not to squirm under her sharp gaze. It felt like she could see beneath my skin, like she was weighing and measuring every thought and emotion I'd ever had. "I should have finished you off at the camp."

I found my voice as Kyle let out a low growl and rounded the car to stand at my side. "Trust me," I said with more bravado than I felt, "the feeling is mutual."

I stared at Sinclair, trying to figure out how she had escaped the explosion at the transition house. Half a heartbeat later, the answer came to me. The attack had never been about eliminating Sinclair: it had been a cover to get her out.

"All those people—" The words caught in my throat as

I remembered what it was like to be trapped while everything around you burned. The terror and complete absence of hope as you struggled just to breathe. "They all died so you could walk free."

She didn't bother denying it. "Do you honestly think any of them wanted the life they had ahead?"

"They probably wouldn't have minded the choice," drawled Jason.

It was oddly reassuring to know his sense of sarcasm could stay intact even when surrounded by men with guns.

My gaze darted from Sinclair to Donovan and back as a horrible realization hit me. There had been time for Donovan and his men to kill Serena and me in the junkyard, but not a single shot had been fired. I tried to think back to what Hank had said about the attacks on the other wolves. *They managed to get three.* Not *kill* three, *get* three. A small distinction that hadn't meant much at the time; now it meant everything.

The attacks on Serena and the other teens from the detention block had never been about tying up loose ends.

My stomach flipped as I clenched my hands into fists. "You want to start again. That's why you went after Serena and the others. You're not trying to cover up Thornhill; you're picking up where you left off."

Sinclair glanced at Donovan. At her nod, he slid his gun free of its holster. "Where is the hard drive?" she asked. "And where is Serena Carson?"

I met Sinclair's ice-blue eyes and tried not to blink as my mind raced. They had snuck up on us in the parking lot, but

I was certain they hadn't been there long enough—or had gotten close enough—to hear most of what Amy had said. And Sinclair certainly hadn't been there when Stephen first told us about the hard drive and what was on it. Why did she want it and how had she known it was important?

A breeze swept through the parking lot, sending a crumpled newspaper and empty soda cans skittering across the asphalt. "What hard drive?" Even to my own ears, the bluff sounded weak.

Sinclair's gaze narrowed as it slid to my right. Eyes on Stephen, she said, "The hard drive and Serena Carson. I won't ask a third time."

Donovan tightened his grip on his gun and thumbed off the safety. The sound it made shouldn't have been audible, but I could have sworn I heard a sharp click—like the sound effect in an old western—as Kyle eased in front of me.

"Wait!" Stephen pushed past us and strode forward. "I'll give you what we have—just let them walk away."

"Stephen?" His name lodged in my throat, a strangled gasp that was more sound than word.

Stephen's back was to us. "It's all right, Mackenzie."

"You don't know who you're dealing with." Jason's voice held the edge of a growl. If I hadn't known better, I would have sworn he was infected. "You can't trust a thing she says."

But a second later, it became apparent that Stephen knew exactly who he was dealing with.

"They don't know where the hard drive is," he said. "They were never supposed to be part of this. Just let them walk away and I'll get you what you want."

"You're making demands?" A small, dark chuckle fell from Sinclair's lips and slithered down my spine. "You don't get to make demands, Stephen. Not after losing the data in the first place. Besides, they have something else we need."

I stared at Stephen's back as the words slowly sunk in. When they did, it felt like the pavement was crumbling beneath my feet. I took an involuntary step back, my shoulders colliding with Jason.

I looked up at him. Shock and anger fought for control of his face as he let out a stream of swear words. "I told you I didn't trust him."

"Right," muttered Kyle. "Because now is so the time for an *I told you so.*"

I eased out from behind Kyle, willing Stephen to turn and look at me. "You lied." The words sliced something deep within my chest. "Everything you said about Flagler. Everything about losing control after Amy's death. How could you have used Amy as part of your lies?"

Though his back was still to me, I saw Stephen flinch. "Things aren't that simple, Mac."

"You're infected and you're working with a woman who tortures and kills werewolves," said Jason. "Seems pretty simple to me."

Stephen turned. "What would you know about it?" He glared pointedly at Jason's neck. "You think the things she's done are any worse than the men who gave you that tattoo? Guys like you are the reason people like me have to hide

240

what we are. At least she's trying to do something to help werewolves."

Jason let out a low snort. "Keep telling yourself that."

Sinclair stepped in before the argument could continue. To Stephen, she said, "You told us you were on your way to retrieve the drive. Where is it?"

All that time I thought he had been checking on his grandfather and he'd really been contacting Sinclair. *Stupid.* I had been so stupid. Stephen's father hadn't sent Donovan after him; Stephen had been working with them all along. He had just lied in the hope we could help him figure out where the hard drive was.

"I thought I had it." Stephen ran a hand over his shoulder as he answered the warden, kneading the muscle nervously. "I was wrong. It's just copies of some of the files. Not the whole drive."

The disdain on Sinclair's face was strong enough to melt flesh from bone. "Where are the files?"

Stephen hesitated. "What are you going to do to them? Mackenzie and the others?"

"They'll be free to go. Once they give me what I need."

The whole country thought Sinclair was dead. She wouldn't undo that by letting us walk away. Once we told her where Serena was, we'd be just another loose end.

"She's lying, Stephen." Kyle's voice was calm and level as he stepped forward, but there was wariness behind each word. "You know she is. And you know Amy wouldn't want this. She wouldn't want anything to happen to Mac or Jason."

It was the wrong thing to say. Stephen turned to Kyle and the expression on his face was so bitter, so lost, that a wave of hopelessness swept over me. "Why should I care what Amy wanted? She sure as hell didn't give a damn about what I needed." He swallowed roughly. "She was just as bad as my father. Do you have any idea what he threw away? What they both tried to take away?"

"Enough." Sinclair placed a hand on his shoulder. "You don't have to explain yourself to them, Stephen. They don't understand. They'll never understand. No one will; that's why you came to me." Almost gently, she guided him off to the side. Once he was out of the way, she gestured at two of the men in the parking lot, waving them toward the rest of us.

The men hesitated until Donovan gave a barely perceptible nod—a gesture Sinclair completely missed—and then moved in to flank us. I bit my lip. Sinclair acted as though she was in charge, but the men weren't taking orders from her.

In front of me, Kyle tensed. A muscle twitched in his upper back and I felt a surge of panic at the thought of what Donovan's men would do if he transformed.

"Where is Serena Carson?" asked Sinclair.

"So much for not asking a third time," observed Jason.

Before the last word had left his mouth, two gunshots rang in the air like thunderclaps. The bullets slammed into Kyle, spinning him around and sending him staggering into me before I could process what had happened.

He fell and I fell with him.

My knees slammed into the pavement. Kyle ended up sprawled on his back with his torso stretched across my lap. His face twisted in pain.

Animalistic, choking sounds clawed their way out of my throat as blood blossomed on Kyle's shirt. I fought with the buttons, my fingers thick and clumsy as I desperately tried to figure out where he had been hit.

Jason crouched over us. He pushed my hands away and ripped Kyle's shirt open. Blood stained his fingers as he thrust the fabric aside. Both shots looked as though they had taken Kyle in the shoulder. Away from his heart. Away from any vital organs. "He's okay. He'll be okay." Jason's voice shook and I wasn't sure whether he was trying to convince me or himself.

I caught a flash of movement over his shoulder and then he was yanked up and back. Away from Kyle. Away from me.

Jason struggled, but the man who had grabbed him was almost a foot taller and twice as wide in the shoulders. He wore what looked like a dozen silver hoops in his right ear, and unlike the other men in the courtyard, he carried an assault rifle. He let go of Jason just long enough to club him between the shoulders with the butt of the gun, practically driving him to his knees.

"No!" My shout echoed in the parking lot as Jason was dragged toward the courtyard.

Kyle pushed himself unsteadily to his feet.

Somewhere, someone else was shouting. It sounded like Stephen.

Rough hands grabbed me and pulled me up. "Move and

I'll shoot her." The words were for Kyle and they did exactly what they were supposed to: they froze him in his tracks.

I started to fight, but stopped when I caught a glimpse of the gun my captor was carrying. The words hadn't been an idle threat.

I threw a desperate glance over my shoulder as I was dragged to the courtyard. Kyle stood ten yards away. Two of the men had taken up positions in front of him, their guns trained on his chest, but he didn't spare them a single glance. Fear flashed across his face—not for himself, but for Jason and me.

Kyle was a werewolf, but Jason and I were his Achilles' heel: all they had to do to get him to cooperate was threaten us.

My gaze was wrenched forward as my foot caught on the edge of a flagstone. I stumbled, but the man gripping my arm kept me from falling. He was smaller than the one who had grabbed Jason, but he still outweighed me by at least a hundred pounds. His skin was darker than the shadows in the corners of the courtyard and his eyes were as black as pitch. Had he been at the junkyard? I couldn't remember.

Stephen said my name as I was pulled past. Donovan's two remaining men stood just behind him. I didn't meet his eyes. I couldn't. As painful as Ben's betrayal had been, it paled next to this. For three years, I had looked up to Stephen. I had trusted him. "Why?" I asked, the word shredding my throat on the way out.

I didn't think he would answer. By the time he did, I was far enough away that I had to strain to catch the soft words.

"Because she's my best hope of a cure. I can't live like this. If anyone ever found out . . . I'd lose everything."

Not *the* best hope. *My* best hope.

In that instant, I hated him. Maybe even more than Sinclair. The warden was batshit crazy, but she wasn't doing this for herself: she honestly believed she could cure LS and help thousands of people. Stephen, meanwhile, only cared about himself.

My eyes sought out Jason. He had been dragged to the fountain. There was a deadly light deep in his green eyes as he watched Sinclair and Donovan walk toward him.

The man holding my arm stopped when we were still a few feet away.

Donovan's eyes were restless, never lingering for more than a second on anyone or anything. Sinclair, on the other hand, had eyes only for Jason and me.

I glanced over my shoulder. Kyle had been allowed to follow just as far as the edge of the courtyard. His gaze met mine for a split second before sliding to the warden. As he stared at her, I could have sworn I saw the wolf peek out from behind his eyes. Sharp and predatory and deadly.

"Where is Serena Carson?" asked Sinclair, her voice every bit as commanding as it had been in the camp.

None of us spoke.

"Do it," she said.

My stomach clenched, even though I wasn't sure what was coming—not until Jason was spun around, not until Donovan strode forward and leveled a sharp kick at the back of his leg.

Jason screamed as his leg gave out beneath him.

I tried to run forward, but the man holding me twisted my arm, twisted it so hard that it felt like my shoulder would dislocate. He placed the muzzle of his gun against my ribs. "Don't even think about it," he said, glancing past me to the edge of the courtyard where Kyle stood.

Donovan forced Jason over the ledge encircling the fountain and shoved his head down while the other man—the man with the earrings—pinned Jason's arms behind his back.

There were only four or five inches of water in the basin, but four or five inches was more than enough to cover Jason's mouth and nose.

"No!" My shout echoed with Kyle's as Jason thrashed.

"Let him up," said Sinclair as Jason's movements began to slow. The men hauled him—sputtering and gasping for breath—out of the water.

Jason leaned on the edge of the fountain and retched.

Sinclair didn't look at him. Or at Kyle. Her eyes were locked on me. I was the one she wanted to break. This wasn't about hurting Jason; it was about hurting me. It was about seeing how far she could push me before I would give her what she wanted. The ghost of a smile crossed her lips, and I knew she was enjoying this.

While Jason was still trying to catch his breath, they shoved him back under.

"Stop it! You're going to kill him!" My voice rang across the courtyard as Sinclair looked on impassively.

Behind me, I could hear Kyle yelling at Stephen, trying to reason with him. On his own, Kyle couldn't take all of the men in the courtyard—not without something happening to Jason and me first—but two werewolves might have stood a chance at turning the tables.

How long had they been holding Jason under? Forty seconds? A minute? How long could Jason hold his breath?

"Just tell me what I want to know," said Sinclair. Her voice was so calm that she might as well have been asking me about the weather.

Jason had stopped thrashing. His body hung limp and boneless over the fountain's ledge.

"The church near the cemetery!" The words were a frantic cry. They ran together and were almost unintelligible. "Please." I stared at Sinclair. "She's at the abandoned church on Douglas Lane. On the other side of town. *Please let him up.*"

"And the hard drive?"

"We don't have it. I swear we don't. I didn't even know it existed until I talked to Stephen. *Please . . .*" The word flooded my mouth with a bitter taste, but I would beg if that was what it took. "Please let him up!"

"She's telling the truth." I didn't turn as Stephen's voice drew closer. "She was friends with my sister. I asked her if Amy had ever told her about a hard drive. It was the first she had heard of it."

Sinclair's gaze flickered to Stephen. "You said you had files."

He hesitated. "They're on two DVDs. In the car."

I counted the seconds as Sinclair considered Stephen's words. When she finally said "All right," I almost collapsed in relief.

The men hauled Jason out of the fountain. He fell limply to the flagstones.

He wasn't moving. He wasn't breathing.

The man with the earrings shot a nervous glance at Donovan. Even the man holding my arm seemed surprised. His grip lessened—just for a second—and I threw myself forward.

I covered the distance to Jason and crashed to the ground at his side. I felt, more than saw, one of the men reach for me, but Sinclair said, "Leave her."

"Jason?" I rolled him onto his back. His face was slack and still, his lips tinged blue. I tilted his head back, desperately trying to remember the first-aid class Amy and I had taken two summers ago. Panic flooded me—so much fear that it was like being ripped apart—but I pushed it away as I pumped his chest, counting under my breath.

There were noises in the parking lot—Kyle shouting, Stephen arguing with Sinclair—but they were a distant, background hum. All that mattered was Jason. "Eight. Nine. Ten." *He'll be all right. He has to be all right. Please let him be all right.* "Fourteen. Fifteen. Six—"

Water burst from Jason's mouth as a spasm racked his entire body.

Eyes swimming with tears, I rolled him onto his side, holding him as more water came up.

"Mac?" His voice was a hoarse croak as he twisted and looked up at me.

"It's okay." I folded my body over him, pressing my forehead to his. "It's okay. You're okay."

I squeezed my eyes shut, holding back the tears, as one thought echoed in my head over and over: I was going to stop her. I didn't care how long it took or what I had to do. Somehow, I would stop Winifred Sinclair from hurting anyone else.

Even if I had to kill her.

"Get me the DVDs."

No. My head jerked up at the warden's words. Whatever was on those DVDs, we couldn't just let her take them.

Stephen hesitated and then turned toward the parking lot. Sinclair stopped him before he took a single step. "Not you. Him."

My gaze darted to Kyle. The sheer fury on his face was frightening. It was impossible to miss the way his muscles jumped and writhed under the sleeves of his shirt. Only then did I become fully aware of the men standing over Jason and me, of the guns that were pointed at us.

My arms tightened around Jason as though I could somehow protect him.

I swallowed. Sinclair might not trust Stephen to hand over the DVDs after everything he had just seen, but she knew Kyle would give her anything to keep us safe.

Kyle's gaze locked on mine. I started to shake my head, but then I glanced down at Jason. They could have killed him. They almost had.

Every person you care about is a weapon someone can use against you. I hated my father's platitudes—especially when they were right.

I didn't watch Kyle turn and head toward the car. I couldn't watch as Sinclair was handed everything. I couldn't watch as she won.

Jason's body spasmed with a cough so fierce that it sounded like things inside his chest were being ripped to shreds. He grasped at my clothes, pulling me closer.

"Jason? Are you okay?" I didn't know what to do. I tried hitting him lightly on the back, but that only seemed to make the coughing worse. He clung to me, and I caught a small flash of blue-tinged light.

His phone. Miraculously, it hadn't fallen into the fountain or gotten wet.

I glanced up. Our two guards still had their guns trained on us, but my body was shielding Jason's hands from view.

I turned my attention back to him just in time to see his fingers dart clumsily across the phone's surface. His hands were shaking so badly that I wasn't sure how he managed to hold the phone without dropping it.

The screen went black.

Jason struggled to slip the phone back into his pocket. I reached between us, helping.

"Thanks," he muttered, voice rough and a little weak. He tensed as he stared at something over my shoulder.

I eased away from him and twisted as Kyle crossed the parking lot, the envelope from the mailbox in his hands.

I started to push myself to my feet, but at a wave from

one of the guns, I settled for kneeling. The edges of flag-stones bit into my knees and the cold from the ground seeped into my bones. Next to me, Jason raised himself to a sitting position, using the fountain for support. His lips were still slightly blue and he was shivering.

Donovan intercepted Kyle before he could get near Sinclair. Given the look on Kyle's face, I couldn't blame him. There were times when it was easy to forget the horrible things Kyle had been forced to do since becoming infected. This was not one of those times.

Donovan took the envelope and peered inside before removing the two DVD cases. He glanced at Stephen. "Are these them?"

Stephen nodded and swallowed. "Yeah," he said. "That's them." He looked oddly beaten down and defeated consider-ing he had been planning on turning the hard drive over to Sinclair all along. He glanced at me and his cheeks flushed. He was only able to hold my gaze for a second before look-ing away.

Maybe watching Sinclair threaten and hurt people he had known for years—people who had trusted him—was just more than he had bargained for.

Donovan glanced at Jason and me as he handed the DVDs to Sinclair. "We should keep at least one of them alive until we check the church."

"Two, I think." Something shrewd and dark shifted behind Sinclair's gaze as it darted between Kyle and Jason. "Otherwise, they don't have anything to lose."

I was *so* going to kill her.

"You said you'd let them go." There was a growl to Stephen's voice. He took a step toward the warden and one of Donovan's men intercepted him. "They told you what you wanted."

"I lied." Sinclair glanced at Donovan. "Kill the wolf."

"No!" The word burst from my lungs just as the world across the river exploded.

19

TIME SLOWED AS A FIREBALL ROSE INTO THE NIGHT SKY— so high that it was visible over the roof of the strip mall. Even on this side of the water, the force of the explosion was incredible. It rattled windows and set off car alarms and distracted Donovan and his men.

The whole thing lasted only an instant, but an instant was all Kyle needed.

He threw himself forward—not at Donovan or his men, but at Sinclair. He grabbed one of her arms and twisted it behind her back. He placed his other hand—a hand that was long and clawed and no longer human—at her throat.

Sinclair was already infected—Kyle couldn't hurt her that way—but he could still rip out her throat.

It was a scene that was eerily familiar; it was a scene that threw me right back to the night of the breakout.

Kyle's eyes locked on Donovan. "Tell your men to let them up."

Donovan raised an eyebrow. He looked unnervingly calm, but when he spoke, his accent was thicker than it had been. "And then what? Do you really think you can just walk out of here?"

"Let them up," repeated Kyle. The muscles in his arm twitched and Sinclair flinched as one of his claws pierced the delicate skin just below her carotid artery.

Donovan hesitated, but then nodded at the two men covering Jason and me. They lowered their guns and stepped back.

It was an improvement, but we were still outnumbered and outgunned. Donovan was right: there was no way we were walking out of here.

I pushed myself up on unsteady legs and reached down to help Jason to his feet. His leg buckled under his weight and I only just kept him from eating the flagstones.

"Knee," he hissed in between swear words as he hopped back on his good leg and lowered himself to the ledge of the fountain.

I bit my lower lip. If we could get Jason to the car . . . I looked up. Three of Donovan's men had fanned out behind Kyle, blocking any escape out of the courtyard.

"Stephen . . ." The warden struggled to address Amy's brother as Kyle's hand tightened around her throat. "You understand the importance of what we're doing. You can't let your sister's *friends*"—she stumbled over the word like it was a foreign concept—"jeopardize that."

"I—" Stephen shook his head. The family resemblance between him and Amy was almost nil—it was like comparing day and night—but in that instant, I swear I saw her in his eyes. He shook his head a second time and took a step back, distancing himself from Sinclair and the situation.

I glanced at the warden. The look in her eyes said Stephen had better run if she ever got free.

Jason grabbed my arm and pulled me down toward him. "Get Kyle and get out of here."

"We're not going to leave you." Had he hit his head when they hauled him out of the fountain?

He tightened his grip on my arm. "Listen—in another minute . . ."

His voice trailed off as, somewhere nearby, tires squealed on pavement. He swore. "There's no time. I sent a 3-1-1. It was the only thing I could think of."

I stared at him blankly. What the hell was a 3-1-1?

Jason let go of my arm and pushed a hand through his still-dripping hair. "All those Trackers covering the street outside Amy's? I told them there were werewolves attacking regs at the strip mall. I told them to come *here*."

Horror and comprehension flooded me as I twisted to glance back at Kyle. Were those headlights on the street?

"You have to get out of here," continued Jason. "Now."

I shook my head as I turned back to him. He was right—we had to get out of here—but we couldn't just leave him behind.

I couldn't leave him behind.

"I'll be all right," he said, reading my thoughts. He pushed me away. "The Trackers will take care of me."

"They're the bad guys."

"Not all of them," said Jason, "and right now we need them." He tried to get to his feet and fell back, cursing. "*I* need them—hell, I can't even walk. Get Kyle and get out of here. If they find him, they'll kill him."

A car roared into the parking lot. A second followed.

"Go!" growled Jason as Donovan shouted instructions to his men. More headlights were visible in the distance. There had been dozens of Trackers at Amy's—God only knew how many were on their way here now.

With a last, anguished look at Jason, I forced myself to move.

"Kyle!"

He shoved Sinclair as I ran toward him, sending her stumbling forward, into Donovan.

I grabbed his arm and tried to pull him out of the courtyard—it was like trying to move a brick wall. "Please, Kyle. We have to go, they're Trackers."

Still, he resisted. "What about Jason?"

"He'll be all right." I prayed the words were true as they left my mouth. Jason was right: he needed the Trackers. He needed medical attention and protection—things Kyle and I were powerless to get him.

For a horrible second, I thought Kyle would argue, but then he let out a frustrated, strangled noise and grabbed my hand. Together, we ran as the first few Trackers poured out of their cars and yelled for us to stop.

I didn't look back. Not to check on Jason. Not even as someone opened fire.

I heard a howl—Stephen?—somewhere behind us, but I just kept running.

* * *

Lungs burning, I sank to the damp grass on the riverbank and fought to catch my breath. It felt like we had been running for hours. In reality, it had probably been less than ten minutes.

I could see the exit for the bridge up ahead. Once we had put some distance between ourselves and the strip mall, I had told Kyle that Trey and Serena were back at my apartment. It was something I had forgotten to tell him and Jason in my excitement to find Amy's mailbox.

Heading to the apartment wasn't up for debate. There was nowhere else for us to go. Nothing else we could do.

My breathing evened out, but my chest still ached. We had left Jason behind. For the second time in as many days, *I* had left him behind.

Kyle stood over me, keeping watch as he swiftly fastened the few remaining buttons on his shirt. Given the amount of blood staining the white cotton, he might have been better off just tossing it into the river. I caught a quick glimpse of his shoulder. Blood had dried on his skin, but there was no sign of the bullet wounds.

"Mac?" When I didn't answer, he crouched down.

Gently, I reached out and slipped my hand under his shirt, placing my fingertips on the spot where the bullets had hit. The skin was as smooth and undamaged as it had looked.

"You didn't have to shift to heal?" I asked, voice far away and shell-shocked after everything that had just happened.

"Not for this," he said, taking my hand and gently moving it away. "If they had hit a bit lower or a few inches in . . ."

"Oh." I didn't say anything else for a long moment. "We just left him," I said finally, dropping my gaze to the grass as I slipped my hand out of Kyle's.

Gently, he reached out and tilted my chin up. "Jason will be okay," he said. "The Trackers can get him to the hospital. They can make sure nothing's wrong."

I nodded. I knew that, but leaving Jason with a group of Trackers still didn't feel right. Sure, they thought he was one of them—for now. But the group was almost as much of a danger to regs with werewolf sympathies as it was to werewolves themselves. I didn't want to imagine what they would do to Jason if they found out his best friend was infected or that he had been involved in the Thornhill breakout.

Thornhill.

My eyes widened. "The DVDs." I crossed my arms over my chest, hugging myself tightly and fighting back the urge to throw up. If Sinclair had managed to evade the Trackers, she had the DVDs. Hell, even if she hadn't escaped, there was no way we could go back for the discs. They probably wouldn't be there, anyway.

Kyle's brows pulled together in a frown.

"You gave Sinclair the DVDs." There was no recrimination in my voice—I would have done the same thing if our roles had been reversed—but a deep sense of loss spread through my body. I glanced down at the river. The water was dark and swift, and the fires on the other side of town were reflected on its rippled surface. The current washed everything away. Every shred of hope.

"Mac . . ." Kyle cupped my cheek with his palm and

turned my face away from the water. With his other hand, he reached behind him and pulled something from the small of his back. A DVD case with the words *Arcade Fire* scrawled in thick, black letters on the front.

Hands shaking, I lifted the case from his hands and opened it. Two DVDs were nestled inside.

It took me a second to find my voice. "I don't understand."

He shrugged and a faint smile crossed his face. "You lied to Sinclair about Serena. I lied to her about the DVDs."

"The concert bootlegs you bought after the Arcade Fire show . . ." I said, wonder filling my voice. A guy had been hawking them out of his trunk in the parking lot. I had thought it was a waste of money—why buy a DVD when half those clips were probably on YouTube?—but Kyle had shelled out twenty bucks.

"Good thing I never clean out my car," he said drily.

In response, I threw my arms around him.

The city was burning and God only knew what was happening back at the strip mall, but maybe—just maybe—things weren't entirely hopeless.

The walk to my apartment took almost two hours.

We made it to the bridge just before the National Guard blocked it off, but progress across was painfully slow. The northbound lanes were gridlocked, and the pedestrian walkway was clogged with people trying to get away from the destruction and chaos on the south side of town.

There was something comforting about being surrounded

by so many people. Even if Sinclair and Donovan had dodged the Trackers, there was no way they would be able to catch up to us. Not in this.

Our appearance earned us more than a few curious looks, but no one asked any questions. Even though the bottom half of my dress was in tatters and Kyle's shirt was covered in blood, there were people in the crowd who were in much worse shape. I spotted three broken noses, five broken arms, and at least twelve black eyes before I stopped counting.

A lot of the people we passed looked numb. Shell-shocked. Just the way I felt. How could Stephen have been helping Sinclair? I understood wanting a cure and the fear of being discovered—especially when your own grandfather was lobbying for tougher regulations against the infected—but how could he have sold us out? How could he have lied to us so easily and how could I have believed him?

Easy, said a small voice in the back of my head, a voice that sounded an awful lot like Amy's. *You believed him because you wanted to.*

Someone collided with my shoulder, hard, and Kyle reached out to steady me as I tightened my grip on the DVDs. I glanced back, but whoever had hit me was already gone, swallowed by the crowd. As far as I could tell, we were the only ones heading *toward* the downtown core, and pushing against the press of people was like trying to swim upstream. I reached for Kyle's phone to call Trey, to tell him where we were, and came up empty.

"Shit." I twisted around, but the ground behind us had

already been swallowed by the throng. "The phone—I think it fell out of my pocket when that guy hit me."

Kyle's mouth pressed into a hard line as he glanced over his shoulder, but he didn't suggest we go back for it. There was no way the phone could have escaped being crushed.

A chorus of shouts rose around us as a man with a megaphone announced that the north side of town was closed off and that everyone would have to head back the way they had come.

I bit my lip as the outraged cries rose to deafening levels. How could they just block off the bridge? *Why* would they just block off the bridge?

A second later, the answer came to me: they were trying to keep the bedlam on the south side of the city from spreading to Hemlock's wealthier neighborhoods.

A wave of acid rushed up the back of my throat. Men were being wasted here when they could have been helping rein things in on my side of town. They were protecting property values instead of people. It was just like what had happened when the werewolf attacks began last spring. The wealthier parts of town had hired—in some cases been given—extra protection. Not a single attack had taken place north of the river.

"It's going to take us all night at this rate," muttered Kyle. He glanced around and then gracefully vaulted over the shoulder-high railing that separated the pedestrian walkway from traffic. He reached back to help me up and then placed his hands on my hips and lifted me down.

We walked on the edge of the outside lane—it wasn't

like the cars were moving.

The closer we got to the south side of the bridge, the more scraps of news we picked up. The fireball had been an explosion at the gas station on Maple. One old man claimed the RfW—Regs for Werewolves—had blown up the station on purpose, but someone else said a semitruck had swerved to avoid a mob of Trackers and taken out the pumps.

No one seemed to be talking about the murder at the fund-raising gala or the disturbance at the strip mall, but that news wouldn't stay quiet long. A murder at a party hosted by the town's most prominent family? That was front-page fodder. God only knew what would happen if the press found out Stephen had been responsible. I remembered the howl I had heard as we ran from the Trackers. Had Stephen been captured? Killed? He had been helping Sinclair and had stood by while Donovan had almost drowned Jason, but . . .

He had asked Sinclair to let us go. He had asked her to let us go and he had hesitated when she told him to stand against us.

That had to make some sort of difference, didn't it?

I hugged the DVDs to my chest. "Do you really think Jason's okay?"

Like the other ninety-nine times I had asked, Kyle's answer didn't change. "He's probably safer with them than with us."

By the time we finally reached the southern edge of the bridge, I agreed with him. No matter how much I hated the

Trackers, Jason had to be better off with them than here. Stepping into the downtown core was like stepping into a war zone. The mingled scents of smoke, tear gas, and burning rubber hung in the air and clogged my throat, while a cacophony of sirens and alarms made it almost impossible to think.

We knew the wolves were planning something for the night of the rally; it looked like they had gotten started early.

Or maybe not . . .

I glanced down as my foot caught on a cardboard sign.

Werewolves Are Human Most of the Time was printed in bold, black letters underneath the RfW logo.

The RfW had been protesting?

Kyle touched my arm and nodded toward the next block. A group—Trackers or RfW, it was impossible to tell—was being driven this way by men in riot gear.

As quickly as we could, we turned off Main Street and headed for Elm.

The damage wasn't as bad here, though cars had been torched and stores had been looted. The looting made things somehow worse. Mindless destruction was bad, but mindless destruction topped with personal gain was insult heaped onto injury.

Even though most of the actual rioting seemed to be contained to the area near Riverside Square, we had to take several small detours to avoid pockets of trouble. We couldn't seem to go more than a block without having to hide from groups of Trackers. God only knew what they were doing to any werewolves—real or just suspected—they found tonight.

Would they drag Jason out on one of their hunts or would his injuries keep him safe? I wished I knew the answer even though there was nothing I could do to change things.

I shivered and touched the compass necklace at my throat as we turned onto Elm Street.

Miraculously, the neighborhood looked like it had been completely spared. Even the cars parked along the sides of the street had made it through the evening unscathed.

For the first time in hours, I felt like I could draw a full breath: Hemlock was being ripped apart, but at least my small corner of it was intact. The thought—and the relief that accompanied it—felt selfish.

My entire body ached, but my steps were lighter as I turned up the walkway to my building. I reached for my keys as we neared the main door, only to realize they were probably still in the pocket of the jeans I had left on Jason's bedroom floor.

I buzzed our apartment and waited for Tess's voice to burst out of the intercom.

Nothing happened.

A small tendril of alarm wound through my chest, but I told myself everything was fine as I hit the button a second time. Again, we were greeted by silence.

Everything is fine.

I avoided looking at Kyle as I retrieved the spare set of keys from inside a fake rock Tess had planted at the corner of the building. I wanted to believe the worry suddenly gripping me from the inside out was unwarranted, and I couldn't do that if I looked at him and saw wariness on his face.

Somewhere in the distance—far, but not nearly far enough—I could hear shouts and the blare of a fire truck. Maybe the relief I had felt at seeing Elm Street untouched had been premature.

My hands shook slightly as I returned to the door and slipped the key into the lock. Despite my throbbing muscles, I raced up the stairs to the third floor.

"Tess?" I strained my ears for signs of life on the other side of the door—the familiar creak of floorboards or the sound of the TV—but it was completely silent.

I unlocked the door, but couldn't make myself push it open. Finally, Kyle reached around me and turned the knob.

Inside, the apartment was dark.

I flicked on the light and crossed the living room. "Tess? Serena?" I checked both bedrooms and the bathroom.

No one was here.

I returned to the living room as Kyle stepped over the threshold and closed the door.

No. No, no, no.

Trey had been at the end of Elm Street the last time I talked to him. They should have been able to get to the apartment. And Tess—I swallowed roughly as I rushed to the phone in the kitchen.

I was halfway through dialing Tess's cell before I realized the phone was beeping: someone had left a message. I entered the code and my cousin's voice began to play.

"Mac—in case you call the apartment and don't get an answer, I'm over at Adam's. I'm fine—he's fine, too—but there are riots down by the river and we figured safety in numbers."

Adam tended bar at the Shady Cat. He and Tess had dated for all of five minutes two years ago before realizing they'd make better friends. He lived on Charlotte Street, several blocks up from Elm. Charlotte was good. It was farther from downtown. Safer.

I bit my lip as I dialed Trey's number. Nothing. I called Eve but all I got was her voice mail.

Not good. So not good.

"Tess is okay. She's staying with a friend." A ball of lead settled in my stomach as I replaced the receiver and turned to Kyle. "But neither Trey nor Eve is picking up their phone."

Kyle crossed the room. He crouched down and retrieved the DVDs: I had dropped them in my haste to get to the phone. "Where did Trey say they were when you talked to him?"

"By the ballpark at the end of the street." I gripped the edge of the counter. "That's only a five-minute walk from here. Ten at the most."

"If Tess had already left, they wouldn't have been able to get in," said Kyle, setting the DVDs on the counter. "They would have had to find somewhere else to hole up."

"Maybe . . ." I was pretty sure Serena had seen me use the spare key before, but it might not have been something she would remember. I glanced at the clock on the micro-wave. It was almost 2:00 a.m. How long ago had I spoken to Trey? Three and a half hours? Four? "But that doesn't explain why they're not answering their phones. With all those Trackers out there . . . or if Sinclair and Donovan got away from the strip mall . . ."

"Their phones might just have died," said Kyle. "It's not like we've had many chances to charge them. The only reason mine was still working was because I had a chance to charge it at Jason's."

"But what about the Trackers or Sinclair?" I tightened my grip on the counter as a horrible thought occurred to me. "Could Stephen have heard Trey say they were coming here? Could he have told the warden?"

Kyle shook his head. "Not a chance. Werewolf hearing is good, but not *that* good. I can hear the other end of a phone call if the person is in the same room, but you were on the other side of the grove. Besides, even if he had heard, he wouldn't have known it was important: Stephen didn't know anything about Sinclair wanting Serena until the strip mall, and I doubt he had time to tell her anything once the Trackers showed up. Even if he did, there is no way they could have beaten us across the bridge."

Everything he said made sense, but none of it did any-thing to ease the worry coursing through me.

I pulled in a deep breath. "So what do we do now?"

In answer, Kyle headed for my bedroom. He came back a moment later, my laptop tucked under his arm. "Now we try to figure out what the hell is on those DVDs—after we get cleaned up."

"You can't be serious." I stared at him as though he had lost his mind as he set the laptop up on the coffee table. "You want to just stay here? While Serena and Eve and Trey are out there somewhere? While Jason is with an entire herd of Trackers?"

Kyle's shoulders tensed. I knew the words and the accusation in my voice were unfair, but lashing out at someone else was easier than admitting how useless I felt.

"I don't *want* to stay here," he said, straightening. The words were slow and careful and a little bit angry. "If I thought there was anything useful I could be doing out there, I'd be doing it. But we have no idea where Trey, Eve, and Serena might have gone. Best-case scenario? They're holed up somewhere—in which case finding them would be next to impossible and would mean leaving the one place we know they might come back to. The only thing we can do is try to figure out what the hell is on those discs. Whatever it is, Sinclair wants it. Maybe even more than she wants Serena. If the Trackers didn't wipe out her and Donovan— if they come after Serena again—those DVDs are the only leverage we have."

I knew he was right, but still, I hesitated. Staying here— safe and sound—while the others were out there felt like giving up. Like abandoning them. "It doesn't feel right." My voice was little more than a whisper.

Kyle let out a deep, frustrated breath and crossed the room. I could see the effort it took for him to push his anger aside as he pressed a kiss to my temple. "Sometimes," he said, "the right thing doesn't feel right at all. Sometimes it feels spectacularly fucking lousy."

Somehow, that didn't make me feel any better.

20

"Any luck?"

I glanced up at the sound of Kyle's voice. His hair was damp and he was wearing an old shirt that I had rescued from the donation pile the last time his mom made him weed out his closet.

Like a gentleman, he had let me have the bathroom first. I had scrubbed my skin and traded my ruined dress for a pair of faded jeans and an oversized T-shirt that hung halfway to my knees. Comfort clothes.

Comfort was one thing I desperately needed. Maybe almost as much as answers.

"Nothing even remotely resembling luck," I confessed, answering his question.

The light from the television cast flickering shadows over his face as he crossed the room and took a seat next to me on the couch. CNN was broadcasting live coverage from downtown. They hadn't shown much that I hadn't already seen or guessed, but I kept the TV on just in case.

I had muted the sound, though. Sound somehow made the images worse.

I glanced back down at the password prompt on my laptop. I had checked both DVDs. Each contained one password-protected folder. Amy had said I'd be able to figure it out, but I had tried at least twenty things so far—everything from the password to her old school email account to the name of the goldfish Jason had given her when we were fifteen. Nothing worked.

Kyle slid his hand over mine. Only then did I realize I had curled my fingers into a fist. "How can I help?" he asked.

I nodded to Tess's laptop, which I had plugged in and set up next to mine on the coffee table. The list of names Ben had given me was beside it. The paper was creased and stained with flecks of blood, but most of the names were legible. "Ben said something about people disappearing in the middle of the night, that those were the names he could remember. I don't know what difference it makes, but I thought that if we could figure out if any of them were inmates at Van Horne . . ."

"That we would know whether or not he was telling the truth about anything?" Kyle opened Tess's browser and then reached for the stale package of donuts I had found in the back of a cupboard. I had already scarfed down three. No matter what horrible things happened, everyone had to eat sooner or later.

"I'm sorry," I said, the words halting and awkward.

"About what I said earlier. I know it wasn't fair. I know you'd rather be out there, too."

Kyle shrugged. "You were upset. It's okay."

I could tell from his voice that it wasn't, not really, but at least he wasn't mad at me.

"Did you try six-eight-four-one?" he asked a short while later, not looking up from his screen. "It's the last four digits of Jason's old phone number. Amy used to use it for passwords until Jason found out and messed with all her profiles."

I gave it a try. Nothing. "I wouldn't know that, though. It has to be something I could guess." I was still wearing the compass necklace. I ran the pad of my thumb over the design on the front as I stared at the blinking cursor. Maybe Amy had just given me too much credit. Maybe I wasn't smart enough to figure it out. I certainly hadn't figured out any of the things that had been going on in her life.

"Mac." Kyle's voice was suddenly sharp. He turned Tess's laptop so I could see the website on the screen.

My breath caught in my throat. Just to the left of a large block of type was a picture of a group of men and women in suits. There, second to the left, was a familiar face: the woman with the glasses who had singled out Serena at Thornhill. The woman we had seen with Amy's father.

"Her name is Natalie Goodwin," said Kyle. "She's a doctor. Before CutterBrown, she worked for the CDC."

I shook my head and reached for the list Ben had given me. Natalie Goodwin was third from the bottom. A wobbly circle had been drawn around her name. "I don't understand. . . ."

Kyle flipped between a number of open tabs. "Ben remembered names—just not the names of inmates. I haven't found all of them—just the ones who have published research papers or who were mentioned in press releases and medical journals—but three of the names Ben circled were at CutterBrown."

"Were?"

He went back to the page with the picture of Natalie Goodwin and pointed to the headline at the top of the page. *Zenith Pharmaceuticals Expands Research and Development.* "It looks like she and two other researchers left CutterBrown to go to Zenith."

"When?" My heart pounded as I searched the screen for a date. The press release was almost a year old: Natalie Goodwin had left CutterBrown well before I had seen her at Thornhill. "It wasn't an affair."

Kyle shot me a confused look.

I set my laptop aside and stood. Pacing, I ran a hand roughly through my hair. "Upstairs, when we heard her talking to Amy's father. She wasn't talking about an affair—or at least not just an affair."

I could feel Kyle's eyes on me as I circled the room. "She said she made a mistake and that she wanted to come back. We thought she was talking about leaving Amy's dad when it was really about CutterBrown. She made a mistake by going to Zenith. Oh my God." I came to a sudden stop. "Cutter-Brown wasn't experimenting on wolves at Thornhill. Zenith was." Kyle looked doubtful, but I was completely and utterly certain. It was the only way Sinclair's connection to Stephen made sense. "Think about it. Stephen said it himself: he's just an intern. If Sinclair was working for CutterBrown, she wouldn't need Stephen to get her information. She could have just asked for it."

Another thought occurred to me. "Where's Zenith located?"

Kyle clicked a link. "Houston. Why?"

"Donovan—the guy with the accent—gave me a business card when he first showed up at Serena's. It had a phone number with a Houston area code."

I walked back to the couch and sat down heavily. "A pharmaceutical company was working with Sinclair—we just had the wrong one."

"And CutterBrown was involved with a camp," said Kyle, glancing back down at Ben's list. "Just not the camp we thought. They were experimenting on wolves at Van Horne."

"Jesus." The word escaped my lungs in a weary rush. "It's like *Spy vs. Spy*."

And something Amy had left us was at the center of it.

"Jason was right." Kyle ran a hand over the back of his neck. "A cure for LS would be worth billions. It makes sense that there would be more than one company in the race for it."

I glanced back down at Ben's list. I had assumed the four-digit numbers next to each name were the numbers of inmates—like the ones that had been on our wrist cuffs in the camp—but they weren't. They were employee numbers, like the number I had seen on Stephen's ID card.

"Ben told me he had to make sure it didn't happen again—that *they* couldn't do it again. He was after the names of the people who had been involved in Van Horne. That was what he was looking for in the study. He was going to go after them."

As I spoke, the screen saver on my laptop—a slideshow Amy had made last year—flickered to life. Some of the photos were completely random but most were of the four of us. Amy had tried to make Jason and Kyle install it on their computers, but Jason had said any screensaver that girly would give his manly gaming machine a complex, and Kyle had refused on grounds that the program she had used had been downloaded from a site that was adware central. I thought the screen saver was cheesy, but I had put it on my laptop to avoid hurting her feelings. After she was gone, I couldn't bear the thought of taking it off.

For a moment, I just watched the photos, hoping Amy's smiling face would somehow make the mystery of the password clear. Some of the pictures were duplicates of ones on the USB key she had given me. After her death, I had stared at them so long and so often that I could close my eyes and recall every detail.

I wanted to remember Amy as she was in those photos, not as the Cheshire cat version that haunted my dreams or as the sad girl Trey had known who had kept a million and one secrets. I wanted to remember her smiling and goofing off. Making screen savers and filling USB drives with photos and music just because she thought there might be something in there that I would someday—

"Oh my God." My voice was a choked whisper. "What was it Amy said in the video? Something about me having the drive and the key?" I pushed myself to my feet, almost knocking over both laptops in my haste, and rushed to my room, where I retrieved Amy's flash drive from its tangle of objects.

"She gave this to me just a couple of days before . . ." I trailed off, unable to say *before she died*.

"A USB key?"

"Also known as a flash drive." I sat back down and plugged the drive into a USB port. "It's just a bunch of music and pictures, but she named the drive." I browsed to the drive on the computer. *MAJiK*. My heart gave a sharp twist. Our initials.

It felt like Amy was in the room with us, like I could glimpse her out of the corner of my eye if I turned fast enough. She had known that I would keep the USB drive if anything ever happened to her. She had planned for this moment.

I clicked the folder on the DVD. This time, when I entered the password, I got in.

A dozen subfolders filled the screen, all of them beginning with the prefix VH. *Van Horne*. Stomach plummeting, I opened the first folder. Inside were spreadsheets and patient files—many of them stamped with the CBP logo. Ben had been at Van Horne. One of the files might even be his.

I opened the second folder. It was filled with dozens of videos. I clicked one at random and an image of a boy strapped to a metal table filled the screen. I watched just long enough to confirm it featured the same sort of torture we had seen at Thornhill before quickly closing the clip.

Proof. The folder was undeniable proof that CutterBrown had been experimenting on werewolves.

I began skimming other subfolders. It looked as though the experiments at Van Horne had gone on for at least four years, stopping only after a test subject mysteriously vanished a year and a half ago.

"Ben. Derby must have paid a fortune to get him out." There were dozens of memos and reports detailing his disappearance—everything from a full security audit to speculation his escape had been an inside job to reported sightings of him. And there was an order to terminate the project—one that bore a horribly familiar signature.

Stephen had claimed his father had started drinking and acting strangely a year and a half ago. It looked like Ryan Walsh's behavior had changed right around the time he ordered the closure of the Van Horne project.

"Back at the strip mall, Stephen said something about his father not giving a damn about him. That he had thrown something away. He meant Van Horne." I ran a hand over the scar on my arm. Ben and Derby; Hank and me; Stephen and Mr. Walsh—why did it always come back to fathers? "Stephen knew they had been working on a cure and that his dad was the one who terminated the project."

Had the warden told him or had he found out some other way? Maybe Stephen's story about meeting Sinclair hadn't been a total fabrication. What if he had sought her out only for her to turn him against his father once she realized who he was and how she could use him?

Maybe and what if. A knot formed in my stomach. In the end, it probably didn't matter how Stephen had found out. All that did matter was what he had done afterward.

Kyle frowned as he read the last report in the folder. "They thought it was a rival company. Corporate espionage. It looks like Amy's father stopped the project because he worried there would be other security breaches, that word would get out about what they were doing."

"They must have flipped when three of their employees went to Zenith." The words were absent, automatic as my attention locked on a JPEG file. It was the only image in the folder. Feeling a flutter of trepidation, I clicked on the file.

Ben.

His blond hair had been shaved down to stubble and he was so thin that his cheekbones jutted out like sharp points. He was all hard angles and skin stretched tight. A living skeleton.

Only his eyes made him recognizable. Clear and gray, they stared out at me from the other side of the camera.

"That's how he was able to work for Amy's family for all those months without her father realizing who he was," I said softly. "He doesn't even look like the same person."

I thought of the things that had been done to Serena at Thornhill and tried to imagine those same things being done to Ben. He had been fifteen when he had gone in— younger than I was now. . . .

The last thing I wanted was to feel sorry for Amy's killer, but I did. I couldn't forgive Ben, but as I looked at the photo,

I felt a strange mixture of pity and regret.

Pushing the uncomfortable thoughts away, I forced myself to close the image and open another file. No sooner had I read the first line then the TV suddenly went out, plunging the living room deeper into shadow.

I reached for the lamp next to the couch and yanked on the pull cord. Nothing happened.

Kyle stood and crossed the room. Shivering, I followed him to the window.

Most of the windows in the apartment overlooked the back parking lot or the building next door, but you could see a slice of Elm Street from the living room. The whole block looked dark. In the distance, behind some of the buildings, I could just see the orange glow of fires.

Somewhere below, there was a tremendous smash followed by the blare of a car alarm.

"Looks like the looters ran out of places to hit downtown," said Kyle, reaching out and pulling the curtains closed as mindless whoops and cheers erupted on the street.

I burrowed down in my oversized shirt. We were probably safe—we were on the third floor and there were two locked doors between us and the street—but what about the others? Jason had the protection of the Trackers, but what about Trey and Serena and Eve?

I knew Kyle was right, that there was nothing we could do, but I wanted to be out there, looking for them.

Heart heavy, I turned away from the window and headed back to the couch. We didn't have long—just until the batteries in the laptops ran out—and we had to get through the rest of the information Amy had left.

Knowing there wasn't anything else we could be doing didn't make me feel better, but I still slipped out the first DVD and inserted the second.

The same password worked for this one, too, unlocking dozens of folders.

I opened the first one. It was filled with PDFs, spreadsheets, and documents. I clicked on a PDF at random and a file came up on the CutterBrown letterhead.

It was an internal memo about a multiple sclerosis study. I frowned at the screen, rereading one sentence over and over. "I don't understand." I highlighted it for Kyle as he crossed the room and sat next to me. "I've got to be reading this wrong. They couldn't have reduced symptoms in ninety-two percent of patients in the test group." I glanced at the date on the top of the memo. The document was fifteen years old.

I bit my lip. Lupine syndrome had only been around for twelve years and the camps for less than that. Whatever this was, it didn't seem to be related to either Van Horne or Thornhill. It was, however, weird. And Amy must have thought it was important. "If CutterBrown developed something that effective, why don't we know about it? Why doesn't the whole world know about it?"

"Maybe the effects were only temporary." Kyle leaned forward, studying the words on the screen. "Maybe the symptoms came back or their reporting methods were flawed."

I closed the memo and opened another. This one was

about a clinical trial for a bone cancer treatment, and it had a similar, unbelievably high success rate. It wasn't until I had skimmed two more files that I realized the clinical trials were all for the same drug—something called ARC42.

"It doesn't make any sense." A crease formed between Kyle's brows. "All of these diseases have completely different causes. Different symptoms. You couldn't develop a single drug that would work on all of them. If you could, you'd be a god." He reached for the computer and went back to the main list of folders.

"Arcadia." We were sitting close enough that I felt him tense. In the glow from the computer screen, Kyle's face looked ashen.

"What's Arcadia?"

He shook his head and ran a hand roughly through his hair. "It's a myth—well, it's a myth and a real place. In Greece." A siren blared outside and Kyle got up to check the window. "There are two versions," he said, staring down at the street for a long moment before coming back. "In one, Lycaon, king of Arcadia, tried to test Zeus by inviting him to a feast and serving him human flesh. As punishment, Zeus transformed Lycaon into a wolf and killed each of his fifty sons."

"Sounds like overkill. Sorry," I added quickly, "bad joke. What about the other version?"

Kyle met my gaze. His eyes looked almost black. "In the other version—in the story the packs tell—Zeus transformed Lycaon into a wolf and cursed his sons to a half-life of being neither wolf nor man. They say they were the first werewolves. Eumon, Portheus, Carteron—the Denver packs are all named for them. They say every werewolf can trace his lineage back to one of the fifty sons."

My stomach flipped. Superstrength, superspeed, super-healing—how many times had I thought that people would line up for LS if you could find a way to harness the benefits while suppressing the wolf? What if CutterBrown had been looking for a way to do just that?

Kyle opened the folder.

It was all there. The making of an epidemic.

Research notes. Genealogy charts and paths of infection. Maps with a scattering of places in the Mediterranean and Europe circled in red. Videos of a man and woman in separate cells. Resignation letters from doctors condemning the work they were doing and internal memos about the legality of the tests they were conducting.

Neither of us spoke; we just stared at the screen, trying to wrap our heads around the enormity of what we were seeing.

They had let it out.

Lupine syndrome had been in the shadows forever. A virus that had been present in a handful of places, one whose spread had been tightly controlled by the people infected. Somehow, CutterBrown had found it. They had been arrogant enough to believe they could manipulate the virus and revolutionize the history of medicine; instead, they had accidentally unleashed LS on the world.

CutterBrown hadn't just been trying to cure LS at Van

Horne; they had been trying to correct the mistake they had made.

A wave of cold swept through me. Everyone who had ever been infected, anyone who had ever died after an attack—CBP was responsible for all of them.

I looked at Kyle. If it hadn't been for CutterBrown, he and Serena would never have been infected and Amy would still be alive. If it hadn't been for CutterBrown, Stephen would never have met Sinclair and Ben might not have turned into a monster. No Trackers for Jason to join and no camps. The entire world would be different.

"This is what Sinclair and Zenith wanted. This is why they needed Stephen." My voice was hoarse. It was an effort to speak. "They thought there might be answers in the original research studies. They had Natalie Goodwin and the other researchers, but they still needed the original data."

"Thornhill is nothing compared to this." Kyle flexed his hands. "Sinclair and Zenith will tear the world apart to get their hands on this disc, and CutterBrown would probably kill us if they knew we had it. It doesn't matter how far we run: sooner or later, someone is going to catch up to us."

I pushed myself to my feet and stared down at him. The answer seemed at once both simple and terrifying. "Then we don't run. We fight back."

21

A FLOORBOARD CREAKED, BUT I DIDN'T TURN, NOT EVEN as Kyle came up behind me and placed his hands on my shoulders, a light touch that helped anchor me.

"You promised you would get a few hours of sleep."

"I promised I would try," I corrected as I stared down at the street through a gap in the curtains. Shadows moved below. Not Trackers—at least not all of them. The smash-and-grabbers were out in force.

What had started as a clash between the Trackers and the RfW had turned into a free-for-all, and it seemed like every thug and lowlife in Hemlock was hell-bent on sacking the town.

"It feels like the end of the world." I wasn't just talking about what was happening outside.

"It's not." Kyle slid his hands down my arms. "The sun will be up soon. Things will be better then."

I wanted to believe him, but I had a horrible feeling that all sunrise would bring was a clearer look at the damage.

"Come back to bed." Kyle threaded his fingers through

mine and gently tugged me away from the window.

I glanced at the couch as we crossed the living room. Kyle had insisted I get some sleep, but he had stayed out here. It was the closest spot to the apartment door and had the only view of Elm Street. It was a defensive position, a spot he could protect me from if the trouble reached our building.

I followed him down the hall and into my room.

The space had seemed strange and a little alien after I had gotten back from Thornhill—almost as though it had belonged to some other girl. It felt that way now. Like the events and betrayals of the past few hours had changed me and I no longer fit.

I sat on the edge of the bed. Kyle leaned down to brush a light kiss across my lips. "I'll be right down the hall," he promised.

I caught his hand as he turned to leave. Even back here, at the far end of the apartment, I could hear the sounds of destruction from outside. "Wait." I shivered; I had ditched my jeans before crawling into bed earlier, and I was suddenly conscious of the fact that all I was wearing was an oversized T-shirt. "Stay with me?" If someone was really determined to break into the apartment, it wouldn't matter what room Kyle was in, and I didn't want to be alone.

He hesitated, his desire to stay warring with the need to feel he was doing all he could to keep me safe. I felt something inside of me crack at the idea that he might say no.

It was like the night after I had almost died in the woods: I didn't want to close my eyes—not if I was alone.

It was weak and stupid and I hated it, but it was the truth.

Kyle cupped my cheek with his hand. "I'll be right back," he said, lightly tracing the edge of my jaw with the pad of his thumb before turning and heading down the hall.

A knot in my chest loosened.

I slipped under the sheets and scooted toward the wall, making room for him.

Kyle came back and set something on the nightstand. "I didn't want to leave the DVDs out of our sight," he explained, kicking off his sneakers. The mattress dipped under his weight as he stretched out beside me.

I shifted closer and rested my head on his chest. The werewolf-quick beat of his heart was comforting. It was strong and fast and true. It was Kyle. Everything he was.

He slipped an arm around me. "You know nothing you said is final, right? All that stuff you said about fighting." His fingers traced light, comforting patterns over my shoulder and collarbone, making me shiver when his touch grazed skin. "You can still walk away. You're not a werewolf: it's not your fight."

"Of course it is." I raised myself up on my elbow. "It involves you and Serena. That makes it my fight. Besides, after what we saw on those discs, I wouldn't be able to live with myself if I just walked away. People need to know how the epidemic started and what's been happening since."

Kyle stared up at me with an intensity that made me blush. "You're incredible. You know that, right?"

I bit my lip. "Good way or bad way?"

In answer, he pulled me down for a kiss that sent sparks racing along my skin and made things inside of me tighten and tremble.

Sirens sounded from somewhere outside, but when Kyle kissed me, it seemed possible to forget—just for a second— how completely messed up the world had become and how scared I was.

It made me want more. More than I knew how to ask for.

I needed to forget. To lose myself. It was the only way I would make it through the night.

Somehow, we switched places so that my back was to the mattress while Kyle's body covered mine. His shirt had disappeared; I couldn't recall either of us breaking apart long enough to remove it. I slid my hands over his chest and along his ribs before gently running my fingertips over the scars on his back.

Kyle moved my hand away, but I shook my head.

Those scars were part of him. They had changed everything, and at the same time, they changed nothing.

They didn't change how I felt.

Outside, the city was tearing itself apart. Suddenly, all I wanted was one good thing to hold on to. Something the horror of the past few days—the past few months—couldn't touch.

I wanted him.

"Kyle?" Warmth flooded my cheeks.

He pulled back so he could study my face. "What is it?"

"I . . ." I swallowed. I wished my life were a movie or one of those glossy TV shows where people always just seemed to know it was time to take things to the next level without awkward pauses and even more awkward words.

"Do you want to stop?"

"No!" The word was a hoarse shout that made me blush harder. I let out a shaky breath. "I want the exact opposite of stopping."

Kyle sat up and stared down at me as though I had randomly started speaking Russian.

Words tripped out of my mouth and over one another. "I mean . . . that is . . . unless you don't want to."

"Mac . . . I . . ." He shook his head.

A surprisingly sharp pang pierced my chest at the realization that Kyle really didn't want this. "It's okay," I said, voice strained as I fought to save face. I tried to tell myself that it was no big deal—so what if the world outside was ending and who cared if Kyle had done this before with someone else—but it was. It was a big deal.

Don't cry, I thought. If I cried, the humiliation of this moment would be utterly complete.

"Mac . . ."

I shook my head and turned my face to the side. I couldn't look at him.

Gently but firmly, Kyle placed two fingers against my cheek and turned my face back to him. "I want to—*believe me, I do*—but I don't have anything with me. I left my wallet at Jason's."

I stared up at him dumbly, not sure what his wallet—or Jason—had to do with anything.

"I don't have a condom," he said, and even in the

darkness, it was impossible to miss the embarrassment on his face.

"Oh!" For a second, I sagged against the mattress in relief and then I swung my legs over the side of the bed and stumbled to the closet. Kyle and I had agreed to take things slowly after we got back, but that didn't mean I hadn't thought about the possibility that something might happen. It didn't mean part of me—a big part—hadn't wanted something to happen.

I stood on tiptoe and fumbled for the small box I had stashed under a pile of old sweaters on my closet shelf. A second later, I turned, foil packet in hand. I held it out awkwardly. "I sort of made a trip to the drugstore. Just . . . y'know . . . in case."

Kyle stood and crossed the room. His jeans hung just a little too low on his hips and the closer he got, the harder it was to think.

His hand closed over mine. "And this is what you want?" He searched my face, looking for any sign of hesitation. "It doesn't have to be tonight. This won't be our only chance. I promise. Whatever happens, we'll be okay."

It was a promise we both knew he couldn't possibly make or keep.

"I want this. I want you." I had never felt more certain of anything in my life.

Slowly, with frequent stops to kiss and clumsily remove bits of clothing, we made our way back to the bed.

Kyle had done this before and I hadn't, but that didn't matter.

Each touch and every kiss was a promise that we belonged to each other. No matter what happened—tomorrow, next week, next year—we would face it together.

I had been brought up to believe that caring about people was a weakness, but loving Kyle didn't make me weak.

It made me strong.

"Not to sound totally shallow, but I always kinda thought it would be bigger." Amy crouched down and traced the letters in the granite. She was wearing a long white T-shirt over black leggings. A blue scarf was wrapped around her throat. It was the only spot of color in this washed-out land.

Everything else was gray.

The sky. The tombstones. Even the grass and the trees.

She pressed her palm flat to the stone, covering up her last name. "So now you know everything. The Walsh family legacy." She glanced at me over her shoulder. "How mad at me are you?"

Her tone was light, but worry clouded her eyes as she chewed on her lower lip. The scarf around her neck changed color, red bleeding through the blue.

I let out a slow breath. I was angry—angry at her for keeping so many secrets and at myself for not noticing how much was wrong—but what good would it do to admit that now? "I just wish you had told me what was going on."

"Me too," she admitted, pushing herself up and turning. "Even though I don't think it would have changed anything—not in the long run. I was always headed here."

"You don't believe in fate," I reminded her. She never had.

"No"—Amy tugged at the scarf and her fingertips came back stained red—"I don't. But I do believe in karma and my dad racked up one hell of a cosmic debt." As she spoke, everything around us changed. The grass became a stretch of rocky shore and the tombstones were replaced by an expanse of water so calm and still that it looked like a plate of glass.

I had been here in a dream once before. At Thornhill. The night I had almost died.

You weren't supposed to feel pain in dreams, but the scar on my shoulder ached.

I picked up a flat stone and skipped it across the water. It bounced three times and then slipped beneath the surface, all without making a single ripple. "You didn't do anything wrong. The universe didn't punish you to get back at your father. That's not how it works."

"Maybe," said Amy, "but that's how it feels. Like I was part of some sort of check and balance. Stephen, too. If it hadn't been for what CBP did, he never would have gotten infected. He wouldn't have gotten infected and he wouldn't have been taken in by Sinclair. In a way, my father lost both of us to the disease he helped unleash."

She began walking along the water's edge and I fell into step beside her.

"So now that you know everything," she said, "what are you going to do?"

"What do you want me to do?" I had already made up my mind—Kyle and I had made the decision together—but I still wanted to know. "You must have had a plan when you addressed that envelope to me and gave me the USB key. What did you think would happen?"

"Honestly?" The corners of her mouth lifted in a sad, bitter smile. "I thought Trey and I would ride off into the sunset and I'd be sending you postcards from Latin America as I tried to forget . . . everything. And I guess I sort of hoped you would be strong enough to do the things I couldn't." She paused and turned over a pebble with the edge of her shoe. "I couldn't hurt my dad. I saw what was on that hard drive and I knew how wrong it all was, but I still couldn't do anything to hurt him. And I wasn't strong enough to stand up to Stephen. Not directly. I knew that Sinclair woman was using him and that what he was doing was wrong, but I couldn't make him see that. He wanted so badly for there to be a cure. For there to be hope."

She glanced up at the sky and waited so long before speaking again that I wondered if she was going to speak at all. "I still care about my father. Is that wrong?"

"No." I didn't hesitate. "He's your dad."

"You hate your father."

"Completely different situation," I said, echoing words Jason had spoken to Stephen in the grove of twisted trees. "No matter what else your dad did or didn't do, he loved you. He loved you and he was a good father. The stuff on those DVDs doesn't change that."

She turned toward the water. "You're going to tell everyone, aren't you?"

"I have to."

"Good." The single word was surprisingly forceful.

"What happens?" I asked. "When it ends?"

"When this story ends, a new story starts. That's how it goes. How it always goes."

"Just for once, I wish you'd give me a straight answer."

"Just this once, I wish I could." She slipped her hand into mine, pressing something to my palm.

I glanced down at the compass necklace Jason had bought for her. "It's yours," I said, trying to give it back.

"I don't need it. Not where I'm going." Her eyes shimmered with tears and she scrubbed at them with the back of her hand, swearing softly. "I never was any good at goodbyes."

"I don't want you to go."

Amy started walking backward. With each step, she seemed a little lighter, like a weight was being lifted from her shoulders. She looked less like the Amy from my dreams and more like the Amy in photographs. "You can't hold on to me forever. Besides, you don't need me anymore."

"I'll always need you."

"You'll be fine. You have Kyle. And Jason. The three of you have one another." A grin split her face. "You're going to have a fantastic life, Mackenzie Dobson. You're going to have a fantastic, amazing life, and I'll be watching."

With a bright flash of light, the shore and Amy burned away.

I opened my eyes and stared up at my bedroom ceiling. Daylight slipped past the edges of my curtains and filled the room. Against all odds, I had fallen asleep.

I raised a hand to my cheek. My fingertips came back wet: I had been crying.

She was really gone.

There were times when I had hated and dreaded the nightmares—times when I would have given anything to wake from them—but part of me didn't want to let them go. I didn't want to let Amy go.

I rolled over, reaching for Kyle. The other side of the bed was empty. I ran my hand over the sheets. They were cold.

My heart gave a small, shuddery skip as I kicked my legs free of my blankets and pushed myself to my feet.

The bedroom door was closed, but I could hear the faint murmur of voices coming from the living room.

Someone else was here.

I glanced at my alarm clock. The power was still out.

I pulled open the door and practically ran down the hall, stumbling to a clumsy stop as I reached the living room.

Kyle was in the kitchen, leaning against the counter. My heart did a small flip when I saw him—one that was half relief and half exhilaration. Logically, I knew what we had done last night didn't change anything, but I felt different in a hundred small ways that I couldn't explain.

Kyle shot me a small, tired smile before nodding toward the couch.

Jason was back. My laptop was in front of him. The circles under his eyes were so dark that they looked like smudges of ink. He looked like hell, but he was clean shaven and wearing fresh clothes. My eyes locked on a black knee brace on his left leg.

"Just a precaution," said Jason, tapping the brace as he followed the direction of my gaze. "They were able to patch me up. They even gave me a lollipop for not crying."

He was all right. He was here and all right and cracking stupid jokes.

I threw myself across the living room and flung my arms around his neck.

"One night apart and you're throwing yourself at me," he said drily.

"I was worried about you, jerk," I muttered, pulling back. "We both were."

"Kyle said to let you sleep." There was an unfamiliar weight to Jason's voice, and the way he didn't quite meet my eyes as he said the words made me wonder if Kyle had told him about last night.

I knew we didn't have anything to feel guilty about, but I was suddenly very aware of my lack of pants. The extra-large T-shirt I was wearing covered more than half the dresses in my cousin's closet, but it was still just a T-shirt.

I grabbed a knitted throw from the back of the armchair and wrapped it around myself as I sat. "Kyle filled you in on what happened?" A blush immediately flooded my cheeks. "I mean about Serena and the others and what we found on the DVDs."

Jason nodded and ignored the blush. He ran a hand over his neck. "I might know where Serena and the others are. Maybe."

Kyle joined us in the living room and twined his fingers with mine as he sat on the arm of my chair.

295

"What do you mean 'maybe'?" I asked, a sinking feeling in my stomach at the tense, miserable expression on Jason's face. "Where do you think they are? What happened last night?"

"Sinclair and Donovan got away—for starters." Jason's mouth twisted around the words. "So did Stephen—after he lost control and shifted. Someone opened fire and it looked like he was hit, but he gave them the slip." He glanced toward the window. "The Trackers are keeping it quiet for now because of all the support they've been getting from Senator Walsh, but sooner or later, it'll get out. Too many people saw him before and after he shifted. If Stephen's smart, he's halfway to Mexico."

He met my gaze. "I was stuck on the north side most of the night, but the bridge opened up again around dawn. The Trackers have a medical tent set up in Riverside Square. They insisted I go get checked out. Afterward . . ." Jason's voice faltered and he shook his head. "They have more than a dozen wolves in a pen in the middle of the square—wolves they caught last night. It's supposed to prove the LSRB isn't doing enough to round up the infected."

I tightened my grip on Kyle's hand. "Serena and Trey? Eve?"

"They weren't letting anyone near the cage—not even other Trackers. And they didn't respond very well to bribery." Jason turned his head and I noticed the beginnings of a bruise rising on his jaw. "But I got close enough to see that at least some of the wolves had black fur."

"That doesn't mean any of them are Serena or Trey,"

I said, trying to sound calm and rational as my heart and mind raced.

"No . . ." conceded Jason, leaning back and reaching into his pocket. "But I found this on one of the paths leading to the middle of the square."

He pulled out a pewter charm on the end of a black leather cord. I didn't need him to turn it over to know there was a symbol etched on one side—a symbol that looked like three interlocking teardrops.

The symbol of the Eumon pack.

It was Eve's necklace.

"It gets worse," said Kyle.

With an effort, I pulled my gaze away from the charm. "How could it possibly get worse?"

"I wasn't the only one trying to get a look at the wolves in the cage," said Jason.

I stared at him, waiting.

"Sinclair was there."

22

BOTH THE MAYOR AND THE GOVERNOR HAD TAKEN TO the radio, urging people to stay in their homes and avoid downtown Hemlock. The Trackers had been quick to respond. They blamed last night's violence—and the continued power outage—on a militant group of RfW members and accused the mayor and the governor of being in the pockets of the pro-werewolf lobby. *The rally will go ahead*, they assured their followers, in some cases going door to door to get the message out. *We will not be intimidated into silence.*

As if the Trackers had ever been intimidated into anything. Jason, Kyle, and I left the safety of the apartment at 4:30 p.m.—one hour before the rally was scheduled to begin—and as we turned off Elm Street, it was clear the mayor and governor had been anything but successful in their pleas.

Hundreds of people clogged the streets—many with dagger tattoos, but plenty without. The closer we got to the downtown strip, the worse the crowds became, until I had to fight against the throng not to be separated from Kyle and Jason.

I tried to tell myself that this was a good thing. We needed Riverside Square to be as packed and chaotic as possible if we had any hope of getting near the cage in the center of the park. Still, being surrounded by this many people who would turn on us if they found out Kyle was infected or that Jason and I had werewolf sympathies made my skin crawl.

At least the crowds made it harder to take in the full scale of last night's destruction. Though I caught glimpses of burned-out buildings and cars, I couldn't linger on any one sight for more than a second or two.

The wall of people ahead of us parted, moving away from the center of the street and heading for the sidewalks as we neared an intersection. I soon saw why: the National Guard had erected a barricade across the street, blocking off all traffic.

"I don't understand." I squeezed past a man who reeked of cigars and sweat as we made our way past the barricade. "I know the Trackers said the rally was still going ahead, but don't the guards take orders from the governor or the mayor? Why block off the street but still let people through? Why not just shut everything down?"

"They don't want a fight," said Kyle, eyes sweeping the sea of faces. "Every network in the country has reporters and news crews here. If they tried to stop the rally and things turned violent . . ."

"Bye-bye reelection," finished Jason. "Besides, there's that whole pesky freedom of assembly thing."

"Wow," said Kyle, "you actually managed to stay awake for an entire civics class."

I was pretty sure freedom of assembly only applied to peaceful gatherings—something I really doubted the Trackers were capable of—but I didn't point that out as I hugged my backpack to my chest. "You do both realize this is the flimsiest plan we've ever come up with, right? I'm not even sure it qualifies as a plan."

"That's what makes it so brilliant." Jason shoved a drunk Tracker out of his way, ignoring the slurred curses that followed. Although he kept saying the knee brace was just a precaution, he walked with a noticeable limp. "Sinclair and her band of merry mercenaries would never expect us to be this stupid. It gives us the element of surprise."

"Assuming the warden is still there," replied Kyle.

"She will be." There wasn't a trace of doubt in my mind. Sinclair hadn't had any more luck getting near the cage than Jason, but that didn't mean she wouldn't try again. They couldn't know whether or not we had gotten out of town. With four black wolves in Tracker custody, the warden had to be considering the possibility that the group had gotten their hands on Serena. Werewolves had a habit of dying when the Trackers got involved, and Serena was far too valuable to risk leaving in their custody. Besides, Sinclair wanted the data Stephen had stolen from CBP and she knew we had at least some of it. We had risked everything to get Serena out of Thornhill: Sinclair had to know she could use her as bait.

We reached Main Street.

"Jesus . . ." Jason's voice—barely audible over the swelling hum of the crowd—was a mixture of trepidation and awe.

"Where did they all come from?" I knew there were hundreds of Trackers in town—maybe even thousands—but nothing could have prepared me for the sheer number of people spread out before us. They stretched for blocks.

I squinted at a nearby group. They were all carrying signs.

INFECTION DOESN'T DISCRIMINATE.

THE CAMPS DON'T WORK.

MY WIFE IS A WEREWOLF.

"They're not Trackers. . . ." My voice was a dazed murmur.

The RfW had come back. Even after last night's violence, they were here.

I slipped my backpack over my shoulder, freeing my hand so I could twine my fingers with Kyle's. Not everyone was like the Trackers; not everyone believed in the camps. Seeing the RfW protest gave me a small spark of hope.

The crowd pushed us forward.

Ten-foot-high interlocking metal fences had been placed between the sidewalks and the street, creating a sort of corral that allowed the Trackers to reach the square without walking through the pro-werewolf demonstration. The setup prevented a physical confrontation between the two groups—at least for the time being—but Trackers still hurled insults and bottles over the fence and the RfW gave as good as they got.

Under normal circumstances, the sidewalks on Main Street were wide enough for three or four people to walk abreast, but the number of Trackers trying to reach the park forced Jason to fall into step behind us. Kyle, meanwhile, stayed on my left, putting himself between me and the members of the National Guard who were stationed every few feet on either side of the fence.

One of the RfW protestors launched himself at the barricade, making it halfway up before a guard pulled him down and swung at his ribs with a baton.

"You know," said Jason from just over my shoulder, "if it wasn't for the tattoos and the homemade signs, it'd be pretty hard to tell everyone apart."

"They're not going to be able to keep control. Not for long." Though it was doubtful anyone in the crowd around us could hear him, Kyle leaned in close. "Do you think this could be why the packs sent wolves? As protection for the RfW?"

I considered it for a moment, then shook my head. "I don't think so." Protecting an RfW protest—even a protest like this—didn't seem like the sort of thing that would require maximum secrecy. It definitely didn't seem like the sort of thing Hank would keep from Eve or reason enough for him to want me out of town before the rally.

Our progress slowed to a crawl as the square came into view. There were more guards here, but they were hanging back, leaving the park completely to the Trackers. The

302

sun set early this time of year—it was already starting to dip toward the horizon—but huge lights had been set up around the square, rendering it as bright as noon. For a moment, I thought the power had come back on, and then I realized the Trackers must have brought generators.

The ever-cynic in me wondered if maybe they had caused the blackout so that they could be the only light in the darkness.

The RfW protest was big—huge, even—but the number of Trackers in the square blew them out of the water. I turned to glance back the way we had come. Hundreds of people packed the sidewalk behind us; what would happen if there wasn't enough room in the square for all of them? Apprehension slid down my spine at the thought of what that many angry Trackers might do.

It was a thought that had obviously occurred to most of the shop owners on Main Street. Almost every store was boarded up, plywood covering doors and windows like people were hunkering down for a hurricane.

A flash of movement in the gap between a sushi bar and a skateboard shop caught my eye. The crowd forced me forward, but not before I glimpsed a familiar figure.

"Mac!" Kyle called my name as I pushed my way to the alley, but I didn't stop until I was in the shadowy gulf between the two buildings.

"What is it?" asked Jason as he and Kyle caught up with me.

A flood of unpleasant memories—memories of the night a Tracker had dragged me into an alley just like this one—threatened to wash over me, but I pushed them back. My gaze slid over piles of flattened cardboard and an old box spring propped up on its end. We were the only ones here.

"I thought I saw something." I ran a hand over my eyes.

"Mac . . . ?" The voice was so soft and hesitant that I almost missed it under the noise from the street behind us.

Serena eased out from behind the box spring, eyes wide and body tense. Her shirt was torn and stained, and her face was streaked with dirt and dried blood. Her gaze darted over us as she let out a deep breath.

"I thought you were Trackers. Real Trackers, I mean," she amended, eyes flicking to Jason's neck as she folded her arms over her chest.

I slipped the backpack from my shoulder and fished around inside. In addition to copies of the information from Amy's DVDs, I had spare clothes, bottled water, and a package of baby wipes—basically everything we'd need if a werewolf shifted and then changed back.

"Here," I said gently, taking out the wipes and holding out the container. "For your face. I have clean shirts, too."

Serena stared at the package for a moment, almost like she was a little in shock, before reaching out and taking two of the disposable cloths. She passed one over her face and it came back covered in shades of gray and pink. She let it fall to the ground and then used the second cloth to clean her hands. Blood lined her cuticles and clung to the lines of her palm.

I swallowed. How had she ended up here—alone—just a block from the rally? "Where are Trey and Eve?"

Serena stared down at her hands. She was silent for a long moment, and when she finally did speak, her voice shook. "I don't know. We were almost to your apartment when this group of Trackers piled out of a truck. They wanted to know what we were doing on the street. They kept making these comments to Eve and me—really horrible stuff—and they had Tasers. It was obvious they didn't really think we were infected. . . . They just . . ." She shifted her weight uncomfortably and it wasn't hard to guess what sort of things the Trackers had said or what they might have been after. "One of them hit me and tried to get me on the ground while another went after Eve. My control slipped. . . ."

She raised her head and met my gaze. "Trey told me to run. I thought he and Eve were behind me. By the time I realized they weren't, it was too late. The Trackers had them."

I opened my mouth to tell her that it wasn't her fault, but Jason beat me to it. "If you hadn't run, you would have just gotten caught with them. It wouldn't have helped anything."

Serena's eyes narrowed. "That doesn't make me feel any better. I left my brother behind. I let him get taken."

"You're sure they didn't get away? Did you actually see the Trackers take Trey and Eve?" Kyle's voice was carefully neutral, without a hint of blame, but Serena still flinched.

"I saw the truck as it drove off," she said miserably. "I was just too far away to get to it."

I wrapped an arm around Serena's shoulders. "Why didn't you go to the apartment or call? Where have you been all this time?"

"Here. More or less." She ran a hand through her close-cropped hair. "I figured the Trackers would take Trey and Eve to the square, but after I got down here, I was trapped. Any time someone saw the blood on my clothes, they got suspicious. This is as close to the square as I've been able to get—not that I had any idea what I'd do once I got there."

I stepped away and pulled a clean, long-sleeved shirt out of my backpack. It wasn't much, but it would at least help with the clothing situation.

Serena took the bundle of fabric. She waited for both Kyle and Jason to turn and shot a nervous glance toward the mouth of the alley before quickly changing.

"What happened after the party?" she asked, rolling up the sleeves to free her hands. The shirt hung off her, but it was a definite improvement. "Did you find anything?"

I gave her the CliffsNotes version. CutterBrown, Zenith, Amy's dad, and Ben . . . I didn't say anything about Sinclair or Natalie Goodwin. I wasn't sure how to tell Serena that the women who had been responsible for her torture were both in Hemlock.

"Shit," Serena breathed.

"There's something else," said Jason, turning back around. His gaze darkened as he glanced at me. "She needs to know."

I bit my lip and nodded.

He started to reach for Serena's hand and then seemed to second-guess himself, letting his arm fall back to his side. "Sinclair is still alive. She's working with the men who showed up at your house. She was in the square

306

earlier—probably trying to figure out if you were one of the wolves the Trackers picked up."

At the mention of the warden's name, Serena went completely rigid. Her eyes widened as she absorbed Jason's words, and then a fine trembling started in her shoulders and radiated down her spine until her whole body shook.

"She's never going to let me go."

Pushing aside his hesitation, Jason took Serena's hand. "She won't have a choice."

Serena let out a strangled, mirthless laugh as she pulled away. "What makes you think anything will stop her? What makes you think she won't grab me—or any one of us—the second we set foot in the square to find Trey and Eve?"

I pulled a USB key—the same USB key Amy had given me—from around my neck. "This," I said. "The whole country believes the origin of LS is a mystery. They think Sinclair is dead and they have no idea what's really been happening inside the camps. That's our insurance policy. We'll get Trey and Eve back, and we'll use the information on this drive to throw Sinclair and Donovan so off-balance that grabbing us is the last thing on their minds."

And even if they did still come after us, even if they got us, the truth would already be out. Some secrets were too big to stay hidden.

The cage hulked in the center of the square, just below the main stage. It was large—at least twelve feet long—but not large enough for the thirty werewolves inside. Most of them were in their wolf form—too scared or too angry to hold back the shift—but six people had retained human shape.

"That's twice as many as Jason saw this morning," said Kyle.

I wondered how many of the wolves were local and if any of them had been sent here by the packs. Most towns had at least a few werewolves, but as far as I knew, Hemlock had only a handful of infected people.

We were ten yards away. The Trackers had finally started letting people near the pen and hundreds of rallygoers were clamoring for their chance to get up close and personal with "the enemy." Most had probably never seen a real werewolf—at least not knowingly.

I shivered. The temperature had dropped with the setting sun and a breeze had started to pick up. It stirred the leaves on the ground and rustled bare branches overhead.

If part of the pen's purpose was to show how terrifying wolves were, it was hard not to see it as a failure. Most of the wolves were pressed up against the back of the cage. They cringed away from the crowd, acting more like frightened dogs on the death row of an animal shelter than vicious killers.

There was only one exception. A wolf with fur the color of cinnamon threw itself against the walls of the cage over and over again, rattling the wire and baring its teeth. The moment it started to calm, a Tracker shoved a baton through the links of the cage, setting it off again.

Could any of the wolves be Stephen? Jason was sure he had gotten away, that he hadn't been injured that badly and was probably putting hundreds of miles between himself and Hemlock, but I still couldn't help wondering.

"There." Kyle pointed to the far side of the cage. "In the corner."

I squinted. In the farthest corner of the cage was a cluster of wolves with coal-black fur.

"Trey's not there." Serena's voice wavered, caught between hope and worry.

"Are you sure?" I asked.

"Positive."

My heartbeat kicked up a notch as I spotted a familiar figure walking the perimeter of the cage. Even at a distance, I had no trouble recognizing Sinclair.

Serena saw her at the same moment. I could feel the subtle shift in the air next to me as she tensed.

Even though Sinclair wasn't a Tracker, people cleared a path for her. It was like she gave off waves of authority. She held something in her hands—a computer tablet—and her gaze darted between it and the black wolves in the cage.

The entire country thought she was dead and here she was at a rally that was being covered by every major news network. She was either very desperate or incredibly arrogant. Either way, if she was here, Donovan couldn't be far. I turned in a slow circle, but with thousands of people in the square, picking out one man was impossible.

Jason appeared at Kyle's side. He whispered something, keeping his voice low so the Trackers surrounding us wouldn't hear.

Kyle said something in reply and Jason glanced at Serena. "You're sure he's not in there?"

309

"I know my brother."

Jason ran a hand over the brand on his neck. "Someone said a group of wolves were moved to the western arch. They were—"

Serena didn't wait for Jason to finish before she started pushing and squeezing her way through the crowd.

Trying to keep an eye on the blur of faces around us, I followed, Kyle and Jason on my heels.

Every so often, I spotted a camera crew. CNN, FOX, ABC. As packed as the park was, people seemed to be giving the reporters plenty of space. The fact that each crew was escorted by their own security contingent of Trackers probably helped.

Applause and cheers broke out around us as gigantic video screens flashed to life on three sides of the square: the rally was officially under way.

Each screen showed scenes from other cities where rallies were taking place: New York, Chicago, Phoenix, Seattle, Dallas—the scenes changed every few seconds.

My steps slowed as I was caught up in the sight of rallies spreading from coast to coast. What if the world had gone too far to change? What if nothing we did made a difference? The thousands of RfW members on Main Street suddenly seemed like a joke.

Jason pushed past me, trying to keep Serena in sight, strides quick despite his limp.

I stared after his rapidly retreating back until he was swallowed by the crowd.

The truth could change people—he was proof of that.

Even after he found out Kyle was infected, I think part of him still believed in the camps. I think part of him had believed right up until he saw what was happening in the detention block.

I reached up and clutched the cord around my neck. Maybe we couldn't control whether or not the world changed, but we could give people the truth and let them decide what was right and wrong for themselves.

"Mac!" Kyle grabbed my arm as the first speech of the night began. "Look!"

I turned back toward the stage in the center of the park but he shook his head. "No," he said, taking my shoulders and pointing me toward one of the video screens.

It was the rally in Atlanta. I opened my mouth to ask what was so important, but then the camera panned across the crowd.

"Hank." My father's name came out a hoarse whisper. He stood in the midst of thousands of Trackers, chanting along, acting like he was one of them. What the hell were the wolves up to?

I didn't have time to give it much thought. The camera moved away from my father, and as I pulled my gaze from the screen, I saw Donovan standing ten feet away. My pulse kicked into overdrive, and I said a quick prayer of thanks that he was looking away from us.

Kyle had already spotted him. "Come on," he said, taking my hand and forging a path through the crowd.

"No longer can we afford to wait for the government and the LSRB to protect us!" Speakers had been erected throughout the park, ensuring every person heard what was said onstage. "Werewolves are a threat to our communities, our children, and our way of life!"

"Just look at Thornhill!" shouted a woman to my left—a sentiment that was quickly picked up by others.

I tightened my grip on Kyle's hand and craned my neck as I tried to catch glimpses of the perimeter of the park. There had to be a spot where they controlled the screens and audio; we needed to know where it was.

After a moment, I spotted it: a long table covered with computers and surrounded by a yellow triangle of caution tape. It was under two sprawling elms, just a few yards to the right of one of the screens.

We needed to get there, but first we had to find Trey and Eve.

Kyle's hand suddenly convulsed around mine, squeezing so hard that I gasped. He let go at once, but he didn't look at me or apologize: all of his attention was focused forward.

I followed his gaze as a scream split the air. The cry was long and ragged and almost inhuman. It pulled the attention of everyone near us. It pulled my attention straight to the large wrought iron arch on the western edge of the park.

No.

My heart stopped and the breath froze in my lungs.

The arch had been turned into a gallows.

23

SEVEN BODIES HUNG FROM THICK ROPES. THEY WERE crowded so closely together that the breeze drifting through the square was enough to make them bump against one another.

Like wind chimes, I thought, dazed. A wave of bile rushed up my throat as Kyle pushed his way forward.

I followed on shaky legs, oblivious to the people I collided with as I made my way to the edge of the crowd.

I couldn't take my eyes off the bodies. Four were in wolf form. Three were not.

The Trackers hadn't set up many lights in this corner of the park, but there was one just a few feet from the west entrance. It lit the bodies like a spotlight.

One figure had been hung slightly higher than the others. Red hair. Small build. Cherry-red Doc Martens.

Black spots danced in front of my eyes. This wasn't real.

Be safe. That was the last thing Eve had said to me.

Despite the crowd in the park, there was a large circle of open space in front of the arch, almost as though the bodies were too much even for most of the Trackers.

The scream came again, pulling people's attention away from the stage.

Someone shoved me aside in an effort to see what was happening.

"Jesus . . ." said a female voice just as someone else asked what the hell was going on.

Clearly, not everyone in the park knew about the bodies. The western arch wasn't visible from most parts of the square, and people were focused on the giant video screens. It was possible most people at the rally didn't know what had happened.

I crossed the empty space. A tremble started in my core and grew in intensity with every step until my whole body shook. Dimly, I registered a female reporter and a cameraman standing in the shadows between two trees, but they were small blips on the edge of my consciousness.

Jason was sprawled on the ground. A trickle of blood ran from the corner of his mouth and he seemed to be having trouble pushing himself to his feet.

Normally, the sight of Jason bleeding on the ground would have sent me running straight to his side, but I spared him only a second's glance before my gaze locked on Kyle and Serena. On Trey.

Trey's body was the second to the left, right next to Eve.

Like the others, Trey had a rope around his neck, but that wasn't what had killed him. The front of his shirt was torn in a dozen places and stiff with dried blood. He had been shot. More than once.

There was more dried blood on his hands and face. Dark patches against his dark skin. His eyes were open but completely devoid of everything that had made him . . . *Trey*.

How long had he been here, like this? An hour? Two? Long enough for the blood to dry. Long enough for the muscles in his body to begin to stiffen.

The body jerked and swayed in a sickening dance as Kyle tried to pull Serena away.

For a moment, I thought she was trying to haul her brother down, but then I realized she was supporting his weight, trying to push him up. It was what you saw people do on TV when someone tried to hang themselves. They lifted the weight so the other person could breathe. But Trey didn't need breath. Not anymore.

Kyle managed to pull one of Serena's hands free and she shoved him. Hard.

That explained how Jason had ended up on the ground.

Angry rumbles started in the crowd behind us.

"Serena . . ." I approached her slowly, hands held up. I swallowed as my vision blurred. "I'm sorry—*I'm so sorry*—but there's nothing—"

"I'm not leaving him like this." The words were a snarl as the rumbles in the crowd turned to shouts.

"Wolf lover!"

"Fleabag!"

"Hang her up next to him if she cares so much!"

I turned toward the words. So far, only a small portion of the Trackers in the park were aware of us, but more were drifting this way. I scanned the growing number of faces, looking for any sign of Sinclair or Donovan.

Kyle moved in front of us, placing himself between us and the crowd as Jason climbed unsteadily to his feet and went to his side.

"Boost me up."

Kyle looked at him like he was crazy. "What about your leg?"

"Just boost me up," repeated Jason, hauling a Swiss army knife from his pocket as he backed toward the arch.

With a nervous glance at the crowd, Kyle followed. He laced his fingers together and squatted down so Jason could step onto his hands, then lifted him up.

Jason made an unsteady grab for the rope holding Trey, and Serena caught her brother's weight as he sawed through the rope.

Tears streamed down her cheeks as she stretched Trey out on the ground. She looked small and lost—even more lost than she had looked in the detention block at Thornhill. A horrible, keening sob came from deep within her chest as she tried to smooth out the wrinkles on her brother's bloodstained shirt.

Careful, Dobs, Trey's voice drifted back to me through the fog of memory. *Nice girls aren't supposed to worry about guys like me.*

Even though I was outside, it felt like there wasn't enough air. I hauled in deep breath after deep breath and it wasn't enough.

The packs had sent wolves to the rallies; where the hell were they? They couldn't all be in the cage. Surely some of them had been in the park when this had happened. Why hadn't they stopped this?

I thought of the image I had seen of Hank in Atlanta and felt a flash of hate so deep that it sliced me to the core. If he had been here with Eve instead of sending her to Hemlock on her own . . .

You know this is your fault, too, added a little voice in the back of my head. *Trey and Eve are dead because you wanted to stay and look for the truth instead of leaving town when you had the chance.*

"Mutt lovers!"

I looked up just in time to see Kyle deflect a beer bottle aimed at Serena.

"Mac! Give me a hand!" Jason had climbed onto the top of the arch and was struggling to maintain his balance as he cut Eve down.

My stomach lurched as her body fell toward the ground.

I caught her clumsily, tripping and falling with her weight. I fought to hold on while every fiber of my body tried to recoil at the touch of her rigid body and dead flesh.

Eve's head fell back and hit the pavement with a dull crack.

It's because they broke her neck, I thought as a wave of dizziness washed over me.

That wasn't all they had done: like Trey, her shirt was caked in old, dried blood.

My stomach rolled. Werewolves could heal almost any wound and could mend practically any bone. Hanging a werewolf might not guarantee death—even if the neck was broken. They had hanged Eve and Trey and then shot them as insurance.

The ground was cold underneath me, but not as cold as Eve's skin.

I caught a flash of movement out of the corner of my eye and glanced up. The reporter and her cameraman were edging closer, trying to get a better shot of Serena cradling her brother's body. My first instinct was to grab the camera and smash it, to keep them from using Eve and Trey as some sort of sick entertainment, but then I realized that I wanted them to film this. I wanted people to see what the Trackers were capable of. I wanted them to see the lives the Trackers destroyed.

Three men with daggers on their necks broke away from the crowd. Jason lowered himself from the arch, wincing as he put too much weight on his bad leg, and then walked forward to intercept them.

"What the hell is wrong with you, Sheffield?" The leader of the trio, a man in a *Hunt or be Hunted* hoodie, put a hand on Jason's chest and shoved. He looked like the kind of guy you found scoring drugs on street corners. "You coming to the rescue of fleabag lovers now?"

"That's her brother." There was a low, dangerous undercurrent to Jason's voice. "Infected or not, he's still her family."

Kyle stepped forward to back him up, but Jason gave a barely perceptible shake of his head.

"That doesn't mean you had to cut him down," continued

the man. "Every one of those fleabags deserves to be up there." His eyes narrowed as his gaze slid from Jason to Serena. "Looks to me like maybe you're starting to feel sorry for them."

Jason shrugged and turned his back on the trio. "Maybe I am."

"We're not finished." The man grabbed Jason's shoulder to spin him around, and Jason came out swinging.

Jason had gotten the crap beaten out of him plenty of times, but almost always when drunk. When he was sober, he didn't pull punches and he was quick on his feet. Even with his injured leg, he was more than capable of taking care of himself.

His first punch took the man on the jaw. A second punch to the gut and the man folded to his knees.

The man's friends started forward but one look at Kyle and they froze.

Jason reached out and grabbed a fistful of hair. He pulled the Tracker's head up, forcing him to look at the bodies still hanging from the arch. "You think this helps anyone? You think this makes a single reg safer?" He yanked up again, harder. "Do you really think they deserved this? For being infected? For an accident they couldn't control?"

He let go so suddenly that the man fell onto his side.

"You're going to pay for this. You'll—"

Before he could get another word out, Jason kicked him so hard that he flipped over onto his back and retched.

Pain twisted Jason's face as he fought to keep his leg

from buckling underneath him, but a split second later, a tight smile tugged at his lips, a smile that said the pain had been worth it.

Jason stared down at the man for a moment as Kyle went to his side, then he shifted his gaze to the semicircle of Trackers that had formed around us. "Anyone else want to try?"

No one moved, but no one turned away, either.

I glanced over my shoulder, to the street beyond the arch. The National Guard was staying out of the square, but they had erected a barricade and what looked like some sort of command center on the corner. They weren't letting anyone in or out of the park on this side.

Disgust and hate flooded my chest. Their command post was within full view of the arch. They must have seen what was happening. Werewolves didn't have legal rights; their deaths apparently hadn't been worth risking a confrontation over.

How could people call wolves monstrous when regs were capable of standing by and watching something like this?

I forced myself to focus. I could give in to the fury and despair washing over me later. For now, I had to push it into a box.

The National Guard's barricade cut off our nearest escape route. We were trapped between a wall of armed men and the thousands of Trackers occupying the park.

It wouldn't take long for news of a wolf-related disturbance to reach Donovan and Sinclair. As insane as it was, I was more scared of them than the Trackers. I had to cut the legs out from under them before they found us.

I pulled Eve's pewter charm from my pocket. I had brought it to give back to her—I just hadn't let myself consider the possibility that we would find her like this.

As gently as I could, I lifted her head and slipped the charm around her neck. Eve cared about the Eumon more than anything. Even in death, I knew she would want the charm to stay with her.

"Be safe," I whispered.

Tears filled my eyes as I climbed to my feet. I brushed them away roughly. There was something I had to do.

"Kyle?" Nerves made my voice a rough croak.

He backed up slowly, not taking his eyes off the Trackers—most of whom were focused on Jason.

"I'm going to the AV booth."

It was enough to pull his full attention. He turned to me, a firestorm in his dark eyes. "What? Mac—no."

I wrapped my hand around the USB key. "One of us has to. Sinclair and Donovan are in the square and who knows how many men they have with them. If they catch us before one of us can do this, or if the Trackers round us up . . ."

Then we were lost. We were lost and the truth would be lost with us.

We couldn't let that happen.

"I'll go." Kyle reached for the drive, but I stepped out of reach.

"I can't protect Jason and Serena. You can."

"Mac, I can't just let you—"

"You have to. I need to do this. We need to see this

through." He opened his mouth to argue and I cut him off. "You can't always be there to protect me." Just like I had to realize I wouldn't always be able to protect him—no matter how hard I tried. I could hear Serena crying behind me and each sob was the twist of a knife. Leaving them felt like running away, but I didn't have a choice. *"Please,* Kyle. I need you to look after them and get them out of the park. Head for the east entrance and get them to the RfW protest—they'll be safer there. You can do that. I can't. You have to let me go."

I didn't need his permission, but I did need him to understand. I couldn't do what had to be done unless I knew he would protect Jason and Serena. Already, the decision was tearing me in two.

The Adam's apple in Kyle's throat jutted out as he swallowed roughly. He knew one of us had to get to the AV booth and that I was the logical choice—he just didn't like it. Almost fiercely, he said, "I'll get them out of the park and meet you there." I knew how much the words—the decision—cost him: it was written across his face. "Wait for me at the booth. I promise I'll meet you there."

I pressed a quick kiss to his lips. Then, before either of us could change our mind, I ran for the wrought iron fence that encircled the park, following it in order to give the Trackers near the arch a wide berth.

I thought I heard Jason shout my name, but I didn't look back. If I looked back, I wouldn't be strong enough to leave.

Dead leaves crunched under my feet as I ran. The noise made me feel disturbingly conspicuous, and because of it, it took me several minutes to realize I was being followed.

I whirled, expecting the warden or Donovan's henchmen. Instead, I came face-to-face with the reporter from the arch.

She was alone, her cameraman nowhere in sight. Her tailored blazer and designer jeans made her stand out from the rest of the people in the park, but on closer inspection, the seam of her jacket was torn at one shoulder and the knees of her jeans were stained with something dark. Mud or blood—it was impossible to tell in the shadows.

"Why are you following me?"

She tucked a strand of honey-blond hair behind her ear, her fingers quick and impatient. I recognized her, I realized. Her name was Sandy Price. She usually covered war zones and protests in the Middle East—big, dangerous stories.

"Because you knew the wolves hanging from the arch," she said. "At least two of them."

"So?"

She crossed her arms and glanced around nervously. Most of the Trackers were sticking to the brightly lit parts of the square and we were off the beaten path. "I thought you deserved to know how they died."

I didn't bother trying to hide the suspicion on my face. "Why would you care?"

"Because someone needs to know. Because they did a brave thing and ended up dying for it."

Something inside of me twisted.

A Tracker strode by within earshot. Sandy Price waited until he had passed before speaking again. "Some of the wolves in the cage were in bad shape. Maybe dying. A few hours ago, your friends helped overpower the guards when they opened the cage door to transfer more prisoners. They had enough time to escape, but they were trying to get the injured wolves out."

I put a hand on the fence, gripping the cold iron in an effort to steady myself. Of course Eve and Trey wouldn't have left people behind. I remembered how angry Eve had been when my father ordered her to leave Thornhill, how she had refused to turn her back on the wolves inside.

The reporter wasn't finished. "The guy your friend cut down yelled at the redhead to run. He tried to buy her time, but she wouldn't leave him."

Trey and Serena will be fine. I promise I'll take care of them. . . .

I squeezed my eyes shut and tried to swallow back a wave of emotion. I wanted to ask the reporter if she had seen the hanging, but I couldn't. I wanted to think of Trey and Eve fighting and refusing to go down, not scared shitless as the ropes were placed around their necks.

When I opened my eyes, Sandy Price was watching me intently. "I'd like to talk to you when this is over," she said. "I'd like to help you tell their story."

I bit my lip. "Why?"

"Because any time something like this happens—and it happens more than people think—Trackers pass it off as the unsanctioned actions of a handful of members. That's what they're already saying happened here. They're claiming a few men took matters into their own hands after your friends attacked." A gust of wind swept through the park, whipping her hair around her face. "People give the Trackers free rein because they're so scared of everything they've been told about werewolves that they see the group as the lesser of two evils. What happened today isn't the lesser of anything. Your friends were trying to help people and they got killed for it. It was an evil act by evil people."

There was something oddly fierce in the way she said the last two words. "Who did you lose?"

Wariness crept into her expression. "Excuse me?"

I shot a nervous glance back at the arch, but we were too far away to see what was happening. I prayed Kyle had gotten Jason and Serena away, that they were all right.

I turned back to the reporter. "The way you talk about the Trackers—it's personal."

A shadow of pain slid behind her eyes. "My fiancé. When we were in college. Trackers found out he was infected and dragged him out of our apartment."

It was possible she was lying, but I didn't think so.

I slipped my backpack from my shoulders and reached inside for a DVD. It wasn't an exact copy of the information Amy had left us—we had stripped out anything we thought might help people duplicate the projects at Van Horne and Thornhill—but it was enough to be utterly damning.

I found a scrap of paper and a pen. Hastily, I scribbled my email address and tucked it inside the DVD case. I didn't know if I would make it through the night, but she was right: Trey and Eve deserved to have their stories told.

"You want a story?" I handed her the DVD. "Keep an eye on the screens and find a way to watch this."

A crease appeared between her brows. "What is it?"

"The story of a lifetime."

Before she could ask anything else, I walked away. Time was running out.

24

THE PRESS OF BODIES MADE ME CLAUSTROPHOBIC. CHEERS and shouts rang in my ears and the too-bright lights made my eyes water. A pro-Tracker band had taken the stage and their music whipped the already chaotic crowd into a frenzy. I was jostled and spun so many times that only the giant video screens kept me from completely losing my bearings.

Never forget the beast that stalks the night.

Remember your duty. Stand with your brothers and fight.

I wondered how long it had taken them to come up with lyrics that rhymed.

Someone hit me from the side. I crashed into the people directly in front of me and was pushed roughly back. I couldn't keep my balance. The crowd shifted and I slammed into the ground.

A foot collided with my stomach as someone tripped over me. The air rushed from my lungs. Retching, I tried to push myself to my feet.

"Whoa there—" Huge hands grabbed my arms and pulled me up. A Tracker with whiskey on his breath and a battered leather jacket tried to steady me. He would have been handsome—if it hadn't been for the bloodshot eyes and the tattoo on his neck. "You okay, sweetheart?"

I twisted out of his grasp.

"I'm not going to hurt you," he said, brows knitting as he raised his voice to be heard over the music. There was a small cluster of scars above his right eye. *From a broken bottle,* I thought. I had seen scars like that before.

"I just want to make sure you're all right," he said. "This is no place for a girl to be wandering around by herself."

"I'm not by myself," I lied. The music faded as a speaker took the stage. "I'm helping with the audiovisual stuff. I'm on my way there now."

The man scratched what looked like a three-day goatee. "Yeah," he said thoughtfully. "Knew I recognized you. You're the one that chick was looking for."

I swallowed. "Someone was looking for me?"

"Yeah. Some woman with a death grip on a computer tablet. It was like she thought I was going to steal it."

"There you are." The familiar voice slid through me like a blade, coming out of nowhere and gutting me on the spot. "We've been looking all over for you."

Sinclair placed a hand on my arm, digging her fingers in so hard that I winced. Her hair was pulled back in an immaculate twist and she was wearing the same trench coat she'd had on last night—though she had added a scarf to hide any trace of her scars. The harsh lights in the square made her look older. Closer to fifty than thirty. The sickly sweet scent of lavender drifted off her skin and clogged the back of my throat. How I had ever managed to smell that scent in Stephen's car and not be suspicious was a complete mystery. I tried to pull free, but couldn't break her grip. She might be a few days away from being a werewolf, but anger gave her plenty of strength.

"Now, Mackenzie," she said as she pulled me deeper into the crowd, "you and I are going to have a nice, productive chat." Her tone was polite—friendly, even—but her mouth twisted around each word, and her blue eyes were as cold and heartless as a winter's sky.

Flashbacks slammed into me, throwing me right back to Thornhill and the night of the escape. The night I had very nearly lost everything. The night I had almost died.

I struggled against the warden's grip as the Tracker who had come to my rescue just moments before trailed behind us. "Is everything all right here?" he asked, a group of friends at his back.

I opened my mouth to say no, but Sinclair cut me off. "This isn't any of your concern. Just go back to enjoying the rally."

The man hesitated, his gaze sliding first to me and then to the hand on my arm. "Looks like the girl doesn't especially want to go with you."

A flicker of movement in the crowd caught my eye. Donovan was making his way toward us, two men at his heels. They were still several yards away; if they reached us, it would all be over. They would use me to get to Serena and Kyle and Jason. They would search me and find the USB key and the DVDs and nothing I could say would make them believe I didn't have the hard drive—or at least know where it was.

Hatred—more hatred than I ever would have thought myself capable of—welled up inside me as I stared at Sinclair. Maybe she had started out with good intentions, but everything she had done was twisted and evil. How many wolves had died for her crazed mission? How many infected people had burned in that transition house just so she could continue her search? Infection hadn't changed her—if anything, it had made her worse.

There won't ever be an end to it, I realized. *There won't ever be an end to it and we won't ever be safe.* Even if I managed to get away—even if we spilled every last secret on Amy's DVDs—we would never be sure that Sinclair wasn't out there. Waiting for us.

It would never be over.

She would never stop and we would never be free.

Unless I put a stop to it. Here and now.

The Tracker with the goatee was still watching us. For a second, I hesitated. I thought of the wolves hanging from the western arch and of what the crowd might do to someone who was infected, but then I reminded myself of everything Sinclair had done to Serena, everything she would still do if given the chance. There was only one way we would ever be safe.

"She's infected!" My voice carried over the crowd.

Five yards away, Donovan and his men froze.

Sinclair twisted my arm. "No more games, Mackenzie. The more you fight now, the more things will hurt later."

Things are going to hurt, all right, I thought, reaching up with my other hand and pulling the scarf from around Sinclair's neck, revealing the tail end of her scars. "See? She's infected! She's one of them!"

Startled, Sinclair loosened her grip just enough for me to break free. She pulled back her hand to strike me, but the Tracker with the goatee was suddenly between us.

He deflected the blow easily as two of his friends grabbed Sinclair. He studied the scars on the warden's neck and then glanced back at me. "You sure, sweetheart?"

I nodded. "I saw her get attacked last month. Check under her collar. There are more scars."

"She's lying." Wisps of Sinclair's hair came free as she struggled against the men holding her. "She has werewolf sympathies."

She tried to shy away as the Tracker reached forward. He pulled aside the collar of her coat, revealing scars that were much worse than the ones that had been hidden beneath the scarf. Sinclair's pale skin looked like candle wax that had melted and cooled. The scars were thick and messy and obviously the work of a werewolf.

More Trackers drew near. Someone in the crowd recognized her. "Holy shit. That's the warden from that camp in Colorado!"

One of the men restraining the warden lost his hold, just for a second, and she raked his face with her fingernails. The man stumbled back, a hand clamped to his bleeding cheek, his eyes wide and terrified.

"She's not contagious yet!" I raised my voice to be heard

over the confusion, but the man turned and ran.

Donovan and his men watched the scene unfold and then melded back into the crowd. I guess their loyalty didn't extend to taking on a mob of Trackers. Either that or they knew there was no chance of recovering Sinclair.

The Tracker with the goatee pulled a gun from the small of his back as more men got the warden under control.

I swallowed as Sinclair cursed me. "What are you going to do with her?"

"Take her to the cage. Don't worry," he added, holding the gun with practiced ease as Sinclair ranted and shouted empty threats, "this is just in case she gets out of hand again."

I wasn't sure if I believed him—not after seeing the arch and not after the warden had just clawed a Tracker—but I wasn't sure if I cared. Sinclair had done truly horrible things and part of me—maybe a larger part than I wanted to acknowledge—felt like she deserved whatever she had coming to her.

I shivered. Maybe I was more my father's daughter than I liked to admit.

I watched until the warden and the Trackers were swallowed by the crowd before turning and heading for the AV booth. Donovan and his men may have allowed Sinclair to be taken, but that didn't mean they were through with us. They worked for Zenith, not the warden.

The trek to the AV table took only minutes.

Given all the money being spent on the rally, I would have expected something a little more high-tech than a handful of computers on a folding table manned by three guys and a girl who looked barely older than I did. I would have at least expected a few Trackers positioned around for security, but there was no one to stop me as I lifted the yellow caution tape surrounding the area and ducked inside.

"No civilians," said the girl without looking up from her screen. The shadows under the trees were dark, but her computer lit her face with a ghostly glow.

"I work for the Walsh family."

"Senator Walsh isn't speaking tonight," said one of the others—a man with a blond ponytail, ratlike face, and lightning-bolt earring.

"I know." I walked around the table so I could get a look at the monitors. The girl snapped her laptop shut so fast you'd think she was reading state secrets. She shot me a nervous, twitchy glance and ran a hand over her neck. I frowned and blinked: the edges of her tattoo were smudged.

"If you know," said the guy with the ponytail, pulling my attention away, "why are you here?" Before I could answer, he raised his voice. "Chrissie, we lost the Chicago cameras. Call them and find out what happened. Tom—swap the Chicago feed with the one from Kansas City until we get the cameras back online. So," he said, and it took me a second to realize he was speaking to me again, "what do you want?"

"Since the senator couldn't be here, the family put together a video memorial for their daughter." I slipped the USB key from around my neck and then hesitated.

What I was about to do would more than destroy

CutterBrown and Zenith: it would destroy Amy's father. Was I really prepared for that?

Yes, I realized, pulling in a deep breath. I would do anything to keep what had happened to Serena from happening to anyone else. I remembered what Kyle had said to me last night: *sometimes the right thing doesn't feel right at all.*

I handed the USB key over.

"No one said anything about this."

I shrugged. "They just told me to deliver it."

Grumbling, he plugged it into his computer and then double-clicked the one file it contained: Amy_Walsh_Memorial.

A series of photos faded in and out. Amy as a little girl. Amy in a kayak. Amy shoving a snowball down Jason's back. If I strained my ears, I could just make out Taylor Swift coming from the computer's speakers.

"This thing is almost six minutes long."

"There were a lot of pictures her family wanted to include, and since Senator Walsh has been such a strong supporter of the rally . . ." The words tumbled easily from my lips. All that time I had spent pretending to be infected in Thornhill had helped my lying skills.

The guy closed the media player, then dragged the video into another window before turning in his swivel chair and handing me back the USB drive. "We'll run it after this speech. Is anyone here to introduce it?"

I shook my head. "The rest of the family thought it would be too difficult to attend."

The man let out a noncommittal grunt and scrawled

something on a piece of paper. He handed the note to the girl with the strange temporary tattoo. "Run this over to the stage. Let them know there's been a change in the lineup and get them to intro the clip."

He glanced back at me. "Anything else?"

"How long until it airs?"

"Ten minutes. Maybe a little longer if the guy speaking right now runs over."

"Ten minutes." I swallowed and nodded. "Okay."

It was enough time for me to get to the RfW protest, but how could I be sure the others had made it there? Kyle was supposed to meet me at the booth. Since he hadn't . . .

Panic locked around my chest like a vise.

What if the Trackers had taken them? What if they were strung up somewhere or lying dead with bullet wounds to their chests? What if Donovan had gotten to them and they were in the back of a van on their way to another detention block?

What if . . . ? What if . . . ? What if . . . ?

As long as I'd had the video clip to deliver, I had been able to keep most of my fear at bay. Now my task was done, and the dam holding all that fear in check was starting to crack.

I pushed the panic aside: I needed to think, and I couldn't do that if I fell to pieces.

"Do you have cameras set up around the square?"

"Of course."

"Do you have one covering the west entrance to the park?"

"You mean where they strung up the wolves?" He turned back to his computer and clicked through windows until a live feed came up. "We have a camera there, but the bigwigs told us not to run footage from it."

The picture wasn't great: The angle was high and strange and the whole thing wobbled as though the camera was shaking. Shadows made it impossible to pick out much beyond the arch itself. My stomach rolled. Two unmoving forms were still stretched out beneath the arch—Trey and Eve—but there was no sign of Kyle, Serena, or Jason.

Good, I told myself. *That has to be good.*

"Some shit went down over there about twenty minutes ago," said the guy, "couldn't tell what happened, but it died down pretty quick."

Without replying, I ducked under the tape and pushed my way back into the crowd.

Kyle had promised to meet me here. Something had to have happened.

Whatever it is, he's all right. They're all right. I said the words over and over under my breath like a prayer.

Anything else wasn't possible.

25

I FOUGHT MY WAY THROUGH THE PRESS OF PEOPLE, HEAD-ing for the western arch in the hope I could somehow track the others from there. It wasn't a great plan—it wasn't a plan at all—but I didn't know what else to do.

I kept glancing at the screens along the sides of the park. One was still broadcasting scenes from other rallies, but the other two were showing the stage in the center of the square. I had been warned the speaker might go over, and he didn't show any signs of slowing down.

"Are you tired of being afraid?"

"YES!" roared the crowd.

"Do you want to take back our communities?"

"YES!"

The chorus of consent was deafening, and each resound-ing "yes" made me flinch.

The arch came into sight as the crowd around me thinned. My pulse thundered in my ears as my eyes passed over the bodies and the area around the entrance. Just like on the computer monitor, there was no sign of Kyle or Jason or Serena.

A patch of nearby shadow moved and I caught a glimpse of broad shoulders and blond hair.

"Jason?" I started forward and then froze as Stephen stepped out of the darkness.

I turned to run, but he was faster.

He grabbed my arm, holding it far more tightly than Sinclair had, holding it tightly enough that it felt like it would snap.

I opened my mouth to yell for help, but something hard and solid dug into my ribs. Without looking down, I knew it was a gun. It seemed strange, somehow: why bother with a gun when you could kill—had killed—with your bare hands?

"Don't even think about screaming."

I tried to swallow past the sudden lump in my throat. "Stephen, what are you doing here? We thought . . . we figured . . . Why are you still in town?"

"Where else was I going to go?" The stale smell of alcohol rode his breath and flipped my stomach. His eyes were vacant, empty. "The Trackers are here to protect everyone from the monsters. That's what I am, isn't it? I'm a monster, aren't I?"

I didn't answer and he pressed the gun more firmly against my ribs. "Aren't I?" he asked again, his voice a growl.

I shook my head. "You're not a monster, Stephen." As much as I wanted to hate him for betraying us and working with Sinclair, he wasn't evil. Selfish, definitely, but not evil.

"You'd say anything right now." His voice was as flat as the expression in his eyes.

I didn't try to break free as he pulled me along the outskirts of the square: it was all I could do just to keep my footing. A few people shot us curious glances, but no one seemed to notice the gun or my distress. There were thousands of people in the park, but not a single witness. "What do you want, Stephen?"

"Just to talk."

He steered me toward the northeast corner of the square, to the row of concrete chess tables. As crowded as the park was, the shadow-filled corner was deserted.

Stephen let go of my arm so suddenly that I stumbled and had to catch myself against one of the tables.

He could shoot me right now. The thought sent a wave of adrenaline crashing through me and was almost enough to make me run. The only thing that stopped me was the knowledge that I'd only make it a few feet before the first bullet hit.

I didn't want to believe Stephen could hurt me, but after watching him stand by while Donovan had practically drowned Jason, seeing the emptiness in his eyes now, I couldn't be certain.

"Sit," said Stephen, gesturing with the gun, "and keep your hands on the table."

I sat, spine ramrod straight and palms pressed flat to the concrete table's checkered surface.

"We came here, once. Do you remember?" Stephen slid into the seat opposite me. He had changed his clothes

339

sometime during the past twenty-four hours, but his eyes were bloodshot and a day's worth of stubble covered his jaw. He rested one hand on the table but kept the other hand, the hand with the gun, out of sight.

"I remember," I said. I pressed my fingers to the table. "Amy wanted to learn how to play, so you took us here. You said"—I swallowed; it was oddly difficult to get the words out—"you said playing in the park was better than playing inside."

Stephen's gaze roamed over the black-and-white squares as though watching a game in progress. "You picked it up so quickly, but you never won. You hated sacrificing your pieces." He raised his eyes to mine. Some of the horrible emptiness had left their blue depths. "I didn't expect you to be here, you know. I never wanted to involve you in any of this."

I had already been involved. I had been involved from the moment Ben had killed Amy, but I didn't say anything.

Stephen passed his hand over his eyes. He looked tired. So tired. "Where are the DVDs, Mac?"

My hands shook on the table. "Why? So you can turn around and give them to Sinclair?" I didn't add that Sinclair was currently in the loving care of a bunch of Trackers.

"Maybe. If she's still willing to talk after last night. If not, I'll find someone else. Someone at Zenith or another company."

I stared at Stephen, desperately searching for some sign of the boy I once knew. "I don't understand. You know what she was doing. You know she was torturing people. Why would you want to help her?"

"Because she's my best chance of not being this way."

"There are worse things than being infected," I said, voice low and careful.

"Easy to say when you're human," he shot back. His gaze slid to a spot just behind my shoulder. "Kyle's infected. Ask him if he wouldn't do the exact same thing in my place."

"I wouldn't."

My breath caught in my throat at the sound of Kyle's voice. I wanted to turn, but I didn't dare take my eyes off Stephen. "He has a gun," I said, voice as calm and level as I could manage. Why were people always pointing guns at me? "Stephen, you're not like Sinclair or Donovan. You're a good person. You don't have to help them."

His gaze cut back to me. "You think helping them is something only a bad person would do?" The look in his eyes was sharp and direct. "Grow up, Mackenzie. You talk about Sinclair like she's evil. Do you have any idea how many wolves die in the camps every month? Fighting, food shortages, overzealous guards, suicides . . . what Sinclair is doing is a few drops in a very large bucket and it at least serves a purpose. A few lives to save thousands. Are you telling me you'd never sacrifice one life for another?"

My stomach churned as I considered his words. Was that what I had done when I turned Sinclair over to the Trackers? Sacrificed her life for ours? Yes, maybe, but it had been self-preservation. Sinclair had gone after us, leaving me no choice. Stephen was talking about the death of innocent people. Dozens, even hundreds of them. Maybe it was tempting to look at people like they were part of an equation, but once you started down that slope, where did you stop?

When I didn't answer, he glanced at Kyle. "Mac can't understand. She's human. But you can't tell me that part of you doesn't know it's worth it."

"It's not." Kyle's voice sounded a little closer. "I've seen what Sinclair was doing to people—what she'll keep doing. Letting her get away with it so I can have my shot at happiness would make me more of a monster than LS ever could."

"You really don't get it. Either of you." Stephen ran a hand through his blond hair, leaving it a tousled mess. He looked angry and a little lost and suddenly terribly young. "It's about the greater good."

"The greater good?" I started to rise from the table and froze as he tensed. "Do you know what was in those files Sinclair had you steal? Did you know that CutterBrown unleashed the epidemic?"

Stephen closed his eyes, just for a second. "Yes."

I chanced a nervous glance over my shoulder. Kyle was standing just behind me. To his left, I could see one of the video screens. It was still showing the speaker onstage with no indication of when—or if—they would get to Amy's memorial video.

I turned back to Stephen. "Your father and the people he worked with helped create this world. And I'm sure they told themselves the same thing, that what they were doing was for the greater good, that they'd cure cancer and MS, and a dozen different things—all while turning a profit. And later? When they tortured wolves at Van Horne? I'm

342

sure they told themselves that they were just putting things right, just fixing their mistakes. The thing no one seems to understand is that if you have to constantly tell yourself that what you're doing is for the greater good, then what you're doing is probably neither good nor great." Slowly, muscles aching from the tension coursing through me, I folded my arms across my chest, hugging myself tightly like I could somehow hold myself together while emotions threatened to pull me apart. "The wolf who killed your sister? He did what he did, in part, because he was infected and then tortured in Van Horne. Your father's company helped create the monster who killed Amy. Tell me how anything about that can possibly be good."

As I stared at him across the table, Stephen's face changed. It became colder and harder, less like the boy I had known and more like a cornered animal. "You're lying."

"Do you really think Mac would lie about Amy?" asked Kyle, voice hard.

As he spoke, the first strains of a delicate love song drifted through the square. A heartfelt voice singing about a doomed affair wasn't exactly what you expected to hear at a massive anti-werewolf rally, and the melody drew Stephen's eyes to the nearest video screen.

He pushed himself to his feet and took several steps forward, the gun hanging loosely in his hand.

I twisted in my chair.

Images of Amy—more than a dozen in all—flashed across every screen in the park. When the last picture faded, text took its place. Statistics outlined the progress of the LS epidemic from a few hundred cases in the beginning to the thousands of new cases reported this year.

The text had been Jason's idea. *Trackers aren't the brightest bunch*, he had said. *You have to help them connect the dots.* Even though the clips were mostly for the benefit of the dozens of news networks covering the rally, I hadn't argued.

The statistics faded out.

The lupine syndrome epidemic began with CutterBrown Pharmaceuticals—a company based in Hemlock—which unleashed the virus. Files flashed across the screen. A moment later, they were replaced with another line of text. *They went on to conduct illegal and unethical medical experiments on werewolves inside Van Horne rehabilitation camp. Experiments continued at Thornhill by Zenith Pharmaceuticals and Warden Winifred Sinclair.*

Stephen turned and stared at us, horror-struck. A scream pulled his attention back to the screen. Larger than life, a teenage girl—a girl who looked like the kind of wholesome teen you'd want babysitting your kids on a Saturday night—filled the screen. The camera panned out as she was forced onto a metal table with steel wrist and ankle restraints. She cried and begged as she was strapped down.

A man in a white coat walked forward with a heavy metal bar. As the girl sobbed and pleaded, he brought the bar down on her legs. Once. Twice. Three times until her legs were broken, misshapen things.

The clip was eerily similar to one we had seen of Serena at Thornhill.

A woman walked forward to inspect the damage as the

girl whimpered and writhed. Finally, after what seemed like an eternity, the girl transformed into a large, brown wolf.

Natalie Goodwin—the woman who had singled Serena out at Thornhill, the woman who had once worked with Ryan Walsh—turned to the camera. "Time to shift: two minutes, twelve seconds."

The clip ended.

It wasn't all the information; it didn't need to be. It just had to be enough to get people talking, to get the reporters covering the rally to dig into CutterBrown and Zenith. It had to be enough to let Donovan and Zenith know that their secret was out. They could come after us, they could try to make another grab for Serena, but people would be watching. It was the story of a lifetime and every reporter in the square—every network in the country—would be chasing it.

Stephen stared at the now-blank screen. It was almost like he had forgotten about us.

I stood as Kyle edged toward me. We both froze as Stephen turned.

"What did you do?" Fear and desperation made his voice shake.

"We told the truth." There was no satisfaction behind the words. Jason had been right: the Walsh family really had always been good to me and this would destroy them. It was almost a betrayal. "I'm sorry," I said, and meant it. "It's over. Sinclair, the cure—it's over, Stephen. People are going to throw a microscope over CutterBrown and Zenith. They'll be asking questions. A lot of questions."

"Do you have any idea what you've done?" He glanced

over his shoulder at the screen and then back at us. "Don't you understand? This was my only chance. The only way I could fix my father's mistakes. The only way I could fix myself." The gun shook in his hand. "It's over now. Everything is over."

Kyle took a step forward as Amy's brother raised the gun.

"Don't." Stephen's voice was sharp and brittle, the sound of ice cracking. Kyle was fast, but he wasn't faster than a bullet.

"Please, Stephen. I know you. This isn't you." The words came out in a breathless rush as my heart and stomach leaped in different directions.

It was like he hadn't heard me. "You were always a good friend to Amy. She needed that." The weight in his voice was crushing and final as the world in front of me narrowed down to his eyes. "I'm sorry," he said.

I squeezed my eyes shut.

Everyone always says your life flashes before your eyes right before you die, but all I saw was Amy as Kyle tackled me to the ground and a gunshot rang in my ears.

It took me a moment to realize that I wasn't dead, that I wasn't even hurt.

Kyle's body covered mine, pressing me to the pavement. I struggled to raise my head as he rolled off me.

Kyle said something, but I couldn't hear him over the roaring sound in my ears.

Stephen Walsh lay sprawled on his back five feet away, the side of his skull a ruined mess. It was a wound not even a werewolf could heal. Blood spread out around him in a growing pool, running along cracks in the pavement.

I couldn't stand; I couldn't seem to make my legs work.

On hands and knees, I crawled to his side.

He stared unseeingly up at the night sky.

Where else was I going to go? I'm a monster, aren't I?

A weight settled on my chest as I stared down at Amy's brother. Stopping Sinclair and exposing CutterBrown and Zenith had been the right choice—the only choice—but Amy never could have guessed this would have been the outcome when she addressed those DVDs.

She never would have wanted this.

I had never wanted this.

I heard Kyle approach, but I couldn't look up. I couldn't look up and I couldn't speak and I couldn't stand.

All I could do was stare down at Stephen's sightless blue eyes.

26

"Mac . . ." gently, carefully, Kyle pulled me to my feet. He wrapped his arms around me, holding me tightly. "I thought . . ." He didn't finish the sentence; he didn't have to. He had thought he was going to lose me. I wanted to return the hug but I couldn't. I was too numb, too shell-shocked. I was frozen.

After a moment, Kyle pulled back. "We can't stay here."

He was right. Even as he led me away, I heard nearby shouts. No matter how crowded and chaotic the park was, a gunshot was too loud to be missed. People were already headed this way.

I wanted to look back; I didn't let myself. Kyle asked if I was all right, but I couldn't answer him. It was as though Stephen had taken my voice along with his life.

Regret filled me. And doubt. But I had made my choices and the only thing I could do now was keep moving forward.

Figuratively, if not literally.

Actually moving forward turned out to be easier said than done as confusion and anger swept through the square. The video had been broadcast on all three screens in the park, and while I had expected some sort of reaction, I wasn't prepared for the magnitude of the backlash that rose around us.

"Fake RfW propaganda!" shouted someone, a sentiment that echoed from person to person until the charge was deafening.

People didn't want the video to be real.

Believing it was fake was easier than accepting the idea that the young girl with the shattered legs could really exist. Supporting the camps was easier when you didn't have to face what happened inside.

"Where are Jason and Serena?" I asked, finally finding my voice as the crowd surged around us.

"Jason was going to try and get Serena to the east entrance."

"*Try?* You didn't get them to the RfW?" I stared at Kyle in disbelief. "You left them in the square?"

He tensed and stopped. Turning to face me, he gripped my shoulders, forcing the crowd to part around us. "If you're expecting me to apologize for coming after you, you can forget it. I got Serena and Jason away from the west arch and made sure we weren't followed. Do you think any of us—me, Jason, Serena—want to make it out of here without you? Do you think any of us could live with ourselves?" He looked like he wanted to shake me; instead he folded me into a fierce hug. "I wouldn't be able to live with myself."

The ice inside of me cracked as the horrible numbness

blazed away. "I'm sorry," I whispered, tears springing to my eyes as I clung to him.

After a long moment, Kyle pulled away. "You'd risk everything to save one of us. You have to start realizing that it goes both ways." He reached out and traced the line of my cheek, brushing away tears. "Now let's go find them."

I nodded and threaded my fingers through his. Together, we pushed our way through the crowd as I filled Kyle in on what had happened to Sinclair.

"Good" was all he said. A single word, but the tone in his voice spoke volumes.

News of the gunshot was spreading rapidly. Stephen's death would be evident as suicide to anyone who saw the body, but people quickly accused the RfW of infiltrating the rally with violence and lies.

Once that happened, it didn't take long for them to begin moving toward the eastern side of the square.

Toward Main Street and the RfW protest.

Last night's riot had involved only a few hundred members from each group. If the Trackers left the square now, thousands would be swept up in the clash.

And Serena and Jason would be swept up with them.

It hadn't occurred to me that our actions could actually make things worse, but that was exactly what the video seemed to have done.

Someone took to the stage to plead for calm. No one listened.

The crowd kept moving, carrying Kyle and me with it.

There was a bench a few feet ahead. I pushed my way to it and climbed up to get a view of the eastern arch. The lights in the park were bright enough to illuminate patches of the surrounding streets.

In the distance, a living wall of National Guards turned onto Main Street. Their riot gear made them look like strange, alien creatures. Creatures with hard plastic shells and stingers.

They would try to keep the two groups separate—even if that meant trapping the Trackers in the park.

We had to find Serena and Jason. We had to find out whether or not they had gotten out of the square.

"The National Guard are flooding Main Street," I said, hopping down. "How long ago did you leave Serena and Jason?"

"Ten minutes. Maybe fifteen."

A spike of fear slid through my chest. Fifteen minutes was more than enough time for a whole life to change. Fifteen minutes was more than enough time to lose everything.

I grabbed Kyle's hand as I followed him back into the throng.

In a last-ditch attempt to keep the Trackers in the park—probably more for fear of a PR nightmare than of any concern for the RfW or the town—the rally organizers shoved the anti-werewolf band back onstage.

It worked. At least temporarily.

As the band began their set, the flow of people streaming toward the eastern arch slowed.

"That won't keep their attention for long," said Kyle as we neared the center of the square.

The band hit the end of their first song. In the lull before the next, I heard the sound of breaking glass and instinctively turned toward the noise.

My stomach dropped.

The cage.

How could we have forgotten about the wolves in the cage?

"Kyle—" I grabbed his arm.

He turned and followed the direction of my gaze. His muscles tensed under my touch: I wasn't the only one who hadn't remembered the wolves trapped in the center of the square. "Shit."

A bottle sailed through the air and shattered against the pen. Another quickly followed. Trackers were throwing anything—rocks, bottles, sticks—in an effort to get a reaction from the wolves behind the wire. A handful of guards dressed head to toe in black looked on with bright eyes and amused expressions.

"We can't just leave them." I thought of Trey and Eve. They had died trying to help the wolves in the cage; leaving them behind wasn't an option.

Only two people in the pen were in human shape.

One was Sinclair. She lay sprawled on her stomach, unmoving as blood pooled beneath her. I couldn't tell if she was dead. The wolves around her were going crazy, snarling and sniffing at the blood. Blood could make control harder—just one of the lessons we had learned in Thornhill.

I waited to feel something—guilt or remorse for turning her over to the Trackers—but all I felt was a horrible sense of relief.

The other person in human form stood with his back to the crowd. His shoulders were rigid and his hands were clenched at his sides. Someone threw a bottle over the top of the wire. It shattered at his feet, but he didn't react.

My heart stopped as we drew closer.

I knew the line of those shoulders and the shape of those hands. If the man in the cage turned his head, I would catch a glimpse of a dagger tattoo and brilliant green eyes.

My hand fell from Kyle's arm. "Jason."

One of the guards strode around the cage. In a flash, he shoved a baton through the wire links, stabbing Jason in the middle of his lower back. The impact was hard enough for Jason to twist and flinch.

The instant he moved, I glimpsed a second, smaller figure in front of him. Serena. She was still in human form, but even at a distance I could see the way her body shook with the effort of holding on to control.

Jason moved slightly, trying to shield her from the attention of the crowd just as she tried to keep herself between him and the wolves in the pen. Jason glanced back, just for a moment, and I made a low, hissing sound at the sight of his battered and bloody face.

Kyle sprang forward. A guard moved to stop him and was sent flying.

Another guard reached for his holster. I ran forward and threw myself at his back, clinging to him like a demented wildcat.

The man was more than twice my size. I managed to hang on for all of twenty seconds before he shook me off.

For a moment, I was airborne, and then I came slamming back down to earth.

My body scraped the pavement and my shoulders collided with the cage a split second before my head hit the ground with a crack. I thought I heard Kyle shout my name, but it seemed like everyone in the square was shouting.

Fingers skimmed my shoulder and I flinched.

"It's me!" Jason's voice was ragged. He was pressed up against the cage, reaching through the links to touch me.

I struggled to my knees. I needed to get to Kyle. I had to help him. Everyone in the crowd had probably figured out what he was the second he had thrown that guard.

"Don't move." The cage rattled as Jason tried—ineffectively—to push me back down with his fingertips. "You probably have a concussion."

"Doesn't matter." My mouth felt like it was full of cotton and blood.

"Of course it fucking matters!"

I forced myself to my feet, clinging to the cage for support as the world around me spun sickeningly. Inside the cage, the wolves were going crazy.

Kyle stood ten yards away, a growing circle of guards and rallygoers forming around him. The muscles in his arms twitched and jumped. If he shifted, they would tear him apart. As long as he could hold on, they would draw things out. They would taunt him.

The confrontation with Kyle had attracted everyone's attention. Even the guard I had attacked seemed to have temporarily forgotten about me. After the hit I had taken, he probably didn't expect me to get back up.

Slowly—partly to avoid drawing attention but mostly because slow was the only way I could move—I edged toward the cage door. "Serena, are you okay? How did you guys get in there, anyway?" The words came out thick and a little sluggish, and it seemed to take more effort than it should have to string them together.

"I'm very, very far from okay. I'm not even in the same country as okay." Serena's voice shook as she stared at Sinclair. A low growl trickled out of her throat.

"Did you . . ." Before I could get the question out, the entire park seemed to flip upside down. It felt like my brains were leaking out my ears. I squeezed my eyes shut and clung to the cage as I froze in place. When I opened my eyes, the world was once again right-side up.

"It wasn't Serena," said Jason. "Another wolf recognized Sinclair and attacked her."

"Is she dead?" I forced down a wave of vomit and started moving again as I tried to divide my attention between watching Kyle and listening to Jason.

"I think so. I'm sure as hell not getting close enough to find out. A group of Trackers followed us from the arch," he continued, answering my other question. "One of them mistook my face for a piñata. Then they said if we liked wolves so much, we should spend more time with them and tossed us in here. They haven't figured out Serena is infected."

I opened my mouth to reply and ended up choking back a scream as a Taser took Kyle in the chest and sent him crashing to the ground.

He's okay, I told myself, letting go of the cage and clamping a hand over my mouth to hold back the sounds trying to break free. *He's been tased before. He'll be okay.*

Forcing myself to move faster, I stepped over the body of the guard Kyle had thrown—he was unconscious but alive—and reached for the cage door.

I was in no shape to help Kyle on my own. The only way I could help him was by freeing Jason and Serena, by letting the rest of the wolves out to create a distraction and maybe gain reinforcements.

The door was padlocked shut.

"Shit."

"The guard had a key," said Jason. "Check his belt."

The pressure in my head grew and the urge to throw up intensified as I crouched down. After an eternity of fumbling at the man's waist, I finally found a single key on a metal ring.

I pushed myself back up in time to see one of the guards pull a gun as Kyle climbed to his feet.

This time, I did scream.

Three Trackers broke away from the crowd and started toward me.

Turning my back on them, I shoved the key into the lock and pulled the padlock free.

I glanced over my shoulder. One of the Trackers lifted a Taser, but he was too late.

The door of the cage flew open and I was knocked back as the entire world went dark.

27

PANIC CLAWED AT MY THROAT. I WAS BLIND. I REMEM-
bered the crack my head had made when it hit the ground.
Something inside my brain had gotten loose or torn or broken.

"Mac?"

I twisted toward the familiar sound of Jason's voice. I
hadn't completely lost my sight, I realized. I could still see
shades of darkness and patches of shadow that seemed to
move.

"Mac? Say something!" Serena's face filled my field of
vision, the whites of her eyes glinting in the dark.

I wasn't blind: the lights in the square had just gone out.
I felt like an idiot.

"Where's Kyle?" I had to swallow twice before I could
get the words out.

Neither Serena nor Jason answered as they helped me
to my feet.

Shouts echoed in the crowd. In the distance, flashlight
beams cut through the darkness.

People began to panic.

"It's sabotage!" someone yelled.

"It's not sabotage!" shouted someone else. "The generators just overheated."

"It's the RfW!"

"It's the National Guard!"

Their reactions didn't make sense. People were panicking because the lights had gone out, but why wasn't anyone freaking over the fact that I had just let thirty wolves out of their cage? Where were the screams and the gunshots?

Unless . . . I tried to recall the exact moment the square had gone dark. The blackout had happened just as I had unlocked the door to the cage. No one was freaking out because no one had noticed the wolves were free. Yet.

My pulse thundered in my ears—a sensation that didn't help the pain spreading across my skull. "We have to find Kyle." We had to get to him before the lights came back on. God only knew what the Trackers would do to him. What they might already have done. My knees went weak.

"I'm here." Kyle's voice was raw and strained and the single most welcome sound I had ever heard as he materialized in front of me. "How badly are you hurt?" He ran his fingertips gently over my forehead; even the feather-light touch made me flinch. "I saw him throw you, but I couldn't get to you."

"She needs a hospital," said Jason. "She has a concussion."

I tried to say that I was fine—or that I would be fine—but a wave of dizziness rushed over me and my legs buckled.

Kyle caught me before I could hit the ground.

He scooped me up in his arms and began weaving through the crowd while Jason and Serena followed close behind.

"Put me down. I can walk." But even to my own ears, my protest was feeble.

Kyle ignored the demand. "We might be able to get out through the western side of the square," he said. "The National Guard probably pulled guards from the barricade and sent them to Main Street."

I heard Serena make a strangled sound behind us. Jason tried to calm her as I struggled to speak. "Kyle, we can't— the arch—"

Even if that side of the park had become our best chance of escape, it would mean walking past Trey and Eve. It would mean asking Serena to look at her brother's body again and leave him behind. We couldn't ask her to do that; I wasn't even sure I could do that.

One of the giant video screens blazed to life, quickly followed by the other two. All three screens showed rallies in other cities while the rest of the lights in the park stayed off.

"What the hell . . . ?" muttered Jason.

I tensed in Kyle's arms, equally confused. How could the screens be on if the rest of the square was without power?

Kyle turned to the nearest screen. We were close enough that the flickering light illuminated his face and the deep frown lines that formed at the corners of his mouth.

Slowly, he lowered me to the ground, keeping one arm

around me for support, not taking his eyes off the footage of the rally in Atlanta.

Atlanta. My heart gave a sharp twist. That was where Hank was.

Something was happening to the crowd on the screen. Pockets of space were opening up as the Trackers broke into dozens—maybe even hundreds—of smaller groups.

The images were without sound, but it looked as though people were shouting.

A moment later, we saw why.

Each pocket of empty space had formed around a single individual. Almost as one, they folded to their knees and transformed. Dumbfounded, I twisted in Kyle's arms to catch glimpses of the other screens where similar scenes in other cities were playing out.

Hundreds of wolves were transforming. Thousands. They didn't attack—not when panic surged around them or when some of the Trackers lashed out—they just peacefully stood their ground.

I remembered the girl at the AV table—the one with the fake tattoo who hadn't wanted me looking at her laptop. This was what the wolves had been planning. It wasn't an attack: it was a mass outing.

Behind me, Jason swore.

A second later, I heard it: a sound like breaking branches—just one or two at first, and then hundreds.

The noise grew until it seemed to come from all sides, engulfing everyone and everything. It was as though an entire forest was being reduced to kindling.

The lights in Riverside Square blazed back to life as, all around us, wolves fell to the ground and transformed.

It was terrifying. And beautiful.

Kyle's arm tensed around me. I could feel the muscles move under his skin and I knew he was fighting the urge to fall to his knees and join them.

"Don't leave," I whispered.

"Never."

Eve and Trey should be here, I thought, tears filling my eyes. *This shouldn't be happening without them.*

Just like the scenes at the other rallies, hundreds of wolves were scattered through Riverside Square. And just like at the other rallies, Trackers edged away, forming small groups as they tried to leave circles of space around each wolf.

The tension was so thick that I could taste it on the back of my tongue.

A gunshot rang out across the square.

"That was the National Guard," said Serena, relying on her wolf-sharp senses. Despite everything that had happened to fray her control, she held on. As I glanced back, I noticed that her hand was twined tightly with Jason's.

There was movement in the crowd as men in riot gear spread through the square. They were ready for an uprising, but when they saw the wolves standing peacefully in place, no one seemed sure what to do.

No one—not the Trackers, not even the National Guard—could take on this many wolves without being decimated.

The image on all three screens flashed back to Atlanta. This time with sound.

A man with shoulder-length brown hair and an impossible amount of grace strode through the crowd and hopped onto the stage.

Ten people followed in his wake. One of them was my father.

Gunfire sounded over the Atlanta crowd, but it didn't seem to faze the man. He walked straight to a microphone in the center of the stage while his entourage fanned out behind him.

He stood there like he had nothing to fear. Maybe he didn't. Maybe anything that happened now was better than a life spent hiding.

When he spoke, his voice soothed and stirred in equal measure. "Twelve years ago, the president of the United States stood here, in Atlanta, and announced the existence of lupine syndrome. Tonight, the Trackers have chosen to hold what they call unity rallies across the country. They want to unite you—regular humans—against what they consider a werewolf threat. They want to unite you in fear and darkness."

Angry shouts greeted his words. Threats of blood and violence were echoed by the crowd here, but even the most skull-thick Tracker knew that attacking the wolves would result in a bloodbath.

Trackers fired the occasional warning shot, but didn't make a serious move against the wolves. For now.

And no matter how loudly the crowd shouted or how

often a gunshot rang out, the man on the stage didn't flinch or back down.

"The Trackers want to unite you against werewolves. We've come here, tonight, to show you that they're too late." He paused for a moment, giving his words a chance to sink in. "You've been told that the camps are the one thing keeping you safe, but there are just as many—if not more— wolves outside their walls. Right now, from one side of the country to the other, werewolves are teaching your children in the classrooms of your public schools. We're protecting your communities as firefighters and police officers. Stocking shelves at your grocery store or mowing your lawn. We are part of your communities and your daily lives, hiding in plain sight. We are your friends and your family. Your neighbors and the people you interact with every day. We've spent too many years hiding what we are, too many years being afraid. Over the coming weeks, we will gather peacefully in cities and towns across the country—just as we have gathered tonight—to show you how big a part of your lives we already are."

A swell of hope lifted me up as he spoke.

I glanced at Kyle. His attention was locked on the screen as though he were committing each word to memory. Even Jason, still holding Serena's hand, looked impressed.

"For years, the Trackers and the LSRB have been telling you that your communities need to be protected, that lupine syndrome is a threat to your way of life. We are part of those communities, we are part of your lives, and we are not going away."

The man strode to the front of the stage and dropped gracefully to the ground. The men and women behind him, including Hank, followed as he made his way from the stage. So did all of the wolves in the crowd.

Around us, the wolves in Riverside Square were doing the same. They slipped away like ghosts, and the Trackers and the National Guard were too stunned to do anything but stand by.

"Everything is going to change," I said, throat tight, "isn't it?"

Kyle held me a little tighter and nodded.

Just for a second, I caught a glimpse of a familiar girl in the crowd. A girl with ink-black hair and a mischievous grin. *You're going to have a fantastic life, Mackenzie Dobson. You're going to have a fantastic, amazing life.*

Standing in the square with Kyle and Serena and Jason, that suddenly seemed possible.

The crowd shifted and the girl was gone.

"It's going to be a new world." My voice was soft with wonder, so soft that only Kyle could hear.

He looked at me and in his eyes I saw an echo of the wordless promises we had made last night. He pressed a gentle kiss to my temple. "It's going to be our world."

Epilogue

Portland, Oregon, Two Years Later

FAT RAINDROPS BEGAN HITTING THE GROUND WHILE I was still a block from my destination. I broke into a jog, clutching my messenger bag tightly to my chest as a bolt of lightning split the sky. The weather report hadn't mentioned thunderstorms, but fall in Portland was nothing if not unpredictable.

A bell jangled as I dashed into the diner. My feet shot out from under me as they hit the wet tile floor, and I ended up clinging to the nearest booth to keep from landing on my butt.

A few people looked up from their coffees and hamburgers, but most stayed focused on their food.

Not my father. "Smooth entrance, kid," he said as I approached the back booth he had claimed.

Rolling my eyes, I shrugged off my jacket and slid into the seat across from him.

Two cups of coffee were already on the table, one full, the other almost empty.

"Did you order food?" I asked.

Hank twisted the heavy silver ring on his right hand. I didn't look too long or too hard at the design etched into the metal. It was the same symbol that had been on Eve's necklace. "I can't stay."

You drove all the way to Portland and can't take twenty minutes for lunch? The words were on the tip of my tongue, but I held them back. Hank was never going to be big on quality time. Besides, ever since Eve's death, he had found it hard to be around me. I was the age she would have been, living the kind of life she might have led if she had lived long enough to see an end to the LSRB. More importantly, though, I was a reminder of the guilt he still felt over sending her to Hemlock.

I didn't like it, but I sort of understood it—at least I tried to.

I ran a hand through my pixie cut and then hauled two things from my messenger bag. The first was a thick, padded envelope. The second was a hard drive. *The* hard drive.

Hank reached across the table and lifted the plastic box. It looked small in his hands, too small to have been responsible for so much.

Now, almost two years to the day that we had found Amy's last message, CutterBrown and Zenith were still under investigation for what they had done—both at the camps and before. Several top executives from each company—including Amy's father—had disappeared. A few had committed suicide. Natalie Goodwin, the woman who had tortured Serena, and Donovan were just two of many employees looking at prison sentences for their actions.

"You actually found it," said Hank, staring down at the drive.

"Tess found it," I corrected. "She was the one who thought to check the house once all of the Walshes' things were gone. It was in the attic, wedged between the rafters."

After the death of her son and the disappearance of her husband, Amy's mother had left Hemlock. Permanently. She hadn't wanted anything else to do with the town or the life she had led. She had cut off everyone and everything—even Amy's grandfather, whose health had never quite fully recovered.

The Walsh family had lost everything—their wealth, their status, even their children—because of ambition and lies. It didn't matter where Ryan Walsh had gone or how long he stayed in hiding: he would spend the rest of his life knowing that his actions had ultimately contributed to the deaths of both Amy and Stephen. I had to believe that knowledge was its own kind of prison.

That night in the square, Stephen had said something about fixing his father's mistakes, but it was Amy whose actions would eventually help set things right. She had discovered the truth and made it possible for others to do the same.

I toyed with my coffee cup and nodded toward my father's hand as he slipped the drive into his jacket pocket. "What are you going to do with it?"

"Find out what's on here that wasn't on your DVDs and make sure it gets into the right hands—or kept out of the wrong ones. Don't worry: I'll take care of it."

A few years ago, I probably would have hesitated to trust Hank with something so important and valuable, but a lot had changed.

After the night of the rallies—the night some people called "the unmasking"—Hank had stepped down as leader of the Eumon to take on a leading role in the fight for werewolf rights. He claimed he did it because he didn't trust anyone else not to screw up, but I knew he was doing it for Eve. He was doing it to try and keep what had happened to her and Trey from happening to anyone else.

Eve had been right: a lot of people had stopped supporting the camps once videos of the tests had become national news. Only one facility remained open—a prison to house werewolves who broke the law or who couldn't adjust to life on the outside—but there was still a lot of work to do. Werewolves weren't being rounded up anymore, but discriminating against them wasn't illegal, and there had been a recent push to implement a sort of national registry for the infected.

I glanced toward the front of the diner where a small sign next to the register read, "Werewolves Welcome." Things were changing slowly, but they *were* changing. And Portland was at the forefront of that change. It was a city with a werewolf-friendly reputation, a city where wolves were trying to create an inclusive community instead of the traditional, almost ganglike pack system. It was the reason Serena and Kyle had wanted to come here after graduation and the reason I had been happy to follow.

Hank drained the rest of his coffee and slid out of the booth. "I'll be in San Diego for a few weeks. The pack leader there is being . . . problematic. I'll call you."

I knew he wouldn't, but I nodded anyway.

He paused next to my seat and put a hand on my shoulder—just for a second—before walking out of the diner.

I watched him through the rain-streaked window as he jogged across the street and climbed behind the wheel of an old Jeep. Like the world, my father had changed, but it was still too early to tell whether or not that change had come in time for the two of us to ever have a real relationship.

"Refill, hon?"

I pulled my gaze away as a waitress appeared at the booth with a pot of coffee. "Please. And could I get a south-west omelet?"

"Sure thing," she said before heading over to another customer.

I pulled out my cell and sent a quick reply to a text I'd gotten from Tess just as I had been leaving my apartment. She had cut back on her hours at work to start taking college classes part-time. "I don't want to work at a place with a name like the Shady Cat for the rest of my life," she had said. Unfortunately, she seemed to spend more time texting me about her cute Intro to Accounting professor than studying.

The bell above the diner door jangled. I glanced up and my heartbeat kicked up a notch as I watched Kyle scan the room. I knew the exact moment he spotted me. Somehow, without moving a muscle, his entire expression changed, his eyes lighting up with a warmth that flooded me from the tips of my toes to the crown of my head.

No matter how many days, weeks, months, or years passed, I still couldn't quite believe he was mine.

I stood as he approached the booth.

Kyle pressed a quick kiss to my lips before wrapping me in a hug.

"Sorry," he said, pulling away a second later. "I'm soaked."

"It's okay." I stole another kiss before sliding back into the booth. "I already ordered," I confessed. "And you just missed Hank."

Kyle unzipped his jacket and took the seat my father had vacated. "You gave him the hard drive?"

I nodded.

"Good." Kyle shook his head. "I know it's been two years, but the thought of it being in your apartment made me nervous."

"My roommate is a werewolf," I reminded him. "Anyone who breaks into our apartment is in for a world of hurt— unless they break in this weekend, since she's going to Seattle on a shopping trip."

"What a coincidence," said Kyle drily. "Jason told me he was thinking of going to Seattle this weekend, too."

"It's been over six months. How long do we have to keep pretending we don't know what's going on?"

"Until one of them breaks down and says something, I guess."

It had taken Jason a year and at least one serious relationship while going to school across the country, but his feelings for me had eventually shifted back to friendship. And it took about the same amount of time for him to admit to himself that he thought of Serena as much more than a friend.

He had never told me just why he decided to join us in Portland, but I was pretty sure frequent late-night phone calls with Serena had at least been a contributing factor. As for Serena, she had fallen harder and faster. Of all the people who had been there for her after Trey's death, the person she kept turning to was Jason. Maybe it was because, out of all of us, he was the one person who didn't try to fix her. He had listened when she needed to talk and had held her when she needed to cry, but he didn't try to put her back together with empty words and promises. He didn't tell her that losing Trey would someday hurt less; he knew better.

"A reformed Tracker and a werewolf." I shook my head. "It's like Romeo and Juliet."

The corner of Kyle's mouth quirked up. "Hopefully with a better ending."

The waitress came back and I fidgeted with the edge of the envelope in front of me as she took Kyle's order. I had some big choices to make. Maybe life-altering choices. Though I had taken a few college classes as a part-time student, I had yet to figure out what I wanted to study or if I even wanted to go to school full-time.

For the past year and a half, my life had been consumed by the contents of the package on the table. Now that things were coming to an end, I wasn't sure what came next. *When this story ends, a new story starts. That's how it goes. How it always goes.* That's what Amy had said to me once. In a dream.

"What's that?" asked Kyle.

I swallowed. Suddenly, irrationally, I was scared to show him. Once I showed him, it might start feeling real. Really real.

With a deep breath, I reached into the envelope.

I pulled out the book and slid it across the table.

Wolf Girl: Secrets and Lies of an Epidemic. Advance Reader's Copy.

Kyle glanced up. "When did you get this?"

"This morning. You had already left for class." I felt curiously exposed, almost naked, as Kyle turned the book over to read the text on the back and then flipped to the dedication.

"For Amy," he read. "In dreams, as in life, you helped show me the way."

"Trey and Eve are in the acknowledgments," I said quickly. "I didn't forget about them."

Kyle shot me a small, reassuring smile. A sad smile. "I know."

The CutterBrown story had consumed the whole country. Amy's family was rich and powerful and politically connected. Her father's ties to CBP—along with the fact that Amy had been murdered by a werewolf—had turned the tale into a real-life soap opera. There was even a movie in the works.

Overnight, anyone connected to Amy or her family

became a hot commodity. It seemed as though everyone from the Walsh family housekeeper to Stephen's high school girlfriend had gotten their fifteen minutes of fame. Once word leaked out that we had been at Thornhill, that we had been the ones to find proof of the Arcadia project, things had gotten really crazy. Jason, Kyle, Serena, and I had been flooded with more requests and offers than we could count. A major network had even contacted us about our very own reality show. I couldn't leave the apartment without being trailed by photographers and reporters, and all of us—Jason, especially—had gotten death threats from Trackers.

In the end, we agreed to do a single interview: an hour-long televised conversation with Sandy Price, the reporter I had given the DVDs to at the rally.

But even as I turned down—or flat-out ignored—hundreds of offers, I still wanted a chance to tell my story. Our story. At least as much of it as I could safely tell.

One night, a few months after the rally, once the attention had started to die down, I began writing about Amy's funeral. Once I started typing, I couldn't stop.

It wasn't the whole truth—I would never tell anyone just how Branson Derby had died or about the man Serena had killed in the junkyard—but it was close. It was the important parts.

Sandy had been the one who had put me in touch with an agent, and she hadn't seemed surprised when three publishers entered a bidding war for the rights to the story. The only thing that did seem to shock her was the fact that I had given away most of the advance.

I didn't want to profit from the things that had happened. They were too horrible. I had kept just enough money to cover living expenses while I worked on the book; the rest had gone to a charity that helped wolves transition out of the camps and back into life on the outside.

It was what Trey and Eve would have wanted—at least I liked to think so.

Besides, I had gotten more out of writing the book than money. The act of writing let me examine things from different angles; it let me revisit the past without drowning in it and had helped me move on.

I studied Kyle's face as he flipped through pages.

Writing our story had helped me come to terms with the past just as moving to Portland, being part of the community here, had helped him come to terms with being a werewolf.

We had each become more accepting of ourselves, and in doing so, had become stronger together.

More companies were working on a cure. Openly. Ethically.

Maybe someday they would find it and maybe Kyle would take it, but whatever he chose, I would be by his side.

Werewolf or reg, it was our actions, not our blood, that defined us.

The world was changing, and Kyle and I were changing with it, but no matter what happened, we belonged to each other.

Acknowledgments

A BOOK DOESN'T HAPPEN IN A VACUUM (THOUGH WRITing does occasionally feel like being jettisoned out of an airlock). So many people deserve thanks for their support and input, but especially:

Emmanuelle Morgen, my fantabulous agent, for believing in Mac, reading early (and unpolished!) drafts, and spending many hours with me on the phone. I was truly blessed the day you picked my query out of your slush pile.

Claudia Gabel and Melissa Miller, my amazing editors, who cared about Mac and her story as much as I did. It's been an honor to work with you over these past three books.

Katherine Tegen for running such a terrific imprint—one I am truly grateful the Hemlock books have been part of.

Tom Forget, Amy Ryan, and Barbara Fitzsimmons in design for making *Willowgrove* look amazing, and Lauren Flower, Casey McIntyre, Onalee Smith in publicity and marketing for getting the word out. Thanks, also, to Kathryn Silsand in managing editorial and Alexandra Arnold.

And massive thanks to everyone else at KTB and HCCB

who had a part in getting the Hemlock trilogy onto shelves. Special thanks, also, to the team at HCC for taking care of this wee Canuck and to Whitney Lee for finding homes for the Hemlock trilogy in other countries.

Huge thanks to all of the bloggers and readers who helped spread the word about the books. I am so incredibly grateful for the support. Thanks, also, to everyone who suggested writing music for *Willowgrove* during the playlist contest, especially Alyssa of the Eater of Books! blog, Charis, Claire Smith, Cate Knox, Jay Uppal, Jade Fuller, Kendall McCubbin, Molli Moran, and Jennifer Nix.

Thanks to Christina Ahn and Cassie Frye for answering medical questions.

Huge thanks, as always, to my friends. Jodi Meadows, Debra Driza, Jamie Blair, and Kate Hart: thank you for putting up with endless emails, circular conversations about plot, and general angst. You are incredible writers and amazing friends. Nancy and Chris: thank you for endless phone calls, advice, and handholding. As always, you guys rock.

Thank you, finally, to my family. Mom, Dad, Sarah, Justin, and Krystle: I would be lost without your love and support. I appreciate it more than you will ever know.